I0678080

When life is a deluge that threatens to take you under, look for God's help to save you!

Liza T. Bergren

DELUGE

Published by BCG Press

6655 Wesley Acres Way

Colorado Springs, CO 80908

All rights reserved. Except for brief excerpts for review purposes,

no part of this book may be reproduced or used in any form

without written permission from the publisher.

This story is a work of fiction. All characters and events are the product of the author's imagination. Any resemblance to any person, living or dead, is coincidental.

Library of Congress Control Number 2025907878

ISBN 979-8-9985037-1-9

eISBN 979-8-9985037-2-6

© 2025 Lisa T. Bergren

The author is represented by Steve Laube.

Cover Design: Timothy J. Bergren

Interior Design: Collin Smith

Cover Image: iStockphoto

Interior Cover Image: Ideogram

Printed in the United States of America

Second edition, 2025

The River of Time Series

DELUGE

A NOVEL

LISA T. BERGREN

For the River Tribe—this one's purely for you, my friends.
Thanks for your passionate encouragement and enthusiasm.

PART I

PREPARATIONS

Late Autumn, 1345

CHAPTER 1

EVANGELIA

"So, what say you, *carina*?" Luca asked me, calling me his *little love*. "Did you not promise long ago that if I returned to you from battle, we would speak of a certain blue dress?"

I laughed under my breath and gripped his arm more tightly, used to his constant teasing. But this specific subject always set me on edge.

We were walking to our favorite hill for an autumn picnic, a habit we'd gotten into since things had settled down on the northern front. For months now, Firenze had kept to their side of the newly reestablished border, apparently content to rest from battle, as we were. And even though the wind now held the chill of deep November, still we came to this hill once a week to gain some privacy.

"M'lady?"

I glanced up at him as we walked, for the first time seeing the intent expression in his green eyes, noting his tone of seriousness. He usually dropped the marriage subject when I refused to engage. He was sweet and sensitive like that. But today the muscles in his jaw tensed, like they did when addressing his men or talking over the day's plans with Marcello. Or when he was thinking about kissing me.

"Oh, Luca. We've addressed this. I said we'd *speak of it*," I said, looking down to the calf-high grasses, brown and dry as autumn prepared to give way to winter. "Make plans. Dream of that beautiful day."

"Come now, love. We both know you promised more than that."

I glanced up at him and then quickly away. "Luca, there is none but you in my heart. But the idea of..." I swallowed hard, feeling the familiar heat of a blush on my cheek. "The idea of...carrying a child, as Gabi is now..." I shook my head. "'Tis enough to anticipate one babe in the face of an uncertain future. We need not tempt God with sending us another."

He shrugged my hand loose, took several quick, long strides ahead to then turn and face me. He held up a hand and I stopped.

"I do not understand," he said, squinting at me. "How does Marcello and Gabriella's joy keep us from our own? *Why* would it?"

I brushed past him and finished our climb to the top of the hill, then flung out the blanket I'd carried, trying to gather my thoughts, my argument. He was right behind me. I sat down and looked up at him, waiting for him to join me. But he stood there with his hands on his hips, clearly wanting an answer.

"Consider it, Luca. There is already enough risk happening in our family," I said. "Remember? With what is to *come?*"

He took a deep breath through his nostrils, flung himself down on the blanket beside me, and rolled onto his back. He shook his head, then shifted to his side, taking my hand in his.

"So we are to be held captive by what is to come, too? Live in fear of what *might* be rather than rejoice in what we've been given for certain? Should we not embrace these years of freedom before it is upon us?"

I gave him a small smile. I loved him. I did. But the thought of being his wife...being intimate with him...perhaps becoming pregnant as my sister had...

Then facing the coming plague...

Not only worried about my family, Luca, Marcello, my future niece or nephew, but my own babe as well...

I shook my head and stood up, pacing back and forth, wringing my hands. "I can't, Luca. Not yet. Not until we are through it. Past it."

He rose slowly, his face full of consternation. I let him approach and gently take hold of my arms, and looked up into the face I loved so well.

"Saints above, Lia, what are you saying? That we cannot wed for...*years*? This illness—you have suggested it would take some time to be through with us, yes?"

I swallowed hard. Would he wait for me that long?

Was I risking...us?

"Do you not see? The plague...Luca, it will take a third—even half—of every city and town and castello. Mayhap more."

"I do." His frown deepened, as did the pressure from his fingers. "But Evangelia, my love, do *you* not see? That means two-thirds, or half, will *survive*." His eyebrows lifted and met at the top in frustration. "And aren't your parents doing everything possible to make certain we are in that portion?"

"What does it matter if we put off our betrothal for a few more years?" I asked, breaking away from him, taking a step back. "We have only been formally courting a year and—"

"For you," he said, cutting me off, making a slicing motion with his hand. He saw my sick expression and groaned, clenched his hand and looked to the sky, then back to me. He took my hands in his, and they felt warm and welcome around my own.

"Evangelia," he breathed, leaning down to rest his forehead against mine. "You've had *my* heart since the beginning. But it does not matter," he said, such pain and angst in his tone that it made me want to cry in earnest. "Because whether I'd been yours for a day or a decade, I'd feel it as an eternity. All I want," he said, lifting a hand to stroke my cheek and look into my eyes, "is to be your husband, and you, my wife. 'Tis all I want," he repeated, so faintly I could barely make out the words. "Please," he said, sinking to one knee, my hands in his. "Please. Will you not trust our future to the hands of God? Will you not be my bride? Now, rather than later?"

My heart pulled at me, begged me to say yes. To nod and watch him rise to his feet, face alight. To have him lift me in his arms and laugh in my ear.

But I couldn't.

I'd risked everything to be here, to stay here, with my family. With him! Wasn't it enough? For now?

I just couldn't put anything else on the line. Not even for Luca.

"'Tis only a few more years," I whispered, begging him with my eyes. "Mayhap three or four? That's all I need. The worst of what is to come should be past us by then."

He let out a sound of exasperation, rose on leaden feet and paced away from me again, his hands in fists at his side. He stood there for a minute, maybe two, before I dared to come up beside him, wrapping my hands around his arm and resting my cheek on his shoulder. "Evangelia. You realize that one of us could die in a hundred different ways even before this plague is upon us? In battle? From another illness? Saints, Lia, one of us could fall down the well while fetching water and break our neck. We cannot live in fear. We *cannot*."

"I understand," I muttered, feeling miserable and guilty. "But this is one risk that we don't have to take. Something we can control. What if we both perish? We can still love each other without the risk of bearing a child who might end up an orphan."

I could feel the rapid beat of his pulse. "'Tis a false belief," he said in a measured way. "We control nothing, my love. Our lives, our futures are in the hands of God, not our own."

I sighed heavily. "I guess we must agree to disagree."

He turned and faced me again, his expression grim. "What sort of nonsensical phrase from the future is *that?*"

I shrugged, feeling the heat of a blush on my face. "'Tis only something we say when we tire of arguing."

"Well, that is not how it is done here. Now. In this place that you've *said* is your own. Here, we discuss until we are in agreement, one way or another."

He was clearly angry, gesticulating with agitated moves. I shifted uncomfortably. He hardly ever was frustrated with me.

He cocked his head and folded his arms. "Tell me the truth, Evangelia. Do you still think about returning? Leaving this and all that threatens us behind? Leaving me?" The last two words were quieter, laced with pain.

I felt heat on my neck and cheeks anew. Until he'd said the words, I hadn't really allowed myself to fully consider it. But yes, it was true. Ever since Gabi had figured out that she was pregnant, I'd thought of the tomb, the time portal, as our escape route if the worst happened. At least for some of us...

"Evangelia," he whispered.

I put my fingers to my temples, massaging away the sudden throb. "Mayhap," I admitted. "If there was no other option. We would *have* to return to the tunnel."

He paused for a long moment, then gently put his index knuckle under my chin and lifted it. "Say that again," he said grimly, looking into my eyes, demanding my honesty.

"If there was no *other* option, Luca," I said again, a bit louder. Feeling the misery. Desperately wanting him to understand, to support me. "If we had to save Gabi's baby, or Mom. Any of us."

It was as if I'd hit him. His green eyes looked into mine, back and forth, before he sucked in his breath. I saw tears rise in his eyes. I'd told him, promised, pledged that I would stay. That my life was here, with my family...with him. But now I'd admitted I kept an exit plan in the back of my mind.

"You would leave me. Leave us," he said flatly. "Uncertain that you could return."

"To save my *family?* Yes," I said.

"A *family*. Of which I am clearly not part," he said.

"No! I didn't intend—Luca, you know what I am saying."

"Do I?" Pain etched every line of his face. He looked down at the ground, digging the toe of his boot into a dry clump of grass, thinking. After a moment, he leveled a gaze at me. "You are right," he said, slowly nodding, and my stomach dropped. "I understand your intentions now, all too clearly. I have been a fool, chasing after you. Losing my heart to you. When you never could be mine forever. I shall leave you in peace now."

"No, Luca," I said, my heart breaking as he turned to walk down the hill, feeling the tearing between us. "Luca," I groaned, a ball forming in my throat.

But he did not turn.

"Luca!"

He left me there, on our picnic hill.

I sat down, alone on the blanket, his form growing smaller in the distance.

And then I gave into the ache inside and wept.

CHAPTER 2

EVANGELIA

M any things fueled my tears.

Frustration that he couldn't understand, wouldn't understand.

Indignation that he'd said he'd wait forever but clearly hadn't meant it.

Anger that Gabi had pretty much railroaded us all into this crazy medieval life.

Irritation that I seemed to get a grip on my fear about the future one week but then fell right back into it the next.

Fear for Gabi's unborn child alongside one of my own...and the idea of placing them in two little coffins.

Yeah, it was pretty dark, I know. But the plague? C'mon, not many American teens had to tackle that big of a threat. I mean, we'd dealt with Covid. But the *Black Plague*?

The thought of how bad it would get made me cry again, thinking about all the people I already loved in the castello, and how half of them might die. Having to bury Fortino had pretty much wrecked us. Same with all the knights who had died in battle after battle, and some of the villagers who had not survived their injuries or illness, no matter how hard my mom tried to save them. We wept over them too.

Then there'd been that time that Luca had contracted what Mom thought had been a minor strain of plague that swept through Italia before, scaring us that it had come early. I remembered seeing him down, weak with fever, with those terrible buboes all over his body...I shivered and wiped my face and hugged myself, rocking slightly. *No, once was enough.* I couldn't share my heart and future with anyone else, besides all the people I loved already. Not fully. I was already exposed on too many fronts. Weak, and practically begging the universe to hand me a nice, fat pain sandwich. And that thought made me cry even harder.

"Evangelia?" asked a tentative voice from a short distance away. "Are you in need of assistance?"

I looked up and saw Adela Forelli and Tomas on horseback. They had started to take a daily ride like Luca and I had our picnics, seeking time alone. It was clear to anyone that they were practically inseparable. Their shared look of worry over me made my throat clog with new tears.

"Nay, I am well," I managed, swallowing hard against the ball in my throat. Tomas—I might've confided in. But Adela? It'd be too weird, given that she was Luca's sister and all.

Tomas looked around, confusion etching lines in his round face. "Where is Captain Forelli?"

"Captain Forelli?" I repeated, stalling for a time. "He's back at the castello. I-I wanted...I decided to take a bit of time for myself."

"Luca knows you are here. By yourself. But he chooses to be in the castello," Adela repeated, clearly not believing me. "My brother wouldn't give you the *chance* to be by yourself if he could be beside you." She cast me a wry grin.

"Yes, well...we had a bit of a falling out." I said the last part in a rush, as if in confession.

"Ah," Tomas said, lifting his chin, his wise eyes seeming to note my tear-stained cheeks for the first time. He looked at Adela again and, after she nodded, Tomas slid from his saddle and went over to lift her down from her mare.

I barely managed to stifle my groan. The last thing I wanted was company, well meaning as they might be. And especially these two. The dynamic God-duo, an ex-priest and an ex-almost-nun. I could practically hear the sermon already. But there was no stopping them. They sat down on either side of me, hugging their legs. At least Tomas had ditched the robe that he'd once worn. Their clothing was simple, but more normal. Tomas's hair was even growing in a bit where he'd once shaved it, an awkward inch-long fuzz that made Gabi and me giggle.

"What has you two quarreling?" Adela asked gently.

I felt the tension gather between my shoulders, torn between sharing everything and telling them to mind their own business.

When I didn't give an answer, Tomas said, "Would it not ease your heart to speak of it, m'lady?" He reached over to pick a long stalk of drying grass and began to splinter off the seed head, bit by bit, letting the wind carry it away.

"Nay, I think not," I said, standing abruptly. "Please, my friends. We packed a picnic that we're clearly not going to eat. The greatest thing you might do for me is to sit here and enjoy this pretty afternoon and eat our cured boar and bread. It'll be quite delicious."

"Evangelia, are you certain—" Adela began.

"Yes, yes, I'm certain," I said hurriedly. I felt badly, cutting them off when they were only trying to help, but I knew that anything I said within Adela's hearing would be repeated to Luca. And Luca and I had shared enough words today, directly or indirectly.

I liked Adela well enough. We got along. But I seemed to stir an odd sense of competition with her. Maybe it was because she'd been gone from Luca's life for so long—off at the nunnery until she realized it wasn't her calling—and had only just returned to find me competing for his attention. Maybe she had thought it was going to be just like it had been ten years ago when she left for the convent. Luca had been only a young teen then.

I bet he'd been adorable when she left—spending his days with Marcello, creating mock battles in the forest, building forts, or finding hot springs to skinny-dip in. It made me smile wistfully, longing for Luca to regale me again with tales of their boisterous boyhood with a big grin on his face. Anything to un-see that look of pain in his eyes...

I glanced back and glimpsed the chubby Tomas gleefully diving into our picnic basket as if they'd just discovered treasure and Adela smiling and shaking her head at him before looking back at me. Seeing me all too clearly, I thought. As the girl who might make her brother happy...or destroy him.

Only one person could help me sort this out. Gabi. But she'd already made her decision, and I wasn't going to bring it up again. I'd agreed to stay here, with her. With Mom and Dad. But I'd never said I'd risk it all. I never said I'd risk my heart. Or babies.

And the thought of watching Luca die...or our child...

Well, the thought of that made my heart break into a thousand little pieces.

GABRIELLA

I hauled the bucket over the edge of the well and paused, gasping. My hand went to my belly, and I looked around furtively. Had anyone seen me pause?

Thankfully, it appeared not. Everyone was busy with preparation for the upcoming harvest feast in the castello, and they were scurrying to accomplish three-times their normal duties... That was why I decided to fetch my own water for my room. The last thing I was going to do was play the whole Lady-of-the-Castello-Card just because I was preggers. I was still trying to get a grip on the idea of it myself, frankly, even though my belly was as round as half a Tuscan melon now. I was just glad I'd stopped feeling the need to vomit my guts out every hour. That first trimester was enough to make a girl swear off sex forever.

But then I caught sight of my husband. And just seeing him stride toward me, every inch of him the most handsome Italian knight I'd ever met, and realizing anew that he was mine, my husband, *forever*...and, well, I knew we'd likely end up with a ton of kids eventually. The guy was just so irresistible. The way he was scowling at me, silently chastising me for drawing a heavy bucket, all love and concern—

"Gabriella," he growled, wrapping one arm around my waist and taking hold of the bucket handle. "What are you doing? You well know your mother said to lift nothing over a stone's weight."

"Everyone's so busy," I said, squirming away, aware that we were already drawing every eye in the courtyard. "The least I could do was fetch my own bath water."

"I shall bring it," he said, lifting the bucket and then picking up the second, which was waiting on the ground. "If you need something during this season of the feast, tell me, and I shall see it done."

As if he wasn't busy enough, I thought, meekly following him. Even though I gave him a tender smile for his thoughtfulness, I hated this new sensation of weakness, helplessness. It brought back memories of being wounded. I much preferred feeling strong, wielding a sword. The whole Little-Woman-with-Child scenario? Yeah, that didn't set well with me.

"Lord Forelli!" Luca called, just as we were entering the turret door that led to our quarters. We paused and waited as he jogged up to us. His green eyes slid from Marcello then back to me. "Lord and Lady Greco have returned from their travels. They sent us an invitation to join them to sup this night."

Marcello glanced at me. Both men were well aware that I preferred to steer clear of our enemy's old castle, Castello Paratore, even if it was now Castello Greco. The walls just held too many bad memories. But I steeled myself.

"We shall go," I said, lightly, trying to take the bucket from Marcello. But he didn't release it until I met his gaze and gave him an assuring smile.

"We shall go," Marcello repeated to Luca.

The captain of his guard, his cousin, nodded once.

"You and Evangelia are to attend as well?"

Luca paused. "We are all invited. But I shall stay here and see to the safety of the keep while you're away, and send others to guard you."

Marcello quirked an eyebrow. "You'd allow Evangelia to go without you?"

Luca took a breath. "'Tis best if the lady and I are not in the same room."

I frowned in confusion, and we both turned to fully face him, but he held up his hands. "Nay, nay. I do not wish to discuss it. Some things are only between the two of us, much as we like to share everything else in this castello."

I pursed my lips. I'd get it out of Lia later. Whatever silly tiff this was, they could just get over it.

"She'll come," I said. "And you must too, Luca. Rodolfo and Alessandra need our support. Let us go and help them celebrate a new beginning for the old castello."

He lifted his hands and cocked his head, a hint of that familiar grin on his lips. But trouble lurked around his eyes. "You know I am always eager to partake in good company, especially when ample wine and food are before us. See if your sister can tolerate the idea. Perhaps if we are seated at opposite ends of the table..."

"It cannot be as bad as all that," Marcello said. "I want you with us. No further discussion."

"Yes, m'lord," he said faintly. His tone let me know it was much more serious than I had thought. What in the world had happened? "I'll have the squires saddle horses for us," he said, "and form a guard as the sun sets."

"Thank you, Luca," I said, reaching out and squeezing his arm. "Might you send a squire with word to my father, over in the storehouse? And to my mother at the tombs?"

"Consider it done, m'lady," he said with a quick bow. Then he turned on his heel and left us.

Mom left each morn for the Etruscan tombs with six men in tow to help her dig. They'd unearthed six of the twelve dome-like structures. Luca liked it because it put some of his bored knights to good physical work each day, even if they thought the project odd and shared superstitious glances. He'd loved putting them to work on the new wing of the castello—the barracks for the knights, the storehouse, the latrine. But as it came close to completion, more specialized work was needed than brute strength, so fewer knights were used—leaving some free to go with Mom.

I checked Lia's room, the den, and Mom's new solarium, but she wasn't to be found. Weary and worried, I returned to our quarters. We'd changed up the rooms since our wedding, adding a library between what was once Marcello's father's cavernous room and the more intimate bedroom that was once his mother's. Here, we had a massive table surrounded by bookshelves, and on one wall, a lovely world map that my parents had found in Rome and made a wedding gift to us. We were delighted to do our part to preserve such a historical treasure. We four Betarrinis were a tad obsessed with its missing seas and undiscovered landmasses and sea monsters depicted in vast swaths of water—oceans that would not give way to the New World for another hundred years or so.

Once in a while we were able to forget we'd traveled back in time nearly seven hundred years. The rudimentary world map, and things like the lack of a real bathroom—were constant reminders. But the pangs of loss were diminishing the longer we stayed. In many ways it seemed like we had always been here. That we were where we had always meant to be.

Marcello was settled in his chair at the end of the table, going through a stack of papers, dipping his quill in ink and signing various documents while Leo, the skinny new steward, stood over his shoulder, quietly introducing one matter and then another. Mostly their business had to do with the harvest and quantities Marcello wished to store or sell, but when I entered, they were talking about a nearby vineyard that had been stripped of all its remaining grapes during the early morning hours as the vintner slept.

"Inform Captain Forelli," Marcello said. "We will not tolerate such thievery. Tell him that I wish for patrols to be assigned through the night, if necessary. It will be good to give the men something to do anyway."

"As you wish," said Leo, who was fairly new to us from Siena. He'd served one of the Nine there until the man took sick and died. Aware of his reputation of having a "sound mind and admirable counsel," Marcello had eagerly employed him. It took a great deal to manage the Forelli estate, and as Marcello prepared to resign his position as one of the Nine, it was even more vital that we squeeze every bit of profit we could out of what was ours.

I turned to my own correspondence, partly wishing I could skip the social niceties expected of me as Lady Forelli. Since it was known that I could read and write, it was understood that I would write to each of the other eight women who were wives of the Nine every month—a task I always put off until the last minute. And it was especially hard doing it this month, knowing that I would soon not have to do this sort of thing after Marcello resigned.

But today Marcello was still one of the Nine, and a messenger was set to ride come first light. I'd procrastinated long enough, totally the laziest lady of the land. But let's face it. There was a part of me that would take a good high school essay assignment over such silly social niceties. *For the love...*

The only girl I looked forward to hearing from and seeing at these gigs was Lady Inirina Spovilie. She lived on the far western side of Siena, in a castello that was a stronghold for the republic—much like Castello Forelli was on the Northeast side—and seemed to be nutsy-in-love with her husband, with his too-big nose and wide grin that made it impossible to not smile when in his company. Lord Manuel, I reminded myself. I was horrible with names. But his wife, Inirina, was the only one of the other eight I enjoyed playing pen-pals with. The rest were old, nosey ladies. Well, not old-old. Most were five to twenty years older.

I sighed, set a sheet of parchment before me, and uncorked my ink. I'd start with Lady Spovilie. Then I could just do abbreviated copies for the rest of 'em. But after I told Inirina of what was to come through the feast—knowing her home was probably in a similar state—and telling her how I was eager to see her attend our Yuletide celebration in Siena, I had a serious Nap Attack. I let a yawn go, stretching, aware that I'd drawn Leo's eye. He was Mr. Proper-Pants. He wouldn't like the lady of the house daring to yawn without covering her mouth, let alone stretch.

I hid a smile and corked my ink, then rose, holding my hands out to my husband until Marcello took them and looked up.

"Leaving so soon, m'lady?" His eyes shifted pointedly to my lone letter on the table, then back to me. He kissed one of my hands.

"I must retire for a bit and rest before we dress and leave for Castello Greco."

He nodded, and I could see some irritation with me in his chocolate brown eyes. It was apparently Seriously Important that I share the latest gossip with these Nine Girls. Maybe he felt it would help him with what was to come. I knew he was sweating the resignation, but sheesh, would a few sentences from me really grease the wheel?

I shoved away my thousandth wish for progressive thought and gave Marcello a small smile. "I shall return, m'lord, to finish the letters before we leave this eve. I promise."

I was rewarded with a small smile before he released my hands and cocked a brow at Leo, waiting for the man to introduce the next item of business. As I eased through the hidden door and into our bedroom, with its ceiling covered in stars and a fire burning low in the corner, I glanced back at him. He was rubbing his forehead as if it ached, listening to Leo drone on, and I bit my lip. In some ways, I wished we could go back in time to before he was in charge of it all. Even if we were in constant battle with Firenze, it had somehow been easier to face the big enemy before us than the hundred niggling things that now weighed on my young Tuscan lord's mind and heart.

He closed his eyes and said something lowly to Leo, and then smiled, clearly having cracked a joke. Despite it all, I still knew him to be the man I loved and admired. Life had changed for us—all of us—but I was right where I was supposed to be.

His eyes found me, still peeking at him from around the door. "M'lady? Are you in need of something?"

"Nay, nay," I said, offering him a tender smile. "I have all I could ever need," I whispered, gently closing the door behind me.

I awakened from my nap an hour later, aware that I dare not return to my lazy, warm slumber beneath the thick covers if I was to make good on my promise to my husband. I went to the buckets of water in the corner and poured one into a basin, undressed, then quickly washed my face and body. The hair would have to be washed tomorrow—I'd never get it dry in time for our trip over to Castello Greco. But I did run damp fingers through it, then thoroughly combed it. Giacinta would come and do something proper with it.

Hopefully, she was downstairs in the lady's maid's room, and not on one of Cook's hundred errands. The most I could do with my hair was a ponytail or braid. I'd need Giacinta if I was to wrestle it into the elaborate knots that were required of the gorget—a sheer throat cloth that was attached to the hair. It wasn't my favorite, but it was respectable, and after shirking my pen-pal duties earlier, I knew Marcello would appreciate the effort. He'd often said he liked how it framed my face. Add to that the fact that we were going to see none other than Lord Rodolfo Greco—a guy who had once done some Serious Flirting with me—and I was all about playing the role of the demure, satisfied matron. Alessandra didn't need to feel any threat or competition from me. Only neighborly love.

I shook out a dark green gown from a trunk, biting my lip in consternation over the wrinkles in it. But I knew from experience that they would likely ease in an hour or two. I'd just get new ones on the ride across the miles, anyway. Lia and I had lobbied for proper closets, but Mom and Dad had nixed that idea with their endless warnings about changing tradition and history. To us, bringing fourteenth-century Italians knowledge about closets before their time seemed minor. And like a big plus for us. But we'd lost that battle, as we had so many others.

Giacinta knocked quickly on the door and peeked in. "M'lady?"

"Oh, good, come in," I said, waving her forward. I turned toward her, the green gown half draped across me. "Is this suitable for dinner?"

"Yes, m'lady," she said. "'Tis a fine choice."

I didn't know why I had asked. There were only about three options. I had a total of ten gowns, a wealth by medieval standards. But most of them were far too snug already on my growing curves brought on by the little lord or lady in my womb.

"I shall summon the tailor and his seamstresses after the feast," Giacinta said, helping me into the gown and beginning to lace up the back as I stood in front of the splotchy looking glass.

I grimaced, feeling the tug and pull. "Oh no, is this one getting too small, too?" I stared in consternation as my breasts pillowed upward from the front. Thankfully, it had an empire waist, and the ample skirt fell directly downward. But the boobage was somewhat alarming. I wanted to be the demure matron, not the neighborhood vamp, right?

"Mayhap it is the last time you might wear it until your baby is born," she said, casting me a rueful smile over my shoulder via the mirror.

I tugged upward on the neckline, but it was useless. "Let's try the gold instead."

"Ahh, it has a stain."

"Drat. Well, the dark purple then?"

"A tear. Remember?"

"But you sewed it up."

"Which makes it suitable for Castello Forelli, but not for a visit to Castello Greco. It might be seen as a slight," she said gently. "This dress is fine, m'lady."

"Are you certain?" I turned back to my reflection.

"I am. Wear the gown tonight and I shall see about letting it out at the seams on the morrow."

"At this rate, I'll be in sack cloth by next week if the tailor doesn't hasten to us."

She smiled. "I doubt that, m'lady," she said, smoothing out my shoulder seams and tugging down the sleeves. Even they seemed tight. It was like my entire body was swelling. Like the week before my period. Except *every* week was that way now. I yanked at my sleeves until they were in place, hoping they wouldn't cut off circulation. If need be, I'd slip into the privy and take my knife to them.

Giacinta set a stool before the mirror and combed through my hair again as I pouted at my reflection.

"I'm a sausage stuffed in too tight a casing," I muttered.

"Nonsense," she said, a tiny smile on her bow of lips. "You are radiant. Glowing."

"Give me another few months. I'll have to stay in these rooms and not come out until the baby is born, or all will talk of the She-Wolf becoming a giant She-Cow."

"I doubt that, m'lady," she said with a smile, winding a coil of hair backward and pinning it at the nape of my neck. "Besides, I thought you were fervently against people making assumptions of others simply because of how they appeared."

"Yes, yes," I groaned, wincing as she pinned a second and then third coil. This is why her hairdos stayed and mine did not. She did not mind inflicting pain on me. I, on the other hand, avoided it at all costs. With three more deft moves, she wound the separate coils into one knot and added a few more pins. All told, I had enough ebony pins in my hair to outfit a walrus with false teeth. You know, a black walrus with black teeth, not ivory. The Darth Vader of walruses.

Where do these hair pins come from, exactly? I had to find out.

"Giacinta, I saw Isabella snitching cakes from Cook's shelves yesterday." The image of the round-cheeked, sweet girl with hair as red as her mama's made me smile. She'd actually lifted a small finger to her lips, sealing me into a wordless secret. And I'd laughed. The girl was all of four years old and as bold as her young mother.

"What?" she said, staring at my reflection with dismay.

"I did," I said ruefully. "I've seen Cook take a switch to the squires for doing the same. I thought you'd wish to warn her. No doubt the girl has simply learned from the other children."

"I'll take a switch to her myself, the little imp," she said, shaking her head as she worked to attach the net to my tapestry cap, worn on the top, back side of my scalp. I winced as she tugged and the hair pulled. "Forgive me," she muttered, pulling anew. I wasn't fooled. She didn't feel a bit sorry. She took pride in the fact that she seemed to be the only one in Castello Forelli who could tame the lady's hair and was gunning to keep that glory. Whereas most days I opted for a quick braid I could do myself, I knew I'd be subjected to this several more times in the next week as the feast went on, and dignitaries and neighbors came to visit.

"There," she said at last, standing back, hands on hips.

"*Grazie mille,*" I said, turning to one side and then the next, viewing with satisfaction the neat coils, knowing they'd stay for a while. *A thousand thanks.* I rose and smoothed my skirts, casting one more anxious glance to my swelling form.

Marcello came in then and caught me staring. "Ah, my Gabriella," he said, coming over and taking me into his arms from behind. Giacinta left without a word. He bent and kissed that tender part of my neck where it met my shoulder, and I shivered in delight. "The best part about

Giacinta doing your hair, is that it leaves all this delightful skin ripe for the taking..."

I squirmed away from him, turned, then wrapped my arms around him, bringing him close for a kiss. "Thank you, husband," I said. *Just when I was feeling fat...*

"For bestowing the finest of kisses?" he said, quirking a brow.

"For being you," I said. I gave him a quick peck on the lips and pushed him away when he tried to pull me closer for something more. "Nay, nay," I said, with mock chastising. "If you continue, we're more apt to end up undressed instead of ready for our journey."

"Would that be so awful?" he asked, pulling at my hips and giving me a sultry look. "We could ask Luca and Lia to give the Grecos our apologies."

I smiled and leaned back to look up at him. "Oh? And what would you say?"

"Brother," he said, crossing his arms and looking to our ceiling, as if dictating, "Please accept my most sincere apologies. I dearly wished to join you to sup this eve. But I found I could not resist the desire to bed my wife."

I laughed and felt the heat of a blush rise at my cheeks. "That would be a fine letter for him to read in the company of my sister and parents."

"Nay?" he said, arching his brow again. He pursed his lips and sighed, looking me slowly up and down. "Ahh, well. Later, then."

I moved to fetch a handkerchief, but he caught my wrist. I turned back to him.

"Later?" he repeated huskily, all seriousness, his dark eyes running up the length of my arm, my neck, my face, as if he were kissing every inch.

"Later," I agreed with an impish smile. "But right *now*, I must go finish those letters I promised you I'd write. So, you know, I am not *occupied* later."

CHAPTER 3

EVANGELIA

"So, what's up with you two?" Gabi said lowly, edging her horse closer, looking at me over her shoulder. "I haven't seen Luca so sad and serious since we were in the thick of battle."

We were on the way to Castello Greco, having just passed the riverbed. Knights flanked us on the front and rear, as well as to either side of us. But I was reasonably sure no one else could hear her. Still, I stole a glance forward to Luca, six riders away. He hadn't even looked my direction when I entered the courtyard. Celso was the one who helped me mount, his face telling me he had been assigned the task and felt awkward performing it.

No one but Luca had helped me mount my horse in months.

"He's angry with me," I muttered at last.

"Why? What have you done?"

I felt a flash of anger wash through me. "Maybe it was something *he* did."

"Okay," she said slowly, clearly not believing me. We both knew that Luca would do anything to please me.

"He's pressing me. For a wedding. Soon."

She faced mostly forward in her sidesaddle, swaying with the gait of her horse, and I admired her profile, the new confidence in her. Marriage agreed with her. Peace, too. Maybe even being pregnant. Why couldn't I share her sense of adventure? Her gambling spirit? Why did I have to think it all through, over and over again, until I had uncovered every tiny little problem—and the biggies too?

"You two have been together a long time," she whispered, giving me a shrug. "You know, by medieval standards."

"I'm only seventeen," I said, hating the whine in my tone.

"Almost eighteen. The same age I was when I wed Marcello."

"And, yeah, look how that turned out," I said, gesturing toward her belly.

She looked a little wounded, her brown eyes searching mine. Then she looked up and around us at the trees, the dry autumn leaves practically crackling in the breeze. "So that's it? You don't wanna get pregnant like me?"

I bit my lip. There was nothing I could say that wouldn't hurt her. Or bring up things that would stress her out. Which wasn't good for the baby...

But what was I to do, lie? Fear of pregnancy was at the heart of it. I loved Luca. I did. But if I married him now, we could have *two* children by the time the plague rolled through. And knowing him, maybe I'd even be pregnant with number three. He was a gentleman with me, always, never pressing me for more than kisses. But there was a heat in those kisses that promised of much more...

My eyes settled on the strong, straight line of his shoulders, covered in the leather breastplate he and the other knights wore any time they left Castello Forelli. His wavy, dark-blond hair had grown out a lot since I cut it—it curled and brushed the high neck of his formal Forelli-gold tunic now.

"So you'll break his heart," Gabi said, nodding toward him then looking back at me. "To avoid the *potential* of your own heart breaking?"

I scowled at her, not wanting Mom and Dad to overhear. The way she said it made me sound a coward rather than cautious. "I think you've risked enough on all our behalf, don't you?" I snapped back.

Hurt washed across her brow, and I wished I could take back the words. But I couldn't. What was it about sisters that made us free to share both the harshest and kindest words? "Gabs," I said with a groan.

"Nay," she said, lifting a hand. "Don't say anything else, Lia. Not now."

I sighed again and looked over at the forest, in the full glory of autumn, with all her colors of gold and pumpkin and sage. I loved it here, I did. But I was feeling stifled again. Trapped. And all this marriage talk made it worse. "I think I need to get out," I said.

She made me wait for an uncomfortably long moment. "Out?" she asked, her tone icy.

"Just for a bit. Out of Toscana. What if...what if we went to Venezia? Before you're too far along to travel? Before..." I let the rest of my words drop. She would understand.

Gabi didn't turn me down right away, but I knew it was a long shot. Mom wouldn't be wild about her taking so long a journey over rough roads, this far along in pregnancy. Exposing herself to God-knew-what in a port city. But we were still a year and a bit away from the start of the plague...

"If we don't go now, when would we?" I muttered.

She stilled and then looked at me, the warmth returning to her expression, a glint of excitement in her eyes. "Do you think? Do you think we could convince them?"

Together, we looked back at our parents, who rode behind us.

"Uh oh," Dad said to Mom, catching our glance. "I've seen *that* look before. What are you two cooking up?"

"Nothing," I said, the pull of a smile at my lips.

"Uh-huh," Mom said doubtfully. She looked so regal in her navy gown. So beautiful beside our handsome dad, as fair in her Danish heritage as he was with his dark, classic Italian genes. I felt the urge to demand they stop, then and there, so I could sketch them, and later paint it, filling in the backdrop of the swelling forest in all its pretty colors. But

Mom and Dad had forbidden me to sketch or paint any of us. We were in the wrong time and place. They wanted no record in the history books, rudimentary as they might be. It was enough that historians were sure to write of our presence. To tell tales of the She-Wolves...

But they looked right, dead-on glorious here, in medieval garb, atop their horses. At ease in their own skin. They filled their days with collecting artifacts and unearthing the Etruscan tombs and finishing the castello expansion project. But they loved it, absolutely loved it all. *Tuscan bliss*, they called it, as they'd always called it, but now it meant so much more...

I wished I could give in to the same. Trust that this ancient past wasn't going to somehow obliterate my future.

"Lia?"

I started, realizing Gabi had said something.

"When would you want to go?" she repeated.

"Uh, the sooner the better, right? For you?"

"Right," she said, thinking. A lovely smile spread across her face as she looked to her husband, riding beside Luca. Evidently, she had an idea in mind on how to convince him. Luca, on the other hand, would likely have some concerns. Or become an outright block. After all, if Captain Forelli wasn't bending over backward to please me, he could become the worst sort of stonewall. The man was as blastedly stubborn as Gabi...

It mattered not. All I had to do was convince Gabi, and the rest would fall into line. That was the way of our family now. Perhaps, I mused, it'd always been the way.

We were crossing the wide riverbed, now nothing more than a foot-wide trickle with little algae-covered ponds here and there, the old boundary line between Castello Forelli and Castello Greco. It had once meant we were crossing into Paratore territory...

"You all right?" Gabi asked, pulling her horse closer to me. She knew this always brought back some fears in me—it did for her, too—even though our old enemy was dead.

"I'm all right," I whispered. "It's better now that it's Rodolfo's and Alessandra's, you know?"

She nodded. "Let's make this the start of a memory makeover campaign," she said with a smile. "Take all those rotten memories with Cosmo Paratore and replace them with better ones with the Grecos."

"That'd work."

I saw Luca at the lead, on the top of the hill just before the road turned and disappeared from sight. He was looking back at me, as if he was wondering the same thing as Gabi. If I was all right. We might not be on speaking terms at the moment, but I felt his love, his care.

What was I *doing?*

Was I driving away my hope at future happiness?

And yet, if he truly loved me, why could we not just keep things the same and marry after the plague was over?

I needed to get out of here, to clear my head. A break from Toscana and, in particular, one handsome, sandy-haired Tuscan with those beautiful green eyes...

GABRIELLA

I liked this idea of Lia's very much. And I was especially glad for it as we passed the Etruscan tomb field, winding our way up the hill and spying the hulking lines of Castello Greco. It kept me from thinking too much about Rodolfo Greco. How it would be to see him again. If it would be weird or awkward between us. If it would be strange, watching him with his new wife, Alessandra.

Marcello had my heart in total, but Rodolfo had been a fling, a serious attraction that died harder for him than it had for me. It had been a challenge every day he was in the castle to maintain a proper distance, to be a friend to him and give him nothing he might misconstrue as hope. I'm talkin' serious boundary lines. But we'd made it work.

If Marcello ever sensed either of us edging near those lines...No, I had to get my mind off it. Rodolfo was kind of like an ex-boyfriend. The road not traveled. *And I love my Road,* I said to myself, staring at the shoulders and profile of the man I adored most in the world.

He shared a smile with Luca, then laughed outright. His laughter came more readily of late—especially when he was away from his desk—and his joy and contentment was contagious. He loved his life as lord of the castello, loved this stretch of peace with the Fiorentini, loved me, loved our baby steadily growing in my womb. Satisfaction practically seeped from his pores.

Only the thought of resigning from the Nine seemed to trouble him. But there was no other option—we had to make a way for him to steer clear of the city, considering what was to come. If he was still at the helm when that ship sailed, he'd ride straight into Plague-o-rama. And my parents had made him see that if he helped Siena prepare for it as we had, it would change the historical course in a monumental way.

As the tall gates of Castello Greco opened and we rode through, memories of the battles we'd fought here with Paratore washed over me again. But they felt distant and resolved, in a way. Healed, or at least heal*ing*. And now that Lord and Lady Greco were home from their travels, it was the perfect time for a sojourn to Venezia. Rodolfo could see to any serious political issues that might arise. Send word to us if there was a problem. In this fleeting season, we might actually be able to simply be tourists, soaking up more of medieval Italia...I knew Mom and Dad would be over the moon at the prospect.

Rodolfo came into view and I hated my sudden nervousness.

"Greetings," he said, standing beside his lovely wife, looking like a fine lady in her new gown. He grinned up at Marcello and after my husband dismounted, they took each other's arm and pulled closer, sharing a kiss on both cheeks. Marcello turned to aid me in dismounting, and I caught Alessandra's eye, smiling in welcome. Her short hair had been slicked back and tucked, creating the illusion that it was much longer;

but I knew it couldn't be longer than her shoulders. She came over to greet me and Lia, and I could see a new measure of joy in her eyes. Peace.

Alessandra: the girl who once hated Greco and then came to love him. I was glad for him. For both of them, really. And with her father disowning her, we were all the family she really had.

"You look well, my friend," I said. "Marriage agrees with you."

She laughed and blushed. "As it agrees with most during the earliest days. Now that we begin our real life—"

"It will be as good for you as it is for Gabriella," Lia said, pretending to not have her own concerns.

Lia and I turned to Rodolfo and nodded. "M'lord," we said in unison, giving him a brief curtsy.

"M'ladies," he said, with a slow, elegant bow. As he rose his dark eyes rested on mine for just a second before he flicked them toward Lia. "Thank you for welcoming us home."

"You were missed," I said. "The boars have all grown fat and lazy, sitting out in the open without you and your lady hunting them."

Rodolfo glanced at his wife with a grin. When he smiled, he was frightfully handsome. And he was hers. *Hers.* Just as Marcello was mine. I was totally good with it. It was just...weird.

Alessandra grinned and laid her arm on her husband's. "Well, we shall have to remedy that at once, shan't we? Remind those boars whose lands they roam."

"Indeed," he said indulgently, turning her toward the castle keep. "Come, my friends, come. The table is set, and we shall feast and properly christen the castello with wine and delicacies."

Marcello offered me his arm, and I settled my hand atop his. We were right together. We'd battled through much to get to this place, this stage of life and contentment. And as we entered the castle, Rodolfo and Alessandra's home, I felt everything had at last come together. Settled. Except...

"What are we going to do about Luca and Lia?" I whispered to Marcello.

"*We* are not going to do anything about them. Let them be, Gabriella. They shall find their own way."

"Nonsense," I whispered back. "My little sister needs assistance. So does your little cousin."

"Your *little* sister and my *little* cousin are full-grown. *And* in full command of their decision-making faculties."

"Hmm. Mayhap."

"Gabriella..." he groaned.

"Trust me. I won't meddle where I needn't."

He shot me a playful warning look as we entered the Great Hall and separated. We women went directly to the cavernous hearth, where a huge fire crackled and spit and danced over a solid bed of red embers. It radiated warmth, and we sank gratefully into chairs set in an arc, six feet back. Mom and Lia were on one side of Alessandra and I was on the other.

I lifted my chilled hands toward the flames and felt my cheeks begin to thaw. A steward came and offered us earthen mugs full of mulled wine and the others accepted it. Quietly, I asked for some warm cider instead. In this era, lots of expectant moms drank wine throughout their pregnancy, but I was taking no chances.

"Brr," Lia said, rubbing her upper arms. "I hadn't realized I had become so chilled."

"We left in summer and returned to deep autumn," Alessandra said.

"A proper time away, I think, for a honeymoon," I said. "Tell us! I want to hear all about it."

She smiled, a bit embarrassed.

"Well, not all about it," I said slyly. "Where did you go? Did you run into any...trouble?" I was careful to not use the word *Fiorentini*, aware that Alessandra's broken ties with her kinsmen would certainly still chafe. The fact that her father had disowned her—believing the lies the Fiorentini had told of her—still ached within my own heart. I had no idea how she could tolerate it. My eyes shifted to Dad, laughing and talking with Rodolfo, patting him on the back. We'd gone back in time to save him. I hoped somehow, some way, Alessandra would one day be reunited with her own father.

"We went south, to Roma," she said, "and stayed with Lord Vivaro."

"Lord Vivaro," I repeated, remembering my own stay with the guy, who could give some Broadway actors a run for their money in terms of sass and drama.

Alessandra's eyes clouded. "Forgive me. Rodolfo told me...I didn't mean to bring up hard memories for you, m'lady."

I shook my head and forced a smile, reaching out to squeeze her hand. "Not at all. 'Tis but a distant memory, a wild adventure. And it was in Roma that Rodolfo set me free...it was there that he managed to sneak in Marcello and Luca, my sister and parents. And now to know that he took you there—the bride who was meant for him all along—well, it all turned out as it ought, yes?"

She nodded tentatively, a hint of worry at the edges of her eyes.

It surprised me, at first, that Vivaro, a Roman with ties to the Fiorentini, had hosted them. But then, the dude was a total salesman, eager to make friends with *anyone* in high places, and Greco was scoring big in a different sector these days...

"Are not Lord Vivaro's baths the most miraculous thing you've ever experienced?" I said, seizing on a common factor we could talk easily about.

"*Yes*," she said, the tension immediately lifting from her face. "They were glorious! Do you think I might convince Rodolfo to install a small version of them here?"

"Of course!" I said. "He would do anything for you."

"Ahh," Lia said dreamily. "And we'd have to visit and join you in them from time to time. You'd become the most popular stop in all of Toscana, being the only castello with a proper Roman bath. Our own neighborhood spa!" she said, adding the last bit in English and looking toward Mom and me.

I returned my gaze to Alessandra, and after a puzzled glance at Lia over her foreign phrasing, she told us of touring the ruins of Roma, of venturing south, to Tivoli, and of its amazing gardens with fountain after fountain. "Surely the best in all of Italia," she said.

"Oh, now that's a place I simply must convince Benedetto to take me," Mom said. "And then?"

"Then we went to Ostia and boarded a ship that Rodolfo hired to do nothing but take us from port to port, south and around to the east coast, all the way up to Venezia." She shook her head, her brown eyes wide and wistful, as if she wished she could return to those long, languid days upon the sea.

"That sounds utterly wonderful," I sighed. Marcello and I had never taken a honeymoon. It wasn't a thing in this era. As soon as we were married, we'd been embroiled in battle; and then with the demands on him in both Siena and here at home, it seemed we never had the time for me to convince him to go away with me for a while. Lia shot me a meaningful glance, and I knew she was once again thinking of a trip to Venezia. And more and more, I was warming to the idea.

"Ladies, would you join us?" Rodolfo called, gesturing toward the long table, now set with dishes that steamed in the chilled air, far from the fireplace. We all rose and went over to where the men waited, standing beside each of our chairs. I felt Lia hesitate when she saw Luca, looking almost sick as he waited for her to approach. *Maybe a trip would help them get past their troubles.* Any idea of them ending up as anything other than Happily-Ever-After was impossible for me to digest. The two were born to love each other. My silly sister just had to accept it...and the risks. Once and for all.

She nodded briefly at Luca, silently thanking him as he pulled out the chair and assisted her to move closer to the table. With the long, heavy skirts we wore, I was always grateful for the help, too. When all the ladies were seated, the men took their chairs beside them.

Servants passed the steaming pots and food on trays and we served ourselves, sliding portions onto our own wooden trenchers. Roast capons, pasta tossed with olive oil and tart, grated pecorino cheese, roasted squash and peppers. It all looked fabulous.

"Did you secure a new cook along your travels?" I asked Alessandra.

"Yes," she said with a triumphant grin. "He is from Sicily and, if he continues to cook this well, I shall weigh as much as a boulder!"

"Nonsense," Rodolfo said, taking her hand and bringing it to his lips. "We shall just ride longer in the afternoons, and we can continue eating all we wish." They shared an intimate smile and Alessandra blushed prettily. How long would it be before she was pregnant, too? As much as I lamented any other children brought into a world before the plague was upon us, I couldn't deny that it would be cool to have a little playmate for my munchkin.

I resisted the urge to slap myself upside the head and instead furiously shoved down a big bite of poultry. Was I really plotting my girlfriends' pregnancies just to score a decent play date? *Sometimes I don't recognize you any longer, Gabs, I swear.*

Leave it to time travel to seriously mess with your head.

"Did you run into any trouble on your journey?" Marcello asked carefully. *From the Fiorentini,* he meant.

"Nay. Two men served as scouts for us and made certain the way was clear everywhere we went in Roma. And once we made port and were at sea..." He paused to share a tender smile with Alessandra before stabbing a bit of squash with the end of his knife. "Once we were at sea, it was as if we left every trouble behind. We chose our ports carefully, of course."

"May it be so for all of us, forevermore," Luca said, lifting his wine goblet in a toast.

"I shall drink to that," said my dad, and the rest agreed, raising their glasses.

But the good vibe ended minutes later as the boys got into some heated debate. The Nine had just voted to back the woolen guild's claim to more grazing land for their sheep, and every lord within the republic was to allow a hundred sheep on their land, free of charge.

"I've never heard of anything so ridiculous," Rodolfo said, leaning back in his chair, his capon bones picked clean. He lifted his goblet and took a drink. "Did these shepherds buy this land? Do they pay to maintain it? Protect it?"

"Nay, but land is difficult to come by for most men, and more and more, it's parsed up into bits too small to feed more than a few sheep. They need a lot of land, freedom to graze. If we want a constant supply of both wool and cloth, and even mutton," Marcello said, leaning back in his own chair, "'tis the only way."

"So we're to have a hundred sheep here?" Rodolfo said. "Eating every blade of grass I'd rather feed my cattle?"

"A hundred for me, a hundred for you," Marcello returned easily. "Is it truly so much to ask?"

"'Tis for a man who prefers a fat *bistecca* to a leg of lamb," Rodolfo grumbled.

Marcello raised a brow. "So serve the lamb to your servants. They won't complain. You'll be getting it at a good price. And the wool and resulting cloth as well. Trust me, in time this agreement will prove to be wise for all of us. Siena will gain strength from it."

Rodolfo moved his head back and forth, as if weighing that thought. Castles took a lot of people to run them; the Grecos would likely employ nearly as many as we did in time. And that meant a great deal of food and clothing were needed as well. Already a hundred or more sheep roamed our hills, and fifty head of cattle. Nearly the same wandered Rodolfo's hills now, too.

His dark eyes moved to my parents as a servant refilled his goblet of wine and our empty trenchers were removed. "I am told that you have been at work in the tombs below us, Lady Betarrini," he said casually.

But I knew that look. There was far more intent behind it than his tone belied.

"As you gave me permission to do," she said carefully. "I am most grateful, m'lord, as it helps further my...studies."

"What is it about the Etruscans that so fascinates you?" This, he directed toward my father. He knew Dad was there as often as Mom.

Dad leaned on the table and lifted his goblet. "How can they not fascinate us? Here they ruled much of Italia for centuries and then disappeared. We wish to know what drove them away, what destroyed their villages, and where they went. Those tombs are valuable clues."

"You are scholars, through and through. Which is respectable in a man and...*notable* in a woman."

Marcello cocked his head and gave our host a long look. Alessandra looked down to her lap, as if anxious, then to him.

"Rodolfo, what is this about?" Marcello asked.

Lord Greco gave him a long, appraising look, and then turned to the steward and two maids. *"Lascia, per favore."*

I stilled as the servants scurried out. What was this?

Had Rodolfo discovered something...about us?

When the servants were gone, the door shut quietly behind them, Rodolfo rose and gestured toward the fireplace. "Please. Join me."

He wanted to be even farther from the door and listening ears. The hairs on the back of my neck prickled in fear. Trying to act casual, we all rose and walked to the fireplace, where the men brought other chairs to close in our circle. When we were all sitting, Rodolfo leaned forward, elbows on knees, steepling his fingertips.

"Alessandra and I have much to tell you. Much that puzzles and concerns us."

"If this is about our excavations in the tombs..." Mom began.

"It is that and more," he said gently. His keen eyes searched her. "You must know that the tales of the She-Wolves of Siena are rather wild in Firenze. At first, I dismissed them all, but there are some that have stuck.

And some that my wife has verified the villagers hold as truth more than lore."

Alessandra met his gaze and then looked to us, nodding once. "Some say," she began, "that the Ladies Betarrini did not come from Normandy, but rather from the tombs themselves. That you are witches who have put a hex on Firenze and hold great power. Over men, in particular."

"Witches?" I said with a scoff. "That is laughable."

"Obviously," Rodolfo said, leaning back in his chair and crossing one foot over his other knee. "But the tombs...One of Paratore's knights swore that you three emerged from the tomb with Lord Betarrini. And that Lord Betarrini was in odd clothing. That day, you killed all but that man. An entire patrol of Paratore knights. It's memorable. And before then, Lord Betarrini was never seen in Toscana. He just seemed to...appear." Rodolfo's fingers made a "poof" gesture.

Mom smiled benignly. "Well, no wonder the Fiorentini talk, if stories like that fuel their fires. And our scholarly fascination does nothing to quell it."

"Nay," Alessandra said, shaking her head. She glanced toward her husband. "Rodolfo gave you permission to dig them out and study them, knowing the Fiorentini were well across the border and few would know. But, Lady Betarrini, people talk." She reached over and took Mom's hand. "We fear for you. Superstition..." She shook her head in frustration. "'Tis aggravating. But 'tis always present. And superstition can drive a mob to do foolish things."

"Indeed," Rodolfo said.

I eyed Marcello. He wasn't offended. Just worried. I didn't dare look at my family.

"In the battle, before you were married," Rodolfo said carefully, "when you ladies left Toscana, you were last seen in this vicinity. And when you returned, you were first seen at Castello Forelli. As if you'd simply appeared again, rather than made the journey in from the coast."

"You of all people have to understand why they had to move as covertly as possible," Marcello said, flicking his hand out.

It wasn't an attack. Just a statement of the obvious. At the time he spoke of, Rodolfo had been working mostly for the Fiorentini, hoping to somehow broker a peace between the republics. Until they made him the scapegoat.

"Had Gabriella and Evangelia been recognized," Marcello continued, "they would have been in extreme danger. And when they returned last, I didn't even hold Castello Forelli."

Greco took a long breath through his nostrils and looked at me and my sister and mother.

We all waited in silence.

"So you are saying," Rodolfo said slowly, fiddling with the thick stem of his ceramic goblet, "that the three most recognizable women in all of Toscana left and *returned* without anyone else seeing them? From the very heart of Toscana? Gabriella, she could pass as one of our own. But Evangelia's fair hair, to say nothing of Lady Adri's..." His eyebrows knit as if it was a puzzle he couldn't yet decipher, and his brown eyes flicked over each of us in turn.

"Yes," Marcello said, setting his goblet down on a side table with exaggerated care. "That's what we're saying, Rodolfo. They are the She-Wolves," he added with a smile, barely covering his rising agitation. I doubted Rodolfo missed it either. "You have seen them in battle. You have witnessed them slip from captivity and cross borders unseen."

"True," Rodolfo allowed.

"They are uncommon women. Uncommon people leave *commoners* to weave tall tales behind them, trying to explain them in a way that makes everyone comfortable. Surely you have not succumbed to the fables of the simple?"

Rodolfo gave him a thin-lipped smile. He wasn't an idiot. He wanted to believe us—his friends, and now compatriots and neighbors—but he wasn't a fool. "There is more," he said slowly.

We watched as he rose, went to the hearth, and poked at a log with an iron tool, sending a drift of sparks up the chimney. And we all waited.

He turned to face us, one hand on the mantle, but his eyes were on me. "We were in Venezia, at court, when we first heard of them."

"*Rodolfo*," Luca said, an edge of warning in his voice. None of us liked how he was dragging this out.

"We learned of some of your kin. Betarrinis."

I froze, wondering if I'd heard him right.

"Two young men found wandering outside of Ravenna. In odd clothing. Telling tales of arriving from a tomb. Of setting their hands on handprints and being reborn into a different...age."

My eyes widened, and I saw his pupils dilate, well aware that he'd hit a nerve. Silence, heavy as death, weighed in the air between us.

And then the room erupted, everyone talking at once.

CHAPTER 4

GABRIELLA

Into the din Dad shouted at us all to be quiet. *"Fermare! Chetarsi!"*

When everyone stopped and looked at him he said, *"Betarrini.*
You're certain their name is Betarrini? Or is it simply a rumor because it
makes for a more titillating tale?"

"We were introduced," Rodolfo said, turning a measured gaze on
Dad, watching him carefully, clearly using each of our reactions as further pieces for his mental puzzling.

"Met them? Where?" Marcello said.

"At court in Venezia. The doge brings them in to show off to dinner
guests, much as he might an elephant or tiger." He turned to Dad.
"When they found out we were of Toscana, they asked after you and
your family, beseeched me, in fact, to escort them to you."

Mom blanched, and I saw that Rodolfo took this in, too, looking
quickly to me. "Are they truly kin to you?" he asked.

"Nay," I said. "I mean, I do not think so…" I sought Dad's help with
a look.

"How old are they?" Dad asked. "What were their given names?"

Rodolfo shook his head. "I never heard them. Did you, Alessandra?"

"Nay."

"The doge simply took to calling them He-Wolves but seemed agitated when they refused to continue telling their tales."

My mind raced. The doge, the Head Cheese of Venice and Genoa, commander of the biggest navy in our medieval world, was not one to mess with.

"How old are these men?" Lia asked.

"I'd say no older than twenty."

Dad closed his eyes and heaved a sigh, as if overwhelmed by this news.

"We must go to them. Surely they're related to us in some manner," Mom said.

"Or it is simply a ruse," Luca said easily to Marcello. "The doge has long been interested in bringing Gabriella and Evangelia to court. You've turned down one or two invitations?"

"Three," Marcello said, nodding at his captain, chin in hand as he stood and began pacing.

Rodolfo squinted at them.

"Those men could be actors," Marcello said. "Weaving an elaborate net so that the doge can finally get the elusive 'She-Wolves of Siena' to court."

"But you've never said the doge meant us harm," I said. "Only that he was curious."

"The man collects people as some women do jewels," Rodolfo said. "It undoubtedly chafes that you haven't yet attended him. He shall endeavor to keep you at court all winter, should you give him the opportunity."

"But he also casts people aside without a thought. Imprisons those who agitate him," Luca said. "Exiles others. I am not certain we should allow our Betarrinis to be any closer to *those* Betarrinis, be they related or not."

"If they are possibly family," Dad said, "we must go to them, Luca. We must." He was frightened. Frightened that these newcomers would inadvertently compromise us and all we'd built here. And his fear freaked me out more than anything.

"The boys—these young men," Mom said. "Were they truly from Ravenna? Or did their accent sound as if they hailed from Britannia and Normandy, as we did?" She held her gaze steady, but I wasn't the only one who noticed her voice rise. I'm sure Rodolfo had.

"I heard nothing of other lands," he said, probably thinking of our whole Britannia /Normandy story anew. "Only Ravenna."

I stood and edged away. I needed some fresh air. Space to think. Mumbling an excuse, I walked down a wide, tall hallway to a small room that functioned as a guest bathroom—little more than a corner pail to squat over, and a wash basin and pitcher—even though I didn't need to go. I leaned my head against the door, my mind racing.

Was it possible? Was there some sort of weird Betarrini gene that allowed us all to time travel? Was the tunnel only open between medieval times and the future? Would it someday close? Were these boys from the year we'd left? Or another? We had to speak to them. As soon as possible.

With shaking hands I poured water into the basin and hurriedly splashed my face before exiting.

He was there, waiting.

Rodolfo. Leaning against the far wall, arms crossed. I could hear the continued, agitated conversation emanating from the Great Hall. Ongoing debate between my family and Luca.

"Will you tell me the truth now, Gabriella?" Rodolfo said softly, unmoving. "About where you are truly from?"

There was no accusation in his tone, only gentle prodding.

"You know where I am from," I said, walking past him. I needed to get back to Marcello, let him field Rodolfo's questions, decide what to tell him—and what not to.

But he hurried after me, grabbing my arm and swinging me around to face him.

I frowned. "Rodolfo, let *go*."

He ignored my demand and instead took my other arm, too. "*Confide* in me," he pleaded, leaning forward. "I want to help. I want to protect you. And your family," he added hurriedly. "You are my kin now, too."

"But they are *my* responsibility first," Marcello said coldly from ten paces behind me. I froze, feeling unaccountably guilty, even though I'd done nothing. "Unhand my wife."

"You are keeping something from me," Rodolfo said, still staring at me, not dropping his hands. In fact, his grip tightened. "Tell me, Gabriella. I've seen things in that tomb that I think you might be able to explain—"

Marcello strode toward us, and I felt the tension of old jealousies, of boundaries crossed—and pushed Rodolfo's hands away myself before my husband reached us. I had to find a way to settle them down before it turned into a fight...

Rodolfo slowly turned toward Marcello as I took my husband's arm. "You tell me then, brother," he said, gesturing in frustration to me. "Tell me *exactly* what is behind all of this. I think I deserve the truth. Because it shall not be long before what affects Castello Forelli affects Castello Greco. And your wife is not truly from Normandy or *Britannia*. Is she?"

"You have all the truth you need," Marcello ground out, staring back at him, cheek muscles clenching. I dropped my hand and stepped back, afraid they were about to get into it physically.

"Why? Why can you not simply tell me? Your sworn brother. Your brother at arms. Your brother who has sacrificed everything for you, for Gabriella..."

Marcello shook his head and sighed. He gestured up and around the opulent hall. "This is hardly a hovel." He sighed, struggling to regain his composure, and then reached out, palm up. "Can you not simply trust me, Rodolfo? Trust us? As you always have before? Have I given you cause to doubt me?"

Rodolfo stared at him a good long while before grudgingly gripping his arm to the elbow and pulling his face close, all sober intent. "You shall tell me before it becomes a crisis?"

"Don't I always?" Marcello asked, a hint of a grin tugging at the corners of his lips.

But Rodolfo wasn't ready to joke around. "Upon my life, Forelli, if this costs me...If Alessandra is hurt in this..."

"She shall not be. Neither shall you," Marcello said, instantly serious again. "'Tis our puzzle alone to unravel, these mysterious potential kin. We shall do our best to keep you out of it. You have my word."

"But I do not *wish* to be out of it," Rodolfo said, brow lowering. "Don't you see? I wish to stand with you. For the first time, I'm free to do so as a fellow Sienese. Why not bring me into your confidence?"

"Because the fewer who know the truth of it, the better," Marcello growled in frustration. "Some things are that way. You know that more than anyone, yes?"

The two stood there, staring at each other. Then Marcello took a deep breath and forced a lighter expression to his face. "It appears we must now take our leave so that we can make preparations for a visit to Venezia. I need you to stand in my stead, seeing the harvest feast through. You shall do so for me? Leo, my new steward, shall be by your side from beginning to end."

Rodolfo said nothing. He looked stricken and frustrated. Then he nodded once and said, "I shall do as you say, brother."

Marcello turned to me, waiting as if I'd just returned to a dance floor after a trip to the bathroom. I walked toward him, my legs feeling like jelly, my nausea—forgotten with my first trimester—suddenly rearing its ugly head again. *It'd be super cool if I vomited my guts out right now. Yeah, that'd top off the evening just right...*

I concentrated on breathing slowly and deeply, in and out my nose, taking comfort in the solid strength of my husband's hand at my lower back. Out in the Great Room, we hurriedly thanked Alessandra, kissing her on both cheeks, and made our way out.

"Well, on the bright side, we won't have to talk the clan into going to Venezia," I whispered to Lia as we entered the courtyard. "It's as good as done."

"I wanted a pleasure trip," she moaned.

"Yeah, well, you can't get everything."

Marcello lifted me to my saddle, and I noticed that this time, Luca wordlessly lifted Lia to hers. Neither spoke, nor looked at each other, but it was as if the threat of this new development brought them a step closer. As if they both needed the other, even if they couldn't admit it.

Rodolfo took Dad's arm and then Luca's. Last, Marcello's.

"Remember, as much as you view the Fiorentini *Grandi* as a nest of vipers, they pale in comparison to the Venetians and their doge," Rodolfo said. "Do not underestimate him."

"I understand," Marcello said, no trace of fear in his tone.

"I hope you do, brother," Rodolfo said, releasing him. "I hope you do."

CHAPTER 5

EVANGELIA

We met up at home, squirreled away in Marcello and Gabi's library, with guards posted downstairs, making certain none of the many people in the castle might wander near enough to hear us. Still, we spoke in hushed voices. Marcello and Dad paced. Luca leaned against the wall, arms folded, watching, waiting. Mom sat in a chair, nervously twisting a handkerchief.

"We have to go to them," Gabi said again. "Bring them here. They must be wild with fear."

Marcello shook his head, chin in hand. "Or would we be safer staying as far from them as possible?"

Gabi and I shared a look. *There goes the trip to Venezia.*

"Their name already ties them to you," Marcello continued. "What if they say—what if they've *already* said things that incriminate them as fortune tellers or diviners? Some might say they're warlocks!" He lifted a hand to emphasize his words, then dropped it. "The doge keeps them as entertainment, much as you might traveling actors. But soon he will weary of their wild tales."

"You've never told us of the future," Luca said evenly, his keen green eyes flicking over me before turning to Dad. "How difficult would it be to believe their tales?"

"Nearly impossible. There are reasons we don't speak of it," Dad said, slicing his hand through the air. "It is terribly dangerous. Not only because it would sound so outlandish, but because it might change the future forever. It's difficult being here, watching everything we do, say..."

"And yet with every day that passes," Mom said, "*they* might be saying more and more."

"Mayhap they're too frightened to say anything," Gabi said. "It took a few days for me to realize—to accept—that I was really here. In this time. But once that happened, I realized that the more I said, the more I might be in danger."

"Me, too," I said.

"Some of us must go, Marcello," Dad said gently. "Surely you see why. They are kin of some sort. And may be in danger. If no one else can go, *I* must go to them. I have no choice."

Mom rose, stately, elegant, and took his arm. "And I will go with him."

"You two aren't going without me," Gabi said. "*Us*," she amended, her pretty brown brows knitting together as she looked from me to her husband. I breathed a sigh of relief, knowing he'd be hard-pressed to turn the three of them down. "Please, Marcello. Please. We must do what we can for them."

Marcello cast a helpless look to Luca, and Luca threw out a hand, saying, "They might be able to contain the damage. Bring these men home, or assist them back to the tomb from which they emerged, so they can return to...Normandy."

Marcello nodded curtly and rounded his desk, uncorking his ink. "Very well. We shall go to the coast and sail for Venezia in two days' time." He looked up at Gabi, pointing at her with the end of his quill. "And we shall use your approaching confinement as reason for our timely return."

She nodded happily and then cast me a sly glance.

I resisted the urge to clap in anticipation. We were going to Venice at last!

For the oddest family reunion ever.

I was so excited about Venice and meeting these new Betarrini cousins that it was hard to get to sleep that night. It all was such a welcome change from stewing over Luca and what to do about him, about the plague, only a couple of years away...what to do about my life in general, really. Now all I could think about was these guys in Venice, and how they were related, *if* they were related and—

Mom took my arm as we crossed the courtyard the next morning. "All I can think about is Venice and all the medicines and herbs I might have access to. But I have to say that Greco's comments last night have me worried. I think he's seen the handprints in Tomb Two. He was putting the new Betarrinis' story together with us, somehow."

"Gabi did say that Rodolfo saw something in the tomb that he thought she could explain. What could he mean?"

Mom stared at me and shook her head slightly, trying to figure it out. "We might want to visit it today. Refresh our memories of everything there, so that when we meet these Ravennans..."

"Oh, Mom! What might they tell *us*? What has happened to the world since we left? I feel like I've been on an island for years without a word about the outside world." I thought longingly of my social media accounts.

"I know," she whispered. "But first, let's pay that tomb a visit while Luca and Marcello are away."

"Where are they?"

"Just on patrol. Making sure the way is clear for us tomorrow and visiting key people in the villages to make their excuses for missing the harvest feast." She gave my arm a squeeze and then went off to her quarters to pack her things. I was already in a royal blue riding habit with a split-skirt—an early introduction to fashion that Gabi and I had insisted upon so we could dodge the stupid side-saddles. I smiled back at admiring knights as I passed, shaking my head a little at how brazenly they flirted with their captain's girl.

Usually, Luca had his methods of keeping the knights at a respectful distance. Up to now, there'd seldom been a time when I didn't feel his presence as a form of protection, whether he was with me or not. But something had shifted. I could feel it. Like a rumbling from deep beneath the earth's crust, dim, strange and unsettling, the change. It stressed me out, and yet I forced myself to lift my chin and keep moving. I had put myself in this position by denying him. I had to stand on my own two feet and hope that somehow, some way, in the right time, Luca and I could find our way forward together.

"Surely it's not as bad as all that," Lutterius said, approaching so quietly I'd missed him. I jumped, and he smiled and lifted his hands to apologize for alarming me.

"Oh, Lutterius," I said, bringing a hand to my breast and shaking my head. "Forgive me. I was in my own little world."

"Well, permit me to escort you out to the bigger world," he said, bowing slightly and offering his arm with a waggle of his bushy eyebrows. It was good to see him in such high spirits, giving me his wide, crooked-toothed grin. Since his twin Georgii had been hanged by the horrible Fiorentini assassins, I'd rarely seen it. I accepted his offer and placed my arm and hand atop his as we walked back through the corridor and into the yard.

"I confess I am most eager to see Venezia," he said. "The other men are envious that we get to attend you and yours."

"As would I, if I were not going too."

Lutterius grinned and opened the door to the stables for me. "No doubt the doge will wish to see Siena's favorite She-Wolf with her bow. I hope you've been diligent in your practice. I'll have a fair number of coins riding on your prowess."

I laughed under my breath. "Why, Lutterius, you know Marcello does not approve of gambling," I said, pretending to shake my head at him. I took hold of my skirts and stepped over the threshold, into the stables.

"One must do what one must when times of peace make a knight's life dull."

I grinned over my shoulder at him, glad that this trip would be a reprieve for him too, and secretly pleased that he so believed in me that he was willing to place bets on my skills. It was then that a man coughed, and we both looked up to see Luca, tightening the straps of his mount's saddle.

I was startled, seeing him. I thought he and Marcello were already away!

"Pardon me," he said, moving between us and over to another horse, running his hand over the Forelli-gold blanket, the saddle straps, the stirrups.

I knew I was blushing, feeling caught, even though Lutterius and I were nothing but friends, and Luca and I were...well, who knew what we were at the moment. Housemates? Friends? Quarreling lovers?

He said nothing more to us, all rigid, simmering anger—*Over what? That I'd allowed Lutterius to escort me? So silly...*But then Luca abruptly left the stables to the courtyard, with hardly a nod in our direction.

Lutterius stared at Luca's back, then to me, clearly puzzled by Luca's cool demeanor. I shoved aside Luca's slight and forced a smile. I'd thought that Luca's anger might have cooled by today, given that he was willing to help me last night at the Grecos' with mounting my horse and been civil during our family "meeting." But apparently not.

"It appears that Sir Luca and I are not on the best of terms at the moment. I hope you shall save me a dance in Venezia, Lutterius."

His face broke out in a wide grin again, and he nodded slowly, even if there was a hint of concern behind his eyes. "You can count on me, m'lady," he whispered, leaning toward me. "We'll shake some sense back into the captain. Mark my words; he won't leave you free to accept dances for long. Especially when those Venetian fellows find out you might be open to invitation."

He waggled his bushy brows again, and I smiled with him. "Thank you, Lutterius."

"No, thank *you*, m'lady," he said, sauntering a few steps off, a new spring in his step, his thumbs hooked along the wide armholes of his tunic. "I'll be the talk of the whole castello when we return."

CHAPTER 6

GABRIELLA

A s soon as I heard Mom and Lia's plan, I was in, of course. So was
Dad. "The tombs are just a stone's throw from Rodolfo's walls," I
said, as we hovered inside the main dome of Tomb Two, in the Etruscan
tomb field. "And he's clearly spent some time in them. Let's figure out
what he thinks I could explain, shall we?"

"The only thing I can think of," Mom said, moving past the other paintings inside the big dome, back to kneel at the entrance, "are
the figures at the mouth of this tunnel. The angels, the Greek, and
the Roman legionnaire. We've long suspected they signify time travel.
Maybe Rodolfo's clever enough to realize the legionnaire post-dates the
Etruscans."

We nodded with her. It made sense that he'd seen it, pondered it.
A memory of him chasing us through the woods, the tracker with him,
studying each broken twig, each pile of disturbed leaves, came to me. In
a way, he was tracking down this path of ours, too. And the stories of us
emerging from the tomb had brought him here.

Repeatedly, I guessed.

"But there's nothing here that *definitively* ties us to that," I said,
looking around.

"Nah," Dad said. "All the guy has is conjecture. And if we don't give
him anything definitive, it can stay that way. I'm with Marcello and Luca
on this. The fewer who know the truth, the better."

"But if we go after those boys in Venezia, Ben," Mom said, "if they somehow tie us together, and they've said too much...." She paused and rubbed her forehead, leaving an adorable smudge on her fair skin. "They could seriously compromise our position."

"That's why it's so important that we get to them fast," Dad said. "Convince them to stop talking, to pretend that they are actors and that it all was an elaborate ruse to entertain the doge or something."

"They've gotta be scared out of their minds," Lia said. "I was."

I nodded. Until I found my sister, I'd been convinced I was living some sort of awful, extended dream. Had the boys been separated too? It sounded like they arrived together.

"There *were* Fiorentini who saw us leave this tomb," I said. "Me, when I first arrived." I gestured toward the mouth of the tunnel. "I had to shove aside the gravestone to get out. And I was in the middle of a whole Forelli-Paratore battle. More than a couple Fiorentini saw me. Dudes who did not die that day."

I thought of the big, hulking knight who almost killed me on several different occasions. How he leered over my skinny jeans and cami. Mentally, I clicked through all the men there that day.

"Most of them are dead now, I think. But who knows? And I'm sure they shared their story while they yet lived. Can you imagine? The tales of the She-Wolves are fantastic enough, but they had some serious kindling for the gossip fires."

"What about the Forelli knights who were here that day?" Mom asked gently.

I thought back, and it made me sad, wistful. Most of them had died too. In fact, all but Luca and Marcello. *They died. Many in defense of me...or Marcello. Or Siena. Sweet Pietro. Happy Georgii. Alanzo. Valente...*

"There was also that lone scout who got away the day I arrived with you," Dad said, chin in hand. "He might still be alive."

"Our story has always been that we slept here, took shelter here," I said rubbing away a tear.

"Which sounds pretty creepy," Lia said.

"And then we have a mother with a fascination for excavating the tombs," I said reproachfully. "Which is all-kinds-of-weird to them."

"Our dealings in Etruscan artifacts serves well enough as a cover story," Mom said, flipping her blond braid over her shoulder.

"Does it?" I asked. "With these new Betarrinis in town? Dudes who said they came through a tomb, too? And probably wearing clothes that couldn't be explained?"

We were all silent for a moment. Marcello had burned the jeans, cardigan, cami and flats I'd arrived in, God bless him.

"Lia," I said slowly, a sudden horror growing inside, "what happened to your clothes when you first arrived?"

She looked at me helplessly. "I don't know. Paratore gave me a gown to change into. But he wouldn't give my clothes back."

My eyes met Mom's, and I felt a little sick. We'd buried hers and Dad's in the woods, and covered them with rocks. They weren't likely to be found. But Lia's...It would've been just like Paratore to hide them away to use at just the right point and time.

"What'd you have on that day?" Mom asked.

"Jeans. A t-shirt. And my purple sneakers." She bit her lip and looked around at us worriedly.

Dad sighed heavily. "Where'd my clothes go again?"

"We buried them as you changed into that knight's uniform."

"And we left that guy fairly naked," he said, pacing now. "If that word got out too..." He rubbed the back of his neck. We'd all thought of these things over the last year and more. We just hadn't dared to talk about it.

"What else could incriminate us?" Mom asked.

Dad resumed his pacing. "I flung my flashlight into the forest. Stupid, I know. I wasn't thinking."

"Where?" I asked. "Do you think we could find it?"

"I doubt it."

"You have that First Aid kit," I said to Mom.

She shook her head. "I hid it too, once I figured out how dangerous it was to have it around."

I frowned. "You're sure no one will find it?"

"I'm sure."

I took a deep breath. "There's no way we could explain it away." I thought of the plastic box—*plastic!*—the imprint and color, the slots and bottles and individually-wrapped products inside. Yeah, if that was found by the wrong peeps, we'd be toast.

"Was there anything else?" Mom asked. "How about when we came back the second time. Did anyone see us leave?"

I flung out my hands. "It's possible. Who knows? There are lots of people in this valley. Scouts. Spies. People on the road. Did you see anyone?" I asked Lia.

She shook her head. "We were on the move right away. Distracted. I don't think anyone saw us."

"But you can't be certain," Dad said quietly.

We heard the horses outside whinny. They must have sensed another approaching. I immediately ducked and crawled out, yanking at my pesky skirts all the way. As I rose, my hand instinctively ran across the sheath that held my sword, comforted by its weight. All four horses stood, ears pricked forward in the same direction. Toward the road that led to Castello Greco.

Toward *Lord* Greco, it turned out, as he languidly entered the tomb meadow, astride an elegant, black gelding.

My family gathered around me, brushing themselves off. We waited for Rodolfo to near, and he paused, leaning down to casually stroke the neck of his horse and then pat it. He smiled at us. "Now why did I suspect that I might find the Betarrinis here, come morn, after our discussions last night?" he asked, his eyes resting squarely on me.

"It's a lovely morning," I said, overly bright and cheery. "We found ourselves restless. So we elected to take a ride."

"To the tombs," he said drolly, lifting his far leg and easily sliding to the ground. He turned and opened a big, leather saddlebag and pulled out a fabric-wrapped package tied with string, tossing it to me. I narrowly caught it.

"You can open it," he said, crossing his arms. "But I suspect it belongs to Lady Evangelia."

My heart faltered, and his eyes narrowed.

He knew. *He knew.*

I turned and handed it to Lia, not wanting her to open it, just trying to buy time to think. We all knew what was inside. I'd felt the familiar weight and give of a rubber sole, her tennies.

"There are only two solutions, as I see it," Rodolfo said gently, evenly, looking from one to the next of us. "Either you're witches and warlock, or there's some strange truth to what the Ravenna-Betarrinis espoused. That you hail not from Normandy or Britannia, but rather from a different...time."

My mouth was dry, my mind spinning. I didn't want to lie to Rodolfo. He was our friend. Our ally now. And yet it endangered him to know. To be in on our secret.

"Come now, Rodolfo," Dad said, stepping forward. "Have you been so deep into your cups this early in the day? I've never known you to speak like a superstitious old man or madwoman. You know our story."

"I know part of your story," he corrected. He moved over to Lia and looked down at her. "Open it."

Casting me a helpless look, she untied the twine and spread apart the corners. A shoe rolled out and onto the ground, practically bouncing. We all stared at it like it was kryptonite, leaching us of any power, any energy.

Rodolfo bent and picked it up and examined it, as if for the first time. "I have been to the finest trading ports of Italia, as well as Normandy and

Greece, but I have never seen anything like this." He lifted the sneaker a bit higher, turning it over to examine the contoured shape of a gripping sole, the stitching across the purple mesh fabric, the neon-green laces. Then he looked at Lia. "Cosmo Paratore told me he'd found you in shoes that reminded him of my family's colors."

"He was a liar," Lia protested.

"He was," Rodolfo agreed. "But in this, he was not. And you, my dear friend," he said, leaning toward her, "are *not*. Please do not begin now." He studied her a moment. "Paratore had decided you were a witch, but you were too lovely to give up; and you displayed no other powers other than the power to beguile a man—a power to which he was willing to be subjugated. So he elected to forget the clothes. Remake you into a proper woman of our lands and use you as a bargaining chip. Until your sister came to save you," he said, nodding at me. "I never heard him say another word about it. But he left the clothes beneath the floorboards of his room. Which I happened upon when we returned from our travels."

He gestured to the other clothes in Lia's hands. "Any one of those pieces would identify you as not only foreign, but...*other*." He handed the sneaker to my dad and crossed his arms. "So tell me. All of it. Where are you from?" He asked the last of it slowly, emphasizing each word, clearly abiding by no further debate. Again, he looked at each of us, one at a time, and I felt like I was in the principal's office.

Dad stepped closer, directly in front of him. "What Marcello said was true. Sometimes, it is best to not know everything. Can you not let this go? Allow us to burn these clothes? Forget you ever laid eyes upon them?"

Rodolfo stared at him. "Forgive me. I cannot. I'd rather know of potential danger, even if it puts me in greater peril."

It made sense to me. He was clever, long used to navigating the complicated waters of being a blood brother to many who were considered enemies and yet loving many on his side of the line too. It was his whole life, really. And he'd lost and gained big in the exchanges that resulted from that devotion. To his mind, how was this any different?

"We are not witches and warlock," Dad said, trying to leave it at that. But Rodolfo forced it. "Then from what time are you?"

Dad searched his eyes. "From a distant future."

Rodolfo scowled in irritation. "How distant?"

"Almost seven hundred years."

Rodolfo's brown eyes widened, his lips parting as he stilled. Then they clamped shut, and his brow lowered. "How is that possible?" he bit out.

"We do not know."

Rodolfo shook his head as he waved at the tomb. "Through there?"

"Yes," Dad said. "It is some sort of portal, a time tunnel, through which we only thought that Gabriella and Evangelia could initiate travel. But now with these new Betarrinis from Ravenna..." He rubbed his temple and looked to the horizon, lost in his own thoughts.

"If only the Ladies Betarrini could travel through it, how did you and your husband arrive?" Rodolfo asked Mom.

"Holding on to them," she said, gesturing toward me and Lia. I still couldn't believe they were telling him. All of it. "Clinging to them for our very lives," she said.

"It's the handprints," I muttered, irritated that he'd managed to get us to spill the beans. Marcello would be ticked when he found out. And yet I couldn't see a way around it. Now we needed to use his knowledge to our advantage. "There's something about the handprint frescoes inside. When Lia and I touch them, they're hot. And we have to touch them *together*. Do you know if there were handprints in the Ravenna tomb our cousins emerged from?"

He shook his head, still looking a bit dazed. "I thought...I thought it was the entrance itself. With the angels, the figures of both Greek and Legionnaire."

Mom nodded, clearly gratified that she'd been right about him noticing that particular element.

Greco's attention turned toward me. "So at any time, you and Evangelia can leave?"

"It appears that way," I said. "Though we have no intention of trying. When we went back last for Dad—we retrieved him from a time before...well, before he died."

Rodolfo visibly paled at this, the first time I'd ever seen him do so in some time. He stared hard at Dad. "Y-you *died*."

"Apparently," Dad said, flinging out his hands. "It happened a couple years later. I don't remember it, because for me, it never happened. They came and retrieved me two years before the accident."

Rodolfo rubbed his face and stared at me, the pieces starting to slide together. "That's why you first claimed your father was dead, but then later miraculously 'found him.' Why your mother was not with you, at first."

I nodded. "But now...Now we're wondering if we're a part of a *big* family that can somehow travel through time. If there are additional tombs, will still more distant cousins emerge? Because that would be rather...problematic. So we must get to these men you met. Find out if what they say is the truth."

"It is," Rodolfo said definitively. "Now that I know all this," he said, waving vaguely over at us and the tomb, then staring into my eyes. "Those men spoke the truth and only belatedly thought twice about it. You must get to them, and then you must get them out of Venezia. Back to their tomb, or this one. Whichever! And *back to their own time*. Do you understand me?"

He was dark and urgent, fear practically seeping from his pores. "Swear they are madmen. Cousins, kin, if you must. But claim they are stark, raving mad." His large hands were on my shoulders. "For if the doge decides there is truth in them... If he thinks that you and your kin have a strange power he could harness to extend his own...Or if he turns against you, you will be in grave danger. Do you understand me, Gabriella?" he asked, shaking me a little, his fingers digging in. His brows knit, and he looked to my parents, to Lia. Then over his shoulder toward his own castle, thinking, I knew, of his wife.

"Yes!" I said in agitation, pushing his hands away. Then again, more softly, "*yes*," understanding his look of angst as the love of kinship and care. For all of us. Not just me. For Siena, and for his new bride, Alessandra.

He turned, went to his saddlebag, and came back with Dad's flashlight. After one last flick of the button and observation of the foreign, miraculous light that came on, he slapped it into my hand. "And destroy *this*."

I lifted the flashlight in my hand, felt the comforting weight of it, the memories it held for me of Dad in so many places, so many archeological sites. In some ways, it represented my childhood. But he was right. It had to go as fast as we could destroy it, in the hottest fire we could find.

"We depart at daybreak on the morrow," I said. "Pray that we can accomplish what we must."

"That I will," he said, with a wonderstruck shake of his head. "Because only God can help you sift sanity from this madness."

CHAPTER 7

EVANGELIA

I pretty much didn't talk to Luca until we were at sea, on our way to Venice. I knew I should tell him of what had happened with Rodolfo, but, well...we were hardly on speaking terms yet. So I let it slide.

· As far as I could tell, Gabi hadn't told Marcello yet either. He seemed free, easy, like he was on vacation as he led her about the deck of the ship.

Lutterius was throwing rotten apples for me, above the waves, and I was practicing, shooting them down, arrow after arrow.

After about ten, I sensed that Luca was behind me. Without turning, I said, above the noise of the sea, "Please, Captain. Won't you join me?"

He hesitated and, after sharing a look with Lutterius, I kept shooting, waiting him out.

Eventually, he dared to join me at the rail, leaning upon it. Lutterius, in deference, handed him his last apple, and then disappeared belowdecks.

Luca gave me a smirk and then chucked it, as high as he could.

I smiled, waited for it to arc, slowly drawing my arrow, and then shot it, just before it hit the water. Arrow and apple somersaulted across the waves and then bobbed there, twenty yards distant.

"Fairly impressive, m'lady," he allowed.

I laughed quietly and then leaned on the rail beside him. "Fairly? What must I do to fully impress you, good sir?"

"You know what would impress me most, Evangelia," he whispered, his green eyes a cauldron of conflict—all at once hopeful and defeated.

"Hmmm," I said with a heavy sigh. "And again we come to that, yes? Our predicament. Please, might we set it aside? Just for a time? Through Venezia?"

He took his own deep breath, staring toward the setting sun, and I admired him from the side as the rays cast a gentle glow over his skin, highlighting the stubble of a sandy-colored mustache and beard.

"Say we set it aside through this sojourn to Venezia, but what then, Evangelia?"

"I do not know," I confessed. "Mayhap nothing will be different. But at least we would have that time together. Rather than endure this dreadful divide where neither of us is happy." I dared to touch his hand with just my pinky and ring finger, and he froze.

Slowly, slowly, we both looked at each other. He moved his long, strong fingers to cover mine, and my heart pounded as he lifted my hand to his lips.

"Ahh, Evangelia," he said resignedly. "I suppose that it is far less trouble to keep you near me, even if I cannot have the promise of your heart forever. It nearly tears me to pieces to stay away from you."

I smiled gratefully. "It was the archery, was it not? That made you give in? Wasn't it my skill with bow and arrow that first made you claim your love?"

He smiled ruefully and looked out to the sea. He still held my hand and I grew quiet, well aware that we both felt wounded, hurt, and it would take a few days to let it fade. To bridge this chasm between us.

Even if I couldn't promise Luca forever, it certainly felt like I was his, and he was mine.

Weren't we?

He wrapped an arm around my shoulders, and we stared out to the endless waves, toward the distant coastline of what would someday be Croatia, and I hoped that we could stretch this Venetian truce into something longer.

Oh, how I hoped.

CHAPTER 8

GABRIELLA

C ome morning, I stared at the roiling waters and fought to keep my breakfast in my belly. I hadn't felt this heave-ish since my first trimester.

Lia joined me at the ship's rail.

"So it turns out," I said, panting, "that pregnancy and sailing aren't the ideal companions."

"Stare at the horizon," she said. "Remember that whale watching trip in California? Keep those eyes on the horizon, not me." I did as she said. "Good. Now, breathe. Slowly. In and out."

Again, I followed instructions, and gradually, my stomach began to settle. The ship felt small, tall and tippy, like a double decker sailboat with two sails. For a time I'd considered going below decks and trying to ride it out, but Mom had tried that and came up, shaking her head. "You don't want to go down there."

So here I'd stood for hours, in the center, at the lowest point. It was mid-morning and we still had the afternoon to go. If the winds remained favorable, we'd arrive in Venice by evening. Silently, I thanked God that we wouldn't be spending another night on this ship. How on earth had Columbus crossed the Atlantic in the *Santa Maria*?

Marcello came to join me after breaking his fast. I'd decided against food, in general, for the foreseeable future. "Are you feeling a bit better?"

he asked hopefully, offering me his arm. I took it and leaned my head against his shoulder.

"A bit," I said.

"Perhaps a morsel of bread—"

"Nay, nay," I declined quickly.

He frowned in concern. "The baby—" he whispered.

"The baby is fine," I said, laying a hand on my belly. "Plenty of mothers are sick for many more months than I have been. It's just the sea."

"Mayhap this was a foolish venture," he chastised himself. "We'd best stayed safe at home."

"And sent my family alone? I think not."

"We could've managed," Lia said defensively. "You simply did not want to miss it."

"Undoubtedly. Between these other mysterious Betarrinis and seeing medieval Venezia, there was no way you were leaving me behind."

"Nay, with what's ahead, I think we'll need every one of us to find our way through," Marcello said. "There are treacherous waters before us, beyond the lagoon and its doge."

We stood there, the three of us for a time, before Luca came up. I breathed a sigh of relief as he stood beside Lia. Whatever had transpired yesterday had apparently helped them make up. Or call a truce. I could still feel tension between them, but it was nothing like it had been.

"What shall we expect?" I asked Marcello. "When we arrive?"

"We'll find our way to a palazzo of my cousins, and they shall make our presence known to the doge. I assume an invitation to court will arrive within a day or two, and we shall find a way to meet these mysterious Betarrini kin. Or at least discover their current whereabouts."

The captain arrived, a folding chair in his arms. He set up the rickety teak chair and gestured toward it. "M'lady, please, take your ease. My own wife is in her last months of confinement, due with our third child at any moment. I know she tires easily, as must you."

"Thank you," I said, sinking gratefully into it. Sitting down, after hours on my feet, felt incredibly good.

Mom and Dad arrived then, carrying water. "Keep sipping at it," she whispered.

I knew they'd devised a method of cleaning the water as we traveled, well aware that it would be difficult for me to stay hydrated. Back at the castello, we could trust the well water. But on board the ship, or on the streets of Venezia, it might prove more challenging. Dad talked about how the Venetians filtered their water, though. They took salt water from the lagoon and sent it through a sand filter beneath the streets, which in turn fed a cistern that supplied a small city block with fresh water.

"It'll actually be much safer than most Tuscan wells," he'd whispered to me.

I sipped from the cup Mom had given me, still keeping my eyes on the horizon as the others discussed what was ahead, who Marcello knew in the city, who we could count on. And gradually, my eyes grew heavier and heavier until I was asleep.

I awakened as the captain shouted directions and sailors repeated commands, hauling sail, belaying rope, tying down this or that. Lia was grinning at me, clapping excitedly. "Oh good! You're awake! Hurry to the rail. You have to see this, Gabi."

Marcello helped me from my chair, and I rose, stiff after apparently passing out for hours. It was a small miracle I hadn't fallen out of it, but I suspected Marcello had something to do with that, as I'd woken up to find his strong hands on my shoulders. I gaped at what was ahead and around us. Ships of all sizes sailed about us, some mere feet off our bow. African ships with dark-skinned men in bright-colored fabric passed us, cheerfully waving. Three ships flying the French flag passed in another.

Our captain was swearing and shouting one command and then a counter command, trying his best to avoid a collision, until at last all sails were brought down and we came to a standstill.

"We await the harbor master to send someone to bring us in," Marcello explained. "In a port this busy, there are papers that must be filed. The Venetians enter freely. We others must squeeze in when we can."

We continued to stare in wonder as small skiffs sailed by at breakneck speed, apparently not fearing our proximity or the lagoon's thick traffic. Men in rowboats heavy with hills of silver anchovies trudged by, heading toward the wharves, their afternoon bounty evident. Others carried goods—boxes of chickens, bales of fabric and cotton, rounds of rope—a floating mercantile of sorts.

"It is magical," I breathed. The setting sun cast a lovely, luminous glow across the water, making the lagoon look like liquid gold and making Venezia's buildings seem warm and inviting. In time, a small sailboat came our way, the harbormaster's flag atop its mast. He waved at the captain and held up a sign with the number "57," and our captain began barking orders, his sailors repeating them even as they hurried to do as he bid. The mood had definitely improved among them; undoubtedly, they were anticipating an entertaining evening in the city. The enthusiasm was contagious.

We moved into the flow of traffic that was heading toward the lagoon's harbor, and I noted that there were poles, some close together and others farther apart, to which boats were moored. The bigger ships—bigger than ours—were positioned farther out, both moored from the front and anchored from the back.

The sailors expertly looped the pole as we passed, just as the sails came down again, and they let out a good deal of rope, gradually slowing our progress. When we came to a full stop, the men wound the rope around a capstan and four took to the wheel, slowly turning our ship around and pulling us into our mooring pole, dimly marked as 57, even as the next ship swept past us to number 58 and did the same. It was a far more organized procedure than I anticipated, but never in my wildest dreams had I really expected the madness that was the lagoon. In our own day, it had been busy, bustling with *vaparettos* and gondolas and even cruise ships, but it was nothing like it was now. The sea traffic was so dense, I thought that, in a pinch, one might be able to jump from deck to deck, until they were all the way to the Rialto.

Two rowboats arrived beside us, each manned by a pair of men. They shouted and bartered with the captain, negotiating a price, until an agreement was made and the captain gestured downward. "Please, m'lord," he said to Marcello, "take your wife and kin first."

Marcello thanked him and handed him a bag of coins, the payment for safely getting us to our port. Soon enough, we were all settled in the boat below, with me feeling particularly proud of myself for getting down the net, preggers, big skirts and all. *Oh yeah,* I thought, *I'm the She-est of the She-Wolves.* I grinned at Lia.

"What?"

"Nothing."

She probably thought she was All That because she climbed it in half the time. *Whatever.* I was still pleased with my surprising feat of grace.

Our trunks were lowered into the boat with us, and then we were off, waving to the sailors, and soon absorbed in the views as we passed. It seemed like the entire world was here in Venezia's harbor. We could pick out what had to be Russian, Chinese, French and middle-English tongues in the first five minutes. The water smelled of brine and fish, but the air was blessedly cool, which kept me from nausea again.

There were merchants ferrying casks of wine and olive oil, skiffs carrying piles of stone out to ships—to serve as ballast weight, I learned from Dad—and others carrying in slabs of white marble. There was chain and rope and bale upon bale of wool. Silk tapestries. Sacks of grain. It was a hive of humanity and trade, and I couldn't help but think that the harbor was a perfect example of why the coming plague would spread so quickly. Everything and everyone was pressed together, sharing space, air, goods, and all sorts of invisible germs with people from all over the world.

For the thousandth time, I wished for hand sanitizer.

"When we reach the docks, you must stick very close to us and keep hold of your purse," Marcello said. "There is an unsavory element here, and they prey upon those who are distracted by the beauty of the city. Be aware of who is around us."

"Sounds just like Venezia in our own time," Dad muttered, but he grinned with excitement as he looked our way. It'd been years since we'd come this far north. I think I'd been about ten, and Lia eight.

The men at the oars took us past the busy docks beside the doge's palace, which led to Piazza San Marco farther down the Grand Canal, and eventually into a small side canal—basically Venice's version of an alley. It was too narrow for the men to use the oars, so instead they stood and used their hands to propel us between the buildings that rose four stories above us. We stopped beside an ornate gate, with mossy green steps rising from the canal waters, up and into the palazzo beside us. A servant appeared, and Lia and I glanced at each other in glee. We were just a few blocks away from the grand plaza, the doge's palace. And staying in a palazzo right on the Grand Canal—with a cousin of Marcello and Luca's.

"We're livin' a serious *dream*," Lia whispered excitedly, as Luca helped her out of the boat and over the slippery little hop to a dry step. We all disembarked and made our way up the stairs, which widened into a grand entrance a story above us. Dad whistled under his breath. Above us, in nine domes nestled between marble pillars, were elaborate mosaics—teeny, tiny, bright-colored tiles that depicted ladies dancing and men lounging, animals of all sorts, and fish and more fish.

"Marcello, my darling!" said a low, melodic voice. "Luca!"

We turned to see a startlingly beautiful woman of about thirty coming our way. She was slender and impeccably clad in a silk gown with a complex weave I'd never seen before. She had a long neck, narrow

nose and high cheekbones, giving her an exotic look. Two black servants appeared behind her, looking half like guards and half like butlers.
They were dressed in flowing Turkish pants, belted at the waist, and
light shirts, which looked startlingly white against their dark skin. They
showed no emotion, no interest really, as if only a word from their mis-
tress would gain their attention. They reminded me of the fierce guards
in Lord Vivaro's mansion down in Rome, and the memory made me
shift uneasily.

Our hostess reached out and took Marcello's hands, kissing him on
both cheeks—her eyes on me the whole while—and then Luca. I noticed
Lia got a similar once-over, but what I sensed in the woman was more
curiosity than anything dangerous. Besides, Marcello clearly liked this
cousin, a young widow who reportedly enjoyed life far more now that
her old tyrant of a husband was dead. Together, they turned to me, Lia
and my parents.

"Lady Caterina Brexiano, may I present my wife, Lady Gabriella
Forelli?"

She curtsied in a regal motion. She seemed taller than I, even if I had
five inches on her. I did my best to mimic her movement, feeling like
an elephant in comparison. But she smiled with genuine welcome in her
eyes.

"And may I present Gabriella's sister," Marcello continued, "Lady
Evangelia, and their parents, Lord and Lady Betarrini?"

"Welcome, welcome," Caterina said, when the introductions were
complete. "My men will show your knights where they may lodge during
your stay here," she said, her eyes flicking over the gold tunics of the
twelve men who traveled with us as guards. "And I shall show you to your
lodgings. Please, follow me."

With that, she turned, her wide skirts in her hands, and we followed
her across the main floor—crafted in a complex pattern of gorgeous
squares and circles—in purple porphyry and marble in olive green, harvest gold, and midnight blue.

"I was sorry to learn of your husband's passing," I said to her as we walked side by side.

"'Tis a blessing," she said under her breath—a wry grin on her lush lips as she crossed herself—"to be free of the old goat. He was as mean as he was rich." Her heavy eyebrows lifted. "And now I am free to enjoy his wealth and run his businesses in my own way."

I laughed under my breath at her honesty. It was easy to see why Marcello and Luca remembered her fondly.

"I am so glad you finally brought your bride to visit me," Caterina said to Marcello. "You've been remiss, hoarding her in Toscana."

"Traveling conditions were hardly...optimal," he said, giving her an indulgent smile. "If I was going to bring Gabriella and her family north, I had to seek reasonable assurance we'd be safe."

Caterina cocked a brow. "Wise, I'm certain, cousin. Lucky for you that the doge holds the pope—and his precious Fiorentini—in disdain. There are few in the city who dare to proclaim their allegiances to Firenze, and therefore, you're likely as safe here as you were at home."

"May your words be true," Luca said.

"Here you are," Caterina said to my parents, opening two wide doors to show them a lovely room with a sprawling four-poster bed and a small balcony over the side canal. "We shall sup in a few hours, but, please, make my home your own. You may wander the entire palazzo, from top to bottom, and should you have need of anything, merely ring a bell," she said, gesturing toward a rope by the door.

"Thank you, Lady Brexiano," Mom said, with a lovely curtsy. I'd have to get lessons from her later. She'd gotten way better at it.

She put Lia in the next room and Luca across from her, waggling her eyebrows as if she expected midnight mischief. Luca just crossed his arms and shook his head in consternation. As much as he loved to joke around, he'd never do anything to put Lia's reputation in danger. Still, a little kissing in a gondola might be just the thing they needed to push them out of their tentative, tense track.

The last room was for us. With a wink, she opened the doors and led us inward, hands clasped, face expectant. The room sprawled before us, and I had a hard time not believing it was the master bedroom. Perhaps she had an identical one on the far side of the hallway. There was a massive four-poster bed with carved headboard and luxurious linens across it, as well as delicate netting across the top, giving it an exotic feel, even though I knew it was used to keep bugs away. Come summer, Venice could be Mosquitoville. That's why Dad insisted we go in the spring or fall.

"Oh," I moved toward the tall windows at the front of the room. "Oh, it's wonderful," I said, taking in the curve of the canal, the multi-colored palazzos lining either side. We weren't just in *Venice*. We were staying in a palazzo during its *heyday*. I looked back at Caterina as Marcello joined me at the windows. "*Grazie*, Lady Brexiano. We might never leave."

"Trust me," she said, coming closer. "When the doge finds out the She-Wolves of Siena are in his city at long last, he might not allow you to leave the Palazzo Ducale. There will be much celebration. He loves nothing more than famous guests, and he's long harangued me to use our family ties to bring you north."

"We can only stay for a week or so," Marcello said, turning toward his cousin, arms folded. "Gabriella being with child, and the winter seas are just around the corner. We'd best be back to Siena in a timely manner."

"Yes, well, I assume you know how the doge is prone to press his own way. There will be business to discuss, trade between the republics."

"I understand. But, Caterina, it is the *other* Betarrinis who have recently come to court that brought us here at all. Have you met them?"

Her long-lashed, dark eyes searched me a moment, then Marcello, then back to me. "I have. They are rather...*unique*. Are they close kin to you, m'lady?"

"Nay," I said, with a shake of my head. "We've not yet met. Honestly, I do not know if they are madmen, latching on to stories of us, or truly two of our own."

"They may well be frauds," Marcello put in, adding to the story as we'd prepared. "Men seeking to gain access to our own Betarrinis."

"Well, they have asked after you," Caterina said. "They fairly demanded to be taken to you, but the doge wouldn't allow them to leave. He finds them intriguing and clearly believes they still have secrets he wishes to ferret out. As I said, he favors any diversion he can find at court, and those two are certainly rare with their wild tales. And likely he knew that keeping them here might bring you northward at last."

"Where are they now?"

"In prison."

"In *prison*," Marcello and I said together.

"Yes," Caterina said, raising a brow. "They ceased speaking at all, in protest that they weren't allowed to leave. The doge had them flogged for their insolence and sent them to the dungeon."

I sighed heavily. "Do you think we might be able to speak to them there?"

She bit her lip and looked tentative. "That would be far more challenging. I expect that the doge will want to observe your reunion with these kin, but I will do what I can to aid you. The doge favors me, and he knows that Marcello is one of the Nine in Siena, so..." She gave her head a little shake. "Give me some time, and we'll see what transpires."

"Grazie," I said, reaching out to touch her arm.

She glanced down in surprise and then to my face, bending her head, all genteel grace, and making me feel like a bumbling idiot. I supposed it was overly familiar to touch her, but she seemed quietly moved by the gesture.

"If there is anything you need before we sup, simply ring your bell. We shall gather in the dining room for our meal when the bell rings three times."

My stomach rumbled, as if approving of the mention of food, and I prayed that she hadn't heard it. If she did, she pretended to ignore it.

Downstairs, we heard men laughing and shouting, and then the scrambling of boots on the marble stairs.

"Caterina!" a man bellowed. "Cat! Marcello!"

Caterina sighed and put her fingers to her forehead in agitation, then looked at Marcello and me.

"Nicolo?" Marcello asked, a wry grin on his lips.

But then the man was there, bursting through the door without invitation, two men with him, four Forelli knights right behind them, looking concerned.

"Marcello!" the broad, short man cried, pulling my husband's face down to him for two exuberant kisses.

"Nicolo," Marcello returned with a grin as the man drew back, hands sprawled out, face filled with joy. "May I present—"

But Nicolo was already turning toward me, bowing. "Lady Gabriella Forelli." He rose, still grinning. "How honored are we to be your kin. I am Nicolo lo Grato," he said, laying a hand on his broad chest. Then he gripped my shoulders and gave me two swift kisses on my cheeks. "Ha!" he fairly shouted to his comrades, gesturing to me. "I would never have believed that I'd one day kiss a She-Wolf!"

I tried to act like Caterina, giving him a regal nod, even as the scent of his wine-laced breath and sweat-stained clothing washed over me. Clearly, he and his friends—who stood behind him, gawking at me as if I had feathers sticking out of my hair or something—had been drinking all afternoon.

"My brother," Caterina said with a sigh. "Come along, Nicolo," she said. "The Forellis have just now arrived. You can speak further when we're at table." She pulled him closer. "And when you've sobered up a bit."

"Sobered up?" he cried, as if she were suggesting something silly. "The evening has just begun!" He turned to his friends, and they smiled.

Marcello waved away the knights behind them, and two disappeared, but the two biggest—Celso and Lutterius—remained on the far side of the hall, arms crossed, ready to come to our aid if these partiers proved too unruly. They reminded me of bouncers at a nightclub.

"Lord and Lady Forelli," Nicolo said, "may I present my friends, my brothers, Sir Cappello and Sir Dalioto."

One stumbled toward me, as if planning on trying to kiss me in greeting, but Marcello stayed him with a hand to his chest. He shook his head as if to say, *yeah, that's not gonna happen.* The man pulled up straight, gathered himself, and bowed from three feet away. The other bowed with him.

"So honored to meet you, m'lady."

"Honored, yes," parroted the second.

"Where is your beautiful sister? The blond one?" asked Dalioto, his words slurring a bit. He was in fine clothing, but was very thin, his face marked by acne.

"Safely in her room, far from scoundrels like you," Luca said, striding in to stand beside Marcello.

"Luca!" Nicolo cried, greeting him with as much exuberance as he had Marcello.

"I thought you were captaining your own ship and off to Africa," Luca said.

"I have been, yes," Nicolo said.

"And he'll soon be off again," Caterina said, hands on her hips, "if he can stay out of his cups long enough to secure his next shipment."

Nicolo waved off his sister, as if she were irritating him. "Time enough for that."

The two shared the same olive skin, the same eyes, but that's where the family resemblance stopped. Nicolo was a few years younger, and his face was much wider than hers. In fact, everything about him was as round as his grin.

"I cannot tell you how grand it is to see you both," he said to Marcello and Luca. "It has been far too long, cousins."

"Agreed," Marcello said, clamping a hand on his shoulder. "But if you shall excuse us, I believe my wife would do well with a rest before supper."

"Of course, of course," Nicolo said, bushy eyebrows rising. He nudged his cousin's side. "'Tis a burden to carry a Forelli in the belly, is it not?"

"Nicolo!" Caterina barked, eyes going wide in horror. If I'd learned one thing, it was that pregnancies weren't normal day-to-day fodder for people to discuss in medieval society. Women did, in private. But men typically gravitated toward the lewd, seeming to feel freer to comment given the evidence of our intimacy as a married couple. Inwardly, it made me want to giggle and roll my eyes over such antics. But for Caterina's sake, I pretended to have not heard him.

"Ahh," he said, waving her off again, hands then going wide. "We are family, are we not?"

Her lips clamped shut, and her eyes shifted to his companions. "Enough. Out. *Out*," she said, shooing them out the door. Once they were gone, their boisterous chatter and heavy boots receding down the hallway, she looked back at us. "If God shall only smile, Nicolo will be at sea again in a few days."

"All is well," Marcello said, his voice full of reassurance. "Luca and I remember Nicolo fondly. And he is not the first man we've seen imbibing."

Luca shook his head, smiled, and passed her to go speak to the Forelli knights outside, giving them instruction. Undoubtedly making certain that one would stay near us, and one would go to Lia's door.

Caterina cocked one brow, long fingers clasped before her. "Yes, well, he shall find his cups filled with nothing but water between now and supper. Do not fear joining us at table."

Marcello laughed quietly. "Thank you, cousin. We appreciate your hospitality."

"It is my distinct honor," she said, bringing a hand to her chest. Then she dipped her chin, took hold of the door handle, and closed it behind us.

We were alone at last, and he turned to trace my cheek and then take my hands in his. "So now you have met some of my kin. What do you think of them?"

"Charming," I said, meaning it. "Both of them."

"You are not offended by Nicolo? Horrified by his antics?"

"Nay, nay," I said. "I think he shall be highly entertaining."

He gave me a grateful look. "He's always been that. He and Luca..." He shook his head. "Let us simply say they got into their fair share of trouble when we were boys together. We might blame him, being the elder, for some of how Luca turned out."

He led me to the windows, where we could look down the *Canalazzo*. I shivered, the moist, cool air of approaching evening giving me a chill.

"Here," Marcello said, wrapping his arms around me from behind. I settled my head beside his chin, loving the sturdy support of his body behind mine. "Better?" he asked.

"Much," I said.

Together we stared down the canal, watching as boats moved back and forth. One appeared to be a sort of floating bridge, with eight passengers all standing as they crossed over from one side of the canal to the next. The water shimmered with the pink light of sunset, and tiny waves from the boat traffic washed against both stone and wood.

"*La Serenissima*," he whispered, the name for Venice meaning *the most serene*. "It truly is beautiful, is it not?"

"It's marvelous. A wonder. So different from Toscana, and yet equally as beautiful."

"Indeed."

His hands moved down to stroke my belly, and I smiled. He took pride in my pregnancy, and he wasn't given to crude jokes about it. I knew he loved this child within me as much as he loved me, and it warmed me to know it. To share it with him. As Tomas had said, babies were a gift, a blessing. And as much as I feared the future, what our child would face in the plague and beyond, I had to trust God that he was holding us all in his hands.

Our days here were so beyond anything I could've imagined or hoped for...being here, in Venice, in the fourteenth century...all of it, from beginning to end, was beyond me, beyond my control. And so I elected to simply appreciate each day for the gift that it was. And this day? Totally Christmas-worthy.

Marcello turned me toward him and cradled my face, his eyes full of devotion. "I love you, Gabriella," he said, bending to kiss me softly, then more searchingly, pulling me closer. "I love you so much that sometimes I think it might tear me apart."

I smiled and kissed him softly. "I hope not. I like you in one piece."

He stared at me intently. "If these new Betarrinis prove a danger to you, we shall sneak out of the city and set sail immediately. You understand me? I will not abide any danger to you or our child."

"I understand," I said, hoping to reassure him more than anything. "Do you think we might be able to see them?"

"I hope so," he said. "But for today, we shall rest from the journey." He led me over to the bed and reached up to unpin the net that held my hair.

I started to protest, knowing I'd struggle to tame it again before dinner, but he shushed me with a playful finger against my lips. Then, one by one, he pulled the pins from my hair, and I closed my eyes, appreciating the sensation of his every touch, the tickle of each section of hair as it tumbled down my neck and across my shoulders. Slowly, he turned and unbuttoned my gown, freeing me of its confines, leaving only the shift for my nap.

But as I sank to the bed and looked up at my husband, who put one knee beside me and slowly pulled off his tunic and tossed it aside—his shirt opening at the nape so that I could see the finely sculpted muscles of his chest—I was well aware that there would be very little napping to be had in this glorious, gorgeous room along the Grand Canal.

CHAPTER 9

EVANGELIA

I rose early, eager to capture the bustle along the Grand Canal from a perch that Nicolo had shown me last night, up on the third floor—or *piano*, as they called it here—in the library. I pulled a lovely, high-backed chair covered in horsehair over to the wide windows and opened the shutters, taking a deep breath of the sea-kissed, cold morning air. Then I settled into the chair and brought out my precious paper, mounted on a board, and a charcoal pencil. My intent was to sketch here, and paint from memory when I returned home to Toscana.

For a long while, I simply stared outward, memorizing the distinct green-blue of the water. The Ottoman-inspired curves and arches formed many of the palazzos beside the Canal and they were painted in sun-bleached red, ochre, or café au lait. Or they were framed in great blocks of natural stone—fresh cream or white, for the most part—or bricks, awaiting a new coat of plaster.

Men greeted one another as they passed in boats, and I decided I'd do two pictures: one of the canal in general, a macro view encompassing as much as I could. And another more secretive view of a smaller canal and footbridge—more of the "insider's" Venezia. I'd have to find just the right spot...but an old photo of Dad's came to mind. Maybe I could convince him to help me find the spot again—if it even looked the same in this era. If not, I was sure we'd be able to find others. For a city teeming with people, I knew I could fill a notebook with sketches of her eerily quiet corners.

I began to work on my drawing of the canal, capturing the rectangular lines of each palazzo, growing smaller in the distance, the curves of the boat lines, the wake spreading behind them. As the morning wore on, more and more boats filled the waterway. Luca arrived, and I thought he sighed in relief, as if he had been worried when he couldn't find me. He gave me a smile and rubbed the back of his neck.

"Good morning," I said warmly, returning to my sketch.

"Good morning," he answered. "You did not come down to break your fast."

"I wasn't hungry," I said dreamily. "Not when there was a feast for my eyes like this!" I said, gesturing outward and returning to my sketch.

He moved to my side and watched as I added line after line. "Will you ever sketch something for me?"

I swallowed a smile. "You mean something like this?" I asked, pulling out a drawing from my small portfolio. It was of a young couple on a hill, overlooking a Tuscan wood.

He cast me a look of suspicion and then took it in hand and studied it for a long time. So long, I shifted in my chair.

"'Tis a fine piece, Lia," he whispered, then looked to the window, as if remembering us being on that hill together and the argument that followed.

I took his hand. "Luca, might you pose for me? Stand still for say, half an hour?"

He cocked his head. "Me? Model for you?"

"You."

"Well I suppose you'd be hard pressed to find another as handsome as I," he said, lifting a brow.

"Truly," I agreed with a smile. "Come with me." I led him out of the library, down the stairs and out the main hall, this time to a street behind the house. We both blinked in the bright, early morning light and looked around. "Are you ready for an adventure?"

"With you?" he asked, cocking a brow again. "Of course." Still, he lifted a hand with two fingers aloft, gesturing to Celso and Falito to follow us.

I smiled with him, and we set off down the alley, entered a wide street—once a canal that had been filled in and covered—and down several blocks. I was in search of the perfect place that only Luca and I would remember. We *needed* this.

"Where are you taking me?" he asked.

"A perfect place," I said with a grin.

"A perfect place," he repeated. "I thought that was any place I was with you." My grin widened. We walked on and on, deeper into the Rialto, even over a tilting wooden bridge that would one day be replaced by the famous white stone bridge. On and on, we went, turning around and going back the way we'd come once or twice when we hit a dead-end. Venice was like that. Full of dead-ends. But the place that I sought was ahead. And when I found it, I stopped so suddenly I pulled Luca up short, practically swinging him around.

"What?" he gasped, surprised.

"Here," I breathed. "This is it."

"This?" He turned and surveyed the view with me. The small canal. The foot bridge. The church and steeple arising beyond the building, curving away from us. The gondolier, making his way through the canal. The sunlight creeping down the western wall.

"There," I said, gesturing toward the small footbridge. "Please. Can you lean against that building, arms crossed, leg cocked like this? You know, like you're always lounging about?"

"You make me sound like a lazy good-for-nothing." He waved at Celso and Falito, and I sensed they were taking up positions a bit away, giving us privacy while keeping watch.

"Hardly. *Luca*," I urged, the sunlight moving down the far wall even as I watched. I demonstrated what I wanted him to do. He pretended to not understand, of course, making me physically position his shoulders against the wall, his leg, his arms, just for the fun of me touching him. And when he was finally as I wanted him to be, he reached out and grabbed hold of my arms.

"A kiss for your model as payment?" he asked, his green eyes searching the empty streets to make certain we were alone. It was early yet.

I grinned and leaned toward him. *This* was more of the Luca I remembered. "A price I'd gladly pay," I said, kissing him softly, slowly, making the most of this exquisite moment with the man I loved.

He took hold of my face with one hand and my waist with another, pulling me closer. Kissing me deeper, more searchingly. It was daring, out in public as we were.

I edged a little away. "Luca," I protested in a whisper. "Celso and Falito are watching. Or someone else may come along."

He smiled and pulled me close again. "Let them see," he said, stroking my cheek before kissing me again. "Let the whole world see. Evangelia Betarrini is not yet my fiancée, but she shall be mine."

"Oh I shall, shall I?"

"Oh yes, you shall." I managed to escape his warm hands and took twenty paces back to the position I desired. There, I settled on a stone with my canvas stretched across a board. I sketched with wild, quick lines, desperate to capture everything about this early morning moment that I could. It was perfect. *Perfect.*

And yet as I sketched, I knew that eventually, I'd have to burn my work. There was no telling what my paintings might do when artists were just now daring to depict a bit of realism. To allow my work to become public might change the whole trajectory of art as we knew it, given that I was so influenced by a modern age. No, this work was purely for my own enjoyment, my own memories. But no one besides Luca and my family could ever look upon it.

Still, I found it fulfilling. Bored, Luca pantomimed passing out, and I laughed under my breath, so glad, so very glad to see him acting more like himself.

Once I captured his basic shape and pose, the essence of him, I moved on to the buildings around him. The sun was rising higher, the entire church steeple bright in comparison to the deep shadows that filled the small canal that ran between three-story buildings. A gondola came around the corner, in the distance, and I hurried to sketch it while he was far away.

"Evangelia," Luca said, sounding worried, his tone hushed.

"Hmm?" I asked, still staring at my canvas.

"*Evangelia.*" He moved out of position toward me, hand out-stretched.

"Wait, wait!" I cried with a frown, worried that I'd still need him where he'd been, that he'd just ruined—

"What is this?" said a provincial tone over my shoulder.

I pulled the canvas to my breast and turned to belatedly see a man in fine clothing, flanked by two others in similar dress, and followed by four knights, so elaborately decorated that they could only be from the doge's court.

The man, with a double chin and flabby cheeks that waved when he spoke, snapped his fingers and then flicked them back toward him, obviously asking me—no, telling me—to hand over my canvas.

"No, *signore*," I said with a shake of my head. "'Tis only for my enjoyment. A folly. A lark," I tossed out.

His small dark eyes stared back at me, unmoved by my attempt at charm. "*Signorina*, I shall give you latitude, assuming you must not know who I am. Now hand over that canvas this instant."

"I beg your pardon," I said, "but I cannot. I dare not offend your sensibilities with my poor attempt at the arts."

He clamped his lips together and lifted his chin. "I glimpsed enough to know that it was far from a poor attempt. Now give it to me."

My eyes ran over his shoulders, the fine fabric, the knights behind him. He was of some rank at court. High enough to think he ruled anyone in his path. My only hope was that he would laugh at my attempt. With a sigh, I handed him my board.

He studied it a moment and then looked to the canal, the bridge where Luca had been, the water where the gondolier had passed. His small, dark eyes moved to the church steeple, then down to my canvas again. I held my breath.

"Pity you are not male," he said, still considering my sketch before reluctantly handing it back. "If you were, I'd place you in a master painter's care for proper tutelage. What is your name? From which house do you hail?"

"M'lord," Luca said, inserting himself. "I am Captain Luca Forelli de Siena de Toscana, and this is Lady Evangelia Betarrini."

"Betarrini, Betarrini," the fat man muttered, over and over again, as if trying to place it. Then his small eyes doubled in size and his hands splayed out. "Lady *Betarrini*? The She-Wolf of Siena?"

"Indeed," I said with a demure nod. Perhaps this key information would help him forget my drawing.

He clapped his ham-like hands together. "What good fortune for me! Come along. I am on my way to see the doge and he shall be thrilled to learn you've finally come to visit our fine city." He took my arm and turned me around, and we were instantly in motion. "With those kin of yours about, he's constantly spoken of you."

"Pardon me," Luca said, racing to catch up and blocking the man's way, his hand on the hilt of his sword. "But we shall have your name."

"My good boy," said the man, placing a hand on his round chest. "I am Lord Gradenigo, *consigliere ducale* of Venezia."

Luca's breath came out of him in a rush. I stared at him as I thought, *consiglee-what?* But Luca's face told me we were in some deep weeds.

"Now come with me. Both of you."

GABRIELLA

Mom and Dad came into the breakfast room as Marcello and I ate delicate slices of bread covered in French marmalade, a taste I couldn't get enough of. I'd already had three slices and was eying a fourth when they came in, faces flushed from the cold, Baldarino and Matteo, two Forelli knights, carrying goods.

Mom had a look of glee on her face and rubbed her hands together when she saw we were alone. Caterina had already greeted us and left to see to some business, and Nicolo and his companions weren't likely to rise early, given the amount of wine they'd consumed the night before. Mom hurriedly moved aside the remaining toast and marmalade—ignoring my frown—clearing the way for her goods.

"You won't believe what we found in the market this morning," she enthused. "The men kindly retrieved them for me."

"Where's Lia and Luca?" Dad asked.

"I don't know," I said. "They left early, together."

"Ahh, well," he said, picking up a basket. He handed it to me. "Here, honey. I always wanted to give you one, but we traveled too much. I can finally make that right."

I looked up at him quizzically, as I felt the light, tightly woven basket. Was something moving inside? Dad looked so proud, so excited...and his eyes were full of love. How glad I was that he was with us, here to experience all of this...to know his future grandchild.

Tentatively, I lifted the lid and peeked inside. "*Oh*," I said, my heart pounding. "Dad! I can't believe it!"

Inside, three puppies all wriggled forward, eager to see me. They were white and black, with the cutest little faces.

"Oh, they're adorable," I said, reaching for the most eager one, who was climbing on his siblings to get to me, hopping. "I think I will call you Desi, for *desideroso*," I said. That meant *eager*.

Marcello laughed beside me and reached for another. "And this one should be Grasso, in light of his round belly." He lifted the dog's face to his, and the puppy licked his nose. He was a roly-poly of a dog, totally adorable.

"Oh, Lia is going to go nuts," I said, reaching for the third, who was trembling in the corner of the basket, as if afraid she'd been forgotten. With a puppy in each hand, I looked up at Mom and Dad. We had begged and begged for a puppy as kids, but it had been as Dad had said. With us gone every summer on archeological digs, it'd been impossible. And Mom had thought pets were a bad idea in this era...given that they were likely to carry fleas, which might be picked up from rats, which might be carrying plague.

"I thought you were against animals in the castle," I said, giving her a meaningful look. With the two knights in the room with us, we couldn't speak freely.

"I've seen some rats and mice of late," she said. "I figure it's best to try and keep the castello free of any rodents at all. But no, they should not be permitted to sleep in our rooms."

"We'll keep them in their own quarters," Dad said with a grin. He lifted a second basket, and I heard the plaintive *meow* of a tiny kitten.

"What?" I said, rising. "Cats, too?"

Dad opened the lid and tilted it to show me, so proud that you would've thought he'd raised them himself. I saw two kittens. "Oh, they're so cute!" I squealed.

"The man said their parents were both excellent mousers. And they're from two different lines, so they can mate."

"We'll be overrun!" Marcello complained, but his smile said he didn't mind.

I looked at the puppies, rubbing their soft fur against my cheek. The poor things might be the first to perish if plague managed to reach us. This was why Mom wouldn't allow us to have them in our rooms or sleep with us. But the plague was still a couple years away. In the meantime, these animals would grow into maturity and likely bring us all joy. I absently rubbed my belly. *And give my child an experience I never had myself.*

"We also ordered all sorts of rare spices and herbs that will be useful," Mom said meaningfully. She opened another basket and began pulling out sacks and boxes of camphor crystals and cloves, as well as jugs of apple cider vinegar and bottles filled with various essential oils, all natural remedies to repel fleas and ticks. The knights were used to my mom gathering such things in each city we visited—usually Siena and Rome. She'd become a kind of de facto doctor, seeing every person in the castle and most of the villagers around us when they fell ill.

She was far more successful than the physicians from Siena, who favored leeches and herbal concoctions they refused to fully identify to my mother because they looked down on her as an untrained interloper. She threatened them with her success. It made me proud of her. Even if she made every one of us eat obnoxious amounts of garlic at practically every meal because of its antioxidants and seemingly miraculous healing powers. Luckily we lived in Italia, and garlic was an easy addition. And if we all reeked of garlic, we didn't notice it as much.

She lifted the last bottle out of the basket and looked at the herbs swirling around inside. "Oil of Thieves," she said in a conspiratorial whisper, handing it to me.

I lifted the bottle to the light, remembering how she'd said the oil was used to combat plague and infection in Europe. I waved the elegant bottle in a circle, watching the citrus peel and herbs float around inside. Venice had the most beautiful glass bottles and corks, waxed into place—something we'd seen little of in Toscana. And here they also had the first true windowpanes—mostly opaque or blue with bubbles, so not clear-clear, but allowing light through. I'd glimpsed a palazzo that boasted glass panes from the top floor down, an extravagance, to be sure. Most still utilized their shutters for night or against foul weather, opening them during the day to allow the sunshine in. For a while in bed this morning, I'd fantasized about bringing some glass south with us to the castello to close in a few windows so it wasn't always so dark, come winter. Or to make Mom's solarium a true solarium, rather than a slightly-lighter-than-most-rooms room. But I knew it was too expensive, and they might not make it through the voyage and then across land without shattering.

That was something I'd never thought about in modern times—how glad I was for windows. Just one of a million things I took for granted...

A messenger appeared at the door and rushed toward Marcello. Frowning, he lifted the parchment paper and broke the wax seal. He unfolded the paper and turned toward the light, then looked at me and my folks.

"Gather your things. We must be off at once. The doge has Evangelia and Luca."

"Wh-what?" I asked. "What do you mean, he *has* them?"

"I do not know," he said with a shake of his brown curls, lifting the paper. "Only that Caterina has sent for us. Mayhap they were discovered on the streets, and the doge was so anxious to meet you, he summoned them to the palace at once."

"I hope that is the extent of it," I said, rising.

"It's all rather kingly, isn't it?" Mom asked, following us out of the room.

"I don't like it," Dad said. "What right has he?"

"The man has every right," Marcello said. "And it isn't just the doge who will find the She-Wolves intriguing. He is but the emblem of the Republic. Right behind him are the noblemen who rule this land and sea. Two hundred and forty of them."

I sighed as we gathered our gifts for the doge—a bolt of fine Sienese cloth, woven with bits of gold thread to symbolize the Forellis, and four ample jugs of the region's finest Chianti wine. We hurried out the door of the palazzo, entering a long skiff on which two of Caterina's men were already perched, ready to row us down the Canal. As our knights entered another skiff beside us, my heart pounded.

So much for easing into the city, I thought. As usual, the She-Wolves' entrance was about as subtle as fireworks above Times Square.

EVANGELIA

I gaped as we were led deeper into the doge's palace, four of the doge's men before us, following Gradenigo, the Consigliere Ducale—who, Luca had explained en route, was some high-powered dude—and four of them behind us. Celso and Falito—stripped of their swords—brought up the rear, looking concerned. They didn't like to be told they were going anywhere that either Marcello or Luca hadn't directed. Especially disarmed.

The gothic loggias looked like stone lace, and gave way to progressively heavier décor as we proceeded inward. The dark, brooding walls and massive wood molding of the future palazzo were happily not present yet...this version of the palazzo was lighter, brighter, with the familiar Italian plaster and big beams across the ceilings. Still, framed oil paintings of past doges peered out at us from under a layer of candle soot as we passed.

We entered one interior waiting room with a merry fire crackling in a white marble hearth. Two figures were carved into it, as if supporting it. After a few minutes, we were led into a successive waiting room, and then another. And so it went, with little explanation, only continuous offerings of food and wine and promises that it would only be "but a moment more." When we reached the fifth waiting room, I decided it was like one of Disneyland's clever lines, wrapping from one section to the next, making you think that the wait was now over, but only sucking you in more deeply. And it was there that Celso and Falito were sent to a separate waiting room "suitable for knights."

Luca was pacing, prattling on about what might have made Lord Gradenigo demand we accompany him. Had there been a standing order from the doge? Was the doge angry with Caterina for not escorting us here immediately? Was it because of my art? And why had they allowed Celso and Falito to accompany us for a time, then separate us?

"Please, please, Luca," I said. "Sit. Stop. You're making me twice as anxious!"

A door opened and a man in uniform bowed toward us. "Thank you for waiting. His Serene Highness shall greet you now. Please, follow me."

We followed our guide through two new doors, this set inlaid with gold. I hesitated at the threshold. The room was the size of a football field, the ceiling soaring fifty feet above us. It was divided into sections, and each section—like the walls around us—had been painted by a master in elaborate frescoes. The scenes depicted battles on land and sea, victorious marches, and processionals outside on the piazza de San Marco. On the far wall, panels depicted a scene on the green Adriatic, a fleet of fierce, fine ships, sailing off into the sunset, their flags proudly displaying the Venetian lion. I so wanted to rush over to them, get closer to see what method the masters had used, but Luca was pulling me along, grunting my name in an effort to bring my attention back into focus.

Twenty men and a few women divided to make way for us to approach the dais, where a man in an odd hat sat in a throne-like chair, his collar high, his salt-and-pepper beard long. He tilted his head up to better hear the man whispering into his ear, and then he was alight, swiftly moving down the stairs to greet us, a wide smile on his face.

I dared to take a breath. Surely a man this glad to see us wasn't bent on harming us.

"My dear girl!" he cried, hands splayed outward, as two servants hastened to catch up with him. I caught sight of Caterina scurrying behind, and two men with my canvas between them, as if arguing who would hand it over. "Welcome, welcome, to Venezia," he said.

I bowed in a low curtsy, thankful for Luca's strong hand in mine. "Your Highness, we bid you thanks for the kind invitation to court."

"Rise, She-Wolf," he grunted. "Let me look upon you."

I did as he asked, lifting my chin and not dropping my gaze from his. He smiled, and I noticed he was about my height and roughly my father's age. He took a turn around me and Luca, as if he expected a true wolf's tail to emerge from my skirts, then came around to face us again.

"You have taken a great deal of time to respond to my invitation, Sir Forelli," he said to Luca, clearly knowing exactly who he was without introduction. Perhaps Lord Gradenigo had told him.

"Constant upheaval between our republic and Firenze kept our attention close to home, *Serenissimo*," Luca said, with a graceful duck of his chin. "Believe me when I say that Lady Betarrini and I would have certainly enjoyed your court far more than the battles we endured."

"Ah, indeed," said the man, chin in hand. He studied Luca, clearly not missing anything, from his easy way with political talk to his proximity to me. He lifted his finger in the air and shook it. "You are not the first one of your kin to enter this court, Lady Betarrini."

"So I hear, your grace," I said, biting my tongue when I felt like blurting, *So...can I see them?* We had to find the right time, the right way to approach it. *Gabi, where are you?*

The man's green-brown eyes twinkled with mischief. He knew I was curious, but he refused to give me any further information. "Over the years, I have heard many tales of you and your sister," the doge said to me.

"People do love to talk," I said.

He smiled a little at that. "You are beautiful, yes," he said, "but you are no finer than many of the women in my court. No more beautiful than my own daughter. Forgive me my disappointment, my dear, but to hear tell of your beauty is to believe that one might see an angel instead of a mere woman."

I suppressed a laugh at this, even as Luca shifted, clearly caught between protesting and remaining silent. "I can well believe it, *Serenissimo*," I said, adopting Luca's title for him. *The Most Serene.* "Clearly, a man with such power as you would draw the finest of men and the most beautiful of women from far and wide." I ducked my head in a way that I'd seen Caterina do.

This made the doge smile. "Beautiful *and* with a measure of humility," he said with admiration. So had it been a test? "That is good, very good."

He offered his arm and, after a second, I realized it was for me. I took it, trying to float beside him, as I'd been coached. "Now tell me, Lady Evangelia, of this other gift, of which I'd not heard. I'd come to believe I knew everything possible about you and your sister without meeting you, but here the Consigliere finds you sketching along the canal and discovers you are a gifted artist."

I laughed under my breath, hoping to diffuse this rumor before it got out of control. *Dad's gonna kill me...* "'Tis merely a hobby, kind prince. And I would be most embarrassed if others were to see it. It is for my eyes alone. Might you permit me to keep it that way?" I dared to lean closer. "I beg you to keep it a secret, Serenissimo. Is there an artist's guild who would admit a female?"

He lifted his chin. "They would if I demanded it of them."

I swallowed hard over my fumble. "Certainly. But you see, Serenissimo," I paused to lift my lashes wide, hoping I looked fetching, innocent, "most men do not favor a woman who presses where she is not welcome. And Sir Luca...well, he already must deal with courting a She-Wolf. That is quite enough of a challenge for one man, without adding another, yes?"

He laughed. "Quite," he said. He stared at me from the corner of his eye, as if waiting, and I saw that he'd led me to the closest fresco. "It is the newest one, created by Nato Natale himself. Do you like it?"

I dropped my arm from his and paced to the left, then slowly walked to my right, taking in each successive panel. The way the man had constructed it, using foreshortening, it appeared that the fanciful loggia had depth, as if we were looking past a group of people in their finery at a party, out the far end, to sea.

"It is magnificent," I said to the doge, meaning it.

He nodded, proudly. "I shall arrange for you to meet him. Mayhap he shall tutor you—in private—as you winter with us."

"Oh, nay, nay," I said, shaking my head sadly. Two things alarmed me; his refusal to drop my skills as an artist and his idea that we were to stay here that long. "I fear Lord Forelli shall not allow us to tarry here that long. We are only to be here for a brief visit this time, but we shall eagerly return for a longer visit in the future."

"A brief visit!" he guffawed. "Many long to linger at court in our beautiful city. I confess I am tempted to take offense with your brief sojourn."

"I am well aware of the honor you've bestowed upon us, Serenissimo." I put a hand to my chest. "I long to stay in your fair city for much longer, but Lord Forelli must return to Siena."

"Lord Forelli may return. As one of the Nine, I am aware how his duties must pull at him. But you, my dear," he said, patting my hand, again on his offered arm, "and your knight, should he be vital to you,"—this, he added with a suggestive waggle of his brows—"may certainly remain here for far longer. Abide with us, in the Palazzo Ducale. Experience the finest that Venezia has to offer."

I smiled, still trying to figure out how to untangle myself. "'Tis a generous offer, my prince. You honor us both. Thank you." I hesitated. "Mayhap you are aware that Sir Forelli is captain of Lord Forelli's guard?"

He lifted his chin, as if understanding at last. "So the man cannot be far from his lord, and the lady cannot be far from her knight," he said approvingly. "You shall give my court much fodder for their romantic chattering."

I smiled. "I seem to do my best in that regard," I said, "wherever I go."

He grinned back at me a moment before his face abruptly clouded. "But what of your art? A talent such as this, even if born to a female..."

"Must be kept to myself," I said, daring to finish his sentence. "Please, my prince. I beg you for your assistance in this."

His brows drew together, and he considered me. "Does Sir Forelli," he said, waving at Luca somewhere behind me, "object to your talent?"

"Oh, nay, nay. But I am already fodder for much gossip," I said, "as you yourself have indicated. And should it become known that I like to draw...and not in a style favored by the masters, people will see me all the more as an outsider. They shall have a whole new reason to chatter on about me. I beg you, Serenissimo, might you keep my secret?"

I stared at him, still with what I hoped were puppy-dog-eyes, hoping I looked as pitiful as possible, so he couldn't help but say yes to me.

His eyes stayed on mine for a long while, and in them I did not see that I'd managed to charm or cajole him, only intrigue him. My dad had told me that a man did not get elected as doge by luck; he was often the most intelligent and wisest man within the nobility, and he was elected for life. Clearly, Doge Andrea Dandolo was no different than his predecessors.

"You, my dear," he said in a whisper, "are quite clever, are you not?"

I gave him a look of confusion, pretending innocence.

"Ahh, yes, there 'tis. You pretend to be confused, to be addle-minded, but 'tis clear you know exactly what you are doing. I appreciate clever women about me. Take Lady Brexiano, for instance," he said, with a nod of approval toward her. She had been speaking with other noblewomen. "Those that flit around without a thought in their head bore me, quite frankly. But women such as you..." A slow smile spread across his lips. "Yes, yes, I am more than glad the Betarrinis have finally arrived at court. And in time, we shall find out your ties to these other kin with their odd stories."

I stared back at him, hoping I looked friendly, demure, unruffled, but feeling my heart pound all the while.

"No doubt you'd like to greet these kin," he said, lowering his gaze, searching mine. "'Tis what brought you north at long last, nay?"

"Actually, Serenissimo, we had already planned to come, so eager were we to visit your lovely Republic. These men..." I shook my head as if concerned... "Should they be telling the truth about their name and in their right minds...Well, let us say we are interested in comparing our lineage to see if we are truly related."

"Indeed," he said. "I, too, am most eager to find out how these pieces of the puzzle fit together. I shall bring you together and observe."

"Of course, your grace," I said with another nod, as if I wasn't thinking *we're totally screwed* in my mind. As if I had no problem with, you know, having the most powerful man in the region listen to us chatter on about time travel and tombs and such...that would be all kinds of awesome.

As he led me back to the others, who all milled about, anxiously waiting on us, he had a little grin on his face. Like he knew he had me. *Awesome, just awesome,* I thought.

And at that moment, I wished I hadn't pushed to come to Venice at all.

CHAPTER 11

GABRIELLA

S o it was that we all moved into the Palazzo Ducale, the doge's men
hearing no arguments against it. Apparently, it had been some sort
of odd royal decree or something, and men arrived behind us at Caterina's place to pack all our things. As soon as we arrived at the palazzo, we
were shown to beautiful guest quarters, and within the hour, all of our
things arrived, too, from our gowns to our new puppies and kittens.

Luca came to see us and told us what had transpired, but Lia was
being held elsewhere, ostensibly greeting the *dogaressa*. We thought it a
means to remind us who held the power over every inch of this city, and
pretty far beyond it.

Dad was pacing. "He wants to know everything about us. He will
watch every move we make, every choice, every purchase, listening to
every word we utter—together and apart—gathering the clues."

Marcello flopped down into a chair. "So, what is there to discover?
Truthfully? You've purchased spices and oils, animals to keep us company in the castello. There is nothing scandalous in all of that. You all know
the story you shall stick to in regard to your history."

Dad stared at me and Mom, switching to English. "I don't like it.
There's something else coming down here. And, of all the men that have
the power to trip us up, this guy," he said, waving about us to indicate
the doge, "has it." He rubbed his temples between his third finger and
thumb, as if massaging away the pain. "I just thought we'd be near him,

maybe meet him once. That he'd be so busy with everyone else at court, we'd be a passing interest, not the main event."

"Parla il linguaggio commune, per favore," Marcello said, asking us to switch to Italian, more than a little irritated. Whenever we lapsed into English, he felt like we were trading secrets. Normally, it was just because we were scared or agitated.

"The doge is far too interested in us," Dad said to him. "Since the other Betarrinis have been here and told him who-knows-what, I cannot help but imagine he suspects we might be similarly...strange."

"You are strange, of sorts," Marcello said, his irritation receding and a familiar smile teasing the corners of his mouth and eyes. He grabbed my hand as I passed and pulled it to his lips as he looked up at me. "But 'tis not beyond the law to be unusual."

"'Tis part of the family's appeal," Luca said, joining in.

"Enough," I growled, pulling my hand from Marcello's and folding my arms. "You are well aware of what unnerves us."

"And so we shall navigate these waters, try to rescue these strange kin of yours—should they *truly* be kin—and be on our way home to Siena," Marcello said. "We have little choice other than to make our way through it."

Dad met my gaze. *The only way through is through*, we mouthed together and shared a rueful smile.

"Usually," I said with a groan, "getting *through* means we end up fighting for our lives at some point."

"Usually," Luca said. "But that also seems to bring out the best of the famous She-Wolves and their parents, does it not?"

"We will fight if we must," Dad said. "But we will use our heads first, and our weapons second."

By evening, Luca was so unnerved that Lia hadn't been returned to us, he took to griping at his men over tiny infractions. The crowds were gathering out in the piazza, getting ready for entertainment the doge had arranged, and I had a sneaking suspicion we were going to be some part of it. We had met him, briefly, that afternoon, and asked about Lia, to which he'd said vaguely, "I believe she is attending my wife."

Caterina gave her head a little shake when I tried to ask if I might join her. Apparently, that would've made him mad or something.

"She is fine in the company of the dogaressa," she said. "There is nowhere safer in the city," she added for Luca's sake.

In our rooms, she urged us to don our finest. We'd be presented to many of the nobles that evening, and after dining with them, we'd go outside to the piazza to join the festivities there. Reportedly, there were fireworks planned, which got Mom and Dad all excited, since they thought only the Chinese had fireworks in this era. But then they grew concerned, as the plague apparently began in China...which led them to confer about dates and what they remembered.

Truthfully, neither of them remembered exact dates. Only vague information. And when I'd been home briefly, all I'd found out was that the plague hit Italy in 1348. We didn't know if that was January or December of that year. All we knew was that 1348 was the year we'd have to pretty much go underground. Bar the gates of the castello and not go out. And that was just two years away.

But we'd seen a "pre-strain" already, when Luca and the others got sick a couple years ago. Were we fooling ourselves that we were safe until the Big Year? Maybe Mom and Dad were right—that if there were Chinese pyro-techs about, the plague might already be present in some fashion. I rubbed my belly, suddenly anxious.

Marcello was there and wrapped an arm around my waist and pulled me close. "Are you well, wife?"

"Well enough. Only worried. I wish they'd let Lia return to us."

"The doge toys with us," Marcello said with a shrug. "Pushes us. Don't let him...how do you say it?"

"Get under our skin."

He shivered, and I smiled, remembering how he thought the phrase was creepy. But he was right. This doge was clever, and he'd likely play every card he had in order to try and corner us, wriggling out any information he could. Because knowledge was power, in this age as in any age. And he clearly wanted to know what we knew about these new Betarrinis...

"Do you think there's any way we can talk to our 'cousins' without someone from the court hearing us?" I asked him.

He hesitated, then his broad fingers slowly rubbed my lower back as if he figured out it was hurting. "It is unlikely. Given how this is unfolding, I suspect the doge himself will be there."

"Can you not request it?" I asked, looking up at him. "As a favor to one of the Nine?"

"Mayhap," he said. "If I am given the opportunity this night, I shall ask it of him. But, Gabriella, even that might not be the best. He will assume we have something to hide, or that we know these men. It well may be best to proceed as if we have nothing to hide, and together, negotiate how we respond."

There was a knock at the door, and Marcello and I parted. "Enter," he said. Four servants did so, carrying trunks in their arms.

When they'd set them down, the man in front said with a grand wave to the trunks. "A gift from the doge and dogaressa. Their highnesses thought you might care to don something special for tonight's festivities. These are for you, Lord and Lady Forelli, and Lord and Lady Betarrini."

"Thank you," Marcello murmured.

The man gave a curt nod and then turned on his heel and exited. Once the door was closed, I scurried over to the first trunk and opened it. Inside was a fine tapestry-like tunic of ivory silk, with a mass of gold thread at the shoulder, and the Forelli coat of arms embroidered across the chest. Beneath it was the softest shirt and leggings I'd ever felt in this era, and gorgeous, soft-leather boots. I held them up, and knew they had to be Marcello's size. "He...He didn't just order these today," I said.

"Nay," Marcello said, taking the boot from me and then the tunic. "He's been anticipating our arrival for some time."

"Anticipating it enough to know our sizes?" I asked. A shiver ran down my back. Could the doge's reach extend all the way down to Toscana? How could he have learned such things?

Tentatively, I moved to the next trunk and opened it. I sucked in my breath, grabbed hold of the gown, and slowly pulled it out. It was magnificent. Almost a bridal gown, in a fine ivory silk with a broad scooped neck, long, tight sleeves and a princess waist. I was relieved to see that—it was a good cut for a girl with a round belly. Down the arms and skirt was a solid ribbon of gold, embroidered with tiny pearls. I reached down and took hold of the slippers and matching headpiece at the bottom of the trunk. Again, the shoes appeared to be a perfect fit. *Creepy...definitely creepy.*

But I couldn't deny that I was excited to put on the new gown.

Two hours later, we were all in our new clothes and led downstairs. But instead of progressing immediately to a great hall of some sort, we were taken outside, to the piazza, where masses of people gathered on all four sides of the rectangular public square, and also filled the *piazzetta*—the small square that jutted off to the side, giving the entire public space an L-shape—along the doge's palace, as well.

There were torches dancing on all the buildings that lined the piazza, and six bonfires in stone pits down the center. The flickering light cast ghoulish shadows across the ancient basilica, which always reminded me of a building that belonged in Istanbul more than Venice—with all its gold, mosaic tile and onion-shaped domes and arches. I thought

I remembered Dad actually saying it was designed after a church in Constantinople....

Noble after noble in front of us was announced by a man in ducal garb, shouted in a high, reedy voice, to which the people responded with applause, cheers, or sometimes jeers. But my eyes were constantly roving, looking for Lia. We'd been reassured repeatedly that she was with the dogaressa, she was fine, and we had edged into territory that might possibly offend our host by continually asking about her...but now, here, we assumed we'd be reunited.

As agitated as I was, Luca was a mess. He was flushed and sweating, even in the chilly November air, so damp that it seemed to seep into my very bones. I thought it silly, the ladies' fashionable gowns with their low- and wide-cut bodices, exposing so much skin, while the men wore shirts and tunics and coats buttoned high up their necks. I pulled my fur stole closer around my shoulders and took a step closer to Marcello, hoping to steal a little of his warmth.

We were next. The name-shouting dude lifted the card Marcello handed him up to the light, paused a moment, his eyes widening and then flicking over us again. He seemed to stand a bit straighter. "The Lord and Lady Marcello Forelli de Siena!"

The crowd seemed to take a collective breath, and chattering stopped. Marcello urged me forward and we descended the steps and entered the piazza, parading the full perimeter like we were exotic animals as people whispered behind their hands. I thought it ridiculous and fought back the urge more than once to just take Marcello's hand and haul him into the crowds. I'd much rather walk the quiet streets of Venezia, leaving this posturing behind us. But one thing kept me here; we had to find Lia. She wasn't with the doge, but then, neither was the dogaressa, that we could see.

"Marcello," I said, under my breath.

"She's here, somewhere," my husband returned. "You must wait, Gabriella. The doge has something up his sleeve, as you say. We simply must wait for him to reveal it."

"If he doesn't do it soon, I believe I shall retrieve my sword and begin tearing through the Palazzo Ducale—and anyone who stands in my way—until I find her."

"That," he said, casting me a loving look, "would not be well received. And you want to meet these mysterious kin, do you not?"

"I do."

"Then play his game."

"How do we play a game when we are not aware of the rules?"

"We discern the rules as we play it."

I stifled a sigh and forced a smile as a lady beside us curtsied and the man next to her bowed. We could hear the twittering as we passed, the crazy whispers of our prowess in battle, the rumors that I was with child, the thought that I was liable to give birth to a werewolf, half man-child, half-wolf. Some wondered over my beauty, seeming surprised that the rumors were true. Others thought I looked more like a man than a woman, given my great height.

It wasn't anything I hadn't heard before. I was used to it, in cities, in villages, where dramatic stories were the centerpiece of every evening's public gathering and much of the gossip shared through the day. And I hadn't exactly lived a quiet, monkish life here in Italia, so this was the logical outcome. I had what I needed at Castello Forelli—all the people I loved best, who truly knew and loved me in return. But some of the gossip still stung a little, as much as other portions made me smile.

People would talk; there was no controlling them. All I could control were my own actions. We came to a stop beside other nobles when we reached the base of the watch tower outside the Palazzo Ducale. Eventually, it would become the brick *campanile*, or bell tower, that was part of the famous Venetian skyline, but now it was a bit shorter, with a wooden spire on top, apparently used to keep tabs on the flow of traffic in the lagoon—sort of like a medieval aircraft control tower. But, you know, for boats.

I looked up with the others, and around to the front of San Marco, the old basilica, with her war-plundered bronze horses at the top center. What was the fuss all about? What were they expecting? Everyone was staring upward, toward the tower, as if anticipating something to emerge there. Was that where they were going to set off the fireworks?

Mom and Dad arrived behind us. "Where is she?" I whispered, knowing they'd be as anxious as we were.

Luca arrived then, too, not part of the announced gentry, given that he had no land of his own. He ran a hand through his hair.

"The dogaressa has been announced. But I cannot find Lia. Where could she be?"

A trumpet sounded above us, and the rest of the crowd looked upward. I didn't like the idea of that trumpeter being so close to the fireworks, but just then I saw a figure in white climb to the railing. With wings. She had huge wings on her back. Two men behind her attached a belt around her to a rope above. My eyes narrowed as I focused on the swooping rope, coming down at a wide angle across the piazza, down to where it was anchored at the center. *It's some sort of crazy-town zipline.* Then I looked back up to the figure, who was taking a bow in hand and nocking an arrow.

"What are they doing?" Dad murmured. "The Flight of the Angel?"

"Flight of the what?" I asked.

"But it's not Carnivale," Mom protested, gazing upward, too distracted to answer my question. That, I knew, was the city-wide festival here every year...at some point in time.

"It doesn't take a feast for the doge to put on a spectacle," Dad said.

The figure shifted, and a man with a torch approached her, setting the tip of her arrow on fire, illuminating her face, the hint of golden hair.

"Oh, no, no, no," I said under my breath.

Because the figure above us—so terrifyingly high above us—was my sister.

CHAPTER 12

EVANGELIA

T he dogaressa gave me no option once she'd come up with the idea. I was taken directly to her dressmaker in the city for a fitting, then returned for a bath, and then hair and makeup so overdone that I looked like a freakish doll.

It didn't matter to her that the Flight of the Angel usually only occurred during Carnivale; it was going to make this party tonight something that people would talk about for years. And given her court—all the ladies parading about with pet monkeys, squirrels and parrots on their shoulders—it didn't take long to figure out this girl was all about the drama. If I wanted her on our side, and if I wanted the doge to introduce us to the mysterious Betarrinis, I had to do this for them. They didn't say it, exactly. But they didn't have to. There really was never a choice.

I looked to the target on the far side of the piazza again. I was to send my flaming arrow flying directly into its center, which would ignite the fireworks. I thought it extremely foolish; if I missed, I could set the building on fire. And in medieval times, a fire in one building surely meant that at least a whole city block could be toppled, if not the whole city. But even this protest fell upon deaf ears.

"There will be many men and the equivalent of a whole cistern of water up there, in case the fireworks spread beyond where they should," countered the dogaressa. "Surely, they can handle one lone arrow."

Still, I hesitated, trying to figure out how to talk her out of it. I imagined a medieval newspaper and headlines. *She-Wolf Burns Doge's Palace to Ground.*

"Come now," she said, so fat that her round head seemed to sit directly on her rolling shoulders, sans neck. "Are the legends of the She-Wolves only that? Do you truly have no talent as an archer?"

"I have some talent," I'd returned.

"Talent enough to kill man after man in battle?"

"A fair number," I allowed.

"Then how difficult shall it be?" she asked, giving me a look as if to say that I was being obstinate. Irritating her, and in front of her ladies-in-waiting, at that.

"Very well," I said. "I'll do it."

"No need to be so reluctant," she sniffed. "It's quite the honor. All the ladies of Venezia compete come Carnivale time to be the one chosen as angel."

"Thank you, Dogaressa," I said with a slow curtsy and bow of my head. And then I'd been sent off to be trussed up like a doll, placed in this gown with its ridiculously long train and now set upon the railing of the tower. In giant wings. With a flaming arrow. Awesome. I refused to look down, or look for Gabi and Luca and my parents. I had to concentrate on the task at hand. Do this thing and move on.

But I let out a little yelp as the men set me free, swinging on the rope, and was conscious of my arrow's fire sending sparks toward my wings. *Good luck not burning to death.* I spun and lost sight of the target as I descended. I only had a few moments longer before it'd be out of range.

People shouted and screamed and clapped below me. My spin ended, and I saw the target at last. With a breath, I let the arrow fly and it arced over the crowd. For a heart-stopping moment, I thought it was going to go low, directly into the marble exterior of the building below it. But it didn't. I'd managed to hook the very bottom of the target and the entire thing burst into flame, and one by one, explosions sent bright yellow, red, and orange sparks into the sky. It was something like a decent neighborhood Fourth of July back home, in terms of scope. No ball field show. But these people, who'd never seen anything like it, cheered like they'd just beheld a miracle. And when I landed at last at the bottom, men surrounded me, kissing me on both cheeks, as if I'd single-handedly saved the city.

Luca managed to break his way through, shoving one man and then another aside, almost creating a brawl, until someone identified him as "the She-Wolf's man." Then the same men he'd shoved aside were clapping him on the back and shoulder, trying to lift him on their own shoulders like some sort of hero.

It was crazy. It was funny. It was wild. And my legs were shaking so hard, I thought I'd collapse.

But he returned to my side. He wrapped a protective arm around my waist, and used his other to make our way forward, toward the church. Finally, we left the biggest partiers behind us, and the crowd split, allowing us a clear vision of the doge, the dogaressa, and two men before them, in chains.

I paused.

Because here, at last, were the new Betarrinis.

GABRIELLA

They made Luca and Lia stop where they were, partway down the piazza. The doge, dogaressa and prisoners were between two bonfires, directly in front of the towering church, topped with its domes high above us. Then they set an apple on each man's head.

"Now be still," said the doge, who was covered by a ceremonial umbrella-thingy held by a man behind him. "If you are still and the She-Wolf of Siena manages to strike the apple off each of your heads, it will be proof that the Lord Almighty wishes for you to have another chance to speak the truth. If she strikes you through the eye, it will be proof that the Lord Almighty wishes for your lies to be silenced."

The crowd around us erupted in excitement, all talking at once. But my attention was on the Betarrinis—or the guys who *said* they were Betarrinis.

The two young men, in dirty, bedraggled, clothes, appeared as if they were shaking already. They were no more than twenty or twenty-two, and with a striking resemblance to me and my dad. I shared a quick look with my father.

"I don't know," he whispered, edging closer to me. "Maybe a distant cousin's kids?"

"You've remembered a cousin in Ravenna?"

"Who knows," he muttered. "I could have distant cousins through-out Italy."

"Serenissimo," Lia said, as the crowd quieted. She waved away the man who handed her a new bow and quiver of arrows. "I have already done what the dogaressa required of me in—"

"And you did a fine job of it," the doge said, striding a few steps toward her. "Ne'er has our city had a more skilled angel descend to this piazza."

The crowd erupted into a new round of cheers.

Lia took a moment to gather herself. Then, "You are most kind in your praise, my prince," she said with a slight bow. "But regardless of my prowess during my descent, I must confess that I feel quite weak-kneed after the excitement. I could not possibly take these two men's lives in my—"

"You shall," the doge said, creepily never dropping his smile. "Or I shall hang them this night for their defiance."

Lia's mouth closed abruptly.

The doge lifted his arms. "You see, you are now able to be an angel of deliverance, if God so chooses. For these two have sorely tried my patience in these last weeks, and I've decided they must either be placed in the madhouse or be hanged. With no family to pay the monthly stipend for the madhouse—unless you, Lady Betarrini, wish to claim them—the only answer is this. I think it rather generous of me."

We all held our breath. One of the guy's apples fell from his head, and he scurried after it, grabbed it, then returned to his knees. A guard placed it atop his head again when he shook too much to do so. What had the doge and his men done to these young men? Our potential cousins?

I moved to step forward, to join Lia and Luca, but Marcello held my arm. "Nay," he whispered. "Your presence will only heighten the tension. This is Evangelia's fight. Let her fight it."

I wrung my hands and stared at my sis. The ridiculous wings made me think of old Victoria's Secret commercials. Except she had a whole lot more clothes on. But would they get in the way of her shooting with accuracy? She'd managed to strike the fireworks target...

"I will not shoot with this bow," she said to the doge, gesturing toward what the ducale knight offered her. "Only my own."

The doge gave her a long, level stare and then nodded to a steward beside him to go and fetch her bow. She was agreeing to it? She actually intended to shoot those apples off?

"And if I succeed," she dared to continue, "the first words the men share will be with the kin they claim. We need to meet with them. In private. For an hour. We need that time to ascertain if they truly are kin to us, and if we should pay for their keep in a madhouse here or in Toscana."

Sheesh, that was smart. I'd never seen her act so strong, and my heart pounded with pride, alternating with panic. I knew she could do it, but with the flickering light of fires, the distance, the stakes...

All around us, the crowd was abuzz, men immediately taking bets for or against Lia. On and on it went, growing louder as people panicked, worried they wouldn't get someone to accept a bet in time, while Luca helped Lia take off the ridiculous wings. Finally, the knight returned with her own bow and quiver.

Lia set the strap of her quiver over her shoulder and slowly reached for one arrow, staring at the young man on the left, a hundred paces away. Mercifully, she let the first arrow go without further pause, hitting the top right quadrant, but succeeding in driving it from his head. He collapsed in tears, falling to his face in relief, but then sat back up, hugging himself, staring in horror at his brother. The other one was younger and now shaking so much that the apple was teetering on his head.

"Be still, cousin," Lia said quietly as she nocked another arrow, her words echoing across the stone tiles. "I can do this," she said, drawing back the string and taking aim. "You may trust me."

The crowd was silent. No one coughed. No one moved. It was impossible, but in that piazza, crowded with perhaps a thousand people, it seemed no one even breathed.

And when she let the arrow fly, it seemed to move in slow-motion for a sec, then picked up speed, driving through the apple and pinning it against the wooden door of the ancient church behind the younger man.

This time, the crowd really did go wild.

CHAPTER 13

EVANGELIA

E veryone moved toward us, from all sides. Luca had no chance against them, though he tried. People were laughing and shouting and lifting me up, chanting, "She-Wolf! She-Wolf! She-Wolf!"

I looked back over my right shoulder, to the consternation on Luca's face, him reaching for his sword—

"Nay!" I cried, "Nay! Please. Let me down at once. Please."

A man with a bulbous nose and deeply dimpled chin near my head heard me and began shouting, "Let her down! Let the She-Wolf down!" He pulled at one man's arms and then another's, joining Luca in the effort, and my heart faltered as I thought I might fall to the piazza's tiles.

But in the end, my body and shoulders were held erect and my legs gradually angled downward. The press of the people kept me nearly aloft, and I'd touch one slippered foot to solid ground only for it to be lifted as the other met stone. They were moving me, slowly, toward the front of the piazza, where the doge and his minions were. I had a brief moment of panic when I realized my bow and quiver had fallen or been pulled from my shoulder, but when I looked back, I saw that people were passing it forward, right behind me.

A hush fell over the crowd as I reached the end of it, to the twenty-foot span of space that separated the commoners from the nobles, who stood on the steps of the church. Luca was spit out of the masses behind me, and hurried to catch up, looking disheveled and frustrated, pushing back a shock of dirty blond hair from his sweaty face.

But my attention was on the doge and the knights behind him, who held the two Betarrini men. I paused and looked the doge in the eye.

"Your challenge has been met, Serenissimo. Now, please honor our agreement by allowing me and mine to have a word in private with your two prisoners."

A cheer went up behind us and I saw the doge's eyes harden. We both knew he had no option. He'd as much as promised. Lips clamped together, he waved one hand of dismissal, and we were all set in motion. The crowd was yelling and applauding and officials were attempting to quiet them, apparently in preparation for a speech or something from the doge. It pleased me...maybe it'd take a while to do what he had to, helping to assure us of the time we'd been promised.

The Betarrini boys were in front of me and Luca, their hands bound, a knight on either side of them with beefy hands locked on their forearms. They kept looking back at me, half in gratefulness, I decided, and half in anger. Maybe they didn't like that I took their lives in my hands. But really, what option did we have? I didn't know if the doge would've ever granted us a private audience, and I wasn't crazy about anyone hearing what we were about to talk about.

I itched in anticipation. Soon we'd know if these two were crazy or fellow time travelers. The thing was, they didn't look nutsy. They looked like...family. A couple of inches taller than Gabi and Dad, with those trademark Betarrini curls, olive skin, and big, brown eyes. Eyes that held no edge of madness.

These guys appeared weary, beaten, scared...but *sane*.

Goosebumps ran up my arm and down my back.

"Evangelia," Luca said, leaning toward me, "Forgive me. I tried to keep them from taking you—"

"I know," I said, giving his arm a squeeze. "In a crowd like that, even the best knight could do little against them."

He gave me a grateful look, but he was still troubled, warily survey-ing the last of the people as we disappeared into the Palazzo Ducale. We turned left, entered a hall to our right and emerged in the center of the palace in an open courtyard. High above us, the sky was a velvet blue, with stars twinkling like winking eyes at us.

We were led up some steep, wide stairs, covered in a barrel-vaulted ceiling, then down another hall, and finally into a room on our right. The ducale knight in charge turned to me.

"You shall find the privacy you seek here," he said, "and we may be assured that our prisoners will not escape. Would you care to have a guard inside with you?"

"Nay," Luca said, stepping forward. "Lord Forelli and I can certainly protect the women."

"As you wish," said the man, stiffly gesturing inward. We walked inside—my folks, Gabi, Marcello, the two new Betarrinis, and Luca and me.

The door closed with a solid sound behind us.

Mom moved to light more candles from the one the guard had given her, while Dad gestured to two chairs across from a settee. The young men settled gratefully onto them, leaning forward to rest their heads on their shaking, bound hands. Luca poured two glasses of water and handed one to each man.

"Drink," he said, and the two obeyed, noisily draining the glasses dry in seconds.

"Any wine?" asked the elder one.

"Nay," Luca said, bringing the pitcher back to refill their glasses. "But now that your tongues are wet, use them. You've managed to spread gossip from Venezia to Roma. Tell us your story. The truth, please. Only the truth." He set the pitcher down, straightened, and folded his arms. "Begin with your names."

"I am Orazio Betarrini," said the elder one, in Italian, "and this is my brother Galileo."

"We are your great grandnephews," Galileo said to my dad, rolling his hand to denote future generations.

"From Ravenna," added Orazio, nodding excitedly, as if that would confirm things for Dad.

Dad remained impassive, crossing his arms. As I looked back and forth between the new guys, I decided it was their eyes that made them recognizable as family.

"We came by accident," Orazio said. "It has been family lore that your family disappeared from an Etruscan dig site and never returned."

"There were Etruscan ruins near our farm," Galileo said. "And we'd always searched them, pretending we were like our famous American relatives."

"Shh," Dad said, gazing worriedly to the door. He sat down on the table between the settee and the young men. "Please, whisper," he said in a whisper himself. "The walls likely have ears."

I moved to the other side of the table. He was right. Doge Dandolo had promised an hour of privacy. He had not promised he wouldn't have spies listen in. And the word *American* would be an odd thing to be bandied about, since there was no such discovered land at the moment. Nor were there likely any Betarrinis in Ravenna, way back yonder in the fourteenth century. Marcello moved a chair closer, as did Luca, and Gabi and Mom moved into our tiny circle.

"Go on," Dad said to Orazio, when we were all settled again.

"My father, he is a farmer. And in plowing the fields this fall to leave them fallow for the winter, he discovered a new Etruscan tomb. It was perfectly preserved."

Mom and Dad shared an excited look.

"And?" Mom said.

"It was a family grave, with many ossuaries, and a skeleton still on a stone in the center, his hands around a sword."

"But it was the handprints among the frescoes that caught our attention," Galileo said.

We all stilled.

"Handprints?" Gabi said, her voice sounding strangled. "What was around them?"

"*Sì*," said Galileo, looking at her. "They were surrounded by stars. A whole nightscape, it seemed."

"And angels, too," Orazio said. "But it was the handprints that we were drawn to. The only other place they'd found handprints was in a tomb field near where you were last seen, before you drove off in a Jeep and were never heard from again. Near two castles—Castello Greco and Castello *Forelli*." He looked meaningfully at Marcello and Luca.

Gabi sat back slowly, her fingers on the arms of her chair, pinching so hard they were turning white. "Castello Greco. You know it as Castello Greco."

"Yes," Galileo said slowly, wondering what she was after.

"He is right," Mom whispered to us. "Angels, and even stars appear elsewhere. But the only place that Ben and I ever saw handprints were in Tomb Two."

"Tomb Two," Orazio repeated, frowning. "How did you know that? You disappeared before it was discovered."

"Because," Mom said slowly, "I discovered it."

"No, some other guy discovered it. Just a couple miles from your husband's last known dig site," Orazio said, nodding toward Dad. "I've read tons about him and the dig. It made him super famous." He tapped his forehead. "What was the other guy's name?"

"Doctor Manero," Dad asked dully, his brown eyes moving to watch their reaction.

"Yes, yes. *Manero*. That's it!"

The breath left Mom with a *whoosh*. Her biggest discovery ever had been commandeered by the jerkiest jerk we'd ever met, Doctor Jerk-Face Manero.

"Don't you see?" Gabi asked her. "It makes sense. We changed everything when we went back and nabbed Dad. You were never there, the year you found the tomb field with Lia and me. But since you've been here, you've done your fair share of excavation—"

"Which made it easier for Manero to find it," Mom finished numbly, rubbing her temples. She looked wan, as if the guy had ripped her off again, somehow.

"Yes," Orazio said tentatively, aware now that he was in tender territory. "He used a drone over the forest. Found it and then became famous."

"Enough about Manero," Dad said briskly. "Get back to the handprints."

"Right," Galileo said. "Well, we visited the Forelli site, which is what they call it now, given the castle and all. We saw a pair of handprints there." His eyes flicked to Marcello. "I have to say, it's beyond strange to meet you. Who knew that we were somehow family?" He shook his head as we all waited. "Anyway, we noticed that there were only two handprints, and different sizes. So when we got home, we looked for handprints like them, and we found them there in our tomb, too, side by side."

"And when we touched them, they were warm," Orazio said. "Or one was. For me. And the other for him."

"Just like for us," I murmured.

"Really?" Orazio asked me.

"Really. And when you touched them together..."

"*Boom*. We were here," Galileo finished, hands splayed outward. "Well, not *here*-here, but on our land. In a different time."

We stared at them for a long moment, all wondering the same thing. Could we trust them? Could they possibly be playing us, having found out our method of time travel somehow?

"What year are you from?" I whispered.

Galileo's brown eyes settled on mine. "2089. And I'm praying you can help us return."

I looked at his clothing, but his futuristic duds were long gone. 2089? They had called themselves Dad's great grandnephews...

"Please don't tell us we're stuck here like you," Orazio said, brows curving upward. "Is there a way to get back?"

"We're not *stuck*," I said quickly, feeling his word as an affront for some reason. As if he was dissing us and all we had here.

Then I looked at Luca. I meant it. Suddenly, I understood. I didn't *feel* trapped. I was exactly where I wanted to be. Couldn't imagine going back. To our era, or these boys'. The idea of it...

I rose and paced away, thinking. It was what I had known all along. I loved Luca. I didn't want to leave him, or even medieval Italy, now. Certainly not my family. But there was something about meeting Galileo and Orazio, the idea of another open time door somewhere, that made it seem more possible to return home. To safety. Security. But was it truly more secure?

As I thought on it, that option came to lack security, too. There were unknowns, any which way I turned.

But it was possible. I could make the leap.

And in that *possibility*, I realized how *impossible* it would be to leave Luca. To leave *us*, and our future together.

I looked to him and found him staring at me. He really was so dang amazing, in so many ways. More manly than when I'd first met him. With those green eyes that seemed to teem with life itself. And the way he was so aware of me, constantly looking out for me...I didn't know how to explain it. But in that instant, I was sure of it. That I had to take the risk. Regardless of the cost to me or him or my family.

Hadn't every single risk we'd taken paid off so far?

"*Che cos'é? Che cosa é successo?*" he mouthed. *What is it? What has happened?*

I only smiled. Smiled so broadly that I thought I might start laughing. He gave me a quizzical look, which only made me think him ten-times hotter.

I'm going to marry this man.

I was going to marry him and take whatever came at us, hand in hand with him. Mrs. Luca Forelli. Evangelia Forelli. Lia Forelli. *Yeah, I could get used to that.*

I focused again on the conversation at hand.

"So we need to get you fellows back to your tomb and home," Dad was saying, stepping forward and cutting the ropes that bound their hands.

But the guys just shook their heads, miserably. "When we came out..." Orazio said and looked to his brother.

"We were so surprised, so completely shocked, we didn't have time to come up with an explanation."

I looked to Gabi. We knew that feeling well. When we first arrived in medieval Italy, I think I'd just repeated something like, "I'm not from here," to Cosmo Paratore in the days after my arrival. And gradually, I figured out that to claim I was from the future would land me in some sort of fourteenth-century psych ward.

"It was our rotten luck to emerge in this time just as a priest and four nuns were passing by on a wagon," Galileo said. "They took one look at us and you'd think they'd seen aliens or something."

"Well, we did walk out of the tomb," his brother said.

"Still. That priest hit the reins across the back of that mule so hard the nuns practically tumbled out the back onto the road." He smiled and shook his head. "We set off in the opposite direction, deciding that the priest and nuns weren't going to be friends, and came across a town that gave us a pretty good idea of what time period we'd landed in."

"We got scared then," Orazio said. "Reality was setting in. But in the dark, we knew we couldn't make it back to the tomb without getting lost." His expression became gloomy. "When we returned there, come morning, it was surrounded by priests and monks. I think they were performing an exorcism."

"What?" Mom asked, rising, looking pale.

"It was that priest and those nuns," Galileo said. "We crept close enough to hear some villagers talking. They thought we were demons, rising from the grave. Or warlocks. They destroyed it to drive us away."

"Little did they know they were blocking us from leaving," Orazio said forlornly.

"We set off walking," Galileo said. "Our only other thought was that we had to get to the Forelli tomb."

"Because of the handprints," Marcello said.

Galileo nodded.

"Indulge me," Marcello said, rising and going to Gabriella. He took her hand and helped her rise and led her to the center of the room. Then he gestured to Galileo, the taller, but younger, brother.

"It was your left hand, yes?" he asked Gabi. She nodded and lifted her hand, palm up.

Eyes wide, Galileo lifted his to lay it against Gabi's. A perfect match.

Marcello waved Orazio closer as he came over to me, doing as he did with my sister, leading me to the center of the room. There seemed to be an electric charge in the air, and I felt a measure of fear before I lifted my palm to match against Orazio's. As if this might change everything...as if somehow, we four might disappear.

I lifted my trembling hand to set it against his.

Again, a perfect match. From the tips of our fingers to the base of our palms.

Our hands grew warm as we stared at each other for a long moment, and again it was his eyes that made me think I knew him from somewhere. That we'd met, somehow, before. But that had to be the Betarrini blood running through his veins. A common gene, reappearing down the family line. The same that made Gabi and Dad look alike, just as Mom and I did.

Slowly, we all let our hands drop, but we only moved a step apart.

"So..." Dad said, pacing excitedly, chin in hand. "Betarrini blood, both pairs, siblings...Are you two years apart?"

"Yes, sir," Orazio said, looking dazed as he stared at me and glanced down at my hand again.

"When are your birthdays?" Mom asked.

We all tensed, waiting for some other cosmic freakishness. But they weren't the same as ours, just a similar span apart.

Dad looked to Mom. "Maybe that's all it takes," he said in English. "The right gene, the right genetic connection with a sibling, and the right sized hand, access to an Etruscan tomb with the prints, and *boom*, you're a time traveler."

"Benedetto," Marcello warned with a sigh of frustration. Gabi quickly translated for the rest as Mom and Dad kept on in excited conference. I knew from experience that it was hard to break into their small circle when they got like this, chasing down a hunch together.

"Gabi and Lia weren't the first travelers," Mom said, shaking her head. "That's what those other symbols in our tomb mean. Why there's a Greek—who *predated* the Etruscans—and a Roman—who came *after* the Etruscans—beside the angels. I thought they'd been added later, by others who somehow wanted to leave their own mark on the tomb. But they appear to have been made at the same time as the rest of the frescoes, by *Betarrini* ancestors. It never made sense to me, either way. Except in this context." She looked around at me and Gabi. "You weren't the first Betarrinis to travel," she said again.

"Nor are you likely the last," Dad said, looking to our new cousins.

"But *we* might be," Orazio said, "if something happens to your tomb and the tunnel is lost to us forever."

"There might be others," Mom said, now pacing the room with Dad. "In our time, many tombs had been bulldozed or otherwise destroyed. But in this time, who knows how many tombs there are?"

That thought gave me both hope and a little dose of fear. The last thing we needed were more Betarrinis popping up everywhere. Not if we wanted to stay here. At some point, they'd be bound to round us all up and waterboard us until we spilled our secrets. I moved over toward Luca again, and seeing my look of fear, he gave me a gentle, reassuring smile. Tentatively, he took my hand. It felt good, so good, for him to hold it again. I never wanted to let him go.

"Please," Marcello said, gesturing toward Galileo. "Resume your story. You were saying your tomb was destroyed?"

"Yes. We set off in the direction of what we hoped was Radda-in-Chianti, which we remembered was near your castello. We had our second batch of bad luck when we met up with a group of actors moving from town to town. They fed us, gave us wine, allowed us to ride some on their wagon, in exchange for a story each night. After a little too much wine one night..." He paused to give his older brother the evil eye. "Orazio here began telling stories of people flying in airplanes and on rocket ships."

Orazio sighed heavily. "And suddenly, we were the favorite storytellers of medieval times. Before we knew it, we were heading north, not south, and we were beaten, gagged and chained when we tried to leave. That is how we ended up in the doge's court. Once here, after a couple of days, we knew we were just digging our own graves, and we refused to say anything. That was when the doge threw us into prison for our disobedience."

"He gets a bit frustrated when his demands go unmet," Galileo added.

"How much did you tell them?" Dad asked hopefully. "Of the tombs? Of time travel?"

"Very little," Orazio said earnestly. "We knew, by then, that we were begging for our own deaths by doing so. But the actors...they swore to the doge about what we'd said. We just refused to back them up."

"What happened to your clothes?" Mom said.

"The actors took them," Orazio said, pushing a curl back from his eyes, frustration pulling his lips into a line.

It struck me, then, that these two would be dang cute after a decent night's rest and a bath. Not that I was attracted to them. I just noticed. And felt a weird familial pride over these new, hot cousins.

Mom and Dad shared a long look. I knew they were thinking we'd have to track down and get rid of those clothes, just as we had our own. There was the incriminating future-factor, but also we just couldn't have jeans or t-shirts or sneakers in the medieval historical record. It'd mess up detail-freaks like archeologists, big-time.

"So how do we do this?" Gabi asked, in English. "Exit Venezia, stage left, with these guys with us? After what just happened out there tonight, his doge-ness is not going to want his new starlet to leave."

"Like, ever," I returned with a sigh.

"He's probably already in the hallway," she continued in Italian, "counting down the minutes on our allotted hour. We knew it was going to be tough to disentangle ourselves. The dogaressa made a point of telling me they had the finest midwives in all of Italia here—that I'd have access to the same midwife who helped her through four deliveries." She stared at Marcello. "I want to be home when our baby comes."

"You shall be," he said, taking her hand, looking a bit pained at having to discuss such intimate details in a public setting. "Rodolfo warned us. The doge likes his court to be the most entertaining and interesting in the world. And our presence certainly aids him in that. We knew we'd be here for a couple of weeks. Let's plan on that and find a way to convince the doge that when we leave, he should send your Betarrini kin with us. Take up Rodolfo's suggestion—to claim them as kin, but madmen. Tell him it's our responsibility to take care of them. If he agrees, he'll gain continued favor from one of the Nine of Toscana and get rid of two prisoners who try his patience."

"Agreed," she said. "I only hope that he is as logical as you are."

We could hear the crowd outside then, even from this inner chamber. While we couldn't make out the words, we could tell what they yelled by cadence alone. *She-Wolf! She-Wolf!*

Gabi's eyes met mine. "It's all you this time, Sis," she said, gesturing toward me. We'd heard a crowd like that before, in Siena. And it had ended with Cosmo Paratore getting his ears cut off.

CHAPTER 14

EVANGELIA

O ur hour with the Betarrini boys was up. We hurriedly promised
to come and check on them the next morning, bringing them
food and new clothing, as well as news on our progress in securing their
freedom. A loud knock sounded at the door.

Luca looked to Marcello, and Marcello nodded.

"*Entra,*" Luca called.

A ducale knight stood in the doorway, with others behind him. With
the door open, we could make out the rock-star-like chant, *She-Wolf,
She-Wolf...*

"'Tis time, my lord," he said to Marcello. "Serenissimo wishes you
all to return to the piazza for the festivities." His eyes moved to me.
"Serenissimo asks that you be prepared for some further exposition of
your archery skills. There are a number of noblemen and gentlewomen
who would like their try at competing with such a formidable opponent."

I smiled, thinking that this time, at least, we could place some of our
own bets. "As long as there are no more apples or people as potential
targets, I cannot see why I wouldn't take part."

The knight looked back over his shoulder, whispering something,
and a man took off. I frowned. What exactly had the doge planned for
me next? Who knew how warped the man was, in his ongoing quest to
have the most unique court in the world?

I was still trying to get over the dogaressa, and all the noblewomen who hung out with her. Five or six of them had squirrels wearing beaded collars and leashes. Some were cute and basically like rodent-sized dogs, but others would alternately relax as the women pet them, and then bite their fingers without provocation. I saw one woman get bitten and fling her squirrel to the ground, then send a servant chasing after it. A parrot flew back and forth across the dogaressa's magnificent room, squawking and leaving a trail of tiny feathers and poop across the ornate marble floor, which again, a servant had to scurry across, cleaning up. There'd also been a ferret in attendance. And the corner housed a huge cage, full of twelve tiny, brightly colored birds.

Luca came over to me and offered his arm. I accepted it. Together, we moved out, directly behind the ducale guards. "You really do look stunning in that gown," he whispered as we walked the hall. "If I died, I'd want to see an angel like you."

I smiled. It was good to hear him back to his normal teasing. But it felt odd, being clothed in white, a color usually designated for funerals in this era. I definitely stood out...but at least I'd ditched the wings. Those things had been heavy—probably a good thirty pounds—and so thickly layered with white feathers that they'd set me to sneezing. I'd practically fallen off the tower bannister before it was time. It was a wonder I'd hit anything I shot at en route down. What a wreck...

"What is it?" Luca whispered, pulling me closer.

"This whole night," I said, shaking my head. "It's so far beyond anything I imagined would happen in Venezia..."

The crowd was so loud as we got closer to the piazza that I doubted Luca could even hear my words. The doors at the end were open, and we could see people dancing, in time with the *She-Wolf* chant, adding instruments as they held hands and wove in and out of other lines.

I glanced back at Gabi, and her eyes were big. She mouthed, *Here we go*...and I took a deep breath.

We emerged, and the crowd went wild, a roar building at the mouth and then spreading to the very back of the piazza until the combined sound was nearly deafening. The doge and dogaressa were smiling and applauding as we approached, the route physically made by a solid line of knights on either side of our path, holding hands to hold back the crowds behind them. From our left and right, people reached past them to try and touch me or Luca. They didn't grab, just touched or patted. It was like walking through a bunch of heavy reeds, blessing us, in a way. I felt as if these were my people. They were with me and for me, as I was with and for them.

I glanced nervously to the doge, wondering how he was going to take that. He'd either want in—and try to cash in on this popularity of ours—or he'd want to take me down a notch. Put me in my place and all. Reestablish dominance. Because this dude was all about the power, from head to toe.

He greeted me as if we'd been gone for days, taking my hands and kissing me on both cheeks. But as I moved to draw away, he pulled me closer.

"Do not test me further, Lady Evangelia," he said in my ear. I just barely made out his words and wondered what they meant as he pulled back and lifted my arm in a triumphant pose, welcoming the crowd's renewed pleasure.

When the applause abated, he shouted, "Our Sienese sister has returned to us!"

Again, people cheered.

When they quieted, he asked in a shout, "But we must know. Are the prisoners madmen, or kin, or both?"

I smiled and thought frantically as the people laughed. "I believe, Serenissimo," I called out, feeling like a stage actor, "that you have found our distant cousins. I am most grateful that you have kept them safe and beg you to pardon them of whatever crime placed them in prison. Please allow us to take them back to Toscana with us where we can care for them. They are clearly not in their right minds."

He smiled, Cheshire-like, and his eyes glinted. He liked this game we were playing.

"There is restitution to be made for their crimes," he said.

"And we shall pay it," Marcello said, stepping forward and taking one knee before him.

This, just as I was thinking of blurting, *What exactly has to be paid for the crime of refusing to tell stories?*

I decided that Marcello's response was probably smarter.

"That is most gracious an offer, my lord," the doge said to him. "I shall confer with my council on the matter. In the meantime..." The doge's lips twitched, and I narrowed my eyes. Just what was he up to?

He turned and brought his palms together, then separated them in dramatic fashion. As if the crowd was glued to his wordless command, they parted and I could see that six people were tied to pillars on the side of the piazza, right beneath the clock tower. Men, all of them, gagged, eyes wide. Knights were placing an apple on each of their heads.

The doge turned back to me and bowed. "Your new friends in Venezia would dearly love to see you repeat your skill with the bow," he said. "Some say that it was a ruse. That you couldn't possibly do what you did, twice. And there are some in the crowd," he said, looking out at the masses, "who feel they were robbed by those who took their bets." He looked back to me. "Given that this is a peaceful, celebratory evening, we thought this the best way to settle the dispute, once and for all."

He lifted a hand to me as I started to shake my head. "Now I know you took issue with taking aim at those who might be kin to you. But these men..." He glanced over to the right with disdain. "These six have been given a fair trial and are condemned for murder. So if you miss..." He shrugged, and the crowd laughed, even as my stomach knotted in horror. I truly thought I might throw up.

"And if she strikes the apples?" Gabi asked from behind me, when I paused for too long. Grateful, I looked over to her. Her demeanor was all princess-pants, while I was just afraid I'd pee in mine. *My big sis. Always there when I need her most.* I managed to turn back to await the doge's reply.

"If she strikes the apples, the prisoner will not be hanged come morn. He will live out his days in the prison."

Gabi paced back and forth, looking thoughtful. "That is hardly a benefit," she said with a playful smile, as if the doge welcomed such banter. "Some would say it's even more trying for your prisoner. And it costs you, Serenissimo, to keep him. Yes? Might you give us another option?"

"Such as..."

"I know!" she cried, snapping her fingers. "In their place, free the six prisoners in your cells who toil there on the leanest of charges. Your people will cheer your clemency!"

The crowd liked that. They cheered as one. *"She-Wolf! She-Wolf!"*

The doge gave her a hard smile that didn't reach his eyes. Because he knew what we knew—Orazio and Galileo's disobedience charges had to be some of the least pressing among them.

"So be it," he said, giving her a magnanimous nod even as I could feel the chill from him. He lifted one finger, and the crowd quieted. "But this time, you use my bow and arrows. There are some that say that your own bow and arrows are bewitched. If that is true, our wager is hardly fair, is it?" His lips twitched with the challenge, and my heart sank.

There was no way out other than to do it his way. Desperate, I turned to Luca, and he leaned toward me. "You can do this, Evangelia. I know you can. They're but twenty paces away."

"But, Luca, if I miss..."

"You shall not. Ask him for ten practice shots first."

"What say you, Lady Betarrini?" cried the doge as the crowd began to murmur in frustration at the wait.

I turned, feeling the tight confines of my fitted bodice. I squared my shoulders and lifted my chin, as I knew Gabi might, were she in my shoes. "If the Serenissimo would grant me ten practice shots first, I shall do my best to put the people's complaints to rest, and free the least threatening of your prisoners," I said, then curtsied low, as if dissolving in a puddle of gratefulness.

The doge smiled and turned to take his bow and quiver of arrows from a knight behind him. "I shall grant you five practice shots. More than enough for the most famous archer of Toscana!" When he gestured me forward, I climbed the steps and took them from him. But he held on to the bow and pulled me forward. "You and your sister are clever, girl. I grant you that," he ground out through clenched teeth.

"We do our best, my prince."

"I bet you do." A grudging smile lifted the corners of his lips. He let go and said loudly, "Now see what the She-Wolf thinks of the finest bow and arrows Venezia has to offer! Give her a target! Make way!"

While men brought targets mounted on hay from the stables, I put on an arm guard in the palest, finest leather I'd ever seen. It looked like it'd never been used and was pretty close to a perfect fit for me. Then I studied the bow, examining the string's elasticity. I pulled it back, getting a feel for the tension. I grabbed hold of an arrow, running a finger over the tail feathers, checking out the weight of the head, the length of the shaft.

The target was ready and placed to the left of the first prisoner. I shook my head in frustration and looked to the sky. Couldn't they have set it a bit farther away for safety? But I'd soon be shooting a *lot* closer to him.

I nocked an arrow and took aim. Breathed in, breathed out, and released. It went high and to the right, narrowly missing the prisoner. He jerked so hard his apple fell. To *his* right, another prisoner visibly wet himself, a stain spreading across his pants.

The crowd erupted, half in glee, half in dismay. But I ignored them, only nocking another arrow, taking aim, calculating the bow's tendency to swing high and right, and then let it go.

I missed again.

This time, only by six inches. But I'd missed. I couldn't bear to look at the prisoners again. It would only remind me of the high stakes of this game...

Gabi came up to me and pulled me close, practically putting her forehead against mine so I could hear her. "You can do this, Lia. You can. Don't get psyched out. Think back to Toscana! Of winning—"

"But that was on our home turf!" I grit out. "With my bow and arrows! This one pulls—"

"And you'll figure out the compensation for it with three more shots. Why do you think the doge gave you his own bow? He knows better than anyone its tendencies. He wants to see you fail. He wants to hold on to our cousins." I stared at her as she cast a furious look over my shoulder at the doge. She was somehow fiercer these days, now that she was preggers. All Mama Bear, looking like she wanted to push me aside and go take down the doge in a wrestling headlock or something. The thought of it made me want to laugh, melting a bit of my terror.

"Listen to me," she said, holding my upper arms. "You have a full quiver. Once you find your compensation, and your rhythm, do not stop. You do best when you're in the zone, right?"

When I said nothing, she repeated, "Right?"

"Right."

"Good. Then get in it and stay in it. Show these Venetians what kind of She-Wolf they have in their midst. And their conniving doge, while you're at it."

I smiled. "On it," I whispered.

She smiled and moved back to Marcello's side.

Again, I settled my feet on the uneven pavers, steadied my breathing, trying to concentrate on only my own, not the collective sighs and gasps and laughs and shouts all around me. I stared at the target and fired again. This time, it went high and to the left. I'd over-compensated. I immediately drew another arrow and fired again. The fourth, the blessed, beautiful fourth, landed dead center. The crowd crackled with shouts, but I ignored them, immediately notching the fifth arrow, and fired, aiming directly above the last. It hit exactly where I intended.

I drew my sixth arrow as I paced to the right, even as the doge was shouting at the crowd to quiet. I fired while I still moved, taking off the first man's apple. The next guy—the one who had wet himself—trembled so hard that the apple fell, but I pierced it at his side before it reached the ground, the arrow tunneling into the wood of a doorway behind him. I dispatched the next three in quick order, never pausing, the crowd becoming nothing but the dim, distant hum of an ocean wave in my mind.

Only before the last man did I pause for a second, recognizing that it would heighten the drama and further secure my favor. Then I let the arrow fly and without waiting for it to strike, whirled and strode the few paces over to the doge, who stood there, mouth agape. I withdrew my final arrow and knelt before him on the stair, knowing from the sounds of jubilation all around me that I had succeeded with the last as well. I lifted the arrow higher to him.

"With one to spare, my prince," I said. And I couldn't keep from smiling in victory, even as my knees wobbled beneath my skirts.

His mouth abruptly closed, and I saw that sincere admiration had won over his wounded pride. I'd done all he'd asked, and the people's complaints would be resolved now. He stepped toward me and took the arrow in one hand, offering me his other. I took it and rose, and the people cheered even more loudly. How did they have any voices left at all?

Side by side, we accepted their praise.

"Clearly," he said from the corner of his mouth, "I've underestimated the She-Wolves of Siena. You are all Firenze fears. And more."

"Better yet," I returned. "We are all that Siena loves. And hope to be similarly loved by our new friends here, Serenissimo."

He nodded, giving me grudging respect. "You and I," he said. "We shall be fast friends. And with me as your friend, you shall not fear Firenze quite as much, yes?"

I flashed him my most winning smile. "With you as our friend, we shall not fear them at all."

CHAPTER 15

EVANGELIA

My nerves gradually steadied as the night wore on. With some food in my belly and a glass of wine, I relaxed into the party atmosphere, dancing with Luca, gently refusing everyone but Lutterius for one brief round. My every emotion heightened as I saw the hope kindle in his eyes in response to my ongoing favor, my ongoing engagement. I even rebuffed Nicolo lo Grato, Luca's cousin, who was clearly miffed and just as clearly back into the wine.

"Saints in heaven," Luca said to me, as he shook his head at another potential dancing partner, warning him off. "I fell in love with you the first day I saw you with bow in hand. But today...Evangelia, I've never seen such grace under fire. You fairly made my heart want to burst."

"Thank you, Luca," I said. "As Tomas says, it is with God's grace that I was able to do any of it. And thanks to Gabi's encouragement. And yours. Without you..." I shook my head.

He moved to touch my face, seemed to remember himself, and dropped his hand. "Without any of us, you still would have done what you had to."

I smiled up at him. And kept smiling as the evening faded into deep night. The Venetians, it appeared, liked to party into the wee hours. But the longer the crowds lingered, the more I wanted to only be away, alone with Luca.

I wanted to be *just us* so badly. It'd been too long since we'd had the chance, since that horrible day of our argument, really. But here, in this city, after all that had transpired, the idea of it seemed hopeless. I fantasized about a lovely, romantic gondola ride, alone with him. But that was for couples of the future. These days, the only gondola-like boats were used purely for transportation, not romantic interludes on secluded canals.

But as we circled in one of the final dances, my hand against his above our heads, our faces inches apart, I dared to whisper, "I need to see you tonight, Luca. Alone."

His eyes widened in surprise.

We broke apart with the next steps of the dance and, when we returned to the previous position, he said eagerly, "There is a small stairway to the rooftop down the hall from your room. Have one of my men escort you up as soon as you can." His eyes were pools of swirling hope, desire, tension.

I nodded.

Thankfully, Gabi soon pulled me aside. "I need to say my good-nights and get this bulbous bod to bed."

"Take me with you, please," I whispered. "I'm exhausted."

"I bet you are."

Marcello and Luca and my folks joined us, and as one, we said our farewells to our host and hostess.

"Until the morrow," the doge said, his face slack with wine and laughter.

"Thank you for a most memorable night," said the dogaressa.

A few more curtsys, a few more bows, and we were finally outta there. I couldn't wait to take off the constricting white gown, to slip on my nightgown, but it would have to wait. Until after I saw Luca. And he said he thought me beautiful in the dress...

I disentangled myself from my family, accepting their last hugs and kisses of the night as if I had nothing else on my mind other than sleep, then closed the door. I leaned my ear against the wood, listening to footsteps fade, doors close, and then the silence. I told myself to count to five hundred. And not the fast way, but the *one-Mississippi, two-Mississippi, three-Mississippi* way.

At about the four-hundred mark, I heard more revelers careen down the hallway and then disappear behind their own doors, but no others. Carefully, I cracked open the door and peered outside. As expected, there were two Forelli knights poised on guard, Baldarino and Lutterius. I exited, trying not to look like I was sneaking.

I closed the door and looked up at Lutterius. "I would like to be escorted to the roof."

He was clearly trying to hold back a grin. "Right away, my lady," he said, gesturing toward the end of the hall. There, I spied the outline of a door in the paneling. Baldarino led the way, and Lutterius remained beside me. By the bounce in their step, it was clear Luca had taken them into his confidence. I knew that I'd practically broken every Forelli knight's heart when I denied their captain and we'd fallen apart. They were hoping this was our big reunion. Just as I was, really.

If he'd have me. If I hadn't hurt him too badly...

Baldarino pushed on the panel and it popped open, revealing a tiny, curving stairway. "Watch your step, my lady," he said over his shoulder.

I followed him upward, Lutterius a few paces behind me, taking care to not step on my skirt's train. Two floors up, we were out on the rooftop of the Palazzo Ducale, and I sucked in my breath. Below us, to the right, in the piazzetta, were the last of the revelers. Some were sleeping on the stones, oblivious to the damp chill of the deep November night. In my haste, I'd forgotten to grab a wrap, so solely focused on seeing Luca I'd been. I rubbed my arms, hoping to generate some warmth, when I saw him turning the corner.

The knights at my side stopped alongside me.

Luca strode up to us and looked to the men. "Grazie, friends. Please form a guard as the Lady Evangelia and I..." He paused to take my hand and lift it to his lips, a wild, hopeful grin lighting up his eyes. "Converse."

I sensed the two men turn their backs to us and take several steps away, giving us a modicum of privacy. There were ducale knights up here too, of course, keeping watch.

But my attention was on one knight alone. *My knight.*

Luca Forelli.

He took my hand and led me to the far edge, where he lifted a blanket. *My thoughtful knight.*

I looked out at the quiet lagoon, ship masts bobbing on the low, slow waves, the water so still that it reflected the three-quarter moon. Sailors' laughter and banter rolled across the lagoon, making us feel like we were all part of some magnificent, wondrous party, far more intimate than the revelry in the piazza or palazzo had been.

Luca lifted the blanket and looked at me. "Cold?"

I nodded.

He unfolded the blanket around his shoulders, the length of it falling to the floor. Then he wrapped his arms around me, enveloping me in it too. "Better?"

"Better," I grinned up at him. I rested my head against his shoulder.

"Saints above, Evangelia," he moaned. "How I've missed you. How I've missed this—being close to you."

"And I, you," I said. We stood there for several long minutes, just appreciating the connection, the shared heat, the familiar smells. I wanted him to kiss me. But that could wait.

"What has changed?" he asked hesitantly. "Why do you again seek my company, my love?"

I took a deep breath and turned toward the rail, looking out at the lagoon again. He settled in behind me, rearranging the blanket to better cover me. Waiting. I leaned back against him, liking the feel of his strong torso, his arms around me, cocooning me, protecting me.

"It's difficult to explain. But I think...I think in meeting Orazio and Galileo, in knowing of this new tunnel and thinking again of going back, of leaving this place..." I shook my head and then looked over my shoulder at him. "It was as if in that moment," I whispered, my eyes not leaving his, "I knew I could never leave. Leave *you*, Luca. I mean, I knew I was staying before. But it was as if...as if I'd agreed to stay for my parents. For Gabi and Marcello. But today...today, it became my choice too. Wholly mine. For me. For you. For us."

"Evangelia," he whispered huskily, his eyebrows hunched, as if every word from my lips was miraculous. "Could it be true? Does this mean that you will be mine? My wife?"

I slowly turned around and lifted my arms to encircle his neck. He pulled me closer, his hands roaming my back as hard and as fast as his eyes searched mine, waiting.

"If you will still have me," I whispered at last.

His breath left his chest in a huff of a laugh, his eyes alight, his grin spreading like a contagion. My knight. The man who could always make me smile.

Then his grin morphed into pent-up desire and hope and joy, all at once. One hand left my back and went to my face, and he cupped my cheek. "Would I have you? Every day, every night, for the rest of my life. My heart has always been yours, Evangelia. You've ruled me, as a queen rules her servant. I live for God, for the House Forelli, and to be your man."

"My heart has always been yours, Luca," I said coyly, smiling up at him. "And now your queen commands you to kiss her."

"Who am I to thwart a queen?" He smiled and leaned closer toward my lips, teasing me, nuzzling me, letting his breath wash over my skin like a caress. I closed my eyes, enjoying the sensation of his proximity at last, the nearness, the heat of him. And then I tilted my head just a bit higher, until our lips brushed at his next pass. He froze in surprise. But without further invitation he kissed me then, in earnest. Plying my lips apart, hungry, searching, demanding.

I thought I could kiss him all night. We'd kissed before, but never with such abandon. He'd always been so cautious, careful with my reputation, my virtue. But now that I was to be his...well, his kisses promised me many days and nights of passion ahead. He pulled back and looked at me in wonder, searching every inch of my face as if I was brand new to him, as if he were trying to memorize me. And then I couldn't stand it any longer and pressed up on my tiptoes to kiss him again.

"Oh, my Lia, my beautiful Evangelia," he said in a whisper, pulling back and gently bending my head to the side. He planted tiny kisses across my cheek and slowly, delectably, down my neck, pausing at the clavicle. There, he hovered. "Please," he said, kissing me there again, the breath from his words sending shivers down my arms. "Tell me that we can marry soon."

"Soon," I said, our years of courting suddenly exploding in anticipation.

"Very, very, soon," he said, moving back up my neck with his tiny, fabulous, kisses. How could lips do such things to a person?

"Here-soon," I said, kissing him on the lips again.

"*Here*-soon?" he repeated, pausing halfway up my neck. "Not in Siena?"

"*Here*-soon," I said in mock demand.

"Yes, my queen," he said, with a grin. "I am yours to command." And then he finished me off with the most knee-weakening kiss of my life, telling me that as much as he said I ruled, he would soon rule me in ways untold.

"Soon, Luca," I moaned. "Marry me within the week."

"My betrothed, so fickle," he said, tipping up my chin to look me in the eye and give me a chance to gather myself. "Cast me aside for weeks. Then demand I marry you within the week."

I gave him a rueful smile. There was no malice in his words. He was like that, too, my knight. Forgiving.

"Forelli knights!" he called over his shoulder, all manly and in control. "Attention!"

I heard the men turn on their heels and face us.

Gently, he took off the blanket and settled it around my shoulders. Then he turned me to face the guys. "May I present my intended, the future Lady Forelli?"

The knights broke out in grins so wide they practically lit up the night, and hooted and laughed as they stepped forward to congratulate us, kissing us both on either cheek, slapping Luca on the back. We bade them to secrecy for the night, until we could tell our family. Luca had long ago sought my parents' blessing, but I knew he'd want their reassurance that they still thought it a good idea. I knew they would. They loved him like a son.

With one last, long look at the magical lagoon, I walked with Luca to the doorway and down the stairs, then along the hall to my room. There, he kissed my hand and held it.

"Thank you, Evangelia. For the greatest honor anyone has ever bestowed upon me. Thank you for trusting me."

"Always and forever, my love," I said.

"Until the morrow?" he asked.

"I do not know if I'll sleep a wink."

"Nor I," he said, reaching up to touch my cheek. "If I do, I'm certain to only dream of you."

"That's no different than before," chided Lutterius with a laugh.

Luca laughed with him, but his eyes never left mine. "Indeed. Until the morrow."

"Until the morrow," I said. And, as I tore myself away from him and made myself shut the door between us, I thought about never having to part from him again, come night. Of going to bed together. Of kisses, and more kisses...

CHAPTER 16

GABRIELLA

I was up before the sun the next morning and found my husband awake, too. He stood over by a window, facing the lagoon. As much as I wished we could have stayed with his cousin Caterina in her palazzo on the Canal, I could hardly complain about our accommodations here in the doge's palace. The view was even more spectacular.

I shifted out of bed, wincing as a ligament in my belly stretched in complaint, then rose and padded over to join him. He wrapped his arms around me and kissed my forehead as I rested my cheek against his chest. My baby bulge felt like a melon between us, but he didn't seem to mind. Together, we watched in silence as the fishermen left the docks for the morning, their chipper calls to one another like sparks in the dark. The air was so cold it chilled my nose, and I snuggled in a little closer to Marcello.

"Cold?" he murmured, shifting his arms to better cover me.

"Yes, aren't you?"

"Here," he said, opening his thick tapestry morning coat—sort of a medieval version of a robe—and offering me his bare chest.

"Ooo, better," I said, settling closer to him. His skin was far more welcoming than the rough fabric. He closed the robe partway around me.

"I'd have to agree," he said, and I could hear the smile in his voice as he pulled me even closer. After a moment, he said, "That was quite a day, yesterday."

"Indeed. I can't stop thinking about it. About Orazio and Galileo. And Lia! I didn't think my sister could surprise me anymore. But she did yesterday."

"She's come into her own. No longer your little She-Wolf shadow, my love. But her own, fine She-Wolf, full grown."

I mulled over his words and nodded. "That's true." I felt an odd mixture of pride and the pang of loss. It was good for Lia, her maturing. It would just be a bit different. A transition for us.

Time and again yesterday I'd taken a breath, about to say something, when she began instead. And she'd handled it all like a pro. Better than I could've, likely. But it was...weird. I'd always been the leader. And yesterday, it was all Lia's show, and my turn to play the supportive role.

I smiled as I thought about how she'd handled it all. About the doge's face, when he thought he had her. Twice. With the Betarrinis. Then with the prisoners and his wonky bow. And both times, she'd shown him who was boss.

"The whole city fell in love with your sister last night," Marcello said.

I laughed under my breath. "I think even the doge fell a little in love with her. But don't tell the dogaressa."

I smiled as I listened to the rumble of his gentle laugh in return. "Luca will have to keep his wits about him in the next few weeks and watch out for her. We all will. Given that Evangelia's proven to be such an engaging guest, the doge will be more resistant than ever to let us leave."

"But it's best if we don't tarry," I said. "Last night I met a noble family from England. They'd heard that we hailed from Britannia and were eager to speak in detail. Only the drama of the piazza saved me from having to share more than I wished."

He leaned back and cupped my face in his hands. "What was their name?"

"Whitehall or something."

"Are they at court? In the palazzo?"

"Nay, not here in the palazzo. And not a part of the inner court. But any larger event with broader invitation? I'd expect them to attend again."

"Hmm. We'll do our best to avoid them, then. Your list of potential enemies continues to grow, Wife. The Fiorentini, the English, the French…"

"It's challenging, coming from Normandy," I whined.

"Indeed. Come, you're still getting chilled, despite my best efforts." He drew me away from the window, where the hint of dawn was on the horizon, casting a rosy pink glow to the sky, shuttering it against the cold air. He pulled me to a settee covered in horsehair by the small hearth and added wood to the glowing embers.

"You and my baby need to get warm," he said, taking a blanket from the bed and settling it over me.

I grinned. "I could become accustomed to such pampering," I said.

"I'm certain you could," he returned, then bent down and gave me a brief, soft kiss, pulled back and looked into my eyes. "I love you, Gabriella."

"I love you too, Marcello."

He straightened. "Now let me see about finding a servant to fetch us a bit of bread and some hot apple cider to break our fast. Doesn't that sound good?"

"Wonderful," I said. Cuddled before a fire with my husband eating breakfast? When did we ever get that opportunity? Back home, at the castello, he always had to be up and eating with the men at dawn. And here we were, in the heart of Venice, in the doge's palace itself, with the morning to ourselves.

But when he went to the door and opened it, Luca was there. "Luca!" he said in surprise, and I turned to look over my shoulder at him.

He took Marcello's arm, glanced at me, and when he saw me with my crazed morning-hair, said, "Forgive me, my intrusion. May I have a word with you in the hall, Marcello?"

Marcello gave him a quizzical look. Why all the formality? What was so urgent? "By all means."

He followed Luca out and quietly closed the door. I threw aside my blanket and ran over to the door, listening at the crack, then grimaced when I couldn't hear anything. I reluctantly elected to pull on a gown and run a comb through my hair as I waited for Marcello to return. I was at a small dressing table, with the best brass mirror I'd ever seen in medieval Italy, working on a particularly stubborn tangle when he returned.

I caught sight of his smile in the mirror and turned to look at him. "What is it? What did he want?"

"A best man."

"A what?" All I could think was that Marcello was the best man. Luca's best friend.

"A *best man*," Marcello said again, more slowly, crossing his arms and grinning.

Gradually, I figured out what he was saying, and my mouth fell open. "What?" I said, rising. "*What?*"

But I didn't wait for him to explain. "Oh my gosh," I muttered. "Oh my gosh!" I scurried past him, opened the door, ignored Marcello's call, and ran down the hall—barefoot—to Lia's. The two knights on duty outside her door looked sleepy and surprised when I careened around the corner, like some sort of crazy cartoon character. I hadn't even bothered to pull back my hair. "I need to see her," I said abruptly to Lutterius.

"Yes, m'lady, I think you do," he said with a wink. He turned to open her door and then closed it softly behind me.

She was still asleep. I stopped short of jumping on the bed, tickling her awake. Because the three, fat puppies were asleep beside her and the four of them looked so peaceful and content, they were practically a picture. One puppy, Desi, lifted his head and yawned, flashing tiny teeth. He licked his nose lazily then set his head down again. Lia's hair spread out in a thick, wavy layer of gold, and there was a tiny smile on her lips, as if she was dreaming about *her future husband*.

That did it. I pounced onto the bed, right beside her, across from the puppies.

She gasped and sat halfway up, then, seeing it was me, sank back to the pillows. "So," she said sleepily, smiling and closing her eyes again. "You heard." The puppies rolled and sat up, yawning.

"No more sleep! Details!" I said, shaking her shoulders playfully. "I need details!"

She giggled and opened her eyes. "All right, all *right*." We each took puppies in our arms as she sat up and told me the whole, lovely, romantic tale of how she finally came to accept that she was destined to become Mrs. Luca Forelli.

"But how?" I asked, wincing as Grasso nipped my finger with his sharp puppy teeth. "How did you finally settle your mind and heart about it? About a possible baby. Because I don't think that Luca's the type of guy to buy into the whole concept of a chaste marriage..."

She shrugged her shoulders. "It just clicked. I was getting close to it anyway. But meeting the Betarrini boys pushed me over the edge, I think. The idea of them going back, entering the tunnel again, Gabs..." She looked to the window, where the sky had become bright with the morning sun, and I studied her lovely profile. She focused her big, blue eyes on me again. "The idea of leaving, truly leaving, terrifies me now. Because to leave Luca..." She lifted her free hand to her heart. "It would break me. And even if I have ten babies by the time this plague finally rolls around," she added in a whisper, "we'll all be in God's hands. I have to trust in that." She shook her head. "I just can't leave him. Ever. Because I love him. With everything in my heart."

I squealed and pulled her into my arms, hugging her. I was so, so glad. And so, so relieved. I knew she had settled her mind at staying here with me. She had to, when I wanted to stay with Marcello. But now, at last, it was her future too. Not just hers because she wanted to be with us, but hers-hers. *Thank you, Lord,* I prayed silently.

I pulled back and ran my hand down her hair. "So...when? As soon as we can get home?"

"No, here," she said with a grin. "Now that I've decided, I cannot wait. I'm hoping we can find a priest and a blue gown and we can get married fast. Today, even."

"Lia! Why? Why not wait?"

"Have you seen my fiancé, Gabi?" She waggled her eyebrows, and I laughed. She shook her head. "No, no—no long engagement for this chick."

"Or..." I said, tapping my lips. It was my turn to look toward the window, thinking. "Yes. *Yes.*"

"What?"

"*Or* you can beg the dogaressa to help you pull off a wedding within the week and send you southward on a fine Venetian ship to begin your honeymoon. If you convince her to make it an event, a party, with the send-off as the culmination, we'd have our exit visa to return to Toscana, with the doge's blessing."

She smiled. "Do you really think that would work?"

"Are you kidding? It'd have to work. He's not going to make a newlywed couple remain at court. And we'll just ride along with you...and bring the Betarrini boys with us. They must have gotten their Get Out of Jail Free card today, thanks to you."

"Let's hope."

"He promised."

"He promised to let the six prisoners on the *least* of charges free. Let's hope disobeying the doge doesn't rank higher than, say, stealing an apple from the produce man."

"True." I rose. "Well, we'd better make ourselves presentable and then figure out how we rope the dogaressa into our schemes."

"Sounds like a plan. Thanks for being happy for me, sis."

"Are you kidding? We're going to be family in a whole other way, now. There will be nothing that can drag us apart after you become Luca's bride."

She grinned at me, and I squeezed her hand. "See you in an hour or two?"

"Two. Luca's going to speak to Mom and Dad again. You know, just to make sure nothing's changed."

"Right." I knew it was only a formality. But if there was one thing medieval men liked, it was a measure of formality. Luca would want to be sure he had their blessing before he moved forward with Lia. This time, he wouldn't want anything to stand in their way.

I left her and grimaced at my reflection in her mirror. I had really torn out of my room looking quite the sight. My hair was a mass of curls, and my feet were bare. I thought about borrowing a pair of Lia's slippers, but she wore a size smaller than I did. I could only hope that nobody else was up at this hour. My room was just around the corner...

I smiled sheepishly when I spied Marcello, waiting for me in the hallway, chatting with the knights. "She is well, m'lady?" he asked.

"More than well, m'lord," I returned with a wink.

Together, we set off down the hall to return to our room. "I'm so, so glad for them, Marcello. I think I might burst."

"Well, that would be rather unpleasant. Bursting, and all."

I laughed and took his arm, and we turned the corner.

And ran right into the first Fiorentini we'd met in Venice.

CHAPTER 17

GABRIELLA

I felt Marcello stiffen before my brain could fully compute who was there, in the very palace with us.

"*You*," my husband said, a sneer of sheer hatred on his face. And then he was in motion, ramming the small man against the hallway wall. He lifted him up, hand under his chin, his face a mask of rage.

It was Lord Barbato. And beside him, Lord Foraboschi. The men who had kidnapped me and tried to marry me off to Rodolfo Greco. But we were not in Roma, we were in Venezia!

"Marcello!" I cried, as the Fiorentini knights went after him, and the Forelli knights pulled at them...

But I knew it wasn't just memories of Greco that infuriated him. These were the men who later kidnapped and abused Alessandra, then defamed her, trying to frame the Forellis. Men who had cost her her relationship with her father. Men who would still like nothing more than to take us down, one way or another.

I loathed them. Seeing them infuriated me, as it had my husband. But this was not the place or time. "Marcello!"

The Fiorentini managed to yank Marcello bodily away.

"Wait! All is well!" I shouted as our knights prepared to draw their swords.

"Give me one reason why I shouldn't break your neck right now," Marcello seethed, still straining toward Barbato while two men held him back.

"Come now, Forelli, aren't we past all that?" sniffed Barbato.

I had to give His Little Lordship some grudging admiration for not shying or backing away. Only in battle had I seen Marcello so fierce.

"We shall not be past *all that*," Marcello spit out, "until you pay for all you have done."

Lord Foraboschi moved toward me and looked me up and down, his eyes full of disdain. "Such a wild thing, your wife. Look at her," he sniffed. "Out in public looking like a wanton nymph of the wood. A barbarian let loose." He gave me a creepy smile. "A She-Wolf in heat."

Marcello wrenched free of the Fiorentini and only my hand against the center of his broad chest kept him from knocking the tall, thin man into the far wall. I was practically squished between them.

"I suggest you Fiorentini clear this hallway at once," I said to both of them, "before there's a scene that none of us wish to create for our hosts. Agreed?"

Lord Barbato gave Marcello ample space as he passed and flicked a hand in the air. "Agreed," he said with a sigh. "Come along, Lord Foraboschi. We shall engage these two at another time." He was two paces away already.

I looked back to our guys, who were now facing off with the four Fiorentini knights, circling, glaring, practically spitting on the marble floor. They all itched to draw swords, and I was only thankful they couldn't, given where we were, and since Marcello and I were unarmed.

Barbato cleared his throat at the corner, and the four Fiorentini reluctantly followed, two of them walking backward, watching us. When they finally turned the corner, Marcello rubbed his face and made a guttural sound of total frustration. Then he looked at me. "Are you well?"

"I'm fine, fine. But what are *they* doing here?"

"I do not know. The doge is no friend to the Fiorentini. But I suppose they are necessary to him for trade."

"And he to them." I tucked my bare toes deeper under the edge of my skirt and ran a hand over my wild hair. "Forgive me, Marcello, for running out like this. I was so anxious to see Lia..."

He shook his head. "Pay no heed to the man's words. He'd have made some derogatory comment, even if you were dressed like the dog-aressa herself."

Still, I was relieved to slip back in our room, close the door and bolt it. Having Barbato and Foraboschi here unnerved me. I thought they'd not have the chance to reach us physically. Not here, not with so many of our own around. But now that we were prepared, they wouldn't catch us unaware again.

Once presentable, and having broken our fast with cider, a roll and a cup of steaming tea from England—the first decent tea I'd ever had in Italy—Marcello and I went to fetch my folks, Lia, and Luca, and tell them of the newest visitors to the Palazzo Ducale. Together, we went to the front foyer, where we were to meet the doge and his minions for a tour of the *Arsenale Nuovo*. They called the shipyard "new," even though it'd been built a good twenty years before, but I was eager to see it. By all accounts, it was a marvel. "The closest thing to the Industrial Revolution we'll ever see in this era," Dad whispered to me as we walked out.

Thankfully, the Fiorentini were not in sight. We processed out in twos, first six guards, then the doge and dogaressa, followed by minions who carried enormous umbrella-like coverings on long poles to shield the nobles from the November sun. Though when I thought about it, even when the sun was not out, they were present. I didn't think I'd like to live with someone constantly covering me with such a thing. It'd be a bit like walking under a perpetual raincloud. I'd be craving my share of Vitamin D, a little sun on my face...

"Gabriella?" Marcello asked quietly. We were about halfway back in the procession of twos, with a total of about forty of us heading toward the Arsenale. "Are you all right?"

"I am well," I reassured him. "Only thinking about those silly *ombrellinos*," I whispered.

He smiled with me. "The most powerful do not need such things to shout about their power."

"Like you, husband."

He lifted a wry eyebrow. "Or you, wife."

"I am not feeling so powerful," I said, resting my free hand on my belly. "Only...bulbous."

"You are hardly bulbous. You are simply round in all the right ways," he whispered mischievously.

We exited the piazzetta and walked down along the front of the Rialto, the busy, green lagoon on our right, alive with so much sea-traffic I wondered that there weren't more accidents. Fishermen were rowing inward, galleys were weighing anchor and lifting sails, and boats of all sizes moved back and forth along lanes marked with white poles. In the distance, I could see our ship, bobbing on waves, glittering under the morning sun.

Up and over two bridges we went, and when we were almost half a mile from the Palazzo Ducale, we arrived at the Arsenale gates. Men guarded it, even as a boat sailed inward, hauling a second one with a broken mast behind it. We gathered around the doge, who waved Lia closer. Luca ushered her over, and I thought that she'd never looked more beautiful, so happy was she. Did the doge think it was all on account of last night? For as much as she'd managed to best him in his challenge in the piazza, he seemed to hold no grudge today. No, her success seemed to garner her greater status in his eyes. *A good thing,* I mused, *if we're to get out of here before winter sets in.*

"In a moment I shall show you Venezia's greatest prize—her prowess at building everything the sea requires, from rope to keel to sail. We harvest our own wood from the Veneto and build the finest ships in all the seas. This is how we've built the strongest navy among any of the Republics. This is why the world fears us."

He gazed around at us proudly. "Even the poet, Dante, wrote of this place," he said to Marcello and me. "You know his words, yes?"

I blanched. I knew *Inferno* a little better than most American-educated students knew it but could hardly quote it. But Marcello cleared his throat. "Indeed, Serenissimo."

"He was a man of your lands, yes?"

"He was. Castello Forelli was honored to host Lord Dante at its table, at times."

The doge lifted his chin in quiet surprise. He gestured with his hand. "You remember the passage of which I speak?"

Marcello thought a moment and then began, "'As in the Arsenal of the Venetians boils in winter the tenacious pitch, to smear their unsound vessels over again, for sail they cannot; and instead thereof one makes his vessel new, and one recaulks the ribs of that which many a voyage has made. One hammers at the prow, one at the stern; this one makes oars and that one cordage twists. Another mends the mainsail and the mizzen...'" Marcello looked back to the doge. The beautiful words were as lyrical as any music, and I suddenly had a new appreciation for the poet...especially when my husband's gorgeous lips were the ones saying the words. "And so it goes."

"And so it goes," the doge repeated, nodding appreciatively. "No doubt the poet's words made you curious to see our fine Arsenale."

"Indeed," Marcello said. "We have been most eager for a glimpse."

"Then come, come, my friends." He turned on his heel, his wife took his arm, and we resumed the procession inward. We passed dock slip after dock slip, men swarming the ships, hammering and sawing. The acrid smell of hot pitch filled the air; and we could see men sweating as they lifted heavy paddles from boiling cauldrons on the dock then scurried toward the ships to swab the planks and joints with the sticky, dark pitch, sealing them. There were long buildings, three stories high, where dockworkers lived, and women of questionable standards in front of them, waiting for their men to return come night.

We passed an acre where women were drying hemp in the sun, twisting the stalks into a yarn-like substance, and then again into thicker strands. Men carried bolts of those strands indoors, into a long building called a ropewalk, where they were braided together in one long length. The workers glanced at us nervously as we passed, clearly unaccustomed to the doge paying them a visit. But we moved on to a sweltering building full of forges, all of the metalsmiths at work on anchors and cleats of every size you could imagine.

The next building was solely for the keel-makers, men who carved the spines of ships from massive trees hauled in on rolling tracks and then rolled them through to the next building, where burly workers created the framework for ships, big and small. On and on it went. Sailmakers. Carpenters in charge of detail work. And then we were at the far side of the docks, next to a lovely, sleek galley.

The doge paused to gaze at me and Lia and smiled benevolently. "It is my understanding, Lady Betarrini, that you have accepted a marriage proposal."

Several ladies gasped behind us and twittered in excitement. My eyes narrowed. How had he possibly learned about it so quickly?

"I have," Lia said, with a glance at Luca and a blush that splashed across her lower cheeks.

"She has made me the happiest of men," Luca said to the doge.

"Indeed," the doge said, lifting a gray brow. "For you'd be hard-pressed to find a finer female in all the land. When word of this spreads, a plague of heartbreak shall be upon us."

"You honor me, your grace," Lia said, her blush spreading further.

The man stepped forward and lifted her chin. "'Twould be my honor to host your wedding. I shall send you and yours off in a ship like this as my gift to you," he said, gesturing toward the one beside us.

Lia managed to pretend surprise. He'd reacted exactly as we thought he might, wanting to horn in on the celebration. I managed to hide my pleasure.

"You are most gracious, Serenissimo," Lia said, with a slow curtsy. "It would be our honor to accept your invitation, but I do not know if it is possible."

The doge frowned. "What could be impossible from a court that can produce wonders such as this?" he asked, gesturing around the Arsenale.

Lia took Luca's arm, as if gathering strength, and Luca smiled at the doge.

"We have loved one another for quite some time, Serenissimo," he said, lifting her hand to kiss it. "It has taken me a long time to convince her to be my wife."

"A She-Wolf is not easily tamed, is she?" the doge asked slyly.

Luca paused as the doge—and then all his minions—broke out into laughter, and we all pretended to chuckle along with him. *Hilarious, that one,* I thought.

"Now that she has agreed to it," Luca went on as soon as the laughter abated, "we wish to marry within the week."

The dogaressa frowned in alarm and the doge's nose twitched, as if he could smell that something was up. "A week," he echoed.

"A week," Luca repeated earnestly. "And then it would be our honor to sail out on your fine ship. We shall be the envy of all as we sail down the coast."

The doge was silent for a moment, and we held our breath. His eyes shifted back and forth, over Luca, then Lia, then Marcello and me. "I suppose you wish to take your Betarrini cousins with you."

"We would," Luca said slowly.

"Very well," he said, lifting a hand and turning. "Take them. I tire of them. Your nuptials shall distract me from my agitation," he said over his shoulder. "It shall be the finest wedding Venice has ever seen." He paused and lifted a finger. "On one condition."

"Anything, Serenissimo," Luca said.

"Not of you, Sir Forelli. This, I ask of Lord Forelli."

Marcello's eyes hardened. "What do you ask of me, Serenissimo?"

"You bring your child to court. I want to meet the offspring of a She-Wolf and one of Siena's Nine."

Marcello paused as we all held our breath. "When the child comes of age," he answered at last. "It shall be our honor, Serenissimo," he said.

I was still holding my breath. *Comes of age? That will be when the child is twenty-one or so, right?* Because there was no way we were coming back here in the next few years, to this future cesspool of all-things-plague.

But I knew he'd had no choice but to promise the man. It was our perfect opportunity to not only leave but leave with the Betarrini boys in tow.

With a grip of his arm, securing the pledge, the doge turned again and led us out.

CHAPTER 18

EVANGELIA

The dogaressa proved to be the dragon lady of wedding coordinators. If I was a daisy kind of girl, she was all Casablanca lily—over-the-top fancy and smelling up the room. Not that they had flowers in weddings in this day and age—the most I'd get was a nosegay of herbs for good luck. Besides, it was November, and while the palace had the occasional bedraggled, exotic palm shipped in from who-knew-where, flowers were few and far between.

But clearly, this wedding was her gig, not mine.

The dressmaker was brought in, and with him came twelve servants, all carrying two bolts of blue material. While I gravitated toward a gorgeous, plain sky-blue silk, the dogaressa was all about a thick navy tapestry-like fabric, with silver thread embroidered into it.

"Look at *this*, Evangelia," she said, running her short, stubby fingers over it in envy. She lifted up the bolt and pulled out a length to drape it across my chest and shoulder. She sighed and her two ladies-in-waiting echoed her, and I knew I was done-for. I cast a glance over my shoulder at Gabi, and she widened her eyes.

"You shall look like a queen," said the dogaressa, shaking her head in wonder.

"Do you think it best, Serenissima?"

"I do, I do," said the matronly, short woman, nodding so firmly that her chin disappeared into folds of flab. She was dressed in one of the finest gowns I'd ever seen, but her dark hair was greasy and she smelled so foul that I could barely tolerate being near her. She ascribed to the common belief that two baths a year were plenty and had already expressed her concern that Gabi and I bathed far more often than was healthy. I'd pretended to agree as if I took her comments as correction, but that wasn't going to keep me from a bath before my wedding to Luca. Nor him from one either. The thought of getting close to him and smelling like this one—dogaressa or not—made me shudder.

"We shall use this one," she said to the dressmaker. "I assume you have designs to show us?"

"Indeed, Serenissima," he said, moving to a leather portfolio. He unwound the long strap from a wooden button and pulled out ten or more pieces of parchment. He looked to me, and down at his sheaf of paper, setting aside a few and bringing the others over to us. Again, it was the dogaressa he showed first. I was apparently a bridal mannequin. I stifled a sigh. I was marrying the best man I'd ever met, I reminded myself. So there was that. And this ceremony was our ticket outta here. Which we needed, especially with the "cousins" in tow...

I looked at the sketches and was drawn to the lines of my normal sort of gown, but the dogaressa was all about the tight undersleeve and the silly, long tippet—a streamer-like piece of fabric that extended off the elbow. I noticed that he had also sketched in a ceremonial bow and quiver of arrows in all of them. They expected me to arrive armed for my wedding? I lifted a brow and looked to Gabi, tilting the paper so she could see it. She pretended to be in awe, covering her smile with her hand.

All of it made me long for my old pair of jeans and a t-shirt more than ever.

"Oh, and her undergown could be in this silk," cooed the dressmaker, reaching for another bolt of cloth. He gestured toward another sketch, where the overgown, lined in fur, came up in the front to about the knee, and cascaded in a V to a short train in back.

The dogaressa nodded excitedly. "Yes, yes. That shall be perfect! Don't you agree, Evangelia?"

"Yes, Serenissima."

The short woman took her pet squirrel from one of her ladies and absently stroked the thing as the dressmaker rang a bell and more servants arrived, this time with shoes. Gabi and I shared a surprised look when we saw that they appeared to have been made for left and right feet—not the standard square or pointed toe that most were. But they were all terribly small. As in Chinese-bound-feet-small. Even most of the little women of medieval Venice couldn't fit in them.

The dogaressa lifted a pair of blue slippers that would match beautifully with the blue tapestry fabric, and then groaned as the dressmaker measured my feet. He frowned and shook his head at my hostess as if there wasn't a chance for us to find shoes. "She'll need to hasten to Cobbler Veraci. He will get them done in time."

"I hope so," she said, casting a disparaging eye at my bare toes. She was just lucky she wasn't dressing Gabi for *Venice's Next Hot Wedding*. Her feet were a size larger than mine. "We'll go immediately," she said.

I hesitated, thinking that we had plans for the day. "Forgive me, Serenissima, but we planned an outing this afternoon. To Borano. I thought I might find some lace for my wimple and veil," I added hurriedly, belatedly thinking of it.

She paused, irritation tightening her features for a moment. "I don't think you should cover much of your pretty yellow hair, veil or no. But off you shall go, *after* we get you fitted for slippers. A bride in our household cannot be married in those frightful things!" she muttered, nodding toward my old, worn slippers. I knew they weren't the best, but I couldn't help feeling a little offended. Besides, any others chafed my toes and gave me blisters...

"Send a messenger to Lord Forelli," said the dogaressa. "Tell him we'll return by the noon hour." She was already in motion, expecting us to follow, and so we did. I knew the guys wouldn't be wild about the idea of us heading out into the city without them, but we had six ducale guards in attendance—four in front of us and two behind—and Celso and Matteo trailed us. At least the silly umbrella-dude didn't come too. It was hard enough to make it through Venice's winding, crowded streets in a procession of any size without that huge thing.

We exited the Palazzo Ducale and turned under the heavy archway that led to the market district of the Rialto. We took a left, and then right, crossed a tiny bridge and paraded down a thin sidewalk alongside a narrow canal. People gaped at us and pointed. Some shouted "She-Wolf! It's the She-Wolves!" when they recognized me and my sister. But we barely had time to wave and smile.

We turned and walked through a brick tunnel, so short that we had to duck our heads, then down a road that again forced us to move into single-file order. This was the street of the *mascherari*, or mask-makers for Carnivale. Through the open doors, we spied gruesome masks with long, hooked noses, spooky white faces with different expressions, along with elaborate masks connected to hats of all colors and embedded with jewels. The dogaressa paused before one. She clasped her hands together and tapped her lips with her fingertips. Then she reached out to one of her ladies and grabbed her hand.

"What if...on the wedding day we hosted a carnivale?"

The lady's eyes widened in excitement. "That would be a spectacle, for certain, Serenissima! We've never had a carnivale before *Martedì Grasso*."

"Well, that would set this apart, would it not?"

"Indeed, Serenissima!" said the lady.

Oh boy, I thought. *The guys are definitely not going to like that idea either.* It was one thing to have a feast and a city-wide celebration like we'd seen the other night. It was a whole other deal with Fiorentini in town. And masks. Potentially *Fiorentini* in masks.

I'd never been a fan of clowns. And masks were vaguely reminiscent of them. Yet I'd always wanted to experience Carnivale, and what an opportunity—to see it in its early stages, before it became the commercialized, touristy event of our own modern era. We wouldn't make it back up north come spring for the pre-Lent festival, and next year was out with what was to come...so this was pretty much my one opp for a while. So when the dogaressa looked to me for permission—not that she actually needed it—I was able to give it to her.

Gabi hooked her arm through mine and stared at me in surprise. "Really?" she whispered in English.

"Why not?" I returned. "The rest of this thing is so far beyond my Pinterest board of wedding ideas it's not even funny."

She laughed under her breath, and we entered the cobbler's store at last. On his shelves were boots and slippers of all kinds, mostly for men. But when he looked up from his workbench and saw who had entered, he smiled in welcome.

"Serenissima!" he cried, immediately coming around and bowing repeatedly. His elderly, drooping eyes moved to us, and then he crossed himself, as if angels had appeared. "The She-Wolves," he breathed.

"Indeed," said the dogaressa. "We are in need of your help, Signore Veraci. Lady Betarrini is marrying within the week and needs to be fitted for slippers to match her gown."

"Of course, Serenissima," he said. "Of course!" He gestured to a chair for her. He took my hand and led me to a wooden step on which he had painted outlines of feet, apparently in different sizes. The paint was well worn and the wood was stained with the oil of what I guessed had been hundreds of pretty dirty feet—based on the clearly delineated toe prints—but I held back my disgust, stepped out of my slippers, and climbed on top.

"Forgive me, my lady," he said, apologizing for his touch on my bare skin as he adjusted my feet to line up with the back. Then he reached for wooden markers with a number on each of them from a rack to his left. "There, I have it," he said. He turned his gaze back to the dogaressa. "I assume you want the finest leather I can find?"

"Actually," she said, moving to lift the flap of a small, square purse at her hip and fish inside, "I was hoping you might dye a leather to match this."

It was a small piece of the blue tapestry.

"Hmm," said the cobbler. "To dye the leather in indigo and get the shoes sewn by…"

"Saturday," she supplied.

He seemed to pale a bit. "Saturday!"

He was beginning to shake his head when she reached back into her purse and produced three gold florins. "To compensate you for putting other orders on hold as you see this one done," she said gently, assuredly, no doubt in her mind that she could make anything happen. "Payment for the shoes themselves will come upon completion."

His small, dark fingers closed around the florins. "Yes, Serenissima. They will be ready on Saturday morning."

"Friday night," she corrected, rising. "Lady Evangelia shall want to wear them a bit the night before to stretch them. No bride wants to be in unworn shoes the day she is to dance more than ever before!"

"Nay, Serenissima," said the cobbler, nodding and bowing repeatedly as we left the store.

I thought we'd head back to the Palazzo Ducale at that point, but the dogaressa had another stop in mind.

"Earrings," she said, lifting my hair and looking at my lobes as if visualizing what would look best. She gaped. "What is this?" she asked, leaning forward to peer at the tiny holes in my pierced ears. I rarely wore earrings to keep from calling attention to them.

"A custom in Normandy," Gabi filled in for me easily. "One we abandoned when we reached Toscana, as it seemed the ladies did not wear them."

The dogaressa frowned. "No lady of Normandy in my court has ever had pierced ears."

"Our parents are merchants," I said. "It was an island we visited that gave us the idea to pierce them." Inwardly, I winced. The more complex the lie, the more challenging it was to remember.

"I see," said the woman. "Well, come along. We'll see what this jeweler can find to suit."

We followed her and moved down the street and along another. As we turned a corner, we saw them. The Fiorentini—Lord Barbato and Lord Foraboschi—and their men. Their eyes widened in surprise...and delight.

"The Ladies Betarrini and Forelli!" cried Lord Barbato, clasping his hands in pleasure, his smile deepening as he saw our two knights, trapped behind four others. He leaned in closer. "What brings you out to the streets of Venezia?"

"We are shopping for Lady Betarrini's nuptials," the dogaressa said, like a proud parent. "You will need your finest, Lord Barbato, come Saturday. It will be the event of the year."

"Indeed, indeed," said the little lord, chin in hand, staring at me and then Gabriella. "The last time I was about to see one of the Ladies Betarrini married, it became quite the event as well." His dark eyes hardened, then, at the memory.

"I trust you shall not interfere with this wedding," Gabi said, edging forward, pressing so close that the little man was forced to take a step backward. "I would hate it if anyone ruined the *dogaressa's* plans for this lovely occasion."

Smart, my sister. Reminding him that messing with us this time was messing with the doge's court itself. I swallowed a gloating grin.

He gave her a confused look, as if he didn't know exactly what she was getting at. "We shall be the consummate guests," he said, with a tuck of his head and a flourish of his hand.

"See that you are," Gabi said, brushing past him. But, as the dogaressa turned to lead us out, he and Lord Foraboschi fell in step with us.

"We are not seeking company, Lord Barbato," Gabi said.

"Only a word, that's all I ask," he said lowly, so as to not to call the dogaressa's attention. "Tell me of Lord Greco. I hear tell he took a bride of his own. The poor waif we rescued?"

"The *woman* you *manhandled* and *abused*," Gabi hissed back. "Say no more, or I'll call my men down on you. Just the thought of Alessandra begs me to pull my dagger and slit your throat myself."

"Here? In the streets?" he said doubtfully. "You are a wilding, true enough. But 'twould cause a most unpleasant uproar and displease our hostess, would it not?"

Gabi's cheeks colored with rage, and she walked a bit faster. I looked over my shoulder, relieved to see Celso and Matteo right behind us now, their hands on the hilts of their swords, awaiting any order from us.

"And you, my lady? I also hear tell that the She-Wolf is not in heat, but soon to have her own litter."

Gabi stopped and turned, clearly enraged. "You, *Barbato*," she said, leaning forward, all in his face, "overstep your bounds."

He glared up at her, obviously itching to move away, but too proud to do it. Celso and Matteo stepped between us and the Fiorentini, pulling Gabi away. The dogaressa turned and began making her way back to us.

"You dare much to offend my lady," Celso grit out.

"Forgive me, forgive me," Barbato said effusively, as if it had all been a misunderstanding, but his eyes were cold. "You shall not have to bear my company for much longer. Good day, ladies."

He cast her a sly look, turned on his heel and left us, just as the dogaressa reached us. I wondered what on earth he meant. Was he not coming back to the Palazzo Ducale? To court? To the wedding? All I knew was that there was something in his tone that sent prickles down the back of my neck...

"Who are those men to you? Do you wish for my knights to go after them?" the dogaressa asked.

"Old enemies," I said, watching Barbato and Foraboschi disappear into the crowds. "But I believe they are leaving the city. There is no need to trifle with them."

The dogaressa sniffed and turned away. "Come along, then."

"What does he want?" Gabi whispered, as we walked, arm in arm. "What could he possibly be after from us?"

"Most likely torment and agitation is all he's after. He's still chafing after we bested him last time, stealing Alessandra away...securing Castello Paratore for Greco. The list is long, in that man's book, in terms of reasons to hate us."

"No more than we have reason to despise the cretin who took Lord Forelli's life," Celso said. He took up a position in front of us and Matteo behind. He spoke of Fortino, and memories of Marcello's older brother filled my mind. Gabi had known him better than I, but I knew he'd been a good man. And the Fiorentini had used him to lure us to a town where they'd managed to kidnap Gabi.

No, there was no trusting those guys. If there were means for them to get to us, to harm us, to bring us down in any way, they'd use them. I sighed. We'd be on public display with this ceremony, distracted...

I could only take comfort in the fact that I was marrying Captain Luca Forelli, and I knew he'd take every precaution he could.

CHAPTER 19

GABRIELLA

We were aboard Caterina's boat on our way to Borano when Marcello and Luca heard about our encounter with Barbato and his bud.

"Why would you not tell us immediately?" Luca asked, frowning.

"There wasn't time," I said. "We reached the palazzo and we only barely had time to change and leave with you."

"What did they want?" Marcello asked, closing our circle.

"To agitate us," I said. "They said nothing of consequence. Honestly, I think he only wants to get back at us any way he can."

"Which is what concerns me," Marcello said.

"And me," Dad added, coming up behind.

"What can he do, here?" I said. "We are under the protection of the doge and dogaressa. He won't want to endanger that."

Marcello crossed his arms. He and Luca were in the casual clothing of the Forelli knights for our outing—leggings and tunics, belted at the waist. Overcoats to shield them from the damp wind. He turned to the rail and studied the horizon of the lagoon, thinking.

"The Fiorentini's relationship with Venezia is tenuous at best. They are here to try and secure a new trade agreement. But what if..." He looked at us over his shoulder. "What if they were here for wicked reasons, and only used that as a shield for their true goal?"

"Surely they would not come all this way just to poke at us?" Mom said. "Firenze and Siena are enjoying their first true peace in years."

Marcello shrugged. "Lord Barbato makes money from battle. He raises horses and has a good deal invested in the metal guild. The more swords his smiths forge, the more he makes. Foraboschi, too. He builds wealth through his mercenaries. Mercenaries who while away the time at home with sparring and eating; these do not make a man money."

This made sense. I knew, firsthand, that the knights we employed at the castello were costly. And yet we had little choice. An unmanned castle was soon a conquered castle. We received a stipend from Siena as an outpost to assist in our defense, but it was only half of what we needed.

"So," I said slowly, "the best way to stir up battle again is to taunt and tease us? That hardly seems enough to instigate a war."

Marcello weighed my words. "They're testing us, trying to find a vulnerability. And likely they're trying to get closer to Galileo and Orazio. I'd wager they've heard the tales they told and would like to see how to capitalize on them as well."

I took a long, slow breath. It would not do to have Orazio and Galileo say anything to the Fiorentini. The guys knew now that they'd said far too much in the early days—and were safely hidden away in Caterina's palazzo until we could leave—but if they were captured...tortured...

Marcello wrapped his arm around my waist and tugged me closer to him. "Cease your fretting, Wife," he said, lifting my hand to his lips.

"If the Fiorentini find out where we've hidden our cousins away—"

"They shall not. Caterina is good at keeping secrets."

I lifted a brow. "And what of Nicolo?"

Marcello and Luca shared a long look of concern. If Nicolo went out drinking, which he was likely to do, and started talking, which he was likely to do...

And yet we'd had no choice. Considering our cousins had just been the doge's prisoners, it was unlikely our host and hostess were ready to give their just-sprung-captives a room beside ours. And we weren't permitted to leave.

EVANGELIA

In Borano, Gabi had a good time wrapping one lace after another over my head and around my shoulders. Obnoxious, heavy lace in ridiculous flower patterns that she knew I'd roll my eyes over... but then Luca approached, face serious, and Gabi and Mom filed out of the room. In his hand was the most precious, delicate lace I'd ever seen. And in this day and age, I knew it'd been stitched by hand, like all the rest. It was like the kiss of an ice fairy, blowing whispery thread atop a surface.

"This is what you seek," Luca said, green eyes glinting as he further unrolled the bolt of impossibly precious lace across his fingers. He lifted it up and across my head, then over, across my face. "Veiled or unveiled, Evangelia Betarrini," he pledged, "I cannot wait to have you as my own."

I stared at him, partially blocked by the veil, and it was oddly moving. Like a precursor to our vows. "Nor I, you," I whispered.

He paused for two breaths, staring at me. "So this is it? The right lace for the veil?"

I nodded.

He grinned and wrapped his arms around me, pulling me close. "In days of old, in arranged marriages, they veiled a bride so her husband-to-be wouldn't back out before the vows were exchanged." He lifted the lace up and folded it back. "If our marriage had been arranged, and I lifted your veil to discover your beauty, I might have fainted."

I chuckled. "My husband-to-be, the prince of overstatement."

"I do not overstate," he said earnestly, cupping my cheek. "Evangelia Betarrini, you are the most beautiful woman I've ever seen." His green eyes searched my face as if he was memorizing every inch of it again. "I cannot wait until you are mine. Wholly mine." A glint sparkled in his eye. "Something tells me the rest of you will be every bit as lovely too."

I could feel the color rising in my cheeks, and he looked gratified. "I love that I can make you blush."

"I imagine you'll delight in that all our life," I said.

He grinned and bent to kiss me. Softly, tenderly. We could hear my family outside, talking with someone, laughing. But it was like they were a great distance away, because my focus was solely on Luca. Luca, *Luca.* How I loved him...how could I have put this off so long? Now that our wedding was almost here, I could hardly wait to kiss him for hours, and let him kiss me...

He leaned back and slowly slid the lace from my hair. I reached up and pulled his head toward me for a deeper kiss. Pleased, he held me closer, then edged me backward, kissing me all the while, until my back met the wall of the house and I was pressed against him. I kissed him and I kissed him some more, opening my lips, accepting his probing pressure, wondering about what it would be like to give my all to him. Just a few days away...

It was a heady thought, that gift. The idea of lying with him, without anything between us. I couldn't wait, on one hand. And on the other, I was terrified.

His hands were so fine, so good. Warm and reassuring, and yet curious and wanting. They roamed my lower back, pulling me closer to him, every action strong, and yet soft. It was as if his touch was demanding, yet thoughtful, all wrapped up in one delightful package. Yearning for more...and yet taking no more than I was willing to give. Again and again I wondered where that line was. And yet, as his lips covered mine and his warm hands roamed around my hips, all I could think was, *I can't wait to be his. Wholly. Fully. His wife.*

It was the first time I'd gone there. I mean, as hot as Luca Forelli was, as much as he made me laugh and was my person, I'd never really accepted that I wanted to be his, completely. And I did.

He wrapped his arm around me, pulling me closer. "Evangelia Betarrini," he moaned, "I cannot wait until you are mine."

"And I," I said, kissing him, covering each bit of his lips, "cannot wait to be wholly yours."

"Truly?" he said, pulling away slightly, running a warm hand over my shoulder and down along my arm.

"Truly," I said.

Then he took a deep breath through his flared nostrils and drew back. Slowly, he reached for the lace on the table and settled it over my head and between our lips, a little swollen from the kissing.

"Soon," he said, kissing the tip of my nose through the lace, "you shall be mine, Evangelia. From the tips of your toes to the top of your head." He leaned forward until his head met mine. He lifted a brow in mischief. "And everything in between."

I huffed a laugh. "You speak of my eyebrows, right?"

"Yes, your eyebrows," he said, one side of his mouth quirking in a smile. "That is what I speak of." He leaned forward and kissed one and then the other, through the lace.

"And my boney elbow?" I asked. "Which will undoubtedly poke you in your sleep?"

"And yes, that," he said, lifting it up. He bowed to give it a kiss as if in homage.

I felt my blush deepen as I thought of going on. "Mayhap we should stop such imaginings. Such thoughts are best explored on our wedding night, not before," I said.

"Indeed," he readily agreed, straightening. "'Tis the sweetest form of torture, to fill my mind with such thoughts before I can act upon them. But rest assured, my soon-to-be-wife," he said, leaning forward to touch his forehead to mine, "I shall act on them. Every one of them."

Now I was blushing for sure, and he laughed in delight.

"The saints bear witness," he said, taking a step away from me, rubbing the back of his neck. He reached out to take my hand. "That I am the most blessed man in all of Toscana."

"Just as I am the most blessed of women," I said, covering his hand with my other and smiling into his eyes.

And I truly felt that way. I couldn't wait—every fiber of my being longed to be in Luca Forelli's arms forever.

CHAPTER 20

EVANGELIA

The next two days were filled with fittings for my gown, completion of my veil, and as much touring about Venezia as we could. But Mom and Dad made better headway in the crowded streets without us, since the Venetians tended to recognize me and Gabi now, swarming us with all their well-wishes. Mom had acquired tons of bottles of oils and packets of dried herbs, which I knew she meant to use as treatments for people back home. Just the thought of it made me long for the castello, which was a nice change of pace. For so many months, I'd itched to leave. Now I only wanted to return. As Mrs. Luca Forelli.

If the Venetians were excited at the thought, the Sienese would be over the moon. And those of Castello Forelli? They'd be crazy-wild. I only wished that Luca's sister, Adela, was here to take part in the celebration.

The morning of the wedding, Gabi and I played in a room with the puppies, laughing as they tackled and rolled over each other, wincing when their sharp teeth bit down on our hands. The dogaressa swept in and *tsked-tsked* me for, "being down on the floor like a commoner," and for "letting those vile things mar your hands."

Like your awful pet squirrel is any better.

She gestured in irritation for us to rise, and we did so, feeling like chastened children. "Come along," she said, over her shoulder. "We have work to do to get you prepared."

I looked toward Gabi in alarm, and she gave me a wide-eyed glance in return. But there was a smile on her face, and she tagged along, which reassured me. Together, we could do anything. Would that change when I married Luca? Things had shifted after she married Marcello...but we'd found our way.

She reached for my hand and squeezed it as we walked the long, dark hallway, following the dogaressa and her ladies, our Forelli knights padding along behind us.

"Why do I feel like I'm going to the principal's office?" Gabi whispered.

I smiled, not daring to respond as the two ladies in front of us sent a reproving look over their shoulders. Apparently, walks down the hallway were meant to be done in silence. Gabi stuck her tongue out at their backs, which made me want to giggle. I covered my laugh with a cough, which made Gabi fairly wheeze with her own laughter, and cough as well. At last we arrived at a doorway, and the dogaressa turned to face us.

"The servants inside here will see to your bath. I will see you afterward, once they are at work on your hair."

"Thank you, Serenissima," I said with a quick curtsy, super glad that I was going to score a bath on my wedding day. When I'd asked about it earlier, my maid had seemed confused and said she'd inquire.

"Are there any other doorways into this room?" Celso asked one of the ladies.

"Only the servant's entrance," she said.

With a nod, Celso dispatched Lutterius to take position at that door, while he turned to guard this main entrance. I noted that Luca had again assigned the burliest of our knights to my guard duty. Maybe because it was our wedding day? I smiled. He was taking no chances that anything might come between us.

We entered the room, which appeared to be an official sort of bathroom, with a ceiling lower than most in the palazzo, perhaps to preserve heat. It featured a large window, open to the lagoon, and two hearths blazing with crackling fires, heavy pots hanging above them. Servants were filling two copper tubs with hot water, and others were setting exotic-looking bottles and bars of soap on a table between them. There were thick cloths meant for towels, so thick they almost looked like the soft Egyptian cotton towels we remembered from home.

But all the women in the room made me shift uneasily. I gazed at Gabi in fear. She'd told me of Rome and how the women had pretty much scrubbed and bathed her in preparation for her almost-wedding to Lord Greco. Knowing my preference for modesty, she gave me an *I'll-handle-this* look and turned to the women behind her.

"I shall see to my sister's needs myself. If you all will finish filling the tub and then depart, we'd be most grateful."

The oldest of them frowned at her. "You do not wish for us to see to her hair at least?"

"Nay. The lady prefers privacy."

The woman clamped her lips shut, clearly offended, and then turned to yank the last pail from the fire and dump it into the tub. Then she shooed the others out and loudly closed the door behind her. Lutterius gave us a nod before he, too, disappeared through the servants' entrance.

"At least she didn't slam it," Gabi whispered.

"You'd think I'd fired them or something."

"They were probably looking forward to bragging rights for getting a She-Wolf ready for her wedding," she said.

"We'll have started new rumors," I said with a sigh. "Tales of me not wanting to be seen naked, lest my wolf tail be visible."

"Or that you're really a man," she whispered, gently turning me around and unlacing my overdress. "Don't worry over it. If you want privacy, you get privacy. It's your *wedding* day. And they'd talk, regardless of what we'd done."

"True," I said, slipping my gown from my shoulders.

"Lucky girl," Gabi sighed, wistfully staring at my full tub. "A bath sounds divine."

"There's another tub right there," I said. "Why not fill it and join me?"

"You think I could?"

"Why not?" I asked her, squaring my shoulders. "This is my wedding day," I smiled, repeating her own statement, "and if I want my sister to not smell like B.O., then it's my right to make it happen."

She laughed. "All right," she said, turning toward the hearth and grabbing a cloth to take hold of the iron handle of another pail. "I'm not one to mess with a wolf on her wedding day."

I finished undressing as she continued filling her tub. As I slipped into the blessedly hot water, any tension I'd felt earlier seemed to melt from my muscles. I went under, holding my breath as I looked up, watching the blurry, painted ceiling dance with the moving water. When I came up, Gabi was just stepping into her tub. Shyly, I hurriedly looked away from her rounding form.

"Oh," she breathed, as the water covered her bare shoulders. She pulled the pins from her hair as I had. "Wish I could make it as hot as yours. But Mom says that's bad for the baby."

"The baby, the baby," I sighed. "Don't you get weary of worrying over the baby?"

"I do. And I don't. It's all good." She dipped under then, wetting down her long, dark curls. She wiped her eyes and reached for the nearest bottle, uncorking it to smell it, making a face and setting it down. "It's like God shifts your heart once you're pregnant," she said, lifting a bar of soap to her nose. Pleased, she settled back against the curved side of the tub and began building a lather in her hands. "Before, you only think of yourself, your husband, your family. But once there's life," she paused thoughtfully, "well, it's like we're built to preserve the next generation. To protect and nourish them. It's like I was always meant to have this baby. Have Marcello's baby."

"Aren't you scared?" I asked, taking the bar of soap from her.

"Of having the baby? Sure. But Mom will be there. And you."

I shuddered. "I dunno, Gabs. You know how I get a little vomit-y…"

"You'll be there," she said, lathering her hair. "It's what medieval chicks do. Tend to each other. Sew up wounds, if necessary."

I sighed and began soaping up my hair. "I don't want to get pregnant. At least not right away…"

"Well, you can try the natural methods. But you see how far that got me."

I nodded. "I will. I guess it's all in God's hands."

"Is that what made you finally ready to say yes to the dress?"

I grinned at her and went under again, rinsing my hair. This wedding was so different than any TV show had ever prepared me to have, it wasn't even funny. When I rose again to the surface, I leaned over the edge of my tub.

"God plopped us into medieval Italy. Found us boys to love. Helped us save Dad. I guess I can trust the Big Guy with whatever comes, baby or not. All I know is that I want to make the most of this precious time before the…you know."

She nodded thoughtfully. "Me, too." She studied me with her big, chocolate brown eyes. "Do make the most of it, Lia. You're marrying an amazing guy today. That's its own kind of fantasy, you know."

"True," I whispered back. Luca Forelli was going to be mine…mine and mine alone.

A scuffle at the servant's door made us both freeze. There was a bam against it, visibly making the wooden panel shudder, then the sound of grunts and hits. "Gabs…" I said.

She was already rising, wrapping herself in a towel and reaching for her shift. The girl was quick, even preggers. But neither of us had weapons.

She pulled on her shift, tossed mine to me and I'd just managed to pull mine down to my thighs—struggling with the fabric that wanted to cling to my wet skin—when they burst through. Four men, one of them dripping blood from his nose, another limping, a gash at his side. But we could see Lutterius on the ground in the servants' hallway.

"Celso!" I screamed.

The door handle moved up, and I could hear him press against the bolted door. "M'lady?"

"Celso, get help!"

The men entered, circling around us, wearing Palazzo Ducale uniforms, but none of them were familiar to us. Thoughts of the men we'd encountered last year in Toscana—Fiorentini assassins—filled me with terror. How I longed for my bow! Even a dagger!

They were silent as they spread out and their silence was oddly creepier than any taunts might have been. I pulled my shift away from my wet skin as the nearest looked upon my bare, dripping legs with lust in his eyes. But these men clearly weren't here to rape us. They were here to kill us. Only that would make this mad attempt worthwhile.

"Celso! Help!" Gabi screamed, reaching for a pail as the men drew wicked-looking daggers. They'd blocked her way to the main door, and it was bolted for privacy. The door shuddered as Celso rammed his shoulder against it, again and again. We could hear him shouting, his voice muted through the cursedly thick door.

"The She-Wolves of Siena," grunted the man in front of me. "You look more like enticing maidens, fresh from your baths, than fearsome warriors."

"You might be surprised," I said, laying hold of a metal pail as my sister had done, our only semblance of a weapon.

"Come now," he said, scoffing at my pail. "Let us see to our business of killing you, and we'll do it cleanly. Die easily, or die in a bloody mess of ribbons, but this day, you *shall* die, She-Wolf."

Another knight joined Celso outside and together, they rammed the door again. It shuddered, and we heard a crack, but it held. There was much shouting outside, directions to go around—

"Now," snarled the leader, and all four attacked us, Gabi and I battling two each.

I dipped right as the nearest man lunged at me, his dagger missing my arm by an inch. But I swung my pail around at him and managed to ram the back of his head. He sprawled out on the floor.

The other grabbed hold of the pail and wrenched it away, tossing it to the corner, and I backed away, snatching bottles and throwing them at him. Then it hit me. "Bottles!" I cried to Gabi.

She seemed to have thought of it at the same time, because she'd leaped to the table already. She tossed me another, and I turned and slammed the end of it against the wall.

A stinky, overly flowery perfume filled the air, and I whirled, sending the substance into my attacker's face. He cried out like it burned him, and blinked at me, looking more fearsome than before. His face turned into a sneer.

The bottle had broken poorly, but it had a jagged edge. Dimly, I knew my hand was cut and bleeding, but my eyes never left my attacker.

The main door shuddered with one slam after the other. Why would it not give way? "*Gabriella!*" came Marcello's voice. "*Evangelia!*"

Neither of us answered. We were too focused on staying alive. I heard Gabi grunt and gasp and the sound of more breaking bottles.

But my heart surged with hope at the thought of Marcello—and maybe Luca—being so close. *Hurry, hurry, love. I can't keep this guy at bay much longer.* Behind him, the other was rising, rubbing his head.

My attacker jabbed at me with his dagger, stepping toward me, backing me into the corner.

"Come now, She-Wolf. Let's end this. Today Siena shall know that Firenze can bring her to her knees any time we wish."

"I think not," I grit out, taking a swing at him with my broken bottle.

Gabi cried out, and I gasped, worried for her, for the baby...I dared to glance her way.

He pounced, then, grabbing hold of my wrist and slamming it up against the wall, the pain of it stealing my breath. Then he slammed my head against it as well, once, twice. I blinked, my vision swimming, trying desperately to focus. The room was spinning, but with a sudden centeredness I wished I could deny, I felt the dagger's edge come across my neck and press in.

"Imagine the story I'll tell," he panted, leaning full against me, driving the breath further from my lungs. "Of slicing the throat of a She—"

I heard the arrow coming and closed my eyes, wondering if it would hit me or him...heard it enter his skull and emerge through the other side with sickening clarity...felt him stiffen and then slump, sliding down and away from me...forced myself to open my eyes and prepare for the next man's attack...

I saw Forelli and Ducale knights flooding into the room and knew the relief of reinforcements, but we weren't free yet—

Gabi. She was blocking one man's dagger strike with her dented pail and kicking at the other. There was blood on her shift...I turned to walk woodenly toward her, operating in a sort of dream-scape, knowing I had to help her, somehow. But I lurched sideways, unable to keep my balance. *My head...*

But then our attackers were turning to fight our knights. And the second door gave way at last, more of ours spilling in, Luca at the front. He ran directly for me, gathering me in his arms, looking wildly afraid, mouthing words, words that seemed slow to reaching my ears. His hands moved to my shoulders and he shook me a little, and I could guess what he was asking—if I was hurt.

"I'm fine, fine," I said in English, looking over his shoulder to Gabi. She was safe too, in Marcello's arms. Celso had one of the would-be assassins on his knees in front of him, hands on his head, yelling at him. But it was like I was under water and couldn't make out the words.

Luca bent and picked me up and carried me from the room. Past Otello, the one who had saved me, still holding his bow. Out the servant's entrance from which the assassins had arrived, down the hallway and into another. We emerged near my room, and he entered, passing the servant with her mouth gaping wide in shock. He carried me to the bed and covered me with blankets, touching my face again and again.

Gradually, I could make out what he was saying. The room ceased spinning. I knew my parents were there, in and out, probably going to Gabi's room too. Ducale knights and servants. The dogaressa. In and out, in a dim, agitated processional.

Through it all, Luca remained. Perched on the edge of my bed, alternately stroking my hand and cheek. Speaking lowly, reassuringly to me.

"Mi sono—mi sono ben, non ti preoccupare," I said at last. *I am well. Don't worry.*

Everyone froze in the room, as if surprised that I was capable of speech.

"You've suffered a terrible fright as well as injury," Dad said, coming to the other side of my bed.

"You can say that again," I said in English, and he smiled. "That was like the worst bath ever."

While Luca couldn't understand my words, the tone of our exchange seemed to give him some relief.

"So..." he said slowly, tentatively checking the back of my head for cuts, "It seems that I must be by your side at all times."

"Indeed," I said, the edge of my own smile helping me breathe more readily. "It appears I'm so popular, everyone wants to come and see me, even in my bathchambers. How is Gabi?"

"Well enough," Dad said grimly. He looked a little pale, knowing how close he'd been to losing us. "She sustained wounds to her arm and leg."

"And the baby?"

"It seems fine. Mom's sewing her up now."

"They were Fiorentini..." I said, shifting, searching every face in the room, suddenly scared one might remain. But Luca had dismissed anyone other than Forelli knights and servants. "Wearing Ducale uniforms."

"We know," Luca said. "They are dead or in the doge's prison. Soon, we shall know who sent them. The doge is nearly tearing off his skin, he's so enraged."

"Barbato and Foraboschi," I said.

"Yes, *yes*. I will hunt them down myself," he vowed, never looking more threatening than he did in that moment. He rose, as if intent on doing so right then.

"Nay, Luca—" I began.

"Nay," Dad said, grabbing his arm as he passed and turning him around. "You belong *here*. With your future *wife*. Leave the Fiorentini scum to the Ducale knights. They shall find them."

Luca paused, tense, momentarily poised to argue with Dad, but soon relented.

"You are right, of course. Forgive me." He ran a hand through his hair and turned back to me, taking my hand again. "You are safe, Evangelia," he said. "You shall be under constant guard until I myself am with you this night."

I nodded. If I'd thought my wedding day was far from the one I'd imagined in contemporary America, I'd been mistaken.

It had just moved into its own zip code of weird and wild.

CHAPTER 21

GABRIELLA

M om sewed up the two wounds I'd received in the fight, one on my leg and one on my arm. We knew we'd offended the doge's own doctor by refusing his services, but we'd seen enough of medieval medicine to know we would do far better on our own. The infection risk alone was enough to convince us.

I tried to bite back my cry as she finished stitching my arm, but it was the absolute worst sensation when the thread pulled through. Excruciating, yes, but also agitating, like chewing on cotton balls. Marcello held my hand and didn't even wince as I squeezed it with all my strength.

"Sorry, babe," Mom said in English, focused only on tying the knot and clipping off the threads with a sharp knife. It pulled at my skin, and I bit back a scream. "I'd kill for some numbing ointment."

"*You* would," I returned, leaning my sweaty head back against the pillows and panting. At last, she was done.

Marcello reached up to wipe the sweat from my brow with a soft cloth, all the more handsome because of his concern. "The...baby?" he asked.

"I'm certain he or she is fine," I said, giving him a reassuring—though feeble—smile. I'd not fallen. Not been hit in the belly.

"He," Marcello said with a small smile, relief flooding his face. "My baby is fine. He is strong. A Forelli." He brought a fist to his chest.

"So you believe it's a little boy now?" I asked, running my hand across my belly in a slow circle.

He reached up to tuck a strand of my hair behind my ear. "An heir for the castello. The people need an heir. And truth be told, I live in fear of a daughter as beautiful as her mother to protect, too." His eyes crinkled at the corners. "But next, we shall beget a girl."

"Babies are surprisingly resilient," Mom said, winding a bandage around my stitches. Her eyes met mine. "But you've felt no contractions, right?"

"Nay," I said with a shake of my head, trying to breathe normally. I was more worried that my anxiety would stress out the baby. My mind was whirling. Over Barbato and Foraboschi. "Marcello," I said, taking his hand. "Why would they go to such lengths? I understand what you said about them prospering from battle over peace, but here? Now? The doge will never allow them in his city again."

The muscles in Marcello's cheeks tensed. "He will banish those two, but Firenze might send others. Where else might they have access to you and yours? Our men would have killed or captured them on sight."

I sighed heavily. We could cut the head off the snake, but the snake would only grow two more...

A knock on the door sent Marcello to his feet and his hand to his sword. "Who is there?" he asked, without opening it.

Whoever it was, they were not enemies, for he unbolted and opened the door, then slipped through. *"Bloccarla dietro di me,"* he said to Mom. *Lock it behind me.*

She did as he asked, then came over to pour me a glass of water. I knew I should get up and act more tough and She-Wolfy, but at that moment, all I really wanted was for my mom to take care of me. I was wiped out. She went and retrieved a brush and began working on my hair, which had dried in a rat's nest in the aftermath of our attack.

"You did well, Gabi," she said. "Protecting Lia and your baby."

"She held her own, thankfully," I said, closing my eyes, remembering. "I had plenty to deal with."

"You two are a wonder," she mused, working out a stubborn knot and reaching for a new section of hair. "I still can't believe, sometimes, that you are our daughters. You're so much stronger than I. So much braver."

"We got it all from you. And Dad."

"Nah," she said with a small smile. "Your dad and I...we have a sense of adventure. But wading into battle?" She shook her head. "That doesn't come easily."

"I've seen you," I said. "You rise to the challenge just as we do. It's not like we go looking for it. We just defend ourselves when necessary."

"And thank God you are so good at it."

"Let's just hope we don't have to do it much more. Life is challenging enough without a bounty on our heads."

"Yeah, well, I'm not sure we'll be free of that any time soon. It seems like it's simply going to be a part of our lives."

I frowned at that, instinctively shielding my stomach with my hand.

"She'll be fine, Gabi."

"So you think it's a girl?"

"Yes," she said, gently nudging my shoulder upward so she could reach the back of my hair.

"Why?"

"Just a feeling. Or maybe it's because I only ever carried daughters, and so I can't imagine a little boy. Whatever. We'd be happy with a healthy, strong babe either way, right?"

"Right." I ran my hand over the mound of my belly and wondered over it. I didn't sense if it was a girl or a boy, really. But as she said, all I wanted was for it to be healthy. Healthy enough to withstand what was to come...And weren't girls stronger than boys? More resilient? Although Luca had survived that earlier strain...

I lifted my hand to my forehead. "So we have to pull ourselves together for a wedding tonight, huh? They're not delaying it?"

"No," she said ruefully. "I think it's a bit like when you got married to Marcello. Lia might be a smidge safer as a married woman. Less of a target once she becomes a Forelli. And somehow, from the outside, our clan becomes more unified. Stronger, by name alone."

"Amazing what a name can do, eh? Though that didn't keep me out of harm's way today."

"No. I suspect it's more of a hope than an iron-clad truth. But we'll take it, won't we? Lia wants Luca. The doge wants the party. We want the party done so we can get the heck out of Dodge. Everyone will be happier come morn. Let's just see Lia through it, okay?"

"Okay," I said. I swung my legs off the edge of the bed, testing my new sutures.

"Careful," Mom said.

"I will. I suppose dancing is out tonight?"

"Are you kidding?" Mom asked, lifting a brow. "There's no way the Forelli boys are going to let you two anywhere near that masked ball. Not after what just came down. And even if they did, your dad and I would refuse you. It's just not smart, Gabi."

"I know," I groaned. Not that I was in dancing shape. I'd pulled some muscles fighting off the bad guys. And with these fresh stitches...it was best to keep movement to a minimum.

Wincing a little, I rose, let my head clear of the initial dizziness, and walked to the window. The day was clearing, the sky a powder blue. Boats skimmed across the water, sails full, reminding me of girls in gowns on a dance floor. It was a shame we'd miss our one true chance at a masked Venetian ball...a predecessor of the Carnivale. But the idea of being out there, among many who might take sides with the Fiorentini—or be willing to accept payment from them—was ludicrous. We had to steer clear of any way we'd be vulnerable. And get back to our Tuscan castello just as fast as we could.

EVANGELIA

The Betarrini brothers were safe, and Luca saw to it that his men moved them to another location in case Barbato and Foraboschi had thoughts about kidnapping them, given that they'd lost their opportunity with us. We knew the brothers' presence in this time only put our plans to stay in medieval Italy at risk; we had to get them out of here and back to their own era.

"Focus on what's ahead," Gabi said, giving my shoulder a squeeze as a maid finished with my hair. The maid had braided a band that crossed my head like a crown—with a strand of pearls in it—and tucked the rest in a net covered in matching pearls. The effect was elegant, and I smiled happily into the brass mirror, gradually feeling more and more myself. I'd bailed on adding the little band of fabric the dogaressa insisted I order from the dressmaker. Just the pearls and netting would be perfect under my veil.

The gown, on the other hand, was something out of a movie. It fit me perfectly, and I felt like a princess in it. The neckline dived in a V to a horizontal band that crossed above my breasts. The bodice was tight, and hugged my torso and hips, yet I could still breathe. The arms were loose and flowing from the elbow, allowing the delicate undergown's arms to emerge from beneath it. The undergown was a navy blue, picking up the darker pattern in the fabric of the overdress, with amazing effect.

"I gotta hand it to her," Gabi said, admiring me where I stood as the maid slipped out the door. "That dogaressa knew what would look good on you."

"She did well, huh?"

"I'll say. Luca will faint dead away when he gets his first look."

"I hope so," I said with a grin. "He'd never live that down."

There was a knock on the door, and my parents came in, Mom and Dad dressed in their finest. Dad took my hand and looked me over from head to foot, shaking his head as if in wonder.

"Evangelia...you're always beautiful. But today, you're more beautiful than ever."

"Good," I said with a grin. "That's the goal, right? To look your best on this day of days?"

"Well, you do." Mom smiled, walking around to study me from every angle. "You're pretty as a picture." When she returned to face me, she took hold of my hands. "You're sure, Lia? Totally sure that this is what you want?"

"Totally," I said, and knew I meant it.

Gabi came over to me with the veil and together with Mom, they gently set it across my head.

Dad took my hand. "To think I might've missed this day..." He shook his head and tears ran down his cheeks. He reached out and took Gabi's hand too, and Mom closed our circle with an arm around each of our shoulders. "I'm so grateful that you two are okay. That you weren't hurt worse than you were."

"Together, we're strong," I said. I swallowed hard past the lump in my throat. Whenever Dad got teary, I did too.

"You are that. But this place..." He lifted his chin, looked to the ceiling and swallowed hard, as if he was trying to get a grip. After a moment, his brown eyes returned to meet mine. "As much as it's meant to me, to us as a family, it's not the safest place for my girls."

"It's the *only* place for your girls," I said, giving his hand a squeeze. "It's where we belong. Come what may."

He smiled and then dropped my hand to wrap me in his arms. "I'm so proud of you, Lia. And I love Luca. You know that, right? He's already a son to us."

"Which is the only way I'd marry him."

He gave me a kiss on the forehead and then moved so Mom could give me a kiss, too. Last came Gabi.

"Thanks for fighting off the bad guys," I said, my voice muffled as she hugged me tight.

"Any time, Sis," she answered, and I could hear the grin in her voice. She backed away, hands on my shoulders. We heard the bells of the basilica beginning to toll, calling us forward. "You ready?"

"Ready as I'll ever be to pledge my life away."

"You're not pledging your life away," she said, straightening the veil over my face. "You're pledging to join your life with his, and gaining Luca's love, forever. If you thought he was devoted before, look out. He's going to be nutsy as your hubby."

I grinned and together, we went to the door. Outside, four knights waited to escort us—Celso, Matteo, Otello and Falito—dressed in their formal Forelli-gold tunics. Otello's eyes widened and Celso flushed when they saw me, and Falito actually crossed himself as if he'd seen an angel. I laughed under my breath, thanking them all as they took their turns complimenting me.

"How does Lutterius fare?" I asked Celso.

"He is well, m'lady. Feeling badly that he couldn't thwart the intruders' entrance, but he'll survive his wounds."

I frowned. "Tell him I understand, Celso. It was one man against four, and he did his best. 'Tis all any of us could do."

Celso nodded. Then Dad offered his arm and I took it, and we were escorted down the hall and the stairs with the beautiful, barrel-vaulted ceiling, Gabi and Mom right behind us. Two knights led the way. Two others protected us from behind.

The halls were oddly silent; every visitor was in the basilica, it seemed. The only living beings we saw were servants at work or knights at intervals, standing guard. More had appeared since the attack—the doge was taking no further risk with our safety. And while they stood at attention, staring straight ahead as I passed, I could sense them watching us closely.

We paraded out to the loggia, with its Ottoman-inspired arches and decorative swirls cut out of stone. The loggia, as modern Italy saw it, had not been built yet, but this was gorgeous enough, the stonework monumental. For a moment, I wished there was a photographer and videographer on site, helping me to remember this precious day. I'd just have to sketch as much as I could as soon as I got home, to help commit it all to memory.

I wondered about the calm pace of my heart. Wasn't I supposed to feel panicky, or be hyperventilating or something? Maybe it was because we'd been through so much this morning...or maybe because what I was about to do was just so dead-on right...but all I felt was anticipation. Glee, sheer glee. It was like I couldn't smile enough.

Dad caught my eye and smiled as we entered the basilica's side entrance, built especially for the doge. We entered and walked directly to the altar. There was no music, no bridal march, but everyone inside stood and a holy hush settled over them all. In a way, it was its own sort of atmospheric music. My heart was already dancing, because I saw my man at the end, with an elaborately dressed priest—or cardinal?—and beside him, Marcello.

At the end of the aisle, Mom and Dad lifted my veil, kissed me on both cheeks, and Gabi handed me a nosegay of herbs. She settled the veil back down over my face and Luca was there, smiling as widely as I was, his eyes alight with wonder. I rested my arm atop his and lifted my skirt with my free hand to climb the three steps. We stood directly below and in front of the cardinal.

The old man had kind eyes, and while my Latin was seriously lacking when it came to following along something this intense and fast, I could figure out enough. There was mention of a man and a woman. Of a union. But seriously, all I had eyes for was my husband-to-be.

This was finally happening.

Me and Luca.

Forever.

We knelt on the step at one point, and the cardinal droned on in a fervent prayer, and while I couldn't understand all the words, I felt the blessing settle over us like a blanket, wrapping around us. A shiver ran down my back. Never had I felt God so close. But here, now, I was so focused on the blessings of my life, it seemed like God was tangibly present. Maybe that was the key.

It almost made my heart explode. Seriously. I'd never felt the kind of joy I was experiencing at that moment. And while I wanted it to go on and on, Luca and I were soon facing each other, the cardinal wrapping our hands with a holy cloth, chanting a litany in Latin; a boy was waving a smoking censer on all sides of us, creating a sweet-spicy cloud of incense around us. In a way, it almost made everyone else disappear. All I could see was Luca, taking my hand, sliding a beautiful emerald ring on my finger, then accepting his own gold-and-emerald band from me. There was some sort of vow that I belatedly accepted, after I realized they were waiting on me, and then Luca was lifting my veil, cupping my face and kissing me, so sweet and tender that it made me tear up.

The people clapped and swarmed around us, offering their congratulations. Luca allowed us to greet the doge and dogaressa, my parents, Gabi and Marcello, but then he took my hand firmly in his and pulled me toward the side entrance where we'd come in. Bells were ringing at a maniacally joyful pace, their deep tolls reverberating in our chests, so loud in the side chamber, I could barely hear Luca. But his expression of joy and peace settled over me, and I merely concentrated on following the knights before us as other ducale knights made a channel through the loggia for us to walk through. The people were in high spirits outside, crowding close to cheer us on and throw flowers at us.

We could hear music and the surge of people laughing and cheering, roaring like the very sea itself. *I'm married,* I thought. *Married. Mrs. Luca Forelli. Evangelia Forelli. Lia Forelli.* I felt like I was floating. The doge and the dogaressa led us upward, and we were again on the roof of the palazzo, the knights on guard turning to smile upon us and applaud. But then the doge and dogaressa led us into another covered passageway, back toward the basilica. We emerged high up in Saint Mark's, turned left, and suddenly we were out above the piazza, between the four bronze horses that had been taken from Constantinople centuries before.

The crowd beneath us went wild when we were spotted. They shouted, "He-Wolf! She-Wolf! He-Wolf! She-Wolf!" in a swelling, disjointed cry that again reminded me of waves—part ebbing, part flowing.

Luca turned toward me, took me in his arms, and thoroughly kissed me, much to the pleasure of everyone beneath us. Then, with a wave, we left the doge and dogaressa to lead the festivities. Back inside the palazzo, there was a table set in an intimate, small dining room, where the sound of the crowd was a muffled roar. At last it was just us—our family. Mom and Dad. Marcello and Gabi. Me and Luca.

"Do you think they'll keep it up all night?" I asked Luca.

"Most likely," he said, picking up the dainty roasted leg of a small hen and biting into it. "They'll be in ill spirits when they find out we're not going to join them. But after enough wine, they'll forget that we were the impetus for this early Carnivale and simply enjoy themselves."

"I wish we could be out there," Gabriella said, accepting a steaming ladle of mushroom soup from a servant.

Marcello laughed without mirth and shook his head. "Think no more of it. You and Evangelia are staying close to your husbands this night."

"Very close," Luca whispered in my ear. I knew I was blushing in response and nudged him in complaint as he chuckled.

"Forgive me for cutting short your wedding, uh, *celebration*, Cousin," Marcello said to Luca, with a wry smile. "But we must sail by mid-morning. Collect the Betarrini boys and depart for Ancona as fast as we can. The sooner we are away from those who assailed our wives, the better."

"Agreed," Luca said.

"The day after we were married, we were at war," Gabi whispered to me, her tone full of consolation. "This is a bit better than that."

I nodded. That had been awful—seeing the guys ride off when I knew Gabi was likely still asleep upstairs, dreaming of her new husband. I'd been so scared that he'd get hurt and not come home to her...

I confess I fairly inhaled my dinner. I was pretty hungry, and I was also a little anxious to be alone with Luca. We'd never been alone for longer than a few hours. Now we had the night...even if it was a short night.

He seemed to be similarly distracted, but picked at his food, pushing most of it to the edge of his trencher, his green eyes straying to me again and again.

"All right," Dad said gruffly, after a while. "Enough of us. You two go, with our blessing."

I grinned at him, and he smiled back at me, like a lord who had just bestowed a gift, which he had, in a way. Luca rose at once—"You need not encourage me further, sir"—and we all followed suit. Luca moved forward to take Dad's arm, and then Marcello's, both of them clapping him on the back and on the shoulder like he'd just accomplished a feat in marrying me. Then he kissed Mom and Gabi on the cheek and turned to me, eyes bright. "Ready?"

I nodded. With a grin over my shoulder to the family, we followed two knights down the hall and up the stairs to his room. Inside, the candles were lit, and there were bedclothes spread over the blanket. Celso closed the door behind us, and Luca slid the bolt closed. He came over to me, wrapped warm hands over both of my hips, and pulled me to him. There was a new measure of claim, authority, power in him, that I found sexy as all get-out.

"Ah, Evangelia," he whispered. "My sweet, precious, Evangelia." He kissed me softly, then more urgently. I matched him with my own desire, pulling him closer.

After a moment, he paused and leaned back to unpin my hair, slowly unbraiding it, then circling around to loosen the net and let the rest of it fall around my shoulders. He tossed the pearl netting over his shoulder, making me giggle, then continued around to my back again. His warm hands rubbed over my shoulders and he leaned forward to kiss me right where my neck and shoulder joined, sending a delicious shiver down my back. "Are you afraid?" he whispered, all careful concern.

"Nay," I said, "not with you."

"Good. There is no need to fear, Evangelia. Only reasons to rejoice..." He unlaced the back of my bodice and slipped it from my shoulders. Outside, through the open window, I could hear singing, a sound of pure joy, while inside, deep within me, my heart seemed to echo it.

Luca pulled off his tunic and then his shirt, and stood there before me, all smooth-chested, muscle upon muscle. Gabi always said she wanted to make a calendar of hot Italian knights...and now I was married to one of them. *Married.* Shyly, I lifted my trembling hands to skim his shoulders and arms, his skin warm to my touch. He took hold of my hand and slowly kissed my palm and then one knuckle after another, his eyes on me the whole time.

"Evangelia," he whispered gruffly. "You have honored me greatly by becoming my wife. Thank you." His eyes glistened with tears.

"The honor's mine, Sir Forelli," I returned, tearing up a bit myself.

He bent and lifted me up in his strong arms, carrying me so slowly toward the bed, I wondered if we'd ever make it there...He seemed to get a bit distracted with kissing me en route. It was like I couldn't get enough of him. When his knees finally met the edge, he tossed me, laughing, into the center of it and hurriedly chased me in, hovering over me, kissing, kissing, kissing...

And for the rest of the night, through fumbling and giggles, and missteps and awkwardness...

And fear and frustration...

And hope and desire...

Through moments that were so crazy, epically wrong...

And eventually, crazy, epically right...

I learned what it meant to be *his*, while my husband learned what it meant to be *hers*...

In the fullest sense of both words.

CHAPTER 22

EVANGELIA

The next morning, when I reached for my husband and found his side of the bed cold, I rose with a start. My first thought was that this was the curse of a Forelli bride—husbands always called to duty—but then I caught sight of him by the window, looking out. He was half-dressed, with only his leggings and shirt on, untucked, and he looked gloriously rumpled and handsome and *mine*.

I swung my legs out of bed and pulled the blanket around me, padding over to him across the cold stone floors, but feeling warm, through and through. He greeted me with a smile and welcomed me by opening an arm to pull me close. I nestled in, my cheek by his neck, and together we looked out at the lagoon, the first light of dawn casting a pink glow over the water.

"Good morning, Wife," he whispered, kissing my temple.

"Good morning, Husband," I said, tugging him close.

His hands roamed over my bare back and he turned his head in order to peer into my eyes. "How does the morning find you?"

"Better than any other," I said, reaching up to kiss his cheek. "I'm Signora Forelli."

"Yes, that you are," he said with a grin, hugging me close. He turned to face me and kissed me. My lips still felt a little swollen from all our kisses last night, but I didn't mind.

"What time do we leave?" I asked, in between kisses.

"In but a few hours," he said, closing his eyes, his lips moving lower, to my jaw, my neck.

"So we must see to packing, getting ready," I said, closing my eyes at the sensations he was awakening.

"Indeed," he said, gently pressing me back and back, toward the bed. "Just as soon as we properly greet the morning as man and wife..."

Three hours later, we emerged from our room, neatly dressed and hair combed—with mine in a new, somewhat-matronly net, courtesy of the dogaressa—and the knights outside straightened. They gave me quick smiles and then clasped arms with Luca, apparently in silent congratulations, and I resisted the urge to roll my eyes. "Bedding a wife" was often the subject of much bawdy conversation in medieval Italy, especially among knights. Marcello and Luca had urged the knights in the castello more than once to keep from discussing it around us, but comments often slipped into the stream of their teasing and story-telling.

I was only thankful that the Forellis' prominence among Sienese society didn't demand that they have a witness for the consummation of marriage—a horror I'd heard about once or twice. Just the thought of it made me blush. It was all so intimate anyway. But to have an audience? A shiver went down my back. Barbato had actually threatened Gabi with that when she tried to escape her marriage to Greco...

Out in the piazza, ducale knights were hauling away a few people who got so drunk the night before, they'd fallen asleep in the streets. I winced as one, covered in his own vomit, tried to wrench away and ended up chest-to-chest with the knight. In disgust, the knight pulled back and struck him across the face, sending him reeling to the stones again. Luca moved between me and the sight and gripped my arm.

"Come along," he urged. "The air on board the ship shall refresh us all."

There was a small crowd awaiting us at the docks, surrounding the doge and dogaressa, who both looked a bit weary after the festivities of last night. Servants stood around them, holding huge canopies above them to shield them from the sun. But I couldn't keep my eyes from the beautiful ship. Crates of supplies that my parents and the men had gathered while in Venezia were tied down on deck, creating a small mound. The puppies cried and yelped from another crate made out of spaced-out slats.

"We have no more room belowdecks?" I asked.

"Not with all our trunks," Luca returned. "This ship is the fastest Venezia's yards has ever turned out, the finest of gifts to us, but she doesn't carry much in terms of cargo."

It was then that I saw her name, painted on the back. *Mare-Lupo*. *The Sea-Wolf.* I grinned and caught the eye of the doge, and he lifted a brow and proudly tucked his chin. Together, Luca and I went to them, following Marcello and Gabi, Mom and Dad. In turn, we gave them our thanks and said our farewells.

"Return to my courts, as promised, with that babe," the doge reminded Gabi and Marcello.

"Just as soon as the child is of age," Marcello said carefully. "It shall be our good pleasure."

The doge reached for his arm. "We shall anticipate your return," he said. "I'll ban every Fiorentini in the city, if necessary."

"That *might* be sufficient to keep our wives out of danger," Marcello said with a wry grin.

"It's a start," Luca said under his breath to me. "Every city is better without Fiorentini about."

The doge and dogaressa turned to us. "Thank you for allowing us to host your nuptials," the doge said, kissing my hand and then covering it with his. "It was a delight to witness it."

"Indeed," added the dogaressa. "The city shall speak of nothing else for weeks."

"You made it far more memorable than I could've ever imagined," I said. "And the gift of this beautiful ship—it's astonishing, truly."

"The least we could do," said the doge. "Return with Lord and Lady Forelli when they come to present their *daughter* to our court," he added. His tone brooked no argument, but his face was benevolent and merry.

"We shall," I said, with a curtsy.

"Go with God," said the dogaressa. "May the winds be in your favor and your marriage fruitful."

"*Grazie mille*," Luca said, bowing to kiss her hand. We turned to Caterina to say farewell, and afterward Luca helped me across the short, steep gangplank to our new ship, where my parents, Gabi and Marcello, and most of our knights awaited. Nicolo lo Grato, Caterina's brother, stood at the helm, looking surprisingly un-hungover. Had he changed his ways in light of this new duty as our ship's captain?

He grinned and kissed both my cheeks. "Lady Forelli," he said. "Congratulations. There is nothing but smooth seas before us. You shall be home before you know it."

"I hope so," I said, turning to my husband with a smile. But it faded as I noted Luca's furrowed brow and tense search of those on board before turning his eyes toward the crowd. I stiffened.

"What is it?" I asked under my breath, following his gaze.

"Orazio and Galileo. They were to be here by now. Falito and Baldarino went to fetch them."

I took a deep breath and continued looking for our cousins among the throngs while smiling and waving as if we were doing nothing more than saying our farewells. Long minutes passed. The doge was onto us, aware that something was awry, that we should've cast off already. He turned to say something in the nearest Ducale knight's ear.

That was when Falito broke through the crowd, red-faced and breathless. Baldarino was right behind him. "They're gone!" Falito panted. He pointed to the lagoon, to a small ship, her sail full, a Guelph cross flapping in the wind upon her flag. "They have them!"

The Fiorentini.

Since they couldn't get to us, they'd nabbed the closest Betarrinis they could...

Galileo and Orazio.

CHAPTER 23

GABRIELLA

"Cast off!" Nicolo cried.

"Aye, Captain," called the sailor nearest the ropes.

Falito and Baldarino jumped aboard, even as the ropes were pulled in from the docks.

"They've taken those you pledged would be safe," Lia called to the doge, appealing to him. After all, he had promised their lives to her in exchange for meeting his challenge. "They're getting away with them!"

"Not for long," bit out the older man. He turned to two men beside him. "Send three of our fastest ships after them at once!"

We were moving out already, sliding out of the docks, the crisp, new, creamy sail filling with the morning breeze.

"Lord Forelli! I suggest you remain here while this is resolved!" cried the doge.

"Begging your pardon, Serenissimo," Marcello called back, after a quick look at me for confirmation. "But when our own are in crisis, it is our way to go to them. We welcome your support, but we shall lead the charge."

The doge lifted his chin, as if surprised that his suggestion would be ignored, but he nodded once in acquiescence. He understood Marcello, respected him. I was gratified at the thought, that House Forelli would have such a stance in this powerful man's mind, but as I turned to face the escaping Fiorentini, growing smaller in the distance, my heart raced. I wanted those naval ships right behind us. We might have a chance of overtaking the Fiorentini, but who knew how many men they carried and how difficult it would be to wrestle away our guys. If we could surround them, convince them that their treachery was hopeless...send them home with their tails tucked between their legs, all the better.

I seethed with anger, that they would sink to such measures. After yesterday...After *everything*, really.

Another sail was unfurled by the five Venetian sailors aboard who would man this ship for us as far as Ancona, and we picked up speed.

"It will be a couple of hours," Nicolo said, "before we overtake them. But overtake them we will." His lips clamped with the pledge.

I looked back. Behind us were the three ships, sails full, Venezia's lion on their flags. *It feels good to have lions behind us,* I thought, *She-Wolves though we are.* I don't know why I was surprised at their speed—their ability to be at sea so quickly. Venezia had the strongest navy in the world.

The *Sea-Wolf* was fast, but we carried a full load. It took an hour to get close enough to see the men aboard the boat we chased.

"We need to get to them before they get to Rimini!" Luca called to the captain. Rimini, I assumed, was the closest port to Firenze. But they'd have to travel overland too—

"We're utilizing every bit of sail we have," returned Nicolo.

"What if it's a trap?" Luca asked Marcello, glancing over at us. "Another attempt to capture Gabi and Lia?"

Marcello shook his head, hands on hips. He looked heroic, a stray curl blowing in the wind. Strong. "I do not think that is the way of it. But just in case..." He looked to me. "Gabriella, I want you belowdecks when we finally reach them. And under no circumstance," he added, lifting a finger to both me and Lia, "do I want either of you without guard."

I shifted, swallowing my irritation. What was I, five? But I knew his concern was fueled by the attack yesterday, and by my pregnancy. "Agreed," I said. Did Lia count as a "guard"?

"Look!" Dad cried, facing the Fiorentini ship, a few hundred yards ahead of us. As one, we all turned.

A fight had broken out on board the enemy ship, and a figure plummeted to the water. The man who had fallen overboard flailed in the waves behind the ship for a moment, then disappeared below and did not emerge again. My heart hammered. "Did that man just—?"

"Yes," Mom murmured, beside me. "Few of them know how to swim. Even the sailors..."

I looked in horror to the swirling water, eddying in rounds of bubbles and waves as we passed. As much as I hated the Fiorentini—hated how they constantly needled us—watching a man die in such a pointless way was horrifying.

Lia cried out, bringing a fisted hand to her mouth, and I looked across the sea again.

We were closer, now. Close enough to see Galileo wrestling with a man, leaning backward over the rail as the Fiorentini knight choked him. I held my breath, as if the man's hands were around my own neck instead.

"C'mon, *c'mon...*" His attacker arched his back, as if hit, and fell away, and we thought we glimpsed Orazio with a sword.

Lia and I shouted, rooting for them. In that moment, it was as if we were in the fight, as we had been so many times before. And our guys—our future-cousins, what kind of chance did they have? Did Orazio know what to do with that sword? Did they know a little Taekwondo, at least?

And then Galileo was at the rail again, rolling over, all legs and somersaulting—

Lia, Mom and I let out a collective scream.

He emerged behind the Fiorentini ship, and the wrestling on their deck ceased as Orazio was grabbed before he could leap overboard, too. Two men lifted bows and began shooting at Galileo, now bobbing in the water behind them, swimming toward us. Arrows sliced the water to his right.

"Nay!" cried Mom.

"Evangelia!" growled Luca.

She was already on the move, reaching for her bow and arrow. But the ship was still just a little out of range. Her first arrow landed ten feet shy of the nearest archer. "Get us closer, Nicolo!" she cried.

The Fiorentini kept shooting at Galileo, but he dived underwater.

"Good man," muttered Marcello. "Stay out of sight just a little longer..."

But now my brain was practically tearing in two. We had to try and rescue Galileo. But that meant dropping sail and letting Orazio slip out of sight with the Fiorentini...

"The Venezians shall continue the chase," Marcello said, as if reading my mind. "They have the numbers to overpower them. We must fish your cousin from the sea."

I nodded. It was the only logical choice, really.

Nicolo steered directly toward our cousin, who continued to rise to the surface, take a deep breath of air, and submerge again.

Lia's next arrow struck the side of the Fiorentini ship and we heard a man cry out. She hadn't hit him. But she'd scared him, buying Galileo precious seconds. Both archers backed away from the edge, watching as Lia nocked another arrow. Had they been in the piazza in Venezia? Had they seen what she could do?

She fired. And this one hit a man in the shoulder, making him wheel backward, exposing Orazio, blood on his face, hands tied behind his back. Seeing him wounded, close enough now to make out his panicked expression, made my blood boil again.

"Man in the water, coming fast!" cried a sailor from atop a sail's crossbeam.

Everyone but I leaned over the edge of the ship, reaching out with hands or ropes or sticks, hoping to grasp Galileo's hand and fish him from the sea. I backed up to the rear of the boat, looking around for something I could use to help.

"Here he comes!" cried Mom.

The entire ship leaned with the collective weight of everyone on one side.

But the waves were at just the wrong angle. I could see it. See how Galileo was struggling to swim closer, unable to reach anything we offered him.

One by one, the sailors and my family groaned in a cascade of frustration as we passed him. He was almost out of reach when I grabbed hold of a round of rope that had been used to tie us to the docks and wrenched it over the rail, hoping, hoping, hoping it might reach him.

I leaned over, wincing, as my belly muscles protested the sudden action. But I heard a shout of hope, then another of victory, and turned my head to see my cousin's hands on the rope, his face rising above the water for air, as the *Sea-Wolf* slowed atop the bobbing waves to reel in her prized fish.

CHAPTER 24

EVANGELIA

The men hauled him in as the Venetians passed us, still in pursuit of the Fiorentini. In the distance, we could see the small port of Rimini, clinging to steep, faded-green hills that plunged into the blue-green sea.

"Gabi," I said, wrapping an arm around my sister's waist.

"I'm okay," she said, rising and wiping her brow. "But that was probably more than I ought to have done."

"I'll say," Mom responded, reproving. Gabi had been instructed more than once not to lift anything over twenty pounds. That rope she'd thrown had to be about forty. "You all right?"

"I'm fine," she said. "And it was worth it," she said with a grin, gesturing to the edge. We all turned as Galileo was hauled aboard, bringing half the Adriatic with him.

"Orazio," he panted as a puddle spread at his feet. "Orazio!" he cried, going to the rail. He turned crazed, brown eyes on us. "They plan to flay him alive in Firenze's piazza! We must save him!"

"We will." Marcello clamped a hand on his shoulder. "The Venetians will overtake them—or at least be right behind them. And we shall be directly behind *them*."

"Rimini is far more friendly to the Fiorentini than they are to the Sienese," Luca said, pacing, as the sailors rushed to haul up sail again.

"Yet Rimini bows to Venezia," Marcello returned. "God has smiled. We shall join in the hunt for Orazio and take down Barbato and Foraboschi, once and for all. This ends today." He looked at Gabi as if he made this promise to her alone. He was as done with the constant threat from those guys as we were.

"They wouldn't truly flay him," I said to Luca, my eyes narrowing in horror.

He wrapped an arm around my shoulders and led me a few steps away from Galileo. "To get to what he knows? To elicit a story that would help turn the people more firmly against the She-Wolves? Yes, yes they would. We must get to Orazio and free him first. Send him and his brother home, to *Normandy*. Before they put you and Gabriella at any further risk. You, my love," he paused to tip up my chin with his knuckle, "must carry on. To Ancona. There you shall find safe passage overland to the castello. And there we shall meet you. With your cousin in hand."

I looked up at him in dismay. We were separating? Going on alone? And yet I saw that we had little choice. He would send the knights with us to keep us safe, while utilizing the Venetian knights to help him take down the Fiorentini, once and for all.

I grabbed Luca's hand. "Without Orazio..." I said, looking back to Galileo.

"I understand. Galileo will be stranded. We'll bring him home, Lia," Luca promised.

We were close enough to see people and horses on shore. The docks of the small port were taking shape, and the Fiorentini were moving in far too quickly, with too many sails still hoisted high. Men on the docks were yelling, waving at them. Did they intend to crash ashore?

In shock, we watched as the keel caught and the whole boat turned—like a ballerina on her toe—and then laid down on her side.

"Orazio!" Galileo shouted in panic. Luca and Marcello held him back, worried he might jump out and swim for his brother.

The bottom of the boat blocked us from seeing who survived, who jumped, who was now swimming for shore. But knowing Barbato and Foraboschi, I didn't doubt they had survived. Rats could swim, right? Brief hope lit my heart that in the melee, Orazio might escape. But then we saw them. Four Fiorentini were dragging him along on the beach, waving away the people who came to them thinking they needed assistance of some kind.

The Venetians headed toward the docks, dropping sail, unwilling to scuttle the doge's ships as the Fiorentini had done with theirs. And we followed suit, dropping sail again to slow our speed for the approach, moving at such an agonizing pace toward the docks that I thought I might scream. Meanwhile, we were forced to watch the action on the beach and alongside the docks like a terrible slow-motion video. They purchased two horses and stole three more at sword-point. We saw them load Orazio, bound and bleeding, on one and disappear down the road toward town.

And the dock was still a hundred yards away.

Luca turned toward me and kissed me, holding my face. "Take your sister and parents home. Go only to the castello. Nowhere else. There I will find you. Understood?"

I nodded. There was a new nuance to his tone—a sense of protection, a right to make certain demands—that I could only attribute to our new marriage. "Take close care, love," I whispered. "Hasten home to us."

"I want to go with you," Galileo said to Luca, eyes clouded with fear and fury.

"Nay," Luca said, nothing in his eyes telling the man he'd consider his argument. "We shall travel faster without you. And if you are recaptured…"

"What if *you* are captured?"

Luca grinned at him. "By a Fiorentini? I think not. They've tried many a time before. Go to our castello. Rest. We shall bring your brother to you as quickly as we can."

"Thank you," Galileo said, still clearly struggling with the idea, but accepting that Luca's plan was best. He offered his arm and Luca took it.

"'Tis nothing. You are family. *My* family now," Luca said, looking back to me. He wrenched himself away, grabbed hold of his sword, and prepared with Marcello to leap to the docks as soon as they could possibly do so. Falito and Otello were right behind them.

I went over to stand beside Gabi, and together we watched as our husbands jumped over the rail to the very end of the dock, running as soon as they found their footing. The others were but three steps behind.

"Go with God," Gabi whispered as they ran up the hill to a corral with horses, the Venetians ahead of them.

"M'lady?" asked Nicolo of Gabi, eyeing the beaches warily. "Shall we depart? Best to be away from these docks, given the company these sailors keep."

"Yes," she said, her hand on her belly, misery etching her face. Clearly, she'd prefer to wait here, or at least watch until they were out of sight, but the captain was right. This town was full of men who wouldn't hesitate to turn us over to the Fiorentini for a bag of gold.

"Make way!" called the captain. "Haul sail! To Ancona!"

"To Ancona!" echoed the other sailors. And within minutes, we were back at sea again.

We made port as the sun set in the west over the rolling hills of Umbria. Nicolo arranged for a month's mooring for our new boat, as well as a guard at night—there were more than a few who might consider trying to steal so fine vessel, freshly launched from Venezia. We paid the sailors who had manned the *Sea-Wolf*—enough for our passage, a couple nights' lodging in Ancona, and passage on another ship back to Venezia. But Nicolo refused payment.

"It has been an honor to serve you," he said, with a slight bow. "Should you find you need a crew for the *Sea-Wolf*, send me word, and we shall come to you."

"*Grazie, Capitano*," I said. For as much as I'd written him off as a drunkard and playboy, I'd been impressed with him on this trip. He'd been a sober and strong leader while on the job. Maybe he only needed the right opportunity, the weight of responsibility, in order to shine. But then, didn't we all?

Dad and Celso had arranged for overland transportation, but with the setting sun, we elected to spend the night in Ancona. We hadn't come all this way in order to be caught on the road home, and we were down to eight knights guarding us. The port was generally friendly territory to the Sienese, but there'd been some unrest of late—with the pope trying to assert more power over the region—and as much as we just wanted to be home, we knew it was best to wait until morning. Besides, I was worried about Gabi. She needed to rest. So did Galileo—exhausted and bruised as he was. And there was a mountain pass between us and home—it'd take all day to get there.

So we found a comfy inn and put our own blankets atop the moth-eaten versions they offered; and just as I was fretting that I'd never get to sleep, wondering where Luca was and how they were faring in overtaking the Fiorentini, I did just that. Fell fast asleep.

I awakened feeling guilty for how easy it had been, sleeping. I sat up and stretched, and saw that Gabi was at the small window, staring out at sea.

"I wouldn't mind it," she said. "After the baby is born and the..." she dropped her tone, "*thing* is past. It'd be good, you know? To sail along these shores on the *Sea-Wolf*, maybe go across to Croatia. And up to what one day will be Slovenia. It's supposed to be gorgeous."

"It can be pretty rough around the Adriatic, I hear," I said. "Who knows what the politics will be like. We'd have to be in fighting shape."

"We will be," she replied, staring into my eyes.

"You're so sure we won't get it. The...*thing*. You, the hypochondriac of the family."

"I'm not sure," she said, looking out again. "I just can't imagine our future here without any of us in it. So I refuse to consider the thought."

I padded over to her and looped my arm through hers and looked down the cliff to the blue, blue sea. "It *is* really beautiful," I said, my tone wistful. "But come, let's grab some breakfast and set out for Castello Forelli. I don't know about you, but I think home will be the most welcome sight of all."

She smiled at me, her brown eyes glowing with warmth. "Eager to move your stuff into Luca's quarters?"

"A bit. And maybe I can stash a bunch of his stuff before he gets home. You know, make a little more room for mine."

"Ahh, yes. The bachelor days are over. No more giant TV screen and old futon couch. No more framed football jersey..."

I giggled with her. "He has his own versions. Armor that he hasn't worn for years but still holds on to. A horsehair couch with a dozen bald spots."

She laughed. "He loves you so much, you could probably toss it all and he wouldn't care. As long as you are in the room when he gets back."

I smiled, and my heart skipped a beat thinking of him coming home, of us sharing his spacious quarters. As captain of the guard, only Marcello and Gabi had bigger rooms. And his had a lovely little view of the northeastern hills, as well as a view of the courtyard on the other side...

I turned to hurriedly dress, but in my mind, I was already in the castello, making his room *ours*. Beginning our life together as husband and wife. Retiring together to a....*Hmmm, we're going to need a bigger bed!* I'd glimpsed it a couple of times, from the hallway, and it was fairly small. Not that he'd complain about that. The thought made me smile.

Oh, hurry, Luca. Please, please find Orazio. Please be safe. And please return to me soon.

CHAPTER 25

GABRIELLA

B y the time we neared home that night, I honestly didn't think I
could be more relieved. Riding horseback all day was never pleas-
ant, but I'd clearly gotten to a point of discomfort in my pregnancy that
made me seriously consider bailing on riding horses altogether until I
was not pregnant any longer. My belly and boobs bounced too much.
My back ached. My hips burned. And that was just the beginning of the
things I was ready to whine about.

We'd run into one band of knights who hassled us a bit on a road
they claimed they owned. But when the Forelli name was mentioned,
they reluctantly backed off, allowing us to pass. The Marche region was
full of little kingdoms, and it was good to cross the mountains and know
that on the downward slope more and more friends of the Forellis would
surround us.

As long as we stayed south of the Fiorentini border.

My heart sped up every time I thought of the guys giving chase to
the Fiorentini, closer and closer to Firenze's territory. Again and again,
I pushed aside horrible thoughts of them getting captured, and what
we would do if that happened. At one point, Dad rode up beside me,
took one look at my face and said, "Rehearsing your troubles, Gabi, is
the worst way to use your energy. Take it as it comes. Don't imagine the
worst. If you have to imagine, imagine the best."

I gave him a grateful smile and focused on that the rest of the way home. Every time I thought about Marcello being struck by an arrow, I pictured his chest plate keeping it from piercing his skin. Every time I thought about my love getting captured, I turned it into him capturing Barbato and Foraboschi. Every time I thought about him dying, not living to see his baby, I imagined him holding our child in his big, strong hands. And every time I saw Galileo look down the road behind us, as if he wished his brother was miraculously approaching, I imagined him running down the road to greet Orazio when our guys brought him home.

Galileo edged his horse closer to mine. "Gabriella," he began earnestly, "I can't begin to thank you and your husband enough. For negotiating our release in Venezia. For going after Orazio..."

"We could do no other. You are our family," I said. "And you wouldn't be facing such trouble if it wasn't for us. We're the ones who led you into that tomb in the first place, right?" I asked quietly, so only he could hear.

He considered this. "Stories of the lost Betarrinis, their ties to Etruscan ruins...ancestors of our own. It was pretty irresistable."

I sighed. How many others might follow? Or would these guys be the only ones with the right genetic makeup and smarts to figure out the time tunnel? It made my head hurt, thinking about it. We could mess history up big-time, we Betarrinis, if the clan kept showing up from who-knew-when to disrupt medieval life. Dad had enough trouble corralling us and keeping us from "infecting history," as he put it. How would he control a bunch of time-traveling Betarrinis?

At last we turned onto a road that screamed "home" to me, and I barely resisted the urge to kick my mare into a gallop. We were only a mile away, then a half mile, and finally, we could see her crenellated walls, her fine towers, and her golden flags whipping in the stiff November breeze. The flags were all the brighter against the dark, brooding clouds. All day we'd worried we'd be caught in a downpour; thankfully, the clouds clung to their heavy loads.

The men atop our walls cheered when they saw us. A call went out to open the gates and by the time we reached them, they felt like the welcoming arms of a mother. We entered and the gray-bearded Captain Pezzati came to me to help me dismount. I wobbled, my legs feeling so weary they were like jello, and he reached back out to steady me.

"M'lady?"

"Nay, I'm only weary."

He insisted on taking my arm until my mother could tend to me, which she did, confidently escorting me through the crowd of welcoming servants and around the Great Hall to our doorway, which led up to our rooms. "Cook," she called over her shoulder, "please send up some hot soup and bread."

"Straight away, m'lady," she said, practically bursting with excitement to see to her task.

I could hear the captain calling for knights to assume formation as we entered the turret. I knew his plan was to send out patrols to hopefully intercept our men returning home—and assist them, should any Fiorentini be giving chase. He'd send them out in groups of six and keep the guys that Marcello and Luca trusted most here with us, as they had instructed. But he was as anxious as I to see the Forellis *all* safely home.

I stopped partway up the stairs and breathed fast, gripping my belly.

"Gabi?" Mom asked.

"Contraction," I panted, feeling the muscles bind from my back forward. "I think."

She frowned. "It's probably just a Braxton-Hicks. Your body beginning to prepare for labor by pretending it's the real deal, essentially. But it's early for that. We need to get you to bed and make sure it's nothing more."

"Give me just a moment," I said, lifting a finger. After a minute, my muscles seemed to relax and I could breathe again. "Sheesh, this pregnancy stuff is a laugh a minute, isn't it?"

She laughed under her breath. "Just wait."

"You sure know how to encourage a girl, Mom."

Her strong arm tightened around my waist and together we made it up the last of the stairs and into my room. I sighed with relief as Mom immediately began to unlace my overdress and unpin my hair. *What would I do without her?* I thought, gratefulness swelling in my heart, despite my exhaustion. There was no fire in the corner fireplace, but the room still felt warm to me. At least it was warmer than it was outside...and once I was in the big bed, under the wool blankets, I knew I'd be toasty within minutes. And hopefully asleep before I quite recognized the fact.

I sank to the edge of the bed, aware that I was still in my road-grubby shift yet not caring. Giacinta arrived with a bucket of water, filled a basin, and carried it over to me with a cloth.

"I'm so glad you're home safe and sound, m'lady," she said.

"As am I." I took the cloth from her hand, dipped it, wrung it out and washed my face, neck and armpits.

"Is Lord Forelli returning soon, too?" she asked carefully.

"As soon as he can. He's in pursuit of some Fiorentini who tried to kidnap our kin."

"Your kin?" she said in horror.

I remembered Galileo, then, with regret. I'd felt so faint... "Giacinta, do you know if my cousin, Galileo, was given a room?"

"Oh yes, m'lady. Lady Evangelia saw to him."

"Oh, good," I said, yawning.

"Do not fret over anything," Mom said. "We shall cover the needs of the castello until you regain your strength." She turned to answer a knock at the door. It was a servant girl with the soup and bread she'd requested of Cook.

"I can't eat, Mom," I said, starting to slump toward the pillows, already thinking of how lovely it would be to fall asleep in my own bed...

"Uh-uh!" she cried, grabbing hold of my arm and forcing me to sit up straight again. "Three bites of soup and half this bread. A cup of water. Then, *then* you can go to sleep."

Giacinta started to work on my hair, combing it out, and the tug of tangles and knots sent little shots of adrenaline through my body. Grumpily, I lifted the wooden bowl to my lips and took my first bite. It was made of squash and sausage and it was delicious. Tasting it made me aware I was hungry. Okay, starving, actually. Soon, I'd gobbled the whole thing down, and in between bites, eaten a good portion of the bread.

"Good, good," Mom crooned. "Feel better?"

"Mm-hmm," I agreed. She let me lie down on the bed as Giacinta stoked the fire in the hearth and then slipped from the room with my empty trencher and bowl. Mom moved to the corner table, uncorked a bottle of wine and poured herself a glass. I felt guilty. She had to be starving herself.

"Mom...you should go eat. I didn't even offer you any..."

"No. I'll see to that in a moment. How's the belly?" she asked, overly casual. Clearly not wanting me to freak. "Any more contractions?"

"Nah. I think it's just that I kinda overdid it today."

"You kinda overdid the whole last week."

I grinned at her, my face half-hidden in the pillow. "I dunno. Political intrigue. Watching Lia zip-line. Fireworks. Crushing crowds. A murder attempt. A wedding. A race across the sea. A drowning man saved. A day-long horseback ride." I turned over, with my hands interlaced behind my head. "Just your average week in Italia."

She smiled and reached over to push some hair out of my face and stroke my forehead and cheek. "Sure you're okay? It really has been a lot for any girl to deal with, let alone a pregnant girl."

"Just tired," I said with another yawn. "But...would you have Lia come and spend the night with me?"

"Good idea," she said. "I'll send her up."

She was almost out of the room when I started. "Mom?"

"Yes?"

"Are you as glad to be home as I am?"

"Gladder, maybe," she said.

I don't know why, but it made my heart smile to hear her say the fake word. "I love you, Mom."

"And I love you, Gabriella. Sleep well. On the morrow, your man will get home."

"Promise?" I asked, knowing she couldn't possibly, but wanting to hear her say it anyway.

"Promise," she said.

CHAPTER 26

GABRIELLA

B ut they didn't come home the next day.

Or the next.

Or the next.

Half out of her mind, my sister spent hours prowling the parapet walkways, as if she could *will* our husbands to emerge from the woods that stood between us and Firenze. Her thoughts were my own, and we gradually steered clear of each other because it just riled us both up to feel the other's angst. And Galileo was as crazed as we were. Several times I saw the knights physically keep him from setting out.

On the fourth day, Captain Pezzati sent out additional scouts and patrols. Three men were equipped to be gone three days, their mission to sneak into Fiorentini territory and find out what they could.

On the fifth day, I awakened early, dressed, and, after pacing my room for an hour, went down to the small chapel. Father Tomas was there—as I knew he was three times a day—on his knees, praying before a tiny altar and cross. I knelt beside him and began my own daily prayer, which amounted to little more than, *Please, please bring them home. Please, God. Please?*

I felt Tomas stir beside me and a rush of cool air as his warm body left my side. I looked up and over my shoulder.

"Do you think this will be the day?" I asked, my words sounding plaintive and weak to my own ears.

He turned and put a hand on my shoulder, his round fingers like sausages. "I do believe it, yes. They are surely well, Gabriella. They shall return to us as soon as they can. Trust in our God, who sees them right now, just as he sees us."

I nodded and stared at the small cross and crucifix on the altar. Was it true? Could he see all of us? Did he truly have the capacity to care for all of us, all at once?

I blinked heavily, feeling a new weariness behind my eyes. I hadn't slept well since we'd returned, missing my husband's reassuring presence in our bed.

"I...I'm afraid, Tomas," I said, rising and moving toward where he stood in the middle of the small, arch-covered room. Pews were apparently a later invention that I very much wished we had.

He studied me with kind eyes and I felt *warmed* by his presence—known, loved. I could see why Adela, Luca's sister, was falling for him.

"M'lady, do you know that God loves you? That he wants the best for you?"

"I do. But does he not want the best for everyone? And yet still, we see heartache and loss every day."

"Indeed," he said thoughtfully. "But our duty is to believe in the best, hope for the best, until that day we must face our own trial. Until then, we must not succumb to the devil's claim on our lives. He prowls about seeking to undermine us. Pressing us to give sway to our worst fears, rather than trust in our Creator. Did he not bring you here, to Toscana?"

I nodded.

"Did he not bring you to Castello Forelli? To Marcello?"

In more ways than you know.

He held my gaze. "Trust the One who brought you together with your husband. The One who shall see you reunited."

I sighed. "Thank you, Tomas."

He shook his head and gave me a small smile. "Not at all, m'lady. It is my good pleasure to offer you succor, meager though it may be." He clapped his hands. "Today is the day. Our friends will return."

"You believe so?"

"With everything in me."

EVANGELIA

Gabs told me all about it. What Tomas had said. It kindled my hopes that afternoon, and I felt a bit lighter as I forced myself to try and read in the den for a time and chat with the knights on the wall, rather than simply stride past them, jaw clenched with anxiety.

They hadn't come home as Tomas had believed they would. And as darkness fell, my stress doubled down. Was I to only share so brief a time with Luca as his wife? Was he lost to me forever?

It was Mom who found me up on the wall, well after night had fallen. I'd donned a woolen cloak, but still my teeth chattered in the face of a brisk wind that smelled of winter. Was Luca warm this night? Or lying somewhere, wounded?

"Lia," Mom said lowly, so many other words lingering beneath my name. *It's time. Leave it until morning. You need to sleep.*

"I know," I said. But I didn't move. She stayed beside me, silent. Waiting. Just reassuring me by presence alone.

"If Gabi wasn't pregnant," I muttered, "she'd be out there. On the search for them. I should've gone with the knights."

"Even Gabi has resigned herself to staying here, where her husband knew she'd be safe. Where he'll find her just as soon as he can get to her. Just like Luca will be hoping to find you."

I heaved a long sigh. "Why do they not send word?"

"Because, for some reason, they cannot." She turned, so that her back was to the wall, and so that she could see my face. "Luca and Marcello know that you and Gabs must be mad with worry. They would not put you through that unless they couldn't do anything else."

I nodded. Crazy thoughts went through my head. A litany of *This is why you shouldn't have gotten married... See? You marry the guy and now you're probably pregnant with his baby and he's dead... Maybe if I hadn't married him, he'd be here, near me... He was so determined to save his wife's cousin, he probably did something stupid... It's all your fault, Lia. All your fault! If you hadn't come...If you hadn't stayed...*

"Come here," she said, opening her arms. I sank into them, holding myself stiffly at first and then gradually relinquishing my pride.

"I'm so afraid, Mom," I said, the words clogging around a ball in my throat. "What if he's hurt? Or...worse?" I gasped with a sob.

"He's not, Lia," she said. "He's simply doing what he set out to do. To free Orazio and bring him home. Which must've proven more difficult than they hoped."

I nodded again, clinging to her words like new islands of hope in a turbulent sea. "Tomorrow? Do you think they'll come home tomorrow, Mom?"

She pulled back and looked into my eyes. "On the morrow, daughter," she said, using medieval jargon to try and set me back on track. "I'm certain of it. Now go and get some sleep. You don't want your new husband to come home to you looking like you haven't slept for five nights, right?"

I laughed through my tears. "I *haven't* slept in five nights."

"Yes, well," she said, brushing my chin with her long, thin fingers. "You can fix that. Go. Sleep. Rather than stand out here, catching your death of cold. And dream of the morrow," she said, leaning closer to me, "the morrow, when your sweet husband returns to you at last."

She was right. Feeling beaten and a little guilty for abandoning my post—and making Falito promise to wake me if they gained word about them—I went to bed. Mom came with me. Either as moral support or to make sure I actually got in bed, I wasn't sure, but her presence reassured me. She helped me undress and slide beneath the cold covers, tucking a foot warming stone near my feet. When I was settled, she leaned down and kissed my forehead.

"It's been some years since you tucked me in."

"Too much?" she asked, hovering.

"Nah. Times like this—every girl needs her mama."

She brushed some hair away from my eyes and then clasped her hands. "Waiting like this," she whispered, "is the hardest thing of all. You are not alone, Lia. Dad and I are praying for them too."

"I know," I said. "Thanks, Mom."

"Anytime, kiddo. Good night."

"Good night."

Gradually, sleep overtook me. I was dreaming, dreaming of being back in Venezia. Of being in the room I'd slept in with Luca, but I was alone, and there was a man creeping in...and then another...and still another. I couldn't move. It was as if my body was frozen, stuck, covered in mud. I tried to cry out as the first man neared me, hovering, hovering, then touching my face and hair...

My belated scream seemed to break me free from my odd body-prison and I lashed out, aiming for the man's face. He caught my wrist, then my other, his grip iron strong. "Evangelia," he said urgently. *"Evangelia!"*

I faltered. The voice was familiar. Known.

"L-Luca?" I stammered, still trying to rise fully from my fog. Was this some trick? Was it truly him? It couldn't be him. He was gone...

"Evangelia," he said, his grip easing as I calmed. He lifted one hand to stroke my face. "It's all right, love. I've returned to you."

A knight pounded at the door. "Captain Forelli!" came his muffled voice. He pounded again on the door...our door. I was in Luca's rooms. Our quarters now.

"All is well!" Luca called over his shoulder, his eyes intent on me. "The lady simply had a night terror." Half of his own face was in shadow—the only light in our room one lone candle—and in my stupor, I still struggled to free myself of the doubt that it was really him.

"La-Luca?" I said again.

"Laluca?" he said, a wry grin transforming his beloved face from concern to laughter. "Don't let the men hear you say that. I'll never hear the end of it."

"It's you," I said in a whisper, reaching up to touch his face.

"In the flesh," he said, waggling his eyebrows. "And speaking of flesh...if you're quite past your fright..." He moved in to kiss me, and I welcomed him, letting the warmth of him—the manly scent of him cover me, remind me, convince me that I wasn't dreaming.

But when his kisses deepened, I put both hands to his chest. "Wait."

He backed off a few inches, waiting.

"Did *all* return with you? Were you able to find Orazio?"

"Yes, my love, yes," he said, placing tiny kisses across my cheek, over the hill of my nose and then on to the other cheek and ear.

"Are all well? Was anyone wounded?"

"All are well," he whispered, his breath hot in my ear. "No one wounded beyond repair." He began to plant tiny kisses down my neck.

"And Marcello?"

He paused and looked up at me. "Are you truly asking about my cousin just as I prepare to make love to you?"

"Is he well?" I insisted. I needed to know. So I could stop worrying on behalf of Gabi, too.

"He is well." He sat up and folded his arms. "Anything else you must know before you allow me to bed you?"

I smiled. "Nay." And then I opened my arms to him.

He needed no further invitation.

But as I returned his kisses, I laughed and cried all at once.

"What is this?" he asked, noticing my tears, pausing. "Am I hurting you?"

"Nay, nay," I said with a contented sigh, placing a hand on either side of his beloved face. "I am only so glad, so relieved to have you home, husband, that it makes me cry."

"Ahh," he said, peering at me as if confused. As if he didn't quite trust that I told him the truth. "Women are truly strange, wonderful creatures, aren't they?"

"I do not know," I said, still smiling/crying/sniffling. "I am one."

"That you are," he whispered huskily, apparently deciding it was okay to proceed. "That...you most delightedly...are."

CHAPTER 27

EVANGELIA

I awakened in Luca's bed. *Our bed.* And this time, he was there with
me.

I laid on my side, one arm tucked beneath my head, staring and
staring at the wonder that was my husband. The man I almost lost by
turning away from him. The man I refused to marry. The man I worried
would never return to me. How could I ever have denied him? He was
wonderful. Funny and thoughtful and loving. And dang cute, too.

His shoulder-length hair curved in waves on the pillow. He hadn't
let me cut it for months, having grown weary of the men's chiding him
for his "sheep-shorn" hair. There was a golden-brown sheen of morning
stubble across his chin and cheeks, and I could see the pulse in his neck.
I loved his nose—long and straight, flaring in perfect nostrils. And his
lips...those lips that formed words to cajole me into laughter or whisper
seductive things in my ears...

Luca's eyes blinked once, twice, and he turned his head to look at
me, as if he'd sensed my stare. "Good morning, Wife. See something you
like?"

"Something I like very much," I said with a small smile.

"No more than the feast that I see before me."

"A feast?" I asked lifting a brow. "I don't know if I care to be
compared to food."

"Nay, nay," he said, his own brow knitting in soft complaint. "There is no finer comparison to a woman. Besides, what more might a man need besides a fine meal inside his belly and a fine wife to warm his bed?" He shook his head a little. "I can think of nothing else."

I smiled. "A roof," I said benignly. "A fire. Clothes."

He let out a scoffing sound and reached out to touch my cheek. "Those things are nice, yes. But if I had you, and I had food, I'd always consider myself a blessed man."

I grinned. "Tell me of it, Luca. Why did it take so long to wrest Orazio away?"

The humor drained from his face, and he flopped over to his back. He opened his arm and glanced back at me.

"Come closer. If I am to tell tales rather than think of other things, I shall at least have you by my side."

I smiled and eased over to him, settling my cheek in the crook of his arm and chest. It felt good to be beside him, to reach my arm across his torso and hold him even as he held me. His right arm, beneath my head, left his hand free to curve up and around my head. He stroked my temple as he stared at the ceiling of our room. Unlike Gabi and Marcello's, it was naught but rough wooden slats and beams. But it felt warm to me, welcome.

"They knew we trailed them, of course," he began. "They took shelter in the first town they could, convincing those within to protect them. It wasn't a heavily fortified town, but there was a decent wall and gates—and too many men for us to conquer. Nor did we wish to invite greater conflict with Firenze."

"A wise choice," I murmured.

"They tarried for days, likely hoping that we would give up and depart. But we did not simply sit there. We became familiar with the road they would need to cross when they finally tried for Firenze. And we laid in wait for the local messengers they sent with missives to Firenze, hoping for reinforcements."

"You killed them?" I asked in consternation.

"Nay, nay. We simply...relieved them of their responsibility. They were told to hide in the woods until it was all over. Our quarrel was not with them, but the men their town harbored. After a couple of days, the Fiorentini knew their missives had not made it through. If they had, men would have answered their call. And the townspeople, agitated when the fourth of their sons did not return, likely were ready to cast them out. They emerged yesterday."

A slow smile spread across his face, and his eyes glinted. "I must say, it was rather delightful. We sprung one trap after another, and within an hour, it was only Barbato and Orazio left."

"Foraboschi is dead?"

"Indeed," he said, practically spitting the word as if he were spitting out the aftertaste of the foul man. "We surrounded them, and Barbato had a knife to Orazio's throat. Your poor cousin was in such poor form that I fretted he might collapse on the evil little man's dagger."

"Orazio?" I said. "He's wounded?" I sat up, my hair falling around my shoulders. I remembered he'd been battered and bleeding days ago on the beach...had they continued to harm him?

"Wounded, yes, but he will recover," Luca said, his eyes drifting down and over me. "Especially once we get him to the tunnel today, right?" He lifted a hand to my face and traced my cheek and neck and shoulder with an uncommonly light touch. "You know how a turn in Normandy can fix a body."

I took a deep breath, remembering it well. Gabi, so near death...

"Still," I said, turning away from him and reaching for my shift. I pulled it over my head and down, ignoring my husband's groan of complaint. "He might need to get there now."

Luca reached out to clasp my wrist. "*Now*-now?"

"I don't know! We need to find out. You told me all were whole and hale last night!"

It was Luca's turn to sigh. "Very well," he said, rubbing his eyes and face. "We'll see off your Norman cousin. But then we return here. To this very room. Agreed? Marcello has relieved me of three days of duty to celebrate our wedding, and I intend to make the most of every hour."

I grinned. "Agreed." I tossed him his shirt and leggings and rose to fetch my bodice and skirt.

It turned out that Orazio was worse off than Luca thought. We found Mom and Dad attending him in the den. He was stripped to the waist, and we could see the dark, ugly bruising that covered his belly like a cloud of poison.

I whipped my head toward Luca. "I thought you said he would be all right!"

"He was! At least he was last night when we returned!"

"He bleeds within," Mom said under her breath as two maids left the room. Luca crossed himself.

"He lost consciousness an hour ago. We'd hoped we could stabilize him overnight, to make it easier today," she said, giving me a meaningful look, "as well as talk to them both a bit before..." Her words trailed off, but I understood. We hadn't had time to make a plan. As much as you could *plan* time travel.

"We'll just have to tell Galileo," I said, my eyes moving to Orazio's brother, passed out in the corner, his face awkwardly against a wall as he slept.

"Lia," Mom said, grabbing my wrist as I moved toward them. "I'm not certain that Orazio will make it," she whispered in English.

"Then we need to get them to the tunnel," I whispered back. "Immediately."

"And how do we do that? Explain that to me. Carrying him out on a stretcher and returning an hour later without him?"

Gabi and Marcello arrived then. "What's up?" she asked in English, joining our circle. Her dark brows arched in concern.

"Orazio's bad," I said. "We've gotta get them to the tunnel. Stat."

"But how will he..." Mom began. "He cannot even stand!"

"Lascia," Marcello said to a knight on guard by the door and another maid, asking them to leave. Both immediately did so, quietly closing the door behind them.

"Cease your use of the foreign tongue," Marcello said to us, lifting a hand to rub his forehead. "Speak in ours."

"We need to get them to the tunnel," Gabi said. "Send them. It shall heal Orazio as it once healed me."

"Were you as bad off as Orazio?" Dad asked doubtfully.

"She was," Marcello said steadily. "Frightfully near death."

I nodded. "He had to put her hand on the print himself."

Dad turned new eyes of respect toward Marcello. "You sent my girl on blind faith?"

"It was our only option," he said, a hint of misery in his eyes at the mere memory.

"She arrived in *Normandy*," Mom said, "with nothing but a scar that looked three years old and a blood stain far fresher."

Dad blanched. He looked to Orazio as Galileo rose. "Then let us get them to it. We'll tell the others we're taking him to a healer." He eyed us all. "It's the truth, of sorts."

Marcello and Luca shared a look, both with hands on their hips. "What shall we tell the men?"

Luca shook his head. "Nothing," he said, shrugging. "We owe them no explanation. We shall send scouts ahead of us, as far as Castello Greco, making certain the road is clear. Then I'll send patrols out with the instructions that anyone not belonging to the castello is to be escorted out of Forelli territory."

"The tongues shall wag," Marcello said.

Luca shrugged again. "The tongues shall wag, regardless."

"We need to move. Now," Dad said, his fingers resting on Orazio's neck, feeling for a pulse. "He fades while we discuss it."

Luca waited on Marcello, and when Marcello nodded, he stepped closer to Orazio. I looked at Gabi. Could we really pull this off? Get him to the tombs, unseen? And get home and come up with some sort of story that everyone would buy? I doubted it. But with another look at the fear on Dad's face, I knew we had to try.

I began covering Orazio up and opened the door to the hall to ask the maid to fetch an additional cloak for Galileo. "We are taking our cousin to a traveling barber-surgeon we met," I said. I turned toward the knight. "Tell the squires in the stables to saddle nine horses."

"Yes, m'lady," he said. I didn't miss that there was just a tiny bit more deference in his tone. Was this what came of becoming Captain Forelli's bride? I didn't know. But I liked it.

We moved Orazio to a hastily made stretcher and Marcello and Luca carried him to the stables themselves. There, Celso and Otello helped them secure it between two horses, a set-up I hadn't seen since the day we brought Gabi home from Roma. Captain Pezzati was arguing softly in a corner with Marcello, clearly perplexed by our plan.

"Enough!" Luca said abruptly, his hand slicing through the air. "It's decided. Simply see it done!"

The elder Pezzati stared at Luca, the ranking captain, his jaw muscles clenching with tension. "Yes, sir," he said, a half second later than was normal. "I shall see it done. May I at least assign four men to attend you?"

"Nay," Marcello and Luca both said at once.

Captain Pezzati eyed one after the other, clearly aware that something odd was coming down, and then turned on his heel and left.

Marcello sighed. He looked to the two knights still in the stables with us. "See that those patrols are thorough in their task," he said.

"Yes, m'lord," said Falito, tense.

Marcello and Luca helped me and Gabi mount. I knew they'd rather we remain here, but they knew we'd never stay. Not when what was about to come down was comin' down. Mom and Dad led the way, exiting the stables and then the outer gates. The entire castello had fallen silent, word obviously spreading that our cousin was nearing death, and we were on a mad, odd quest to get him to an unknown physician. Tomas and Adela watched us go, his arm around her shoulders, questions in their eyes. We ignored them, pretending not to notice.

Outside the gates, Marcello looked up. "We shall return by nightfall."

"Yes, m'lord!" called Otello. "Go with God and may the young Lord Betarrini be saved."

Marcello nodded, and we headed out. As we traveled the well known path toward Castello Greco, once Castello Paratore, I found myself praying for Orazio. It was nothing more than a simple petition—*Please save him, Lord. Please let the tunnel work for them as it worked for us. Please, please, please...* But it gave my heart a focus even as my mind whirled.

The half mile to the riverbed and the climb up the hill to the tombs seemed to take longer than ever. It was cold, our breath fogging before our mouths and from the horses' nostrils. I tugged my cloak closer, shoving away the sensation that it was the cold of death rather than the cold of winter upon us.

But finally we were there, and it appeared as if the Forelli patrols had done well in clearing the way. We'd not encountered another traveler or villager upon the road and timed our entry to the tomb meadow so that the guards on the wall of Castello Greco did not see us. Swiftly, we rolled away the rock at the mouth of Tomb Two and entered, one by one. Luca dragged Orazio in, his hands beneath the man's armpits. Marcello was last. "No one else in sight," he confirmed in a whisper as he straightened inside the narrow passage.

We all looked up to the handprints. "Do they look like the others?" Mom asked Galileo.

"Yes," he said with a nod. "Nearly exact." Faltering a little, he approached them and reached up to the larger print on the left.

I held my breath.

We all held our breath.

"It's warm," he said after a tense moment, relief sending wrinkles to his brow as if he might cry. "Hot," he amended.

Mom and Dad went to him. "You know what to do," Mom said. "We're counting on you."

I squinted, wondering what she meant. Counting on them? For what?

"Do not forget all we spoke of," Dad added.

"I will not," Galileo pledged. "We owe you our lives." He took Dad's arm and pulled him closer to kiss both his cheeks. "You *can* count on us." Quickly, he moved to do the same with Mom. I knew they'd been spending some time together these last days as we awaited the men's return, but what exactly had transpired between them?

"We must make haste," Luca said grimly, his hand on Orazio's neck. "He fades..." He rose, and together with Marcello, they each took an arm over a shoulder and lifted Orazio between them. Marcello took his right hand in his own and lifted it above the print, just as he had Gabi's. Chills ran down my body at the memory.

"Wait!" I cried. "How is it that you did not go with Gabi, last time you held her?"

Everyone froze.

"How is it that you did not travel back in time with us, as Mom and Dad did when they held on to us?" I pressed.

Marcello frowned and looked to Gabi, searching his memory. After a moment, his dark brows lifted. "I believe I held her...but it was as if I offered her." He shook his head, eyes locked on his wife. "I offered her to God. I didn't try to hold her. Keep her."

Gabi nodded slowly, her eyes running across Orazio, who was inhaling in a rasping gasp now. "That's it," she said. "Hold him upright, but do not hold him tightly," she said. "We don't want to lose you, too."

"Nay," I said.

"I understand. Are you ready?" Marcello asked Galileo.

"Thank you, everyone," Galileo said, looking each of us in the eye. "For everything."

"Just go. Live to an old age. And speak not a word of it," Luca said gruffly. "We need no other visitors from *Normandy*."

Orazio began to convulse, a terrible gagging sound coming from his throat. The men struggled to hold him.

Galileo looked to Marcello, panic in his eyes. "*Ora.*" Now.

Marcello dragged Orazio's hand down, fingers splayed, as he had once done with Gabi's.

A blinding light flashed, and we were all pushed back, as if a sonic wave had come through. The sound was like a deep-timbered burst, making our ears pop.

I blinked rapidly, trying to force my eyes to adjust to the semi-darkness again.

The Betarrini boys were gone.

CHAPTER 28

GABRIELLA

We all took a collective breath. Lia had hold of my arm, as if she'd feared I'd fall, but I felt oddly steady on my feet. A smile spread across my face. "We did it."

Dad tucked his head and lifted a hand to the prints where, seconds before, Orazio and Galileo had stood.

"Well, *they* did it," I amended.

He stepped forward and peered at the handprints from inches away, as if there'd be some clue as to their odd power.

"Do you think it will save him?" Marcello asked, turning grave eyes on me. He looked a bit wan, and I understood that he was remembering me disappearing from his arms, as Orazio had just done.

I went to him and wrapped my arms around his muscle-bound torso. "I hope so. I think...I think because they were able to...*travel*, because Orazio yet had that strength in him, he's likely to survive. I imagine even now they're emerging from the tomb, trying to sneak by archeological site guards."

The Betarrini boys had told us that in their time, decades after we'd left, there was nothing inside the tombs. Everything had been removed by archeologists to museums and labs to be examined. But the frescoes had remained. And those prints...They'd not seen them in any other Etruscan tomb find, other than the one they'd used and this one.

"Think they made it back to their time? To the future?" Lia asked. "Or ours?"

Dad scowled at her. "Wonderful. They might not only mess with one segment of history, but another."

"They'll take care," Lia said. "You drilled it into them, right?"

"At least they yet live," I said with a sigh. "The rest is in God's hands."

Dad gave me a long, thoughtful look. "Indeed."

"What now?" I asked Marcello. "If we return right away, everyone will wonder about a physician we trust, so close to the castello. People far and wide might set out after him, in search of a cure for what ails them."

"We tarry a while," he said. He looked around the dome-like tomb. "But not in here. Let us ride a few hours. We shall place rocks on the stretcher so that it appears as if a man is still atop it. If anyone sees us, mayhap they shall not remember we were fewer in number than we claimed."

It was as good a plan as any. I knew we were in pretty sketchy territory. We just needed a story we could all stick to.

I gathered up my skirts and crawled out of the tunnel and emerged outside, blinking in the bright light of a frigid November morning. While it was still cold, the sun was climbing, doing its best to dispel the worst of the chill.

But I started when I saw him.

Because Lord Rodolfo Greco stood there, arms crossed, waiting for us to exit the tomb.

"Rodolfo," I began.

He held up a gloved hand, shushing me as effectively as a stern principal. Marcello crawled out to join me, but Rodolfo looked past him, waiting, waiting...

I knew, then. He'd seen us enter. With Orazio and Galileo. And now he was witnessing exit without them. I sighed, not really in the mood for another Greco inquisition.

Mom and Dad came out. Then Lia and Luca.

Rodolfo shook off Marcello's hand and ducked his head into the entrance, hand atop the doorway, peering into the dark. He looked back to us. "So 'tis done? They've gone? Back from whence they came?"

"'Tis best you do not know the specifics, brother," Marcello said slowly.

Rodolfo moved closer, inches from his face. "I," he said, "of *all* people, have proven worthy of knowing specifics. *Brother.*" He practically spat the last word. But I knew it was fear that drove his fury. "Tell me all of it," Rodolfo grit out. "Those men? I assume they were your Betarrini cousins?" This time he looked to me.

I gave him a slow nod. He already knew of the tomb's capability, but why was I reluctant to share more?

His dark eyes returned to me and my family. "So it is something within your blood that enables this witchcraft?"

"'Tis not witchcraft," I said, starting to reach out to touch him and then thinking better of it. "We said no spells. Indeed, we had no idea what would happen when we first laid our hands upon the prints. All we know is that it takes two of us, and the right two of us. My mother and father cannot do it. Only Lia and I, together. Only Galileo and Orazio, together."

"Then how does it occur? What is your explanation?"

"I know not," I said, with a slow shake of my head.

"The light I saw, the sound..."

"The moment it occurred," I said. "The moment that Orazio and Galileo left us."

"They simply disappeared, as if struck by lightning?"

It was as good an explanation as any. I nodded.

"The one was injured," he said, mumbling, as if overwhelmed by a cascade of thoughts. Then he straightened, head cocking toward me. "As you were once. After your injury. After you'd been stabbed and poisoned..."

He'd apparently heard of that night. Known of me, of Lia, before we'd ever met. It made sense. We'd swiftly become the target of every Fiorentini, and he'd been one of them.

"The journey seems to heal as well as...*move* us from one time to another."

Rodolfo searched my face. He took a breath, then two, and turned from me, staring up in the direction of his castle, hands on his hips. From this particular location we were hidden from view. At last, he looked at us from over his shoulder, turning to face Tomb Two.

"We must destroy it," he said. "If word gets out, if they find the evidence here..." He gestured toward me and Lia but spoke to Marcello and Luca. "They'll come for them. Fiorentini and Sienese alike. They'll no longer be the She-Wolves. They'll be named *witches*, blamed for every manner of ill fortune imaginable. You know how the simple-minded talk."

"Nay," Mom said. "You cannot!"

"You cannot destroy it," Dad added. "The site is too important."

"Why not?" Rodolfo asked angrily. "Your daughters have married well. Gabriella grows heavy with child. Your life is here now, is it not? What value are these old tombs in light of your family's future?"

Dad opened his mouth to say something, then his lips clamped shut. He and Mom looked miserable. I could see their devotion to preserving history at war with the reality behind Greco's words. Yet they were both visibly resolved to stand against this. For two reasons: the tomb represented our own escape route should the worst happen. Not that I could ever imagine using it. And I knew my parents had a hundred questions about the tomb, the portal, they were dying to answer.

Rodolfo's dark brow furrowed. I knew he was trying to figure out why they would cling to it. "'Tis due to the fact that the tomb might still be useful to you," he said softly.

"It saved Gabriella once, as we hope it just saved Orazio," Marcello said. "Think, man," he said, reaching out toward Rodolfo. "Wouldn't you do anything to save Alessandra if you could?"

"Even if it meant that I might lose her forever?" Rodolfo returned. "Leaving me to the stake and fires at my feet, named a sorcerer? A warlock?"

"Even then." Marcello's earnest eyes drifted to me. "Would it not be better to know your woman lived, even if she couldn't be with you? Either way, you lose her, but one way, you have hope."

Rodolfo rubbed his face and kept staring at Marcello. "Gabriella and Evangelia are safer than ever as your brides. It's been relatively peaceful with Firenze, aside from this last attempt in Venezia. Why do I sense you fear something bigger? Some greater fear? Have there been additional threats against you and yours?"

"Nay, nay," Marcello said. "It is but the concern of a father-to-be, with soon not one to love and protect, but two."

I wondered if I was the only one who heard the bit of forced cheer in his voice, meant to cover the lie. Rodolfo seldom missed such things.

His keen eyes moved over the rest of us. I lifted my chin and took Marcello's arm as if warmed by his words, but it didn't feel authentic, real. More like I was some lame actress in the high school play.

"You are from the future," Rodolfo said softly, almost reverently, his eyes widening with slow understanding. "Therefore, you know what the future holds."

I scowled. "We know some things, Rodolfo, but precious little. Almost seven hundred years divide your time from our own. And while my parents were Etruscan scholars, they knew only basics about this particular time period. It is our aim to not change anything in history by what we do know. Simply being here we have already changed aspects of the future, and we are trying to keep from changing more. So you must not ask us, friend. We cannot tell you of it. We have not even told our husbands. It is best for everyone if we do not."

A shout sounded from the woods. At a distance, but it spooked us.

Luca looked to Marcello. "Patrol. One of ours. Let us hasten to the old hunting hut. Take this eastern path to avoid the knights of Castello Greco seeing us."

"We are not finished—" Rodolfo began.

"Enough!" Marcello interrupted, agitated, then softening his tone. "We shall speak of it another day, if we must. In the meantime, I ask that you keep it in confidence."

Rodolfo hesitated, then nodded once, clearly unhappy that he could not press us further. Ferret out the piece he sensed we kept back...our knowledge of the plague.

But we were already turning from him, going to our horses. Luca's suggestion of the old hunting hut was a good one. It was small and in poor repair, but it had a fireplace and a mostly intact roof. We could get warm, at least, as we waited for some hours to pass before we returned home.

Rodolfo followed us down the hill and stood there, arms folded, looking up at me. His expression confirmed this wasn't over.

Marcello edged his horse between me and Rodolfo, basically severing his stare. "Brother," he said. "Do I have your word? You shall keep silent on this?"

"For a time," Rodolfo said, "*brother*. But we *shall* speak of it again."

Marcello sighed and looked to the gray skies. "Why must you always need to know every single nuance of a matter, Rodolfo?"

"Because it has kept me alive to date," he said. "And now I, too, have a woman I am responsible to protect. If this knowledge you keep will aid me in that matter, then I shall insist upon knowing it."

"Until later," Marcello said, clearly irritated by his press.

"Until later, then. Go with God."

"And you," Marcello snapped, wheeling his gelding about and leading us into the trees.

I could feel Rodolfo's eyes on me as I urged my mare forward, too.

But I didn't dare look back.

PART II

HORIZONS

Winter 1345 - Spring 1346

CHAPTER 29

EVANGELIA

It said something of the trust and regard the people of Castello Forelli granted us when they did not ask more than once where we had left the Betarrini brothers. Luca passed it off as a matter of security, keeping their whereabouts a secret, and this made sense to most of them. I knew Captain Pezzati was still frustrated to not be in on it—and irritated that we'd taken the risk to set off without guards—but within a few days, all was back to normal.

Days passed into weeks.

Weeks evolved into months.

Marcello arranged for a letter to arrive, written in a foreign hand with a wax seal none of us recognized, and Gabi and I read it aloud to Mom and Dad within earshot of Giacinta and Cook, the two greatest gossip-sharers in the castle. We were confident that all would soon know that Orazio had made a full recovery and that he and his brother had made their way to Pisa to set sail to Normandy.

"That is the best possible word to receive," I sighed, imagining what it would be to know that the boys were truly home and well. It made me think of what Luca and Marcello went through, sending us off, not knowing if we even lived through it.

Married life was so fun, my heart so settled, that my memories of why I'd ever put it off seemed to fade in my mind. Luca was attentive and tender and only teased me about how I made our quarters far too womanly for his taste.

"Only because you now live within these walls," he said, kissing me last night, "can a man tolerate it."

I'd replaced a few threadbare window tapestries—what were once family heralds, I guessed—with newer, thicker, longer ones imported from Holland. They depicted romantic scenes from aristocratic country life, and I marveled at what they'd been able to accomplish in thread and design, as well as how much warmer our rooms were now. But from the way my husband carried on, you would've thought I'd painted the room pink. They'd cost a great deal, but Gabi and I still had gold of our own, and I hadn't even asked him before purchasing them from a merchant in Siena. Now, I knew, I'd have to get him to agree on such things if I wanted to avoid his endless teasing.

My monthly Friend came and went as the months went by, and I decided that Mom's advice on natural birth control was working, given the few nights Luca and I were simply content to snuggle.

Snow fell periodically, but it never lasted long in Toscana. Still, the days were short, the fires heavily banked to warm the rooms, and peace continued to reign between Siena and Firenze. We considered it a miracle, of sorts, and we settled into daily routines.

Marcello and Luca often had to spend time in Siena. With Marcello being one of the Nine, he was working really hard to get a few key things in order before he resigned from his post. Mom and Dad often went with them, still working on supplying the castle for what the men had come to call "any siege," as they watched barrel upon barrel stack up in the storehouse, wondering at the folly of it after a while. I heard them talk. They understood provisions to withstand a siege. Thought it wise. But none of them had seen provisions for *years* of war, for which we prepared. They obviously thought it a waste, overkill.

The guys hated to leave us, but now that Gabs was getting closer to having her baby, there was no way to take the day-long trek on horseback.

While I would've liked to go to the city to be with my husband some, or shop with Mom and Dad, I volunteered to stay with her so Gabi wouldn't be alone. It made Gabs crazy, and she paced the perimeter of the yard, or up atop the wall on warmer days, truly like a She-Wolf trapped in a cage.

"*Pregnancy*, they call it," she groused to me that morning. "It's more like *prison*."

I laughed and sympathized with her, but amidst our ongoing peace with Firenze, I relished the relief of responsibility. I helped Cook bake bread a couple mornings a week, but mostly I was free to sketch and paint in our new solarium, which I planned to do today. It wasn't long before Gabi arrived, wringing her hands over her basketball-of-a-stomach.

"Let's go see Alessandra," she said, moving over to the thick, milky glass discs from Venezia—a gift from the doge—that now made up most of the windows of Mom's solarium. "It's been so long since we've had the chance to be just us girls. I want to take her that new book of poetry. She'll love it."

I frowned. "Castello Greco is only a couple miles. But it's still a couple miles. Sure you're up for that?"

She rubbed her belly. "We can take it slow."

"Are you sure, Gabs? What about...Rodolfo?" We'd done pretty well avoiding any opportunity for further discussion with the man since that day at the tombs. We'd seen the Grecos almost weekly, but it had always been in the company of many others. Alessandra seemed blissfully unaware we were at all at odds with her husband.

"He's in Siena with the guys. I overheard a scout say he'd seen him there. And I'm going to go crazy if I don't get out of here," she said, eyes wide.

"I dunno, Gabs," I sighed, weighing her need with my responsibility as stand-in guardian. "The last thing we need is for you to fall off a horse, a month before your baby is due."

"Maybe I should fall off on purpose," she said, misery etching her tone. "Get this baby moving. How can I get any bigger? My boobs are busting out of my dress and this belly..." She groaned, even as she continued to stroke it. "I'll never be the same!"

"Probably not," I said with a grin, rising to take her hands. "But you really have never been prettier, Gabi. All rosy cheeked and cute curves. And the way the guys fall all over themselves to try and take care of you...It's true what they say. Everyone loves a pregnant woman."

"Humph," she said, still stroking her belly. Her skirt's gathers seemed to emphasize the roundness. "*Cute curves*. That's a polite way of saying *fat*."

"You're not fat! You'll have that baby in five weeks and you'll be back to normal a few weeks after that. And less grumpy."

She let out a long breath. "You know what would make me less grumpy? A *walk*. To Castello Greco. C'mon, Lia," she said, her whole face settling in for some serious begging. "Let's go see Ali. She's gotta be bored, too. She wanted you to give her some archery lessons. Or we can play tric-trac if it's too cold to be outside. Or poker. I don't care! Just something to get me out of this funk."

I laughed. "All right, all right. Settle down. But let's take bags with a change of clothes. That way, if you're too tired to make the walk home, we can stay there overnight."

Her face lit up with victory and she clasped her hands together before pulling me to her to kiss both cheeks. "You're the best sister ever."

"Yeah, yeah," I said, already feeling a measure of foreboding that I'd just given in to something I shouldn't have.

⁓ᗣᕫ

We set off an hour later, with twelve men as our guards—Captain Pezzati wouldn't accept any other option. I guessed I was as excited as Gabi for an outing and a chance to talk—really talk—with Alessandra. I knew it'd been tough for her adapting to life among the Sienese, shirking her Fiorentini roots. But she'd seemed to do a bang-up job of it. And she clearly loved her husband. Just the thought of them, and the small, secretive looks they shared, made me smile. Both had been in serious need of love. And they'd found it.

It made me think of Luca, long for him...If there was one thing medieval Italy seemed destined to do, it was help people in the ways of love. As we picked our way down the road, pausing periodically when Gabi had Braxton-Hicks contractions strong enough to steal her breath, I contemplated that thought. Even the knights who protected us on the road—six ahead and six behind—seemed to either have a love interest in the villages about or maids in the castle. Castello Forelli would've made a crazy-great setting for a series like *Downton Abbey*, I thought. We were all so intimately wrapped up in one another's lives...

"You know what I love best about being here?" I asked Gabi, as she blew out a long breath and rubbed the bulk of her belly.

"A certain knight?" she asked, raising a brow.

I glanced past her to the two closest knights within view, waiting on us, while giving us a measure of privacy by staying a bit away. "Well him, *yes*. But it's being together as a family. Living life together, you know? Not just Mom and Dad, you and Marcello, me and Luca. But all of us. The knights," I said, waving forward, "the maids," I said, waving backward. "The stewards, the squires, everyone. It's like living with a great, big family. We never had that, back home. Mom and Dad never connected with our relatives."

We returned to our easy pace along the path, among tall oaks that had long since shed the leaves that crunched beneath our slippers, and a few evergreens.

"Back home," I went on, "we didn't even know our neighbors. I mean, beyond names."

Gabi nodded. "I think this is how we were meant to live," she said. "In community. Taking care of one another. Sharing. Loving. Celebrating and grieving together. I think it's part of what drew me here and convinced me to stay."

"Me, too."

We walked for a time in silence. "It's good here, Gabi. I'm glad we came."

"I'm so glad," she said, sliding a smile in my direction.

We picked our way across the dry riverbed, and I thought that soon after the baby came—which seemed to be our every measure of time of late—water would flow again, filling its banks. I liked when it was full, and I determined that Luca and I would take to river excursions for our picnics, when weather cooperated. There was something about moving water that soothed and restored me. And I wanted to fill my sketchbook with lively images of it.

I even liked the process of watching it ebb and dry up, I decided, as we left the stony bed behind us, climbing up the path toward the tombs. It was another part of life I liked here, the way we measured the passage of months by the weather—and not just a superficial understanding of the weekly forecast, but a primal knowledge of the cycle of seasons that fed the earth, which fed the fields, which led to food on our tables. That was something that most kids back at Boulder High would never really get. Not really. Even with all their eco-friendly ways. Most had parents bringing home six-figure salaries, and the closest they got to their food source was Whole Foods. It was a start on what was unfolding in me, this tie to the earth, but it was only a start.

Gabi paused at the meadow with the tombs and cast a questioning glance back my way as if to say—*Want to stop?*—but I shook my head. The last time, watching Orazio and Galileo disappear...even the thought of it made my stomach vaguely queasy. Because now the thought of me and Gabi putting our hands on the prints...leaving Luca! It made me tear up. *Please, Lord,* I prayed. *Make a way. Keep us from ever ever ever having to leave. I couldn't bear it. I couldn't bear it...*

Gabi glanced back at me. "Lia?"

"It's okay," I whispered. "I'm okay. It's just....passing the tomb. Thinking of leaving again..."

She turned to me and took me in her arms, which was a bit odd of late, with a basketball between us. "I know," she said simply. And I knew she did. More than that, for the first time, I fully understood what it had taken for her to leave the second time. The first, she thought she might be in love with Marcello. The second, she knew. She *knew*. And still, she'd found it within herself to go. To go with me to try and get Dad. Because we couldn't do anything else.

Because we couldn't do anything else.

I guessed that was a key. And I silently marked it in my head and heart as a hallmark for future tough decisions.

We journeyed on, up and over the hill, with periodic stops and patient waiting by our guardian knights. I knew they were probably half-bored out of their minds, but also probably half-delirious with the opportunity for a real task. Marcello and Luca and Captain Pezzati kept them busy with daily training. But most of their days were filled with normal castle life, and with no battles on the horizon, it was dull for a knight. There was a tension among them that I thought might grow increasingly challenging as this peace continued.

We neared Castello Greco, her towering gates soon before us. With her entry perched on the far side, her gates were taller than any other I'd ever seen. I pushed aside the memory of Gabi above, dangling over the edge as Cosmo Paratore—once my captor, then hers—gripped her by the arm on the night the castle fell to the Sienese. I pushed aside the vision of Dad, injured after a sword blade pierced his upper chest—a wound that had to heal the old-fashioned way, through normal time, and had healed reasonably well. But we'd been so scared. So. Scared. Thinking him dead, after all we'd done to save him.

So...yeah. This castle carried some baggage with her. But when our knights announced us, as the newish gates opened with a tremendous groan and creak, and we saw Lady Alessandra Greco awaiting us, practically dancing on her toes with pleasure, I smiled. We were remaking our memories of this place. Filled with good people. New days and nights and celebrations. And this would be one of them, I decided.

I saw that she held a small girl by the hand, a child no more than about three. She was precious, all dark skin and long, curly hair, in a tiny, perfect dress.

"Who is this?" I asked, leaning in to kiss Alessandra on either cheek.

"This is Chiara," Alessandra said. "She has come to live with us."

Her eyes told us there was more to the story, but it would have to wait—she didn't want to talk about it in front of the child. The girl whined, and Alessandra lifted her up and onto one hip, cradling her close, murmuring to her. "I'm so glad you've come to visit," Ali said, smiling at each of us.

"We missed you and thought you might be lonely," Gabi said, "without Rodolfo at home. We didn't know little Chiara was keeping you company! Would you mind if we spent the day with you, and possibly the night?"

"Mind?" she returned. "That would be grand." She turned to the steward at her right. "Agostino, we shall set a special supper this night for the three of us, in the small hall? See that their men find provisions in the gatehouse?"

Her words held power, but her tone was questioning. Clearly, she was still getting used to being lady of the house. I held back a laugh. That was never something that Gabs struggled with. But it would've been for me, and my heart went out to her. Maybe Gabi could give her some pointers.

As soon as I'd thought it, Gabi was on it. "You must drop the question from your tone," she said quietly, slipping her arm through Alessandra's as we walked. I followed them. "The lady of the house never questions herself, only directs."

"Which is challenging, m'lady," Alessandra returned, "when this lady questions every word she utters."

Gabi lifted her head, as if in surprise. "Alessandra," she said, "the thing that struck me most when we met you was your singular purpose on the hunt. I think it's what struck your husband, too. In that same way, you must address your household. The key aspect being that it's *your* household. Rodolfo likely cares primarily for the knights and your security in terms of household duties—the walls, essentially. Everything within these walls is *your* realm, yes?"

Alessandra mulled over her words, looking somewhat troubled. "Would that your words be true. My husband cares for the walls, the territory, the border. But I daresay he cares for everything and everyone inside, too. There seems to be naught that escapes him. He is uncommonly aware, uncommonly *keen* to things that are by degrees...off."

We were silent, all lost in this thought. For it was true. Rodolfo Greco *was* uncommonly attuned to nuance. Detail. It was why the Fiorentini sent him after us, years before. He was like a hunter, or a detective. Gathering clues. Guessing at logical paths. Deducing. The Sherlock Holmes of the Middle Ages.

I was glad he was in Siena. For a time, we girls could put off thoughts of the future and simply concentrate on the present. And to me...well, it was the closest thing to a slumber party that I'd had in a very, very long time.

CHAPTER 30

GABRIELLA

C hiara was a delightful child. She coyly played hide-and-seek with me as we ate, ducking under the table and then peeking out. We soon learned she was an orphan, and Rodolfo had simply brought her home to Ali a week past when he couldn't find another to take her in. Her mother had died in childbirth and her father, in his grief, had drunk himself to death. When Rodolfo rode through the village, he'd found Chiara, dirty, crying and hungry, in the road. Few of the villagers wanted another mouth to feed...they were only interested in boys, who might better help them till their fields or harvest their grapes. And as the nearest lord, they figured Chiara was Greco's responsibility.

When Alessandra finally got the child to sleep, she returned to us.

"So," I said, "you went from newlywed to new mother. How are you faring with that?"

"Ahh," she said wrapping her arms around herself and shaking her head with a grin, "I could not be happier. After losing my mother, my brothers, and then my father..." Her voice caught, but she swallowed hard and continued, a tight smile on her lips. "To me, this is as if God has given me a new beginning. Hope," she added. "I dream of filling this castello with babies in time. I want lots of little Grecos about!"

As if in response, my baby rolled within my womb. Ali's delight over insta-motherhood made me suddenly eager to have my own child in my arms. "I'm so glad for you," I said, reaching out to squeeze her arm.

"'Tis wonderful for all *three* of you," Lia added.

"What did Rodolfo think?" I asked. "Of adopting the child?"

"He seems a little in love with the girl," Alessandra said. "He smiles all the time. And he is glad that we could help Chiara when she had no kin to turn to. You should see the girl with him. She follows him around like a little puppy!"

We stayed up late. Alessandra was deeply in love with her husband, still as ga-ga at the mention of him as Lia was with Luca. We shared stories and giggled, and Lia gave her an archery lesson by torchlight, keeping her enthralled with her account from Venice all the while. Ali was a quick-study and had obviously been practicing with her bow, for she was as good as I was now. She watched Lia's every move, asking her questions about handholds and tension on the string.

I didn't even try to enter in, finding it impossible to properly hold the bow with my belly getting in the way. Lia attempted to cajole me into trying it by holding it at an angle, but I refused. Besides, my back ached and it was hard to stand for any length of time. I was happy to simply sit and watch them, laughing with them.

Soon after, we headed to bed, pausing at the top of the stairs.

"I'm so glad you're settling in here," I said to Alessandra. "Close to us. I'm so glad you are our friend."

"As am I," she said, shyly placing a hand on her flat belly, making me a little envious.

Thoughts of the plague taking Rodolfo, Alessandra, or little Chiara crowded my mind, but I quickly shoved them away, forcing a smile.

"We best get to bed, Gabi," Lia prodded. "You need rest." We continued down the hallway to our guest rooms.

We said our *buona seras* and then went to our chambers.

I waved at the knights, who were just trading off shifts, shut the door, slid the bolt closed. Then I flopped down on the bed and promptly went to sleep without bothering to get undressed.

I awoke far later than I might have at home. Back at Castello Forelli, a maid arrived shortly after sun-up, every morning. But here, no one had knocked, and I hadn't heard a thing outside. Feeling creeped-out—as if I might have somehow been left alone in the castle—I moved to the door, listened a moment and then unbolted it and peeked out.

Falito startled, as if dozing on his feet, and straightened. "My lady?" he asked, concerned.

"Oh, good morning," I returned. "It was so quiet I thought mayhap you'd left me."

"Nay, m'lady," he said sternly, as if I'd just offended him by suggesting such a thing.

"Good, good," I murmured. "Is Lady Evangelia still asleep?"

"Nay, she accompanied Lady Greco and little Chiara on a walk."

I let out a sigh and shut the door. Blinking, I undressed down to my shift, threw my rumpled gown to the bed, went over to a small table, poured water from a pitcher into a basin, and quickly washed my face and under my arms. I dried off and pulled out another gown, a deep burgundy that was so well made it managed to make me feel decent in it, even with my protruding belly. This one had no gathers at the front, falling from an empire waist straight down, and I hoped it made me look a bit less like Her Whaleness. Around adorable little Alessandra, I always felt Amazonian...and the pregnancy just made me feel all the bigger.

I combed out my hair but knew I would never be able to wrestle it into more than a semblance of a knot. *But it's just us girls this morning,* I decided. *No worries.*

Slipping my feet into my tapestry flats, I was out the door, telling Falito my plans from over my shoulder, even as he hurried to catch up with me. The other knight was gone, presumably watching over Lia. Ever since the attempt on our lives in Venice, the knights were crazy vigilant. Irritatingly vigilant. Away from home, I understood it. Back at the castello, and even here, I thought it ridiculous, but Marcello had been adamant.

"Do you know where Evangelia and Alessandra went on their walk?" I asked, still walking.

"The western woods," Falito said. "But m'lady, I'd expect them back at any moment. Mayhap if you simply wait here..."

"Gabriella," called a man's voice.

I froze for half a sec then continued, electing to pretend I hadn't heard him as we rounded a corner.

Because I knew it was Rodolfo.

"Gabriella!" he called again, this time clearly in the hall behind me.

I looked to Falito, who stared at me in confusion, wondering why it took Lord Greco twice to stop me. Wringing my hands, I glanced back at Rodolfo and forced a smile. "You've returned, m'lord," I said.

I had to face him.

Without my sister.

Without his wife. We hadn't been alone since...Roma.

"Come," he said, gesturing to his den. "I have need of you."

I swallowed hard, resting my hand against my rounded belly, tightening with another Braxton-Hicks, this one especially fierce. *Did he mean...No. No, of course not.*

Slowly, I walked back to him and entered, Falito right behind me.

"'Tis all right, Falito," Rodolfo said. "The lady is safe with me."

"Begging your pardon, m'lord, but I am to stay with my lady at all times, even with friends."

Rodolfo looked to me, waiting.

With a sigh, I turned to Falito. "Please wait outside the door for me. If I have need of you, I shall not hesitate to call."

Grim-faced, Falito paused. "My lady—"

"If I have need of you, I shall *call*. Be at peace."

Falito reluctantly turned on his heel and slipped out, slowly closing the door behind him.

Rodolfo leaned against the table that served as his desk, folding his arms. "Where were you going in such haste?"

"To catch up with your wife and my sister," I said. "I overslept, and they went off to walk with little Chiara. I am so glad, Rodolfo, that you took her in. It was most kind."

A small smile danced on his full lips, and his eyes softened. "It's been a blessing to us as much as her. I think...I think Alessandra needed a child, to settle her. To give her focus here." He gestured about. "'Tis much to take in when one has been raised in a small cottage."

"But she is faring well," I said. "Adapting?"

"She is," he said with a nod. "But now that I have a family to protect, I am all the more concerned." He crossed his arms and pinched his chin as he studied me. "'Tis the reason that I called you in here, Gabriella. You've avoided me for some time. Since that day in the field of tombs. When—"

When he'd pressed us for the truth. When he realized we were from the future. "Yes, yes," I said, glancing back at the den door, praying Falito wasn't listening in.

Rodolfo frowned and then stepped closer to me, maybe so that he could speak in a quieter tone. Still, it made me uncomfortable. I resisted the urge to back away from him. Wished with everything in me that Lia and Alessandra would get back. Tried to find the courage to look him in the eye and failed.

"Gabriella," he whispered, reaching toward me and then, thinking better of it, dropping his hand. I stared into his dark eyes. "Tell me what I must know," he said. "To keep my family safe. What is to come? What do you so fear?"

"I cannot," I whispered, shaking my head. "It shall change things."

His dark eyes searched mine. "You are my friend. You are Alessandra's friend. There is something ahead of us that makes you afraid for all of us, yes?"

"I cannot tell you," I said, fighting tears. "Do not ask it of me."

"It is plain that Castello Forelli prepares for siege. The additional knights. The storehouse with food and medicinals. The new latrine and well. When, *when*, is this war upon us? Is it the Fiorentini who shall overtake us?"

My eyes widened. *This* was why he pressed. He feared that our enemies would take the upper hand in battle. And if they caught the Grecos...their end would be as grim as it would be for us. Perhaps even worse. Because they were thought of as both enemy and traitor.

I took a deep breath and paced to the window, thinking. What would it hurt for him to think it a battle? Was it not wise for the lord of a castle to fortify and be prepared for anything? And yet would that not likely change history in another way, if Castello Greco became as strong as Castello Forelli? Thinking it all through, from every which way, made my head hurt.

"Gabriella," he said, laying a hand on my shoulder.

I turned, thinking to make him drop it, but he just took my hand in his. Even took hold of my other hand.

"You shall tell me, Gabriella," he said, begging me with pain and necessity in his eyes. "I shall have the truth. If the Fiorentini capture Alessandra, or Chiara..." His voice broke, and tears welled in his eyes. I saw, with some relief, that he pressed on behalf of his wife, his new daughter—not in some odd pursuit of me.

"They would subject them both to the vilest of treatment, Gabriella." His face reddened. "They would give her to men to have their way with her before making me watch her die. They would murder that precious child for carrying my name. Please. *Please.* I must know."

I swallowed hard around the lump in my throat. I could feel a Braxton-Hicks coming on, the muscles at my lower back tightening...

"'Tis not that sort of battle we shall face, Rodolfo," I whispered. "That which you suppose..."

He frowned, his hands tightening around mine. "Nay?"

"Nay." I lowered my head, shaking it.

"Gabriella," he said, his tone now full of warning.

"I cannot tell you."

His hands moved to my shoulders, and he shook me a little. "You must. You *must*."

"Nay! Nay!" I tried to wrench away, but he held fast. "Unhand me! *Rodolfo!*"

Falito pounded on the door. "M'lady?"

Remembering himself, Rodolfo dropped his hands and turned partially away. "Forgive me," he whispered.

I took a deep breath. "All is well, Falito!"

Rodolfo looked contrite and frustrated. One hand went to his hip, the other to massage his head. "Please," he said, dropping to one knee before me. "Please," he whispered.

I stared down into his handsome face.

My friend.

Marcello's blood brother.

How could I keep it a secret? If it might save him and his family?

"'Tis the plague," I whispered, feeling the gates within me burst.

"What? The *plague*?"

"Worse than anything you've ever encountered. Ever seen," I said, tears now rolling down my face, imagining our lovely valley, all the villages and families that would endure illness, death.

He swallowed hard. "When?"

"Two years from now it shall reach Venezia, Pisa, Ancona, Sicily. Within months, it shall sweep through all of Italia. And this is the worst part," I said, so faintly I wondered if he could even hear me. I stared into his eyes. "It shall remain with us, like a hungry tiger, *with* us inside the cage. For four years. And in that time, it shall take one-third of our friends and family members. Even half, in some cities."

His lips parted, his eyes widening in horror, then growing distant.

He rose painfully, as if he weren't in his late twenties, but rather an old man, then he returned to rubbing his head.

"We shall leave," he said, looking at me over his shoulder. "We must all leave. Take to the seas and outrun it."

"Nay," I said with a small shake of my head, rubbing my lower back, suddenly killing me. "There is nowhere to go that it won't either await us or come after us. 'Tis a battle for the whole known world."

"Known world," he repeated, his eyes hardening. "What of your world, your land? We could go there."

"Nay," I said. "I don't know if it would work and—"

"Gabriella," he said quietly, walking toward me. "Don't you see? I speak not of the tomb. I speak of going elsewhere, in *our* time. Far away. We could all set sail and go to your land—the *unknown* world. From whence you came."

"Nay," I said, shaking my head, with a small, hopeless laugh. I was pretty fuzzy on a lot of history and how we might screw it up. But I was totally sure that Dad would freak if we suggested we beat Christopher Columbus to America. And the pilgrims hadn't exactly had it easy. "Nay," I said more emphatically as his jaw tightened, preparing to wear me down. "'Tis impossible. And even if we did go, 'twould only present us other battles."

I sighed and reached out to lay a hand on his forearm. "What lies ahead of us is frightening, for certain," I said. "But 'tis a known battle. And Marcello is provisioning to protect any of his brothers who have come to our aid at risk of their own lives. He feels he owes it to you, as do I. You and Alessandra shall not be alone. When this evil comes to our valley and hills, there shall be room for you and your little girl within our very own walls if need be. But, Rodolfo, you must not tell anyone of this. Not even Alessandra."

He scowled. "I cannot keep this from her."

"You must!" I felt the familiar tightening at my back then, but this time, it was ten-times stronger.

And when it wrapped around, under my belly, deep within, I bent over, gasping. A second later, my water broke, a rush of warm, clear liquid running down my legs and pooling on the granite beneath me.

"Gabriella!" Rodolfo cried, gripping my arms, even as he picked up his boot with distaste. "What is *this*?"

I groaned, half mortified that it looked like I just peed all over his floor, and half in terror as the realization of what was happening solidified in my mind. I swallowed hard and looked him in the eye. "I am in labor," I said.

"You are *what*?" he said.

"The baby! My baby! The hour is upon us! I'm about to give birth!"

And never, ever had I seen Lord Rodolfo Greco look so scared.

CHAPTER 31

GABRIELLA

H e picked me up in his arms and carried me to the door. "Falito!"
he bellowed, kicking the door. The knight opened it so fast that
he nearly hit us. He stared at Rodolfo in open accusation as we swept
past.

"What is it? What has happened?" he asked, following behind us.

"Fetch the Ladies Alessandra and Evangelia. And send a man for the
village midwife. Lady Gabriella's baby is coming."

I might've laughed at the straight-shouldered, strong knight paling
so fast I thought he'd faint. But I was in the middle of another contraction. I tried to breathe through it, worrying that it was upon me, so soon
after the other. Weren't they supposed to be farther apart? Wasn't that
what Mom said? Farther apart and then getting closer, the nearer I came
to actually giving birth?

Tears streamed down my face as the contraction clenched at my
belly. It felt like the worst cramps of my whole life. But more tears came
as I fretted over the baby, coming now, weeks before he or she was due.
Was she big enough, strong enough to survive? Did we get the birth date
wrong? We hardly had access to ultrasounds and data to tell us...

I let out a strangled moan.

"Hold on, Gabriella, hold on," Rodolfo said through gritted teeth,
carrying me down the hall. "You shall be all right."

"My baby," I said through my tears as he laid me down on the bed I'd slept in last night.

"She shall be all right," he said, squeezing my hand.

"She? She?" I laughed through my tears. "Why does everyone insist they know 'tis a girl?"

"Because she must be," he said, casting me a wry grin as he pulled a handkerchief from a pocket and handed it to me.

I turned over to my side, panting, trying to get my head together. "My mother. I need my mother. Please, Rodolfo. Can you send a rider to Siena to fetch Marcello and my parents? These things can take tah—" I winced, fighting for breath. "Time."

But my last word emerged strangled from my throat as another contraction took over. I panted, feeling like an idiot, but not caring. This kind of pain was Scary with a capital S.

"Never mind," I said, catching hold of his hand. "Get that midwife here first. And send for Giacinta and Cook from Castello Forelli. I don't want to deliver this baby on my own."

A sly, satisfied grin took over his face. "Another fierce She-Wolf, howling in."

Hilarious, this guy. Suddenly the most intense man I knew thought he was a laugh-a-minute.

"Rodolfo!" I cried, grabbing his tunic and pulling his face close to mine. "Go and fetch them at once!" I demanded. "Yourself, if you must!"

"So be it," he said, fear and concern sobering him at last.

I released him. "Go! Go!"

And the man scurried out as if he were but ten years old.

The next contraction wracked me, and I cried out. All I wanted was for it to go away. Or stop.

The pain. God in heaven, the pain....

Falito peeked in, looking flushed and sweaty, despite the chilly winter day. "Ladies Evangelia and Alessandra are on their way, m'lady."

"Good," I managed to say. "Thank you. Now can you kindly close that door and stay on the other side of it?"

"Yes, m'lady," he said, looking like I'd just given him the moon by excusing him.

I rolled onto my hands and knees and rocked, wondering at the excruciating agony at my lower back. Was something wrong? Was this normal for women in labor?

Alessandra and Lia arrived, faces pale with alarm, all nervous energy. Behind them were an army of maids. Two carrying a brass bathing tub. Four with eight buckets of steaming water. Two more carrying piles of linens.

Lia rushed straight to me, stroking my head, pushing the hair from my sweating face. "What has happened?"

I sighed and then clenched my teeth as I could feel another contraction building pressure across abdomen and back. "Water broke," I grit out. "Contractions coming fast. Much faster...than what Mom said."

Her blue eyes widened with alarm. "How soon might we expect the midwife?"

"An hour, mayhap two," Alessandra said.

My eyes met Lia's, and I shook my head as I panted through the next contraction.

Would she get here in time?

Could I do this without Mom?

Without a midwife?

And away from home?

I looked at my sis and our friend.

"Let's do this," I said, leaning back on the pillow as the contraction built to a crescendo. I cried out, gripping Lia's hand.

"It's so early!" Lia said, fretting through every syllable. "It's early, right? Really early?"

"Who knows?" I cried out. "It's hardly an exact science here," I said in English. "No ultrasounds, no charting. We're working off best-guess-es."

"Best guesses?" she said. "We can't do this, Gabs. I can't do this. What if something goes wrong? What if—"

"Lia," I said, gripping her hand with mine. "I need you to be the strong one here. A *She-Wolf.* I've seen you do it before. Do it again. *Now.*"

She hurriedly nodded and seemed to get a hold of herself. "Okay. Okay. I've got this. Want a bath? It might ease the pain. I mean...is that okay?"

"Think it's safe?" I asked, looking over to the inviting water, steam rising. "I mean, now that my water's broken?"

"What do I know?" she said, any measure of confidence in her tone slipping.

"Forget it," I said. "Let's not risk it." *Oh, Mom, Mom, where are you? I need you! Marcello!*

But thoughts of my mother and husband were soon usurped by the pain, the mind-stealing, breath-robbing pain. No sooner had I caught my breath then another contraction was upon me. I could feel the baby shift, lower, and the pain eased a bit, by degrees, even as the contractions wracked me, one after another.

Rodolfo had joked about this little She-Wolf, roaring in. And he appeared to be right.

EVANGELIA

As much as I thought that Gabi would have this baby within the hour, it went on.

Hour after hour...after hour.

Contraction after contraction.

For a time, they came faster. And then they stalled.

It was comforting when Cook and Giacinta walked through the door, but after changing Gabi's bed linens and her position, we all pretty much settled into watching the ongoing torture of sorts, via each contraction, making her face clench in half-terror, half-misery. I held her hand, trying to hide my grimacing at how she bore down upon my fingers. Cook left to make some sort of soup in the kitchen that we could easily down as we kept watch with Gabi. Alessandra dabbed her forehead with a cool, white cloth. But mostly she knelt at her bedside and muttered prayers in Latin. Giacinta joined her.

Oddly, it blanketed the room in a sort of comforting embrace, those prayers, uttered in the ancient tongue. How many mothers, aunties and friends had offered up other prayers like them, begging God to see us, rescue us, deliver us?

Hour upon hour we moved through—me, half desperate for Gabi to deliver, and half-desperate to put it off. What did I know about birth? Delivery? Was something wrong? Is this when they decided to do c-sections? Why did Mom have to be so far away when we needed her most?

Deep into the early morning hours, there was a knock upon the door.

I lifted my head, knowing my hair was going in a hundred different directions and basically, I looked like a mess. But I wondered...hoped...*Mom?*

It was Marcello, and behind him, Luca, who cast me a smile before he was shut out again in the hallway. Greco hovered beside him, looking anxious.

"Where are my parents?" I asked Rodolfo, looking over his shoulder at the closed door.

"They were away from Siena for the day," he said distractedly. "We sent men. They'll be here on the morrow."

On the morrow? We needed them now!

Marcello rushed over to Gabi, who was sweating and grimacing through another terrible contraction. I followed. The midwife was on her other side, stroking her arm, encouraging her through. Alessandra hovered behind the little woman, handing her fresh linens before she asked for them. How did Ali know what to do? Had she helped deliver other children in the village? I felt desperately out of place, completely inadequate.

"My love, is this not early?" Marcello asked, when Gabi's contraction ended, and she caught her breath. "I thought we didn't expect the babe for a month yet."

"We didn't," I muttered, bone-weary, unthinking. "Until Rodolfo upset her and—"

I caught myself before I finished. In a quiet moment, hours past, when it was just the two of us, Gabi had told me what had come down. How Rodolfo had pretty much forced her to tell him about the plague. But I shouldn't have let on...*I shouldn't have let on.*

Gabi stared at me, as if I'd just betrayed her, even as another contraction was upon her, making sweat pour from her brow and her red face clench up. Marcello's jaw muscle twitched in silent fury. "I shall return to you upon your call," he said, kissing her forehead.

My eyes locked with Alessandra's.

I'd just screwed up. Big-time.

I chased Marcello from the room, closing the door behind me as Gabi wailed. All the way down the hall to where he backed Rodolfo up against a wall, shouting accusations.

"How could you?" he growled. "My wife...in her fragile state! What did you say to upset her so?"

Rodolfo lifted his hands. "Marcello, I—"

Marcello struck him savagely across the face, sending him sprawling.

"Marcello!" Luca cried, grabbing him. Rodolfo looked up at him, cradling his bruised cheek, his eyes sparking with their own, cold fury. He was on his feet in seconds, and the two circled, hands clenched.

I burst between them. "Cease this! Cease!"

But they spoke over me, around me, and I could feel their joint frustration and anger as clearly as if I'd slipped into a hot cauldron of boiling water.

Marcello took my arm and wrenched me to the side. "See to your wife, Luca. This is between me and *him*."

I stared back at him, barely recognizing my brother-in-law. What was wrong with him? Surely he didn't think that—

"You provoked this!" Marcello cried, poking Rodolfo in the chest. "You set her into her labors, endangering both my wife and child!"

"Nay!" Rodolfo said. "Nay. I merely wanted to know—"

"Wanted to know what? Why prey upon a woman, when you could ask me, man to man? Why wait until your brother is away, before you corner his wife?"

"Corner? Nay, Marcello. I merely wanted—"

"Falito told me! All of it! How you brought her to your study, closed the door! How Gabriella cried out for you to *unhand her*. And then Evangelia confirmed my fears." He leaned closer. "You have never quite given up on Gabriella, have you?"

My eyes widened in horror, as did Rodolfo's. I could only be glad he spoke in a hushed undertone as Gabi wailed, down the hall, blocking Alessandra's hearing.

"Nay, brother," Rodolfo said, shaking his head. "You do not understand."

"Oh, I understand," Marcello sneered, grabbing hold of Rodolfo's tunic in both fists and shoving him to the wall. "You have always wanted my wife, haven't you? And when you couldn't have her, you waited to exact your vengeance. Waited, until I was away from home. Waited, until she was at her weakest, so close to the delivery of our child...to prey upon her. Press yourself upon her. Bring her such trial that she went into labor far before she should have!"

Marcello's face was an inch from Rodolfo's. Luca and I gaped in horror at them. *He didn't just say that,* I thought. *Please tell me he didn't just say that...*

Rodolfo stared down into his friend's eyes for a long moment, not moving to defend himself. "You are not yourself," he mumbled. "You misunderstand my intent."

"You intended to have her as your own. If I had not come to Roma, you would have forced those nuptial vows," he said, spittle flying in the torchlight.

We all froze for a moment, remembering that day. Remembering how close to the precipice Rodolfo had come, to either giving into the Fiorentini or giving it all up for us. And yet, and yet...he was the one who had snuck us into the church, found us access, made a way to free her. Right?

"I wed *Alessandra*. 'Tis she who holds my heart," Rodolfo growled and shoved him back, slamming him into the far wall. Marcello faltered, gained his feet and rammed into Greco again, at the belly, until he hit the other wall.

"Nay!" Luca cried. "Brothers! Nay!"

He managed to get between them, a hand on each man's heaving chest. "This is a *good* moment!" he gritted out. "A fine moment! Within these walls—once the domain of our enemy—Marcello's babe, his heir, is about to be born! And you two are fighting like two belligerent bulls! This is not the time and place! *This is not,*" he said again, lowering his voice, "*the time and place.* Marcello," he said looking to his cousin, "you have spoken rashly. Rodolfo," he said, looking to his friend, "you have acted out of turn. Both of you owe your brother an apology," he said, face reddening with fury. "See to it."

The men shifted, but Luca held his place, panting with the effort. "Brothers..."

Marcello heaved a sigh and wrenched away from Luca's hand, stepping away a few paces, hands on hips. He lifted his chin, staring at the ceiling, then down to the floor. "Luca is right. I was...rash. Forgive me, brother."

The words were lacking *oomph*, spoken as a boy told to do what he must by his mother, not as a man who believed what he said. And while I hated that, it was true. Rodolfo had always had a thing for my sister. He loved Alessandra. I knew that was also true. But some feelings died hard...and while Marcello loved both his wife and the brother of his childhood, a man could only tolerate so much.

Rodolfo ran a hand through his black hair and then rubbed his face. "I did press Gabriella for information I had no right to press her for, without you in attendance. Forgive me. I never meant..." He looked toward Marcello.

Marcello turned halfway, as if listening, but did not meet his gaze.

"I never meant to send her to her labors early, Marcello. Please, believe me in that. I would never do anything to harm Gabriella or your child. Or you. Truly."

Marcello blinked several times, looked down, then strode away, toward Gabi's door, laying his palm and forehead upon it as she wailed in agony.

GABRIELLA

Lia returned, looking peaked, but I had bigger things on my mind.

Like the fact that I was having this baby. That he or she had shifted, further down. It was happening, finally.

I was just glad Lia and Cook and Giacinta were with me. If I couldn't have Mom and Dad—who had apparently gone off to another Etruscan site—these were the girls I wanted with me.

"Thank you for your help," I said to the maids, who'd gradually congregated in number around me, like some kind of freaky peep show was on. "Please, take your leave. Only the midwife, my sister and my friends should remain."

They filed out, reluctantly looking back at us, some appearing as if they might like to truly help, others like they were just sorry to miss the big moment. I didn't care.

"This baby is coming. You'll stay with me?" I asked, panting.

My sister squeezed my hand. "Of course."

Alessandra nodded gravely. "Yes, yes."

"May I keep holding your hands?" I gasped. "I know they must be like chopped liver right now..."

Alessandra gave me a curious look at my phrase, but she took my hand in hers. "Squeeze as hard as you want. I held my mother's as she birthed my brothers."

The knowledge that she *had* witnessed birth bolstered me. Lia and me? Yeah, we'd sworn off pregnancy in total after watching a few YouTube videos. And now here we were...

The midwife moved down between my knees, coaching and cooing to me in alternately soft and commanding tones, bringing me through one contraction after another. Encouraging me to rest in between. To breathe. To pray. And then...to push. Push, with the contractions.

"'Tis time," she said.

I clenched my teeth as a strong contraction started to build. At the same time, I bore down, pushing, pushing...And then it blessedly eased.

"Breathe, Gabi," Lia said, as I leaned back against the pillows when the contraction had passed, gasping for breath. Alessandra wiped sweat from my forehead and cheeks.

I panted, trying to shore up the energy for what was ahead. And when the next contraction came, I bore down and pushed. And then with the next. And the next.

The midwife let out a little cry, her face lighting up with excitement. "Here comes our little lord or lady! I see the head."

I pushed, and I pushed, and I pushed, much preferring this round to the hours of ongoing contractions the midwife called transition.

We were in a rhythm now.

There was focus, rather than sheer, terrifying pain.

A goal. The baby was coming.

"Here are the shoulders," the midwife said, her tone soothing, joyous. "The baby 'tis almost here. One more push, m'lady. Just one more."

And then I felt the relief, as the babe was finally free of me. It was done.

Lia was crying and laughing, all at once, as the midwife lifted the babe up so we could see.

"A boy," she said. "A precious boy."

He-Wolf, I thought, collapsing backward, eyes still hungry to watch my son every second, catching my breath as he took his first, scrunching up tiny cheeks and eyes to wail his complaint against this cold, bright air after so many months of comfort and warmth within my womb.

Alessandra and Lia were both hugging me and kissing me at once and we all laughed through our tears.

The midwife produced a sharp dagger and held it in the flames of the hearth, then cut the umbilical cord. She tied a clumsy knot and rubbed him down with a linen, removing most of the white, pasty film that covered his body. Alessandra gently lifted him in two hands and encouraged me to untie my gown. Lia helped me pull the straps of my shift down, and Alessandra laid the child against my breast to suckle.

Overwhelmed, exhausted, stunned, I seemed to be little more than putty in their hands, content to do whatever they asked. All that filled my mind and heart was that I was a new mama. With a baby Forelli at her breast.

He squirmed against my skin, and all I could do was wonder at the miracle of him. The perfect, precious gift. Ten toes like tiny little roly-poly bugs. Ten fingers, stretching in complaint and then clenching into tiny fists. Swollen newborn eyes, momentarily opening, staring at me, as if recognizing me, *knowing* me, but at the same time trying to get to know me.

"A boy, Gabs, a *boy*. I was so sure he was going to be a girl," Lia said in English, snuggling close to my side. She laughed softly, tears still rolling down her cheeks.

"Mom and I did, too," I said, tracing the side of his precious little, round face. "But now that he's here, it's like I've known all along. My son. Little Lord Forelli."

They helped me cover up and ran a brush through my hair before ushering in Marcello. Mom had talked me out of inviting him into the labor process, knowing it might change custom if one of the Nine did such a thing. But I felt a pang of loss that he hadn't been here to share it with me. It had been horribly hard and scary and amazing and awesome all at once.

My husband's face was a mass of terror and triumph—and in seconds my pang of loss was gone. He cupped my face, tucking hair back behind my ear, before turning to gaze upon our tiny, perfect son with me.

And we were all still for a sec.

One, precious, perfect second of recognition. Of the miracle of a new life, a new soul, born among us.

"What shall you name him?" Alessandra said, after that moment, bundling soiled linens and pulling them aside, into the corner.

I looked to the babe in my arms and smiled, a tear running down my cheek, love swelling inside me so big I thought I might burst. He was so wonderful. It was such a miracle. My son, *our* son.

I looked into Marcello's eyes and smiled, remembering another special Forelli son. We'd not spoken of names much. It had only led to disagreement.

But it was so clear to me now.

I laughed, tears welling in my eyes.

"Fortino?" I asked him, my cheeks wet, then looking back to our child, knowing it was intrinsically right. "Fortino Betarrini Forelli?" I whispered.

"Fortino, sì," Marcello said, his tone warm and assured at the right-ness of it.

I pulled our tiny son close to kiss the dark, damp curls, plastered to his round head in places, wisping in others. "Welcome, little Fortino. We're so glad you're here. Somewhere, up in heaven, your uncle is celebrating too."

CHAPTER 32

GABRIELLA

M arcello left me—to go hand out cigars? Drink brandy? I had no idea...this birthing chamber was just clearly the domain of women in medieval Italia and he'd gone beyond his bounds. With swift Italian-mama actions, the midwife saw to the grossness that was the afterbirth. Afterward, she washed me and massaged my belly with the relaxed moves of one who did it every day, telling me it was good for the uterus, it would ensure I'd have many more babies in the years to come.

"I shall be content with just this one," I said, lifting the baby a little, so glad—*so* glad—it was all done.

She grinned then, showing her missing teeth. "He is a fine boy. Good and strong," she said, flexing her arm muscles. "His father shall be proud. But a mama needs many."

I grinned. "Mayhap. 'Tis difficult to think beyond this one."

"Keep massaging your belly," she said to me sternly. "Until you can feel it soften. Eat good, red meat every day. Drink milk, lots of milk. You need it as the child needs it from you. And two glasses of wine, one in the morning, one at night," she added, lifting two fingers, and then tucking the far side of my blankets in and under the mattress.

I frowned. I was pretty sure the Surgeon General wouldn't approve of that last advice. "Wine?"

"One for the mama," she said with a grin, "and one for the babe," she added, leaning down to affectionately squeeze his little foot.

I smiled. I wouldn't take that last advice, but I loved the spirit in which it was given.

"Does he look small?" I asked her, worriedly looking at my son. "Did he come too soon?"

"Heavens, no," she said, crossing herself. "The Lord brought him on the day he was destined to arrive. And this child is perfect. To me, he seems full-formed." Her dark eyes looked me over, and a bit of doubt creeped into her face. "And yet for one as big as you…" She shrugged and leaned down to take the baby from me without asking.

Quickly, she stripped him from his blanket. The baby squirmed and then his tiny lips curled into a mewl of complaint, but she ignored him. Her round hands covered his shoulders, probed his belly and, unceremoniously, his little man parts. She turned him over on one palm and forearm, running two fingers down his back. Then she turned him back over and pulled his mouth close to her ear, not seeming to hear his cry, only the air coming from his lungs. At last, she smiled and cradled him close, cooing and cooing, bringing his complaint to a stop.

She tossed me a satisfied smile, waving away my concerns with her fat fingers. "The little lord is perfect. Fully formed. No need to worry, Mama Forelli."

"*Grazie mille*," I said, watching as she swiftly bundled him again and then settled him in my arms.

She waved my thanks off even as she backed away. "I shall stay here for the day, unless I am called to another. If you have need, send for me, yes?"

"Yes, thank you," I murmured.

Lia arrived again, two steaming buckets of water in her hands. And Alessandra with more fresh linens.

"We thought you might like a sponge bath," Lia said. "I think you're supposed to avoid bathing for a while, but we can do our best."

"That would be wonderful," I said. My only reluctance was releasing the baby when the time came. But I could see Lia, holding him, bonding with him, and it was almost as good as holding him myself.

Almost.

I stepped into the tub, and Alessandra passed me soap, which I lathered on a cloth and washed my extremities. Gingerly, I bathed, feeling new aches and pains, as well as my odd, flabby belly, reminding me of a deflated balloon. I hoped it'd deflate a lot more in time. I massaged it, as the midwife had instructed, thinking how nice it felt to be free of the burden of carrying a child within, and how much nicer it was to look upon my sweet baby boy instead.

"Oh, you are going to be a ladies' man," Lia said, nuzzling him. "With that dark hair and those dark eyes...And your auntie will make certain that only the best come near you."

"May I hold him?" Alessandra asked shyly.

"Of course," Lia said, offering the child up to her.

Our friend took him and carried him over toward the window, holding him close, looking natural with him in her arms.

"Just think," I said. "Within the new year, you'll likely have your own baby."

"Would that it be true," she mused. Her eyes sought mine. "At least your trial is over."

"True enough." I used a sponge to scrub my neck and shoulders, then rinsed off with a wet cloth. The girl was holding my son. *My son.* It was real. It had happened.

"He is beautifully formed, Gabriella. He doesn't seem a bit too small."

"You believe so?" I said, worry creeping into my mind and heart again. This child needed every week of growth he could get between his birth and what was to come...Strength. Immunities.

After I toweled off and donned a clean shift, Ali brought him back to me and settled him in my arms. Lia returned then and climbed onto the bed beside me, which the maids had swiftly changed, whisking away the old, bloody and soiled linens. I set little Fortino on the bed between us and carefully unwrapped him. His legs and arms were skinny, his belly rounded. I saw now that the umbilical cord end was tied to a tiny stick, which was how they encouraged it to wither and fall off, leaving behind a rustic sort of belly button. Was everyone an Outie in this era?

It'd be fine with me. I couldn't wait until he was healed and I could kiss that sweet belly button and watch him smile. I leaned down and kissed his little toes. "How can I fall in love twice in this life?" I said to Lia, happy tears welling in my eyes.

"He already has my heart, too," she said, taking my hand and squeezing it, still staring. "Can you imagine it? The little guy will fairly bust with all the love he's going to get at Castello Forelli."

"Indeed," I sighed. I leaned down and took his hands in mine, admiring the eensy, almost translucent nails. He squirmed, and his tiny face squinched up to complain about the cold air across his bare skin. I laughed and cooed and pulled him into my arms, rocking a little, and he soon settled down to sleep, his tiny chest rising and falling.

"Is this all they do all day? Sleep?" I asked.

"If the Lord is kind," Alessandra said. "Why don't you try and rest while he does, Gabriella? You've been through quite an ordeal."

"Good idea," Lia whispered, kissing his head. "Marcello will soon return, I'll bet. He went home to give the good news to our people. We'll leave you two alone for a while. Sleep. And ring the bell or shout if you want or need us to return."

"All right. Thank you."

After they closed the door, I settled down on my side, nestling little Fortino close to me. Lightly, I stroked his cheek, cupped his head with my palm, watching as he stretched and then went on slumbering.

A tiny miracle. My tiny miracle.

Thank you, Lord, I prayed. *Thank you for protecting him. And me.*

I was well aware how many women died in childbirth or afterward in this era. But everything seemed fine. I felt well, strong—crazy-tired, sure—and crazy sore, like an alien had just burst through my body. But all in all, okay. I stretched out my arm above my baby so I couldn't roll over on him and settled my right hand on the other side of his body. I could feel the steady, staccato beat of his heart, the quick rise and fall of his tiny lungs.

He was here. Whole. And mine. Ours.

Our son.

With that thought, I slept.

Sometime later, my son—*my son!*—awakened me with his pitiful mewling cry, rousing me from a faraway dream. It took a moment for me to remember where I was and what had happened—but then I saw that Marcello had climbed into bed with us. He looked with fear upon our squawling, unhappy babe, but it seemed oddly natural to unlace my gown and bring the babe to my breast. He wandered a bit, but then latched on, and I smiled as he suckled hungrily.

Marcello watched, brows raised, and then a slow smile crossed his face. "A miracle, really. All of it. From start to finish."

"You think so?"

"I know so. Do you not?"

I gazed down at our son. "Yes," I said, nodding happily. "I do."

Come morn, after Marcello had dressed and gone again, a knock sounded at the door. "Lia?" I called.

She peeked in. "You two okay?"

"We're fine," I said, smiling again at my baby. "Just doing something totally weird."

"Weird?" she asked, closing the door behind her.

"Yeah, you know. Feeding a baby. With my *body*. Which is producing *milk*. Isn't that weird? I think it's weird."

"I think it's wonderful," she said, going to the hearth to set new wood atop the glowing embers. I looked to the window. Late morning, by the looks of it. Were our parents on their way yet? I was so eager for them to meet their grandchild.

She edged over to me as Fortino, sated, pulled off the breast, his head lolling to one side. "Ooo, may I hold him?"

"If you'll try and burp him first," I said, wrapping him up and handing him over.

She lifted him up to get a good look at his face. "Think he'll have brown eyes?"

"Between me and Marcello? I think so. He'll be as dark as yours will be fair."

She shifted but remained silent. I knew she didn't want a baby—wanted to wait, if she could, until after the plague came and went—but now that I was through it, all I could think about was the joy of it all, the sheer joy. And I wanted that for my sister, too. Surely God wouldn't allow all this to happen...me to come here, fall in love with Marcello, marry and have this babe...just to take him from me. Would he?

I frowned, thinking of the stats. One-third of the population. How many mothers who truly loved their sons with everything in them would watch their children die? Or die themselves? Somehow, that seemed even harder to me. Feeling myself fade, knowing I was leaving this precious child motherless...

"Gabs?" Lia asked me, growing concerned. "What is it?"

"Oh," I said, shaking my head, "nothing. Nothing."

"You looked sad..."

"I'm fine," I said, moving to the other side of the bed, climbing out. The last thing Lia needed was to hear me fretting about the plague and what it might do to a family. I knew firsthand what it was like trying to do birth control the old-fashioned way, and Fortino was the result. If Lia and Luca were doing the same...well, chances were good she'd end up pregnant at some point soon, too. The only true birth control in this era was to avoid your husband altogether. And the Forelli boys? I blew out a breath and smiled. Yeah, neither of them would freely choose abstinence.

I moved to the fresh gown Marcello had brought me from Castello Forelli. Lia would lace me up when she decided to set down her nephew.

I grinned. Who was I fooling? I'd probably have to call for a maid or wait for Alessandra. I looked in the dim looking glass at my reflection, my hair a crazy mass of curls, and attempted to brush it. Rather than fight it, I decided to dip my hands in the basin of water and wet it partially down, giving in to the curls. Marcello always liked my hair down anyway. And in this intimate space, when he came back to collect us...it'd be okay, I figured. Even if the rest of the medieval matrons disapproved of a girl with her hair down.

I forced myself to eat some of the food that Alessandra brought us; but mostly, I paced and dozed and stared and stared at my little son. All I wanted was for my family to gather, for all of us to get back to Castello Forelli. Once there, surrounded by all I loved most, I believed I'd feel settled. But as the sun set, Lia looked over at me on the bed.

"It's getting dark, Gabs. It's not safe for them to travel. I think you should just try and sleep. They'll surely be here soon after sunup. They're likely halfway between here and Siena already."

I nodded, feeling ridiculous about how sad this thought made me. Of course they couldn't travel after dark. These winter days were short, and they'd probably stopped at the inn, halfway home. I didn't want them to get hurt, riding after dark. But still...my heart was like a stubborn two-year-old, wanting what it wanted.

And what I wanted was Mom and Dad.

All of us home. Now.

CHAPTER 33

GABRIELLA

We departed the next morn, Marcello lifting me to my side saddle, and then taking Fortino from Alessandra's arms to lift him up to me. Little Chiara cried, sad that we were taking the *bambino* away, reaching for us. Her heartfelt tears melted my heart. Alessandra picked her up and kissed her cheek.

"'Tis all right, Chiara," I said. "You and Alessandra will come and visit us soon. Yes?"

Ali smiled and nodded eagerly. "We shall let you get settled and come and visit in a few days." She held up three fingers to Chiara. "We'll go see little Fortino in this many days, yes?"

Chiara sniffed and stuffed two fingers in her mouth.

Rodolfo was stiff and distant, only giving me a quiet nod and smile as farewell. Maybe he felt guilty...but honestly? I knew what had driven him to push me. He only wanted to protect his family. And holding little Fortino close, I couldn't blame him a bit.

Marcello tied my mare's reins to his saddle, leading us, and I knew he felt every measure of pride in bringing us home as he did upon the morn after a victorious battle. Forelli knights in full golden regalia rode before and behind us, ready to escort their littlest charge home. Every one of them wore the wide grins of proud uncles. Not even the gray and cold, foreboding late-winter day could dampen their moods.

I glanced back to Rodolfo and Alessandra, knowing I could never thank them enough...grateful that the man had ridden after my husband and fetched the midwife and my sister. With some relief I saw both Grecos smile up at us, and Rodolfo bent and took little Chiara into his arms, drying her tears and waving as we exited the gates.

As we rode out, I wondered if I'd made a terrible mistake, telling him of what was to come...and yet, I didn't feel guilt. Only hope that someone else might have a fighting chance to battle what was to come, that it wouldn't catch my dear friends unaware. I thought of telling Marcello what had happened as we passed the tombs, but didn't want anything to mar the day. Marcello would be frustrated by the potential risk of my disclosure, I thought, but he would understand. And if there was one of his brothers that I thought he'd tell himself, it'd be Rodolfo.

I shivered and pulled my cloak closer, looking down at my son's tiny face. He slept, unaware that he was going home for the very first time to the castello that would one day be his. My heart swelled with joy, even as I obsessed over the idea of getting close to a roaring fire in the hearth of the Great Hall and driving away the chill that was settling in my bones.

As Castello Forelli came into sight, her golden flags waving in the stiff wind, I saw that every possible person was now bundled and waiting on her walls. When they saw us, they cheered, their combined voices warming the chilled air with the name *Forelli! Forelli! Forelli!*

Never had I had a more joyous sense of home.

The gates were opened, and maids and squires and knights and cooks and stewards all spilled out in a continuous stream, surrounding us. Surrounding us, welcoming us, begging for peekaboo views of the tiny "prince," as I'd taken to calling Fortino...

Behind us, the gates closed, and then, I saw them, Mom and Dad. They waited by the big doors of the Great Hall, stately, as if they were presiding over the castello in our absence. But I could tell by their expressions that they fairly burst with anticipation. And judging from their appearance, they'd only arrived shortly before us. Mom, with her normally perfect braid, had blonde hair sticking out all over the place, and her dress was rumpled, even dirty. Dad, well, he looked like he'd risen from his bed and hadn't given a thought to changing his clothes or combing his hair. But I didn't care—I was just glad they were home, finally ready to meet their tiny grandson.

Marcello pulled to a stop, dismounted, and then came to me, easing me down, the baby still in my arms. We shared a grin, and I handed him his son. Marcello cradled him, lifted him a little and began turning slowly.

"My people, please welcome your future lord, Fortino Betarrini Forelli!"

There was an audible gasp, then sighs, and people were clapping and crying, pressing in, kissing our cheeks, touching the baby's head...And then they made a way. A visible passage for my parents. We moved toward them, my eyes on Mom and Dad, wondering anew at the gift this moment was. When I came here, I had no father. He'd been long dead. And yet he'd been restored to me, as Mom had been restored to me in another way altogether.

I had to hand it to them. Both looked first at me, as if the babe wasn't there. They reached out to me, Mom cupping my cheek, Dad taking my arm, and pulled me to them, even as they ushered us inside, out of the wind. "Gabi," was all they said. But it was enough. And yet in the utterance of my name they'd seemed to have said, *We're proud of you...We wish we had been with you...what is this gift?*

"*Madre, Padre,*" I said, *Mom, Dad...* "This is your grandson."

We circled in close. I soon sensed Lia and Luca moving in, too, with me and Marcello, surrounding the babe.

"And now we are seven," I said lowly. I looked at each of them.

"A holy number, Tomas would say," Marcello whispered, stroking his son's head.

"A perfect number," Mom said. Eagerly, she gestured to Marcello, silently asking for her grandson—with a hopeful "May I?"—and he happily complied. She cradled him close and Dad wrapped an arm around her shoulders, tears streaming down his face. I'd never seen him cry so much.

"Do you know?" he whispered, turning red-rimmed eyes toward me. "Do you know what this means to me? A moment I could so easily have missed. Would have missed. To see you with my grandson," he said in a hush, and we were all crying then. "So perfect. So perfect! Oh, how I love you all!"

We pressed in, none of us willing to let the moment slip away.

"A new generation upon us," Marcello said, holding his gaze on each of us a moment, letting it sink in. "Hope. Do you feel that, my family? *Hope.* Cling to it. Do not let it go. Regardless of the dark days ahead. When we feel despair, when we feel loss, remember *this*. Hope. Light. It fairly blinds us now, but some day we will need to hold this memory in our hearts. Remember it. *Remember* it."

I stared at him.

And I thought that never, ever, had I loved Marcello Forelli more than I did in that moment.

PART III

PESTILENCE

1348

CHAPTER 34

GABRIELLA

It came to Italia as we expected.

Months after Marcello had resigned his post as one of the Nine, ignoring the confusion and outrage of the other eight. In the last hundred years, such a resignation had never been witnessed. But we knew there was no way we could be in the city when it arrived. It was the only way to ensure a chance at survival.

It came when our son, Fortino Betarrini Forelli, had grown a mess of curls and the fiercest determination to defy every parental directive sent his way, and delighted in tottering after Chiara Greco—a soulful, thoughtful girl of five—who doted on the little boy as if she were the mother hen, and he, her chick.

It came just when we were hoping we were wrong, or something had changed and it wasn't going to come after us like a dragon.

The Black Plague.

The darkest of terrors.

It was as if we were caught in the web of some horrific prophecy, hearing news of its arrival along our coastal cities, and moving swiftly, striking down one in three. January swept into February, spreading the plague among those who huddled around winter fires. It reached further, deeper, in March into April. But summer was the worst.

Come the heat of August, the cities keened their collective horrified, mourning cry.

And Marcello paced.

Paced and paced, torn between the knowledge he held and the history unfolding before him, powerless to stop it.

Worse, he began to drink, into the night, alone, staring into the fire. Glass after glass of wine, calling for more when the carafe was empty.

His republic called for him, begged him to return, hoping that he or the She-Wolves knew of some magical fire-retardant to the inferno unfurling all about us. But there was nothing. Not even the knowledge within my parents' minds could stave off what was to come. What they built within Castello Forelli, and by repetition, Castello Greco, was merely their best guess at a defense.

Food. Water. Medicinals, in the most basic sense. Armory to withstand a prolonged siege.

And so we waited. Listening as it closed in, a narrowing funnel, the danger ever nearer, soon within a few days' ride.

Then it arrived within our borders. Toscana. Then within reach of us, in the northeast.

Messengers arrived.

Messengers we would not admit.

We demanded they break the wax seals and read the words aloud from the other side of the gates.

It came to us, story after story of disease and death.

But still, Castello Forelli would not open her gates.

We listened.

We returned missives.

We distributed food.

But we would not open our gates.

CHAPTER 35

EVANGELIA

At first, the men watched in mute disbelief as Marcello and Luca turned those at our gates away. Out of respect, they did as they were asked, but I could see them peering after their captain and lord in complete confusion. It was so out of character for the Forellis—to reject those in need rather than greet them with mercy—that I guessed they simply hoped it was a phase of sorts, and that Marcello and Luca would soon give in.

They did not.

They had no choice, really. To take to giving away food and medicines would mean that anyone with need—and there would be many, in time—would take to camping outside our walls. While the walls were tall and thick, Mom and Dad had been clear; they didn't want those who were sick right outside. It was simply too close. People, even people who were well, inevitably attracted vermin. And vermin inevitably made their way through the tiniest of cracks and through the thickest of walls.

For a time, Marcello sent crates of supplies to the villages within our lands—Cavo and Annini and Carini—weekly. A knight would volunteer, load two mules, take them to the villages, and then spend a week in the hunter's hut to be certain he had not taken sick. For months, they all returned. Then one did not, and the system failed. Because when the next knight went out, he found the last one dead in the hunter's hut, hauled him out and buried him, then got sick himself. He ended up at our wall, begging to be admitted.

Luca refused him. "Forgive me, brother," he said. "For the good of all within, we cannot. Go and make your peace with God, and find a good place to lay your weary head in the woods. We shall pray for your soul."

He'd left the wall, then, not looking at anyone else. Not even me.

Over the weeks that followed, the knights' and servants' disbelief and confusion turned into simmering indignation...

...then despair...

...then resignation...

...then apathy...

...which was the toughest of all for us to take.

"We came here to embrace *life*," I said to Gabi, under my breath, as we took our daily walk around the perimeter of the castle. "To take what came to us, even if it meant facing death. Remember? That's what we said. We wanted to hold on to that feeling of living, truly living, rather than just making it through the day. That's what we discovered here. That's what we wanted to hold on to. Now, we have none of that. We live, but it is as if we are half-dead!"

Gabi set down little Fortino and rolled the leather ball for him, and he happily chased after it, kicking it, in that awkward, stiff-legged way of toddlers. But she said nothing. Because she was thinking? Or disagreed?

Four knights passed us, with nods of greeting, and I remained silent until we were beyond them.

"Back home," I continued, "People get home from school and work and just drive inside their garages, barely waving at neighbors. Never taking the time to get to know them. Remember? We hated that. But now, how are we any different? You and I both know that we're staying off the wall because we can't stand it. Turning away from everyone out there. It's easier for us to stay down here, pretending they don't exist."

She shook her head. "You think I don't live with that guilt every day? My husband's guilt? No one feels this weight more than Marcello. No one. Have you seen him? It's eating him alive."

Her eyes told me it frightened her far more than I knew.

"We simply have to weather this, Lia. Make it through. No, it's not how we want to live. But if we want to *live*, we have to stay the course. Remain strong. Keep our eyes on the horizon and keep setting our feet toward it, day by day, month by month, year by year. Not just enduring but waiting with expectation for a reprieve. For change."

"This is only year one," I whispered, more a thought I was digesting than telling her anything she didn't know.

Gabriella just bent and scooped up squirming Fortino and kissed his neck, then held him up to me. "This is what we will concentrate on through the year and beyond. New life, even in the face of death."

I took Fortino in my arms. He patted my cheeks. "Awww, Via," he said, unaccustomed to me not greeting him with a smile and assuming something was wrong. "It's okay," he said in English, having learned our automatic comforting words. "It's okay."

I stared at his big brown eyes, the glossy curls that looked like they'd come off of big rollers. Felt the comforting, compact weight of his little body. Knew that I'd die to save him, as I would any of the rest of my family.

"It's there, Lia," Gabi whispered, slipping her arm around my waist. "Life. It's just going to be a little less *obvious* for a few years."

GABRIELLA

Whereas I came to accept it, Tomas and Adela only became more agitated as the months passed.

Quietly married just as the plague began, they looked like anyone else in the castello in their simple garb. But deep inside, they remained the holiest people I knew. And it was that pull toward grace and mercy that called them *outside* the walls.

Time and again they approached Marcello and Luca. Together. Apart. Begging them to open the gates to those who were in need. Citing Scripture. Citing basic moral code. Citing civility. Humanity.

Until they gave up and one day, were in the dining hall, trunks packed, asking to be released. "We cannot remain," Tomas said, lifting his chin and sad eyes to Marcello. "We can no longer turn our backs on our sisters and brothers."

Adela wrapped her hands around Tomas's arm, but she looked as resolute as he was.

"Leave us," Marcello growled, speaking to every knight and servant in the hall, but only looking at Tomas and Adela. I tensed. He'd already been drinking for a while. I knew, from experience, that it was never best to approach him at this hour of the day.

In two minutes, only family remained, and the heavy door was shut. Everything but the crackling fire in the huge hearth was silent for several heavy seconds.

Luca stepped down from the dais and went over to them, trying to intervene. "You cannot leave. 'Tis the only way to weather this storm—to remain in the shelter of this castello. You know this. For months people have approached the castello, ill, dying. But we remain strong!"

Adela moved to take his hands, looking up at him. "But we are called to *enter* the storm, brother. The Lord calls us to those in need."

Luca shook his head. "'Tis not the way of wisdom," he said, his voice trembling with fear-borne-rage. "Look what happened to our men we sent out with supplies! Do you wish to invite death to visit?"

"We do not fear it," she said. "The Lord shall protect us or he shall smite us, but whatever comes," she paused to take Tomas's hand, "we are ready to accept it."

"What we cannot accept is remaining here," Tomas said. "No matter how great our love and respect is for you, brothers," he said, nodding to

Marcello and Luca and Dad, "and you, my sisters," he added, looking to me, Lia and Mom, "we cannot ignore the need of those outside the walls."

"We are not ignoring them," Marcello said, rubbing his face, his eyes purple-ringed and bloodshot, "we simply cannot aid them in the way you wish."

"You are not aiding them at all, now," Tomas returned. "I do not understand this and cannot live with it. They need us out there, Marcello."

"They need to see us and feel our touch," Adela said.

"You cannot!" Luca cried. "That is akin to taking Death as a dance partner!"

"Our own blood brothers may have taken ill by now," Tomas said, methodically rolling up his sleeve to show the triangular tattoo that he, Luca and Marcello all carried. "We shall go to each of them, shelter with them for a time, and minister to those in need around each of their homes."

Luca was shaking his head. "I forbid it," he said, angry and desperate. "As Adela's last male relative, I forbid it."

Adela's grip on Tomas's arm tightened. "I answer only to my husband and my God now."

"You are a fool!" Luca said to her. "You nearly died, that day, when you were in the hands of the Fiorentini. We saved you! And now you toss away your life?" His face and tone turned to pleading. "I know this makes no sense to you. I know it feels wrong. But I beg you, sister, brother, to trust us in this. 'Tis the only way to preserve our lives. To stay away from those who ail."

"Those who give away their lives shall gain it, and those who cling to life will lose it," Tomas said, and I assumed it was Scripture he quoted.

Luca stared back at him. "Are you so ready to give away my sister's life? Do you care so little for the gift and beauty of your bride?" The last words came out in a sneer, and he stepped closer to the shorter, pudgier man.

Tomas did not react. "I would give my own life to save your sister's," he said. "I love her with everything I have in me. God has graced me mightily," he said, looking down at her, "with the gift of a wife. But he has spoken to us. And he calls us not to remain here, but to go out, to where there is need. He has called us not to minister to the healthy, but to those who ail."

Luca sighed heavily and stepped away, lifting a hand. "Cease. No more of the Holy Writ. Please."

"You object to it," Tomas said gently, "and you refuse to look upon our brotherhood marking, because you refuse to face the truth. You know righteousness. You know what you are called to do...to serve. But you are at war with your own hearts."

Marcello shook his head, his eyes hollow and distant. "You do not know the whole of it."

I stared hard at him, wondering if he would cave, tell them at last what it was that we faced. How the plague would last. And last, and last...this battle against the unseen enemy.

But he did not.

"We do not know the whole of it," Adela pressed, looking not to him but to Luca, "but you will not tell us all that you know."

"Or believe you know," Tomas said. "Only the Lord knows what lies ahead of us."

Or those who come from the future, I thought. But it caught me, that thought. Did I know, truly know, all? We only knew a portion, really. The main, overwhelming, scene-stealing storyline. But what sorts of subplots might weave their way beneath, adding texture and depth in the next few years? The thought gave me an odd surge of hope. Could the plague be our backdrop, but not the stage itself?

"We shall not keep you here as prisoners," Marcello said, his face slack with weariness and defeat. "But just as I begged you to not go to

Rodolfo Greco because I feared the worst—and you ended up on the wall, with a noose about your neck—so, now, do I beg you not to go out there."

Tomas stared back at Marcello, remembering. He had been so close to death that day. One push away from strangulation atop the wall of Castello Paratore.

"We all were spared that day, were we not?" Tomas asked softly. "Every one of us. Could the Lord not spare us again?"

I thought about it. Dad taking the sword through the chest. Me hanging over the edge of the precipice. The rocks launched from the catapult, so narrowly missing us. The knights who came against us, thirsting for our blood.

And yet we had made it through.

"The Lord gives and the Lord takes away. 'Tis never ours to hold, regardless of how we like to pretend it is," Tomas said.

Silence settled around us like a misty fog.

"You shall go, then," Marcello said, a note of hope entering his voice. "And be our emissaries? Would you do that for us? Take supplies to the villages, rather than bring the infirm to our gates? We would supply you weekly and—"

"You cannot allow this," Luca sputtered, turning to him. "This is my sister we speak of! And our brother!"

Marcello's jaw tightened. "'Tis not my decision. Castello Forelli is our sanctuary, not their prison." He gestured toward Tomas and Adela.

Luca let out a groan and paced away, rubbing his face, his head. I wrung my hands, knowing there was no way for me to make it right.

Adela went to him, though, and again, took his hands. "Please, brother. Send us forth with love and hope and prayers of blessing and protection. You think we do not fear? We are human yet," she said, with a small smile. "As apt to fail as any other. But please, Luca. Please. Send us with your love and blessing."

Luca stared at her, then folded her into his arms, holding her for a long moment. "Adela, Adela," he whispered, kissing her head. "I shall miss you. *And* your idiot of a husband," he said, reaching out an arm to him.

Tomas took it. And again at the gates as they departed.

But when the gates closed, I wondered if I'd ever see them enter through them again.

⁓⟋⟍⁓

They survived for months, out beyond our walls. At first, staying close to us, in and around the Forelli villages. Then farther afield, among the blood brothers who still lived. They had promised to stay away from Siena, their only concession, finding more than enough to minister to beyond the city gates.

Everywhere they went, they cared for the people. Fed them. Wrapped the horrific wounds. Buried them. Moved on.

And then a week passed, with no word from them.

Then two.

Then, the hardest of message of all came from Conte Lerici.

Plague was upon their house.

Half were dead.

Adela and Tomas among them.

GABRIELLA

And so it went.

People approached our walls.

People departed.

Some were well, whole.

Others ill and spent. Dying.

In time, we could smell the stink of the dead even from within our walls. At first, I dared to walk the parapet, taking in the image of men, women, even children, outside our gates, dying or dead. The bodies thrown into horrifying heaps. The living, begging to be let in, as if we held the secret to healing. To freedom.

Which we did, in a way.

Quarantine.

No one in or out. It was the only way. The only hope for us to weather this storm. This was why we had laid up provisions.

Marcello—with the aid of wine consumed until he could fall into desperate slumber—ignored the summons to Siena, as a former one of the Nine. Stories from there were horrific. So many dead within days that the morticians and grave diggers were overwhelmed, many dying themselves. There were too many to remove, far too many.

And so the dead rotted.

In the slums and in palazzos alike.

Death came hunting, consuming entire flocks and with no discernible pattern.

Ravaging our people over and over.

And over.

Month by month.

Year by year.

Our only break from the despair was little Fortino, and now the second child, growing steadily in my womb.

But would my children live to see the world beyond our gates?

The fear that thought brought to me—of watching a child die in my arms—was a different kind of plague upon my heart.

PART IV

INFILTRATION

Spring, 1350

CHAPTER 36

EVANGELIA

I would say, later, that we sought each other out as comfort.

A respite in the storm.

Luca and I took ease in each other's company, fiercely, defiantly. Claiming life, love, in the face of so much death and destruction. We found solace within one another's arms. With him I knew peace and satisfaction and such deep connection...and glimpsed life, as it should be.

But two years into the plague, when I knew I carried Luca's child—and Gabi was well into her second pregnancy—I wept.

Because all I could see before me was devastation.

Disaster.

Disease.

Destruction.

Death. The antithesis of this new life, tingling within my womb. I cursed God. Cursed him for bringing this to us, when he knew, he *knew* what we faced. Why taunt us with hope? Delight? When we well knew what was before us.

For two years, the plague had ravaged Toscana. We were all but cut off from Siena, the messengers arriving farther and farther apart. Today we'd heard news from the city that Siena's priests had decreed the Roman statues within Il Campo a pagan curse—the likely cause of the plague—and the ancient, priceless figures were destroyed and chopped to bits in order to be secretly added into a supply of building material for Firenze's walls. Because Firenze had not yet been hit as hard as Siena.

Such was the thinking.

Pass off our curse to our enemy.

And now, Il Campo was denuded of the statues that had once given her such countenance, such grandeur, stature. A simple, barren shell of what she once was, I figured, remembering it from modern times. I'd wondered what had happened to all of those beautiful marble figures. Now I knew. They'd been chopped to bits.

"Such superstitious fools," Marcello groused, deep in his cups that evening. Luca and I shared a worried glance. We'd watched the depression slowly take hold of him. It wasn't good for a man like my brother-in-law to be cooped up in a castle for so long. In fact, it seemed bad for all of us. A pall hovered over the entire castello.

"Thinking they might play God," Marcello grumbled, lifting his glass and draining it.

"You cannot truly blame them," Gabi said with a sigh. "They're desperate." I thought about the Forelli palazzo on Il Campo, sitting empty, the furniture all covered with linens, the servants long since let go.

At their feet, Fortino chased two oddly shaped dice, shaking them in his hand and letting them loose, motivated by the knights around him who idly betted on his toss.

"And now the Nine are but Four," Luca said, pouring more wine for himself. He eyed Marcello carefully, twisting his goblet between his palms. That had been in another message. A new, desperate call for Marcello to resume his seat, resume leadership.

Marcello lifted red-rimmed eyes to look at Gabi, the question unspoken.

"You cannot," I whispered, knowing it wasn't my place to enter the conversation, but finding I could not remain quiet. "You cannot go," I said, louder this time.

Because if Marcello went, I knew Luca would go with him.

Beneath the table, Luca took hold of my hand and squeezed it.

Marcello swung his legs over the back of the bench and rose, shuffling over to the hearth. He put a hand on top of the mantle, as if hanging on for strength, and the firelight danced across his handsome—though weary—face as he sipped again from his cup. Looking as if she'd aged ten years, Gabi went around to bundle little three-year-old Fortino up in her arms and hand him to his nursemaid.

Mom and Dad rose, tension evident in every line around their eyes and mouths. The Great Hall cleared out, every knight and maid aware of the stress building between us. I knew they'd likely stage eavesdroppers outside the door, but they'd give us the illusion of privacy. Every one of them had agreed, once the plague arrived in Italia, to keep to the castle. To not see friend or family until the last known victim was buried for three months. We hadn't even seen the Grecos, who were attempting a similar quarantine across the valley.

Everyone in the castello had agreed to it, but I knew it was difficult for them, as it was for us, two years in. They were probably half hoping that this would break our steadfast desire to keep our gates so stubbornly shut. Despite the terror outside our walls, most medieval minds could not quite get their heads around the concept of how disease passed from one to another.

When it was only the six of us, Marcello spoke, head down. "I must go to them. They are devolving to madness. Who knows what else is happening in the city and the Republic?"

"Nay, Marcello, nay," Gabi said, taking his arm. She gently turned his face toward her. "You cannot. You know what it could mean."

"I know what turning my back on my kinsmen means," he said. "Look at me!" he said, lifting his arms to her, his face full of self-loathing.

"I cower here, day by day, and only manage to welcome another because of *this*," he said, lifting his cup. With a sneer he threw it into the massive hearth, where it broke into pieces, the red wine sizzling against the back of it.

We all stood there, in silence. Relieved it was out in the open, at last. That Marcello was willing to face it. But now what?

"What can you do for them?" Gabi asked. "There is no nobleman with the power to keep them from this pestilence. It strikes where it wishes. They'd be safest in their country homes, outside the city."

"As it was for Castello Gallo and Castello Rizzo?" he bit out, and I felt the pain in my gut over that again, even as Gabi recoiled. Two of Marcello and Luca's blood brothers and their families, decimated by the plague. Both messages had been unclear if there were any survivors—only a plea for prayer, and a tone to each note that felt like a farewell. We could do nothing but send food and medicines to the survivors.

That aspect had been the worst part of this whole deal. Keeping the guys from telling all their brothers—men who had ridden to our aid, saved us from certain death. If we'd told any more, it surely would have significantly changed the outcome of these horrific four years. Our friends would likely have lived, yes, but history would be irrevocably shifted. It had been bad enough that we knew, that Gabi let Rodolfo know. No others could be told.

Today, along with news from Siena, there was a note from Sir Mantova—the man who had arrived with the catapult in the last battle here, to save us—that his house, too, had been struck.

This was what weighed so heavily on Marcello, what drove him to drink so much, night after night, and what was pushing him over the edge now. He was clearly haunted by the specter of his brothers going down, one by one...when he'd been in a position to potentially save them. Haunted by giving up his seat on the council of Siena, as one of the Nine, in the face of the worst crisis they'd ever seen.

"Tell them," Luca said.

We all looked to him. Tell us...*what*?

Marcello sighed heavily and looked around, as if he sought a new goblet of wine.

"Tell them," Luca repeated.

Marcello scowled at his cousin but then seemed to give in. "There is more," he said at last, clearly working the words over in his mind. But I noticed he elected to stare into the fire rather than look at any of us. "These last months, Firenze has rallied. The plague seems to have left her gates and not returned. While our beloved city is finding it difficult to bury her dead." The words came out of his mouth in a tortured mix of agony and bitterness.

We were all silent. How could this be fair? Why would God not strike them as he had us? Maybe the priests hadn't been so far off, smashing their statues of gods and goddesses as both a token offering and a curse...God seemed to be judging on a whim anyway.

Luca crossed his arms and faced us. "Siena is at her weakest in decades. And Firenze is feeling her strength return..."

I shook my head. "You don't think...They wouldn't..."

His worried green eyes shifted to me. "I do. And they would."

"It's madness!" Gabi cried. "If they attack Siena, they might gain a city, but they'll return home with an enemy that would take them down from within."

"But do you not see?" Marcello said dully, staring unblinking at the fire, gesturing at it as if he could see the Fiorentini within the flames. "They do not understand that." He finally turned toward her. "They only see opportunity. *Think*. Think of Lord Barbato and Lord Foraboschi. The lengths they went to in Venice to strike at you and yours as a means to engage in battle again. And now...this. Siena practically open for the taking."

Gabi swallowed hard. "Then she shall fall. But we remain. Safe. Here."

He shook his head, a tiny movement. "You do not understand. If Siena is attacked, and I do not go to her aid, we shall be labeled bigger cowards than we already are."

"And far more threatening," Luca said, "as *traitors*. Punishable by death."

"But he...But he is not of the Nine!" Gabi protested.

"But he is still a loyal son to Siena," Luca returned gently. "And expected to act as such. For if he doesn't, it shall not go well for him. And therefore, us."

"So one way or another," Gabi said, so quietly that I almost missed it, "Siena claims you."

Marcello tried to take her elbows in his hands, but she wrenched away, shaking her head. "Nay, Marcello. Nay."

"I am sorry, Gabriella. Truly, if I saw another way..."

She backed up as he advanced, his face a mask of apology. "You cannot," she insisted, shaking her head. "You know you cannot."

"I go now and attempt to lend aid, and hopefully live through it, or I remain here, a coward waiting for them to come and retrieve me so they can cut off my traitorous head. What say you, Gabriella? Which is better? Which is better for our son?"

She shook her head and stopped her retreat, giving in to tears, then. Mom and I cried with her. Luca put a strong, bracing arm around my shoulders and curled me into his chest. Over his shoulder, I watched Marcello wrap Gabi in his arms.

"I must go," he said, kissing her hair as he wept, too. "I must go and do what I can to shore up the city."

"But what of us?" Gabi cried, desperate. "What of your sons?"

"What of you?" he repeated softly, tucking a strand of her hair behind her ear. "This is as much for you and yours, beloved, as 'tis for me and mine. If Siena falls, if Firenze owns us, whom do you think she'll come after first? Who shall be the first prize she claims? You? Evangelia? Our little Fortino or tiny Benedetto?"

He shook his head, his hands dropping into fists.

"Nay. I must keep them as far from our gates as possible. And that begins by making certain Siena remains strong. Soldiers must be hired, trained to replace those who have died. Commerce must resume, as much as possible. Strategic relationships with Roma, with Venezia, with Pisa, must be built. Those are tasks for a man who has done them before. And I must teach the sons of the men who have died to take their fathers' places."

Gabi wasn't a crier, but the wrenching sobs that emerged from her throat ripped me to shreds. She cried as if he were dying in her arms already. As if every dream had died. And it tore at me, made me fight for breath, even as bile rose in the back of my throat.

I looked up to Luca, forcing myself to determine what I suspected was true. And with one glance, I knew.

CHAPTER 37

EVANGELIA

I wrenched away from him, making it only a few steps before I vomited across the floor.

"Oh, Lia, Lia," Mom soothed, coming over to me. "My goodness, I know this is hard news, but to be this upset?" she asked.

She helped me straighten and then seeing my face, understood. I'd not just puked because I was stressed out about Luca going—though I was—it was more due to my pregnancy, which I hadn't told any of them about. Not even Luca.

Mom swallowed hard. "Oh, honey," she said, pulling me into her arms. I cried harder then. "Oh, honey," she repeated, rubbing my back.

"What?" Dad asked. "What is it?"

I looked at him and then at the others, focusing on Luca. Hoping it would change his mind to go. "I am with child."

Luca's eyes widened, and then a smile broke out across his face. He came over to me and lifted me in his arms, turning me in a slow circle, face exhultant. But it gradually dawned on him. Why I wasn't excited now. Slowly, he let me slide back to the floor but held on to me.

"'Tis difficult news, Evangelia, to be certain. In these times, with what we face..." He reached up to wipe my tears and cup my cheek. "But 'tis good news too. Do you not see?" he asked lowly. "'Tis a sign from God. Hope for us. Could there be anything sweeter than another tiny Forelli about the castello?"

"Nay," I said, still crying.

He kissed my cheeks, my forehead, pulling me close. "'Twill be all right, sweet Evangelia. Trust me. Trust the One who brought you to me. The One who has seen fit to begin a new life," he said, placing a warm hand across my stomach, "even as we face so much death."

I swallowed hard, trying to get a grip. "Do not go," I said, clenching a handful of his gold tunic. "Please do not go, Luca," I whispered.

"I must," he said. "My place is with Marcello. And I agree with him—his place is in Siena. We shall not stay away long. And when we return, we shall stay in the hunter's hut for a time, to make certain we carry nothing foul back with us."

I thought of him in Siena. I thought of him so close, at the hunter's cabin, and yet not able to return to me. I thought of being pregnant—never so closely tied to him—and yet soon, to be so far from him.

And then I started crying in earnest.

"Is this how the She-Wolves of Siena truly want to see their husbands off?" Mom asked, after it'd gone on for a couple minutes.

I think after all the many months of being strong, and both being so scared and sad, that my tears basically fed off my sister's and hers, mine. I'd get a grip and then hear Gabi choke on a sob, and then I'd lose it again, and vice versa. But thank God we had Mom to pull us together.

"Now, girls," she said, taking a swift breath, collecting herself. I saw her own face was tearstained too. "While Marcello and Luca collect what they must for the journey come morn, we three must pack some things to help them while they're away. Come with me."

We swallowed hard and followed her out, our husbands looking grateful to her. They probably hoped their mother-in-law would fix us up and return their normal wives to them, not these crazed, hormonal, despondent, sniffling messes. And we did have to pull it together. I knew that. I just couldn't seem to do so.

To me, Marcello and Luca were heading into some scene out of *The Walking Dead*. All I could envision were the refugees that continued to come to our gates, begging for help, for food, for hope.

"How are they going to steer clear of everyone who might be infected or carrying the plague?" I asked Mom as we entered the storeroom. She took a wooden crate and began gathering supplies.

"They won't," she said. "That'd be impossible."

"But then..."

She glanced at me. "They'll need to be strong. Stay strong. I believe Luca might have an edge. If it was an early strain of the plague that he caught those years ago—and it sounded like it was—he might have some immunity."

My heart pounded with hope, but I said nothing, conscious that Gabi was listening. *What of Marcello?*

"In fact," Mom continued, settling two bottles of Oil of Thieves in the crate, surrounded by straw, "you all were exposed at that point, right? There could be something in our vaccines that aid us. And maybe Marcello is immune. He got close to Luca, right? When he was sick?"

Gabi nodded. "Very. He practically carried him."

Mom touched her hand. "I find hope in that. You can, too."

"Thanks, Mom," she said, closing her eyes for a moment and pinching the bridge of her nose. "I needed something like that to hang on to."

"Me, too," I said. "Now what can we help you pack?"

"Food, in that crate there. Wine. I don't want them to have to hire servants or shop much in the markets."

"If Siena still has a market," Gabi said.

"Any way we can keep them out of the public will be beneficial. Gabi, grab a bag of the dried oranges. Vitamin C, in case this monster is pneumatically spread."

"Pneumatic?"

"Some say it was fleas and it was transported by bite and blood. Others maintain it was spread like colds—sneezing and coughing. I say we shore your boys up for either version."

"I'm down with that," Gabi said. "So...linen, too? To cover their faces?"

"And soap. Blankets from here," she directed me. "Those we know won't have fleas inside them."

One of the cats walked in as we worked, weaving in and out of our legs. Every night Mom and Dad combed all the dogs and both cats, searching for fleas. Blessedly, they'd been free of them. But they still periodically dabbed orange oil onto their bellies and legs, just to make certain. Or combed soda ash through their fur. Fleas, apparently, hated orange oil and soda ash.

Mom was already putting orange oil into the box, along with two bags of lime powder—which we periodically swept across every inch of the castello floor—soda ash, two braids of garlic heads, and several jugs of apple cider vinegar. Tiny vials of the outrageously expensive tea tree oil and lemon grass oil were the last to go in. She packed straw into all the empty corners and then secured the lid.

We all looked at one another. The boys had probably packed and would want to get on the road as soon as morning. Which made us all reluctant to go out and face them. Mom took our hands.

"You both married well. They're strong. They're smart. And they know how to use all these medicinals. I've taught them myself. Have faith in them."

Come morning, we all dragged out to the courtyard, watching with dull eyes as horses were led from the stables. Two patrols would accompany our guys. I could tell the remaining men envied them. They itched for new activity, real battle, anything to save them from the monotony of the castle...even if it meant facing death.

Luca took my hand and led me away to where we were partially hidden by a wall from the mass of people. He pulled me into his arms, and we just stood there. Still. Silent. Aching.

"You keep my baby safe," he said at last, pulling back to look me in the eye. "I want to see a bump instead of your beautiful flat belly when I return."

I let out a small laugh. "I shall do what I can."

"See that you do. In fact, I'd love to see you fat. Chubby, at the very least. It would make you all the more delectable. Curving even more in all the right places."

That made me laugh outright. "Be careful what you wish for, Sir Luca Forelli."

He smiled, his eyes crinkling at the corners in the way I so loved, and lifted my hand to his lips. Then he took my hand firmly in his and led me to the center of the courtyard, where everyone was gathering to say their last farewells.

I closed my eyes, wanting to memorize the feel of his hand around mine. So warm and strong...My husband. Would this be the last time he touched me? Would he die out there? On the road? In Siena? Or was it possible...could he possibly be immune?

He leaned down, touching his forehead to mine.

"I'm not much of a praying person," I whispered, "but Luca, I'll be praying that you will be protected, and wise about choices you make, and above all, shielded from the illness."

"And I shall echo those prayers for you as well, beloved." He brought my hands to his lips again and then tore himself away to mount up.

I'd take any help God was dishing out if it meant that Luca would return to me. *Return to us*, I corrected myself, and found my hand straying to my stomach, as I'd seen Gabi do so many times during her own pregnancy.

"I shall send word," Marcello said to Gabi. "Once a day. By carrier pigeon to the village, not here." He knew Mom didn't want any more birds flying in here if she could help it. We'd long since shuttered the dove cote and killed any bird that knew Castello Forelli as home. "I'll share all I can."

She nodded, clearly trying to hold back tears, and the nursemaid brought Fortino forward for his father to kiss him. He did so, on both cheeks, then bent to kiss baby Benedetto.

"You are the man of the castello, Fortino. See that it remains safe." He smiled, obviously kidding, but Fortino nodded soberly and then reached for Gabi. Marcello bent and kissed her tenderly as the knights all mounted up. Luca turned to me.

"Farewell, beloved," he whispered, kissing me once more, lightly, almost reverent.

"Return to me, Luca."

He didn't promise, only flashed me a smile, then mounted up. In seconds, they'd ridden out, and the gates were immediately closed, the massive crossbeam sliding back into place. Dad came over and wrapped an arm around my shoulders, holding me, as we stood there, silent.

And for a moment, I didn't worry about Luca dying. I envied him, the ride, the freedom. How long had it been since we'd ventured out of the gates? More than two years now. I felt like we'd just been locked up in a tomb.

I wondered...was it better to go out and face death? Or hide from it, hoping it wouldn't come hunting?

CHAPTER 38

GABRIELLA

W e waited for four days to hear from Marcello for the first time. I was nearly tearing my hair out, about ready to saddle Zita and go galloping toward Siena, because he'd promised—*promised*—to send word. What had happened? Why wasn't he sending messages? Did he not know that his silence would be driving me mad?

I was up on the wall again, watching the road that led to Cavo, the little village that should have received at least three messages by now. Apparently, he'd forgotten the awesome spectacle that was the Wrath of Gabi. Apparently, I'd given him the impression that communication was optional.

Something terrible had to have happened. Something horrific, something awful...

I could feel how tense I was making the men, hanging out there, hour after hour, in the cold. Two offered me their capes to wear over my own, but I refused. I knew they had to be twice as chilled as I.

Fortino was wailing somewhere below, probably because his nurse-maid wasn't allowing him to have everything he wanted, which seemed to be particularly frustrating for a four-year-old. Within, I felt the same frustration. I wanted that message now. Needed it. *Please, Lord...*

"M'lady," Captain Pezzati said, coming over to me and turning to face the outer wall at my side. "Mayhap the dove keeper has met with some sort of...obstacle."

I stared at him for a long moment, horror overtaking me. *If the plague had gotten the dove keeper...*

No, he was fine. He was in Cavo, a village miraculously untouched by plague so far. We'd taken Signora Mancini a cow and two sheep and a crate full of baby chickens that first year after her husband died, and I knew she made a living in Cavo, now, off the milk and eggs and wool. It had worked so well, we'd taken to providing similarly for any widow of a Forelli knight who perished. There'd been ten since that day. Valente and Pietro and Giovanni among them. More had perished in the battles with Firenze, but many died as bachelors.

I thought about all the men riding out with Luca and Marcello. They'd all volunteered, Marcello said, and most were unmarried. But I knew that three had wives. What would happen if the plague came to our castello? Struck one after another down? How long might we manage to provide for widows and orphans before the coffers were empty? We'd had a couple of challenging years ourselves. More men and maids to pay; no crops to harvest. No pay from Siena, now that Marcello wasn't one of the Nine. Only a stipend, as an outpost of the Republic, to aid with the keeping of additional knights. But even those payments had grown less frequent as the city struggled to negotiate the trials this plague wrought.

I stared at that open, empty road, as if I could will the elderly dove-keep to appear. I thought of his kind, droopy eyes. His keen interest in everything that happened at the castello. His joy at the feasts we held on the high holidays.

I knew he'd come, if he could. Or at least send someone.

"Send a knight to Cavo," I said to the captain. "A volunteer. Tell him not to enter the village, but to call out to the first person he sees, staying at a distance." I reached out to touch his wrist. "He must keep a fair distance between him and any other, you understand?"

"Yes, m'lady."

"And if the village is clean—if there's no plague there—see what has come of the dovekeep."

I forced myself to go downstairs. To eat some meat and some bread at noon meal. To play with Fortino, chasing and kissing him as if there was nothing at all to be concerned about. All the while I kept listening for a knight to approach, for a shout at the gate, but all was silent. I felt the seconds tick by, and when Fortino had gone off with the nursemaid to play, I couldn't tolerate it any longer. I swept my cloak around my shoulders and climbed the steps of the turret. I resumed my position at the wall, and Captain Pezzati silently stood beside me, arms folded. Watching. Waiting.

"There," I whispered, finally seeing a figure in the distance.

A Forelli knight, golden tunic just barely visible.

But I frowned. Because he was riding fast, kicking up a cloud of dust behind him.

Our knights traveled at a canter when on duty, unless—

"Open the gates!" the captain bellowed. "Men at the ready!"

I saw them, then. Twelve knights rounding the bend in the road, chasing our man. One taking aim with his bow and arrow...

"M'lady, you must take cover," the captain said sternly, grabbing hold of my elbow and trying to shove me toward the turret. "Enemies approach!" the captain bellowed at his men. "Archers, on the double!" The walls were a mass of movement, everyone slogging toward their stations, moving sluggishly, as if awakening from sleep. It had been months upon months since they had to run.

"Go, m'lady!" Captain Pezzati barked at me. But he was too busy to worry about me for long.

I tore down the turret stairs, flattening myself against the wall as twelve men ran past me, carrying bows. Then I emerged through the fortified door into the courtyard.

The nursemaid, Mercede, carried Fortino, who was crying. Her eyes were round, her face pale as she watched men and women run across the courtyard as the main gates slowly opened.

"Get those gates closed as soon as he's in!" Captain Pezzati bellowed to the men below.

"Yes, sir!"

"*Sbrigati!*" I said to her, urging her to hurry. "Go to the tunnel. 'Tis likely a misunderstanding, but in case it isn't...Prepare to lock yourselves in the tunnel. Do not come out until I come for you myself."

"Yes, m'lady!"

I shoved back the knot of guilt for not taking Fortino myself, for not comforting him as he wailed and reached for me. But I was lady of this house, and there was no way it was coming down today. I strode over to the Great Hall and into the armory, where a man was handing out weapon after weapon. Spying me, he turned to the corner where my sheath and sword were stored. He handed it to me, a slight smile on his lips.

I laughed under my breath as I strapped on the sheath, even as I strode back out to the courtyard. Our man would enter at any moment.

"He has...he has a child with him!" Captain Pezzati cried. "Nay! Nay! Shut the gates! Shut them!"

The men, at the ready, began pushing the massive, metal gates closed again, but at the last second, our knight burst through, hunched over, his golden tunic a mass of blood, three arrows in his back. In his arms was a small girl with a mass of black curls.

I looked and then did a double take.

It was Chiara Greco.

She looked healthy, just scared sick. Her dark eyes found me and stared. "*Per favore,*" she mouthed over and over again. *Please. Please. Please...*

"Send them out! Send them back out!" Captain Pezzati was screaming down at the men in the courtyard. Cursing like crazy, when I'd never heard him say a foul word in my life.

I knew he feared what had just happened—in two years, we'd never admitted another who hadn't spent a good week in the hunter's hut to make certain they did not carry the plague. But I ran to them, fear gripping my hammering heart.

The knight looked down at me, eyes already beginning to roll back in his head. "Fiorentini," he grunted, a bubble of blood appearing at his lips. "Lady Greco met me..."

And then he collapsed to the ground, pulling Chiara with him. I caught her, pulling the child into my arms.

"They stay! Shut and bar the gates!" I screamed, even as the knight at our feet breathed his last. I stared at the arrows in his back as the gates were closed and the metal bar shoved into place.

"Chiara, Chiara," I said, rubbing her back, holding her tight. "Where is your mama? What has happened?"

The little girl was sobbing, her words coming in gasps. "We...ran...through...woods. Mama...and me. Bad men...coming. Papa said...we...must."

I looked up at the grizzled Captain Pezzati on the wall, putting it together. The twelve chasing our knight. No messages from Cavo. Lord Greco, sending his precious family away from the most protected place they would ever have. Only desperation would have led him to send them to the woods. Only the Fiorentini...

Or the plague.

"Prepare for siege!" I screamed.

CHAPTER 39

GABRIELLA

T he men hastened to do as I'd ordered, even as Captain Pezzati shouted the same command. Arrows came a moment later, missing all but one man on the wall, then cascading inward in a harrowing fountain of death. Mom and Dad found me recklessly trying to drag a knight into the doorway of the Great Hall, out of some dull sense of duty. From far away, I noted that I must be in shock.

Mom gripped my wrist. "Gabi, leave him! He's dead!" She wrenched me around, toward safety.

Together, we ran for the Great Hall.

I looked back. Little Chiara, barefoot, dirty, stood where I'd left her. Arrows continued to rain down about her, and stuck in the dirt at an angle, like some curious contemporary art exhibit.

"Chiara! *Sbrigati!*" I cried, waving her forward.

She took a faltering step and then another, her filthy hand going to her lips.

"Gabi, is that Chiara *Greco*?" Mom asked, alarm filling her voice as she joined me in the doorway.

I didn't answer. I knew that if she stayed out there much longer, I'd see the child pierced. I ran, feeling an arrow miss my head by inches. The sky was filled with them, our men mostly taking cover in the face of them. How many Fiorentini were outside our walls?

The twelve I'd seen in pursuit of our knight had been but the first...

I paused, catching sight of an incoming arrow, and that pause saved me. I wrenched the child's arm, pulling her up and into mine, even as I ran back to the Great Hall.

Panting, I looked at Mom and Dad, who stared at me and the girl.

"Are the Grecos *here*?" Mom grit out, frustrated, torn. She worked at a wounded knight's back, breaking off the head of an arrow as he groaned in agony. Given that we'd successfully kept out every outsider for more than two years, I thought she was showing remarkable restraint. Maybe because our infiltrator was all of five years old.

"Nay. She was rescued by our scout, who died out there," I said, nodding to the courtyard. "I don't know what's become of Rodolfo or Alessandra." I knelt in front of Chiara again and tried to get her to look into my eyes. "Sweetheart, please tell me. Is your mama alive?"

She nodded. "I...think so."

"Where? Where is she?"

"In the woods," she said. "She told me the bad men would follow her. She said to run to Cavo and not stop."

"What did you see there, Chiara? How many knights were there? Were they all Fiorentini?"

She only stared at me, silent. She was in shock. Stunned. What had she seen? What had left her unable to speak?

I took her hands in mine. "Chiara, where is your papa?"

Still, nothing but silence. Just fresh tears, breaking my heart. I pulled her back into my arms.

"The scout," Mom said, still working on the knight. "Where had he gone?"

"Cavo," I said dully. "He went to see why we'd received no word from Siena. And now we know why. Firenze is on the move. They're cutting us off."

"But how would they know?" Dad asked. "That we're not receiving carrier pigeons?"

"I don't know," I said. "Maybe they don't. Maybe they're taking out any men between us and Siena. I just have a really bad feeling. A really bad feeling..."

This attack. So soon after Marcello and Luca had left for Siena.

No doubt the Grecos were under similar attack.

Lia arrived in the doorway, breathless.

"They need you," I said to her. "Up on the wall with your bow. Take out as many out as you can, Lia. As many as you can. Because I think..." I paused, staring at the child. "I think they're here for us."

Castello Greco.

And Castello Forelli.

And the She-Wolves of Siena.

And... The thought of it brought me up short. *Fortino.* My precious boy, all dimples and brown eyes with his low chuckle. What might they do to him to get to us? I remembered the cage, the taunts, my near-death experience in Firenze.

It would be the triumph of the decade for our enemies if they were successful. Sacking our castles. Capturing any one of us. A distraction in the midst of the devastation the disease wrought. A centering. They'd claim God's favor.

And perhaps...perhaps they'd be right in doing so, if God allowed it. *Please, God, don't allow it. Help us. Help us...*

CHAPTER 40

EVANGELIA

S o...having morning sickness and trying to be a She-Wolf archer was
a harder combo than I thought. Bile rose in my throat, and I nearly
blacked out when I saw what approached us from all sides.

Hundreds of Fiorentini.

But I made myself stop, breathe a prayer, and in a few moments I
knew I felt sharper than I'd been in years. Since Venezia, really.

Attentive to every movement, every sound.

Perhaps it was the spark of battle, real threat, not just endless practice
or exercise, that brought it all into focus...

Captain Pezzati insisted I stand mostly behind a stone barrier. But I
still managed to take down at least twenty men in the first hour of our
attack, while but five of ours had either been wounded or killed.

I edged around the corner of the parapet, trying to get a grip on what
we faced. I was still a bit stunned that we were facing warriors at all. How
had our enemy fielded an army while fighting the plague, too? I knew
that Firenze hadn't been as hard-hit as Siena, but...this?

I studied them, making quick calculations, wondering just how
many were at our walls. I leaned down low, making my calculations.
I'd seen fifty men. There were likely five-times more beyond them, held
in waves. Luca and Marcello had taken twelve men with them. We had
thirty-six others.

Thirty-one now.

Part of me wanted to just shout at all the guys to take cover. But that wouldn't work. If we didn't actively guard the wall, they'd attempt an ascent.

The squires arrived, arms full of enemy arrows they'd collected below. They dropped piles off beside me, and the other archers and I grinned at the sight. There was something especially sweet about taking down our enemy with weapons sent against us first.

"Castello Greco has been breached!" cried a man.

"Greco's flags are down, Fiorentini flags in their place!" cried another, firing an arrow.

My heart surged with terror. Where was Rodolfo? Was he dead? Or worse, captured? How had Chiara gotten to Cavo? Had Alessandra somehow escaped and fled to the woods? Tried to reach us? Castello Greco and her knights were strong. If she could be breached, so could we.

An iron claw shot over my shoulder, arced down, and clattered against the stone wall inside. I whirled and tried to wrench it away before it grabbed hold but failed. The rope grew taut. On the other side of the castle, I saw a second claw had been shot across that wall. And with a sinking heart, to our south side too.

The claw nearest me scratched its way upward until it caught on the far side. Otello scurried over to me and crouched across from me on the parapet. "You take out whoever's climbing this while I saw through the rope."

I nodded once, rose, turned and aimed, but could only let one arrow fly before ducking, since three others were aimed at my head. I let out a cry of frustration and fear. Otello was only halfway through the rope. How were others doing on the other sides?

Concentrate on this one alone, I thought. *One at a time. Just do this and move on.* I hitched up my skirts and crawled five feet to the side, hoping I might surprise them and gain a couple of seconds to get a second arrow off.

"Stones!" Otello bellowed to the nearest squire. "We need stones!"
I saw it, then. What had alarmed him. The rope was moving.

I rose and fired one arrow and ignored the three archers below, turning to target me again as they spied my new position. I was rewarded by seeing my first arrow sink into the chest of the first climber and was pretty sure that my second probably found its target too—one of the enemy archers.

Two squires arrived, arms full of stones, faces taut with a combination of fear and hoped-for glory.

"There," grunted Otello, gesturing with his head to right below the rope. He was still sawing, three-quarters of the way through. "Let them have it, just as we practiced. Drop the rocks atop them and then take cover, *fast*."

"Yes, sir!" they cried. On the count of three, they rose and pelted a man below with their rocks. We heard a cry and then a volley of arrows shot over their heads as they stared at each other, wide-eyed with glee. I rose at that moment and got two arrows off as the archers reached into their quivers. *This could work*, I thought.

"Again, boys, again!" I cried.

We repeated the exercise, and finally, finally Otello got through the rope. We heard the screams of men falling. I wanted to give Otello a high-five, but he was already surveying the other ropes and claws.

"Come with me to the eastern wall, boys!" he cried over his shoulder to the squires.

The boys hurriedly grabbed their remaining stones and ran behind him.

Dad arrived, grim-faced, but I thought I saw an edge of relief in his eyes to see me, alive. Hunched over, he went from one downed man to the other, passing two dead before he found one wounded. This one he dragged by the feet toward the turret door, then picked him up across his shoulders, squeezed through the tiny doorway, and disappeared. I assumed he and Mom were setting up a triage wing. But if it got any worse, we might soon need them up here with us.

I swallowed hard as I glanced down below and saw the woods teeming with bodies. *Yeah, we might need every able body up here in a sec.*

I resumed my shoot-and-take-cover mode, relieved to spot those at the south wall repelling their attackers. Across from me, Otello and the squires had reached the eastern wall. With luck, they'd take care of it as they had the others.

Another of our knights, Baldarino, took a particularly brutal arrow into his eye and out the top of his skull. He screamed and whirled his arms backward, then fell over the inner wall to the courtyard below. I winced, swallowed against the bile rising in my throat and let out a cry of rage. Rising, I drew an arrow and began running down the wall, shooting arrow after arrow after arrow, pausing only to kneel, fill my quiver again, and then resume my run. I made it to the other side of the castle, all the way to the gate. Then turned and repeated my run.

The men cheered as I passed, chanting *She-Wolf, She-Wolf, She-Wolf,* as they continued to unleash their own arrows upon our enemies. I smiled, even as Fiorentini arrows got so close to me that I could feel them *whoosh* past my head. When I got back to the western wall, Gabi was waiting by the turret. She handed me a skin of water and gave me a small smile.

"This preggers thing is working for you," she said under her breath. "Looks like your mad ninja skills are better than ever."

"Hope you're right," I said, after swallowing. "Because we're going to need it. Take a look." I gestured over my shoulder.

"As bad as I thought?"

"Nah. Worse," I said.

Gabi edged her nose around the corner, pulling back when an arrow shot past her. "How many?" she asked quietly, any trace of humor gone.

"I don't know. They keep to the trees, but I'm guessing by the numbers in these forward forces that they might have close to five hundred."

Having caught my breath, I nocked an arrow, ducked around the corner and shot it, then returned to face her. "Gabi..." I reached out to touch her arm. "I think Castello Greco fell."

"What?" she asked, her brown eyes flying northward. She licked her lips, and I knew she'd seen the Fiorentini flags. "No! No, no, no..." she groaned, her face a mask of pain. She knew what I did...If Rodolfo and Alessandra survived, if they were taken to Firenze...their deaths would be agonizingly slow.

She rubbed her temples, and her eyes moved to me, panic within them. "We have to go and find them...figure out..."

I nocked another arrow, turned, aimed and shot it, then returned to face her. "I know. But we kinda have our hands full *here*, Gabs."

She swallowed hard, her face paling. "They'll kill them," she whispered. "If they don't have them already...Chiara's here. Alessandra might have escaped."

"Let's hope she's far from here." I resumed shooting, letting her come to the conclusion I had. The Fiorentini were coming for us, too. And as much as we wanted to help Ali, we had to concentrate on our own.

I paused after I glimpsed a man below who appeared to have a bruised face. Turning, I dared to peek at him again. Then, as the arrows came at me, I crawled a few paces down the wall and dared a peek at another. *There.* Buboes. Black, bulbous, hideous lesions along some of their necks.

Only their intense hatred could fuel them to move beyond the confines of their disease.

I sat down, my back to the wall, trying to piece it together.

Then I looked at Gabi.

"Gabs, they've hired dying men. The men attacking..they're all sick! Infected!"

New horror entered her eyes. It was her turn to look...and look...and look again. Like me, she put her back to the wall and sank down, thinking.

"They must have promised them something. Or their families something, if they did this," I said. I nocked another arrow and then another and then another, shooting the men below. I noticed now how they were a bit slow to react. Sluggish. This was why I'd taken down a man with nearly every arrow I shot. Not because I was some freakin' awesome She-Wolf. But because my enemies were sick. Probably feverish and dizzy. *Slow* to climb the ropes.

A clamp arced over my shoulder and grabbed hold of the inner wall. Gabi immediately set to sawing it through with her blade. "So if they're sick..." she said, "then all we need to do is hold them off for a few days until they're too sick to fight."

"Sure, no problem," I grit out, turning to take aim and shoot, then whip out of range again. Five arrows sang through the gap in the wall. "Except some of them seem to be faring better than others."

"They're using the sickest," she said, a piece of her curly hair falling in front of her face as she sawed, "to weaken us. They know they're dying anyway...why not die in glory, trying to take us down?"

I turned and looked down the wall, wondering where the squires and their rocks were. Where the men were. And then I saw. Five new claws had sailed across the wall—one on every sector. Everyone was busy. How long could we keep them from breaching the castello?

I eased up, peered over the edge, and let out a little scream. There was a man just three feet below me, his eyes red-rimmed and hollow. He raised a battle axe and made a hasty attempt to cut my head like a Tuscan melon, but I dodged him, and his axe struck only the stone beside me. Holding the rope with only one hand sent him awkwardly twisting to one side.

"Now that's not nice," Gabi said, ramming her sword down on his wrist.

I heard men shout below him and suspected my sister had not only managed to take him out, but others below.

"Nice work," I said, offering her my fist.

She brushed my knuckles with her own, panting, as arrows soared over our heads. Then she positioned her sword behind her and rose, swinging at the rope with all her strength, a beautiful arc that had to have left her hands and wrists aching. All but the last strands gave sway to her strike. More arrows came past us as she knelt. She shouted at the nearest squire.

"Go down to the kitchens! Tell them to boil every pot of water they can and bring it to us when they're hot!"

"Yes, m'lady!"

"You intend to scald them?" I asked.

"Yes," she grit out. "I only wish I had huge vats of oil. Go. Tell Pezzati what we think is happening."

"On it," I said, partially rising. But when she moved to the rope, I urged her to pause. If she waited a minute or two, until others climbed the rope, she could cut the last remaining strands of the rope *and* a few men.

Her eyes met mine. "Got it. Go!"

I gathered myself, nocked another arrow, and began my run down the parapet toward the gate where Captain Pezzati, red-faced and sweaty, was shouting orders to the other side. I saw that the majority of our archers were on either side of the gate, continuously shooting. And then I finally recognized what I heard. *Boom...boom...boom.*

They had a battering ram.

I swallowed hard as the gate shuddered with each strike but held.

Oh, Luca. Come home, I thought. *We need you. We can't hold out for long. Luca! Luca!*

I prayed they'd learned of the Fiorentini invasion and were on their way back to us even now. A man beside me took an arrow, and I eased him to the stones below, examining his wound, his face. It was Alanzo—steady and strong Alanzo—and I wanted to weep as he gasped for breath, holding my hand in terror. The arrow had pierced his lung.

"Kill me," he gasped, his voice raspy, thick with blood. He gripped my hand. We both knew that a strike through the lung was a slower death. But most often, it *did* mean certain death.

"I cannot," I said, sorrow in every syllable. I wished Mom were here, that she could slip him some medicinal that would at least ease his pain or make him sleep until death took him. I cried out, frustration overwhelming me.

The captain looked down at me, and I knew I had tears streaming down my face. "M'lady?" he said, gripping my arm. "Are you harmed?"

"Nay, I am well," I assured him, reading the fear in his eyes. "'Tis Alanzo I grieve."

The man was shuddering now, in my arms, and I held him tight, gritting my teeth. "The Fiorentini...They are all ill, Captain! They've put their sick troops forward, to wear us down," I said. "To sicken us too!"

Captain Pezzati's gray eyes scanned the wall, thinking. "All this time, keeping the ill from our gates," he muttered, lowering his head and rubbing the back of his neck, "just to have them bludgeon their way in."

Bludgeon. Climb. Crawl.

"How long..." I gasped, "can the gate hold?" I tried to get a better grip on Alanzo, crying now as I attempted to keep him from thrashing as he drowned in his own blood, wanting it to end—*God of mercy, please take him....*

Grim, Captain Pezzati leaned across his torso to aid me in holding our fallen friend. "We could hold them off for a good while yet," the captain said. His grey eyes met mine. "But I agree with you. There are many out there, behind these."

Alanzo gave one last shudder and then slumped in our arms, the life leaving him like water pouring from a pitcher. Feeling that—a soul leaving his body, the hollow of what remained—stole my breath.

I scrambled a few steps away, nauseous.

Captain Pezzati held his fallen friend and crossed himself. Then he looked me in the eye. "While we can hold for a time, we need to be prepared. When I whistle, you gather up your mother and father, your sister and nephew, and you prepare to fight your way out. We shall surround you with every able man left. If the castello falls..."

"She cannot fall!" I cried.

He took Alanzo's body and shifted it to the edge of the parapet, out of the way, crossing his hands over his chest in the way of the dead, then stared grimly back at me.

"If she falls, I shall not see you fall, too. You must be away, m'lady. Somehow. Some way. I cannot face Captain Forelli with word that his wife has been taken. Nor Lady Gabriella, Fortino, and her parents. But you all must be together. Ready to fight to the end. Understood?"

I looked past his shoulder, at the men fighting, shouting, edging past, ducking. It was like they moved in slow motion. Sounds dimmed. I knew every one of them would die to save us.

I lifted my eyes to the skies. Gray clouds gathered, and there was just a bit of daylight left. Come night...I shuddered at the thought. But with the hours left, and with every ounce of strength I had, I would fight. Taking a deep breath, I rose, refilled my quiver, and went about my task again.

CHAPTER 41

GABRIELLA

C ook sent eight terrified maids to the wall with buckets of boiling water, and we took to dumping them atop the men who tried to climb their way upward. I winced as they screamed, but I knew none of them would hesitate to kill any one of us...or worse. Blessedly, Cook also sent two maids up with loaves of bread and cold water for each of us to take hurried gulps and bites.

I hadn't even realized I was hungry. Or how tired I was, until I'd stopped for a moment. The siege had been going on for more than four hours.

We'd probably killed a hundred or more men outside. Eight of ours were down, leaving us with twenty-seven fighting men, plus Mom, Dad, me and Lia. The bad news was that Lia had been right...the men behind the first waves were stronger, less sick. They came at us, faster, more powerful by the hour. If their attack continued, unabated, I figured we could stand for another hour, maybe two, if we were lucky.

I wracked my mind for a way out. If nothing else, I had to stall for time. To give Marcello and Luca time to return to us, with aid. Or at the worst, put off that horrible thought that Captain Pezzati had given Lia—that we'd try to fight our way out.

I knew that we'd all perish in that scenario.

We'd be brave, for sure. It'd be epic.

But we would all die.

I made my way toward the gate, and when Captain Pezzati turned to take a drink, the maid visibly shaking by his knees as arrows flew over her head, I said, "Fly the white flag, Captain."

He paused, slurped from the scoop, and wiped the excess off his lips with the back of his hand. "M'lady?" he asked, cocking his head.

"Give our enemy the signal, Captain. I want to know who 'tis behind this attack before night overtakes us. I want to see his face. And I want to buy Marcello and Luca time to return to us."

"M'lady, we do not even know if Lord Forelli has—"

"Lord Forelli hasn't heard word from us for days. He shall be on alert. Mayhap he has even sent scouts to make certain all is well."

Captain Pezzati's gray eyes widened slightly with the edge of new hope.

"Fly the flag," I repeated. "I shall know who dares to attack us now."

"Yes, m'lady," he said, with a genteel nod. He turned and went to a box beside the gate wall, opened it, and removed a musty, moldy ivory flag. He pulled down the golden Forelli flag, replaced it with the ivory, and raised it. It hung, limp, lifeless. But in moments we heard shouts from below and the arrow fire ceased. No more iron claws came loping over the wall. Everything became still.

I ran my hands through my hair, aware that it had all come loose through the long hours. Shook my head, at the mad futility of trying to be a lady in the midst of battle and giggled. And then I rose, slowly, my hand on the cornerstone of the gate pillar, as if every Forelli who had ever resided within these walls might grant me strength.

Captain Pezzati took to my left side, Celso to my right. I could smell them, rank with sweat. Or was it my own stink? I knew I hardly looked like the lady of the house, my hair in full disarray, my dress soiled and bloody.

I scanned the men circling our walls below. The Fiorentini remained still, their hands at their sides. Some hunched down to watch.

"I am Lady Gabriella Betarrini Forelli," I called. "I shall speak directly to your lord!"

There was a pause. Some of the men looked over their shoulders to the woods.

After a moment, Lord Barbato strode outward, cape over one shoulder, hands casually crossed on the pommel of his saddle. Two men flanked him, looking strong and determined.

Barbato, I seethed. *Of course it's him.* I found hollow comfort in the fact that at least Foraboschi was dead.

They stood directly below me, just forty feet away, and I ached to give the nod to Matteo to take him out with an arrow.

"'Tis enough, Barbato," I called. "I don't wish to kill any more of your men. Go home to Firenze."

Low laughter rumbled below while my men remained silent. I knew they were busily bandaging wounds, gathering additional arrows, just as mine were.

"These men are here for one cause only, m'lady. To rid this corner of Toscana of the traitorous Grecos and our greatest enemies, the Forellis. Come now, my lady." He spat out *lady* like it was a foul word. "End this folly. You know you are outnumbered."

I paused. "And yet we shall still relieve *you* of a great number of your men if we decide to fight to the death." I turned to walk a few paces to the next space in the wall, killing a bit more time, milking it.

"And why must we be enemies? Have we of Castello Forelli not spent years in peace with you, our neighbors to the north? Is not your truest goal, Lord Barbato,"—it was my turn to spit out his name—"to make war and line your own pockets? Is that not why you are here?"

His face soured as he studied me in the torchlight. "Our enemies are not those of Castello Forelli. 'Tis you, Gabriella Betarrini Forelli. And your sister. The witches of Siena."

I blinked, uncertain of what I'd heard.

"We are here for the witches of Siena, those who have brought the plague to our lands!" he cried, looking along the wall to my men.

I blinked again.

He was pinning the plague on...*us?*

"I know not of what you speak," I said. "Has the plague taken *your* mind, sir? Are you a madman now?"

"Only if you have bewitched me as you have so many others," he said with an angry slice of his hand. There was grumbling assent all around him. Obviously, he'd been spreading these lies for some time. This, *this* was why the sick fought for him. They believed Lia and I had brought the plague to Italia!

"This plague came from the Orient, not from a She-Wolf," I said with a scoff. "Think on it. It came first to Venezia, to Sicily, via the ports. Not from within. Not from *here.*"

He lifted his chin. "And yet rumor has it, that not one within your castello has fallen. In over *two years* of the pestilence among us. I know not of another household like it, other than yours and Greco's. 'Tis witchcraft, through and through. You have cursed even your own Sienese, and we are here to rid our lands of our enemies, once and for all. In time, even our Sienese brothers shall bless our names for ridding them of the She-Wolves and this wretched curse."

I wanted to laugh. He was crazy. And yet the story of the statues in Siena, of sane priests doing insane things, made me pause. This was a crazy time. *Cuh-razy with a capital C.* All around. They might really succeed in this attempt to pin the Black Plague on us. And Barbato would see us killed, as he'd hoped all along.

A rider came up behind him, from the main road, and dismounted. He scurried over to Barbato's back and said something to him. Barbato only partially turned but was clearly listening. His lips twisted into a grimace.

Agitated, he clamped his lips shut and turned his head to hear the man out. After a long moment, he looked past the man toward what I thought was the direction of Castello Greco. *Rodolfo...Alessandra...*

One of his men came over to him and spoke as well. Then the man strode away, and I could hear dim shouts.

"They're pulling out some of the men," Captain Pezzati said out of the corner of his mouth.

"It's Castello Greco," I murmured. "I think something might have gone wrong there."

"We can only hope," he said. "If they have to take half their men, or even a third—we might have a chance."

Barbato turned back to me, only one man beside him now. "Surrender, Lady Forelli. If you and your sister come with us, we shall leave Sienese lands immediately."

I returned his steady gaze. "I need an hour to confer with my family."

He let out a scoffing laugh. "I am no fool, m'lady. You are a woman who knows her mind. Tell me of it."

"I have changed," I said, as sweetly as I could. "I must speak to my family, and the men. I am but a woman, my lord far from home."

He laughed again, shaking his head, a hand on his hip. He lifted it then, speaking to his men. "See that? Even now she attempts to beguile and bewitch with her womanly ways."

"Let me take him out now," Matteo ground out, his hand tightening around his bowstring. "He should not be allowed to utter such foul words."

"Nay," I whispered. "'Tis a game. Allow me to play it." I turned to pace back to my original spot, Pezzati and Celso trailing behind me. "Tell me, Lord Barbato," I said. "What experience do you have in dealing with witchcraft?"

He paused and frowned. "I have no experience with witchcraft, woman, other than my dealings with you."

"'Tis a weighty accusation."

"Indeed. But I know not of any others but you and other Betarrini ilk who emerge from *tombs*. One moment there. Another moment, not." Agreement rumbled through the ranks below.

Sneering faces. Hatred. They believed his lies. *Believed* them.

And this was why Barbato went to such lengths to capture Orazio and Galileo—to force them to confess to witchcraft. To tie it to us, in time.

I bit my cheek and forced a laugh. "You are touched in the head," I said. "No one comes and goes from tombs. We've merely studied them, as scholars do."

He laughed and lifted his hand, pacing. "Do you hear her, men?" he cried. "Have you ever known a woman to learn her letters and numbers, let alone claim to be a scholar? This is a woman who has left her gentle ways behind her. She is a witch. She is *other*. Or she is a man and has engaged in the foulest of intimacies with Marcello Forelli."

I kept pace with him from above. "I am every bit a woman as each of your mothers!" I cried.

Lewd comments and cries reached our ears, and every one of my men tightened with rage.

"Steady," I growled as I passed them. "Let them taunt me. I am wasting time. Steady," I repeated.

I turned outward. "I bore a son, more than three years past. Do witches bear children? Nurse them at their breast?"

Again, more lewd comments.

All for the cause, Gabi, I told myself, bearing it. Not reacting. Not calling for arrows to rain down upon their disgusting minds.

Barbato was laughing, shored up by our banter. When I returned to the gate, he said casually, "My men wonder if you would be so kind to disrobe, Lady Forelli, so that we might judge for ourselves if you be but man, woman, or some other creature."

I laughed and shook my head. "You poor, simple-minded fools. So ready to accept the word of a man who builds his treasure off the backs of men who soldier for a cause. Do you not see?" I cried. "Do you not recognize that you are being used?"

"Enough!" Lord Barbato yelled. But I ignored him.

"Do you not see that Barbato and his friends make piles of gold florins from sales of swords, bows, arrows, shields, while all of you earn...what? A good name? A small portion of land? A few pieces of silver?"

"She wields her tongue like a sword," Barbato bellowed. "Guard your ears! Do not listen to her, she—"

"He uses everyone and everything he can for his own gain!" I cried. "He has used your sick brothers in this fight against us! We who only wish to live as your neighbors in peace!"

"Quiet, witch!"

"Think on it!" I cried, swiftly walking the parapet. "Think on it! Has Siena once brought battle against you, in these two years past? We have not! We have not! We have left you in peace! Just as we ask you to leave us in peace!"

"That is enough!" Barbato roared. "Enough! Surrender now, witch, or prepare to be breached and hauled out behind our horses in chains."

It was my turn to emit a sarcastic laugh. "If I surrendered to you, Barbato, I doubt you would grant me any honor. I remember it well, Firenze's *hospitality*."

His face reddened, his horse shifting beneath him. "Then do I correctly understand you? You shall not come down? You shall not surrender?"

"I told you. I need an hour to confer with my men and family."

"You toy with me, witch." His face tightened, and he lifted his arm.

All the men came to their feet and all of mine straightened, readying themselves.

And then the attack resumed in earnest.

CHAPTER 42

GABRIELLA

As we did our best to fend off our attackers, I thought of Captain Pezzati's plan. To break out of the gate and fight our way out.

I knew that it meant our men would die in front of the castello rather than inside her walls. It would be a heroic way to go, but it would not spare them...nor us. Because I knew we'd still be outnumbered, and in time overcome. No, our best bet was to fight as long as we could, then retreat to the fortified inner portions of the castle and pray the doors would hold until Marcello and Luca could come...and that Barbato wouldn't think of burning us out.

Lia returned to my side, panting, plainly weary. Her fingers were bloody from the continuous shooting, as were those of all our archers. It was getting so dark out it was difficult to see farther than the ground, and it was bitterly cold. There was the scent of snow on the wind. Yeah, that'd about cap off this perfect day...a good, old-fashioned blizzard. That'd be fan-freakin'-tastic.

Hope that my husband—and reinforcements—would come this night waned in the face of our bleak reality. Barbato was not calling off the attack. They'd come, and come, and come. They shifted in the deep shadows of night, while we had to have some light, to make certain we didn't take down our fellow Forellis rather than any of the Fiorentini who made it across the wall. And that made us an easier target.

I shook my head at Captain Pezzati and Lia as more arrows shot past them and two more claws crossed the walls. So far, only one stream of Fiorentini had managed to breach us using that method, and we'd cut down the five men who infiltrated us. But it didn't keep them from continuing to try. They knew what I was just realizing—in time, we'd be too weary to cut another rope, drop another rock, toss another pail of boiling water. In time, two or three streams of men would infiltrate the parapet, and others would follow.

"Under cover of darkness, m'lady," Captain Pezzati began, as a man behind him was hit in the shoulder, and another eased him to the parapet floor, "if we could get you far enough into the woods, you might have a chance to escape."

"Nay, that's madness," I said. "'Twould be preferable to die here, fighting, than to watch you all sacrifice yourselves as our living wall."

Lia nodded in agreement. "So we take refuge below, when we can fight no longer?"

I stared at her. There was one other option. An option that only she, my parents, Luca and Marcello knew of. A narrow escape tunnel out from under the new wing of the castle. It might get us far enough to do what Captain Pezzati proposed.

"I think we make them *believe* we're inside the fortified portion. We leave everyone in the castello there. But we take Mom and Dad, the children and a few men, and go to the tunnel."

"But 'tis *unfinished*," Lia said. "There are days, mayhap weeks of digging left."

"What tunnel?" Captain Pezzati grunted, his eyes narrowing.

"Not if we go directly up," I said to her.

"Directly up," she repeated. She edged around the wall, peering into the darkness to the northeast, as if trying to make her best guess as to where the tunnel ended and where that would put us.

"Of what tunnel do you speak?" Captain Pezzati growled again.

"Shh," I said, eying the nearest knight behind him. But he appeared to not have heard. "'Tis a narrow siege tunnel. Created for just this purpose, bit by bit, by only our closest kin, so that no one would know but us. For just this reason."

"But 'tis *unfinished*," Lia said again, clearly getting angry. "It gains us nothing if we do naught but rise directly in front of Barbato's tent."

I sighed heavily and rubbed my forehead. "Do you have a better idea?" I asked in English, flipping my hand out to her. "We're not gonna make it 'til morning, Lia."

She stared back at me, her blue eyes flicking back and forth, thinking, thinking...then she looked to the captain.

"You could...seal it behind us. The tunnel. The castello might be overrun, but they would not find us there." She glanced at me. "They could simply return the bricks to where they now lay, behind us."

She proposed a tomb, of sorts. The mere thought of a confined space with so many bodies made me gasp for breath. But I grit my teeth and nodded. Only one thing made me smile.

If we were breached, *when* we were breached, the Fiorentini would not find us within.

And they really would think we were capable of a very dark magic indeed.

CHAPTER 43

GABRIELLA

We fought for hours, but as they sensed our strength fading, they brought ladder upon ladder to the wall, and we knew we could not keep them all away. We were down to twenty men.

"Come away, m'lady," Captain Pezzati said, gripping my arm.

I wasn't arguing. It had to be near three in the morning, and I knew our battle was lost. I only hoped that Marcello, Luca and any Sienese knights he could muster were on their way. Across the castello, on the far wall, we saw Fiorentini streaming in, like ants climbing up and dividing in either direction, a constant line.

We raced down the turret stairs. At the bottom, a man prepared to close and blockade it, as I knew they would do in this main section. Here they had access to water and double doors. Mom and Dad were there, tending to the wounded, having wisely placed them in this Last Resort wing. As soon as she saw us, Mom rose and came to me.

"We are overcome, then?"

"Yes. We'll leave them here," I said, gesturing to the knights and servants. "I must get to the children and then we will take shelter in the fortified tunnel."

I ran across the courtyard and encountered two Fiorentini. Despite my weariness, I knew they stood between me and my sons. I ducked the first man's swing and struck at the second man, missed him, but turned the sword hilt in my hands and stabbed him in the back with one mighty thrust. I yanked it from his body and rolled to the right just as the second man brought his battle axe downward, missing me by inches. I was on my feet. I attacked the knight, and unbalanced, he backed up. To his misfortune, it was right into Celso, who finished him with one deft blow.

I went to the turret door and slammed my hand against it. "Mercede! Mercede!" I called the nursemaid. "'Tis me, Gabriella! Open the door!" Desi and Grasso, two of our terriers, followed behind me, barking.

"M'lady?" came Mercede's tentative, frightened voice.

I turned and struck down another Fiorentini who came at me, his neck grotesque with big, black buboes. He lifted his sword belatedly, and my own sliced his neck. Blood and pus squirted out in a broad, disgusting sweep. I almost vomited at the smell that ensued. Was that it? Had I just gotten infected?

I rammed against the door. "Open it, Mercede! Now!"

I heard the bolt slide open and I yanked open the door, taking weepy Fortino into my arms while the baby slept—blissfully unaware of the danger—in Mercede's. The dogs were barking. "M'lady!" Mercede shrieked, and I instinctively ducked, a knight's sword narrowly missing my own neck and crashing into the wall above. Thankfully, Celso was still with me and took him on.

I took Fortino's chin in my hand. "Hold on to me," I said. "No matter what happens, don't let go!"

He nodded, big tears slipping down his face. I swung him onto my back and his small hands knotted beneath my chin, choking me, but I didn't care. That choke meant that my boy was with me, alive.

"Chiara, stay with Mercede!" I cried. But I knew my directive wasn't really necessary. The girl clung to the nursemaid in stark terror.

More Fiorentini swarmed the courtyard. Lia was on the far side, firing arrow after arrow, and I concentrated on her. "Follow me!" I screamed to Mercede, and we ran.

"Down, Gabi!" Lia cried when we were halfway across. I ducked, praying Fortino wasn't sticking up too far, and heard two arrows whistle past us in quick succession, then men crying out as each found their mark.

"Run, Gabi! Run!" Lia shouted, turning to shoot to her left, then swinging to the right.

I ran toward her like a high school quarterback spotting the end zone, praying Mercede and Celso were right behind me. Desi and Grasso scurried along beside us, growling.

"Gabi!" Lia said, looking left.

She took down one knight, the force of her arrow spinning him away from me but wasn't fast enough to catch the second. He barreled into me, tackling me to the ground. I heard Fortino cry and felt his grip break at my neck. I immediately turned to crawl toward him. He was on his back, eyes wide, the wind plainly knocked from his little chest.

Celso blocked a blow that would have killed me for certain, and then Dad was there, scooping Fortino up in his arms, offering me a hand. "C'mon, babe. Time to go."

I took it, and he yanked me up and through the tunnel doorway. It slammed shut behind us. I blinked in the torchlight, taking stock while looking about in my shell-shocked fog. The dogs circling around my legs. Fortino, in Mom's arms. Dad. Lia. Mercede and the baby. Countless wounded, each with a sword in their hands or near them. "Celso," I mumbled. "Celso!"

I turned toward the door, but Captain Pezzati blocked me. He shook his head as the second door was shut and locked. "He shall see to his duty," he said grimly.

Celso had chosen to stay outside. To defend the door as long as he could. To defend us and give us a few more precious minutes.

I wept at the thought of him, gasping for breath. So many men–brothers, really—now dead or dying. My eyes swept across the wounded and ten weary but hale knights. Fifteen more were maidservants, stableboys and squires.

"Come, m'lady," Captain Pezzati said, gripping my arm again. "We must get you to that inner chamber."

"Nay," I said, shaking my head. "We shall not leave you or them."

"Should this last segment of the castle be breached, we shall fight to the last, even the wounded among us, to defend you," Captain Pezzati said. "You may trust us."

"I do trust you," I said. "Every one of you. And you may trust us too. We shall not abandon you."

Captain Pezzati's face reddened with frustration. He turned his grip on my arm, and I knew he was preparing to drag me to the tunnel, if need be. "Our duty is to Lord Forelli, and his priority was your safety."

I wrenched my arm away. Strength rose within me as passion and understanding and life flowed through veins that seemed long-empty of late. "You are our family," I said, looking at each of them. "You are our brothers. Our sisters."

I looked to Mom and Dad and Lia, then. Making sure I wasn't alone in this. Each of them nodded an assent. Only the children made me pause. But this was right. Good. I was as sure of my course as Tomas and Adela had been when they left us. *I can do no other.*

"Close and bolt the second siege doors," I said, looking to the far end of the tunnel. "We shall remain with you until this is done."

The men looked bleak. Several women were crying.

"What does it matter?" Giacinta said, her daughter, Isabella, in her arms. "They shall kill us whether or not you are here. Why not take shelter? Save yourselves! Take the children with you!"

The girl clung to her mother's waist, weeping.

"Nay. We shall not leave you," I ground out. "Together, we shall fight. Marcello and his men must be on their way to us by now. They must. We will simply hold out long enough for them to come to our aid. And we shall do that together."

We heard the muffled crack of a door—the outer one?—and all looked to the secondary door. I'd never been more grateful for reinforcements than I was in that moment.

And yet I was aware of Celso and others who had not made it inside with us. Would any of them survive? I had to fight the urge to fling open the doors and charge out to lend my sword to the cause again—only Captain Pezzati's firm commands stopped me. He reoriented the Betarrini-Forellis to the very center of the room, with the wounded on either side of us, and able warriors on each end.

He set up Lia and Matteo behind four crates, giving them a barrier on either side, and the ability to shoot in both directions. But I knew the swordsmen at the front would largely keep them from doing any good until we were desperate indeed. The two set to work, gathering arrows into neat stacks that would allow them to reach and draw without pause.

I settled Mercede in the very center, holding my boys. Isabella and Chiara were on either side of them, sandwiched by Mom and Dad. Then I reached down, kissed Fortino's forehead and caressed his cheek. "Try and sleep, little man," I whispered.

He blinked laden eyelids, as if fighting the urge already—he only needed my permission. Miraculously, he seemed to have forgotten the tension in the air, the rhythmic pounding that now sounded on the outer door, the gasps and quiet sobs of frightened women. I prayed he would close his little eyes and sleep through the worst of what was to come. That he wouldn't see any more bloodshed this night, that he would awaken to me and his papa holding him close.

The door cracked and groaned and gave way.

The sounds of our invading enemies drew closer, just one fortified door between us now. It took maybe twenty seconds for us to hear the Italian version of *heave-ho* beginning, and the rhythmic battering ram was now before us, visibly setting the heavy timbers to trembling with each blow.

But they held. God bless them, for minute after minute, they held.

It was the massive hinges that eventually gave way.

And all at once, the door crashed down between us.

Our enemies charged with a horrifying yell.

Matteo and Lia each let an arrow fly and then another, over our kneeling knights.

Our enemies came, but given the confines of the tunnel, could only move in three at a time. According to Captain Pezzati's plan, our forward knights blocked and struck, then dodged when they wearied, allowing three others to take their place. In this manner, seven or eight of the Fiorentini were killed, creating a sort of human barrier.

But we were soon down to ten men.

The fight went on and on, the sick knights on the attack truly seeming like zombies to me. There was a desperation in their eyes, a final mission that led them to expend the last of their energy on this terrible battle. And the sickly sweet stink of rotting flesh—that unique odor that I knew I'd forever tie to the Black Plague—filled the tunnel.

"So much for quarantine," I muttered to Mom, as she moved into position beside me. She had her battle staff ready. Dad remained beside the children, their last hope at protection. Fortino and Chiara crouched behind him, rocks in their small hands. *Deliver us, Lord. Save us. Please.*

Two of the wounded knights who had been carried into the tunnel managed to get to their feet, their swords plainly heavy in their weary hands. But they stood on either side, our last semblance of protection. Any able-bodied maidservant, footman or squire already stood in front of them. The sight of it made me weep.

"Come back here, behind us," I said to them all. There was no way I'd stand behind them and see them cut down. Not when I was still able. "Please, all of you. Protect the children. They are the future of Castello Forelli." *They are our future.*

They reluctantly shuffled behind the boxes, behind Lia and Matteo, and we moved out in front of the boxes in their place. I could see that two more of our wounded had died in the last hour, their faces now a waxen, stiff mask. Four of our knights at the front had fallen, leaving six.

"Kneel, Gabi," Lia said. Matteo told Mom to do the same thing. Captain Pezzati took a knee. Now that there were fewer knights at the front, it just might be possible...

Captain Pezzati shouted, "*Une, due, tre!*" On the count of three, Matteo and Lia let their arrows fly, trusting the knights at the front had heard their captain over the grunts and groans and curses and wails in the fray. At the last possible moment, they ducked, and the arrows pierced their adversaries. Those knights backing them up leaped over them to attack the Fiorentini. Again, on the count of three, two more arrows took down two more of our enemies. And in this fashion, we seemed to hold the line for several more minutes.

It didn't take long for the Fiorentini to see what was happening and duck on the third count, but there were so many behind them that the arrows inevitably found a mark. And those strikes became a good distraction of their own, forcing men to shift and carry their comrades away, or climb over their dead bodies, yet another barrier.

Otello and Lutterius were two of the three knights we had left at the front. As if sensing that they neared the end of our defense, the Fiorentini surged, sacrificing those ahead of them by pressing inward, burying our knights and dead with their own.

We hadn't seen it coming, this mad scrambling rush over both dead and living.

Chaos ensued in the flickering torchlight and deep shadow. Action became like a slow-motion sequence in my mind. Arrows flying by our heads. Swords coming so close to my neck and arm that thin lines of blood followed them, like a pencil's trace on parchment. I waded forward, well aware that my parents and sister were near. That my son was behind me, and I had chosen to remain here, rather than hide away.

A sick feeling filled my stomach as I struck one man after another, wounding and killing, wounding and killing, wounding and killing.

Had I been wrong? Was this a terrible mistake?
Would we all die?

CHAPTER 44

EVANGELIA

I could see Gabi slowing, her movements becoming laden with weariness, her reactions perilously slow, even as I could feel the rising tension among the maidservants and footmen and squires behind me. The Fiorentini tried to cut them down with a few deft blows. It was a farce, putting swords in their hands. I simply could not let them get any closer.

My desperation led me to take increasingly dangerous strikes, over the shoulders of my sister and the two remaining knights—Lutterius and Otello. Anticipating their moves, the sweep of their strikes, and following it with deadly accuracy with my arrows. Never had I felt more in tune with my bow. The thrum of the string, the growing numbness in my fingers as I drew and drew and drew again...it was like I was a machine, my mind a computer, narrowing in on a target, firing. It helped that the target was essentially a wall. Basically any arrow I fired was likely to strike someone, somewhere. And so far I'd managed to miss my own.

But my attention was on Gabi. Time and again I saved her from a certain death blow. I desperately wanted to call to her to fall back, to come back to us, but I couldn't take the second's time to pause—I knew it was far more effective to continue as I was, trying to take down her next adversary.

Otello was struck across the leg and Gabi turned to him, distracted.

"No," I whispered, shooting another arrow. I reached for my next, but the stack was gone. I glanced behind, and Chiara handed me one. "Another," I grunted to her, turning and aiming.

But I froze as my sister was stabbed in the belly with a dagger. Her head flew back, her mouth gaped open. Her attacker sneered and leaned into her.

"Nay!" I screamed, letting my arrow fly, piercing her attacker through his neck. Otello leaned forward and, with a cry, peeled them apart, going down between them. Mom grabbed hold of Gabi's armpits and dragged her backward, Lutterius desperately trying to defend them.

"Loro vengono," I grunted to those behind me, weeping as I continued to fire. *Here they come.* When they were too close, Matteo and I took up swords and leaped over the boxes to protect Gabi, sinking against the side wall, gasping.

I ducked to miss the strike of the first knight upon me, a skinny man about my dad's age. As I rose again, I glimpsed Chiara and Isabella's round eyes, peering over the edge of the crate in terror. I glimpsed little Fortino, witnessing the worst night of his short life. And I thought about the child in my womb, and how much I wanted to meet him or her. How precious a child was. How precious *my* child was.

"You shall not..." I began to bark out in gasps as I went on the offensive, "take us...today!" I repeated it, over and over, striking down one knight and then another and then another. "You shall not...take us...today!"

But even my last reserved surge of energy was short-lived. Battle was out-and-out exhausting, and we'd been at it for most of a day. I could feel the Fiorentini beginning to press forward again, my short gains lost in moments. And gradually, dimly, I began to accept that we might die here this day. *At least we're together,* I thought, distantly, like I was thinking of another family entirely. *We arrived together. It's fitting we go out together.*

Only the thought of Luca and Marcello, of leaving them as widowers, kept me from dropping my sword and giving up. Again and again, I forced myself to parry a strike. To duck. To twist. To lean back. To drive my sword forward. I was just adequate with the sword. But wherever Barbato had dredged up these men—they were worse. And so even in my exhaustion, I held my ground.

The pink light of dawn began to cast the men before us in deep shadow, making them faceless. I struck one down, and then another, and blinked, wondering if I was seeing things. Wondered if I'd been wounded and was dying. Because behind those that still attacked us, it seemed like there were fewer to back them up. More light streamed in, across the heaps and piles of dead and wounded that now filled the tunnel waist high.

I continued to respond in automatic fashion. Lifting my heavy sword with trembling arms. Bearing the brunt force of a strike that sent a chattering wave through my arms, shoulders and back. Shifting to attack again.

When there were but six before us—was it a mirage?—Mom reached out and gripped my wrist as I again brought my sword down upon the next man. Her voice came to me as if through water, and I looked to her, confused, dazed.

Then back to the man before me.

His face came into focus and again, I blinked heavily.

It was Luca.

"Evangelia," he said, easing the sword from my hand and tossing it aside. "It is all right. You have done well."

I looked dumbly from Luca, to Marcello—just catching sight of Gabriella and running toward her—and the other Forelli knights. Out in the courtyard, I could see more Sienese knights.

In the center of them was Rodolfo Greco.

"Papa!" Chiara shrieked, running past me and out to Rodolfo. I stared as she dodged the wounded and hopped over dead men, struck by the horrific sight. No child should have to endure such trauma as she had...Was this what our child would have to become accustomed to?

Marcello reached Gabi and gathered her up and into his arms. Mom followed them out of the tunnel.

I could hear women crying behind me, sobbing, saying relieved prayers of thanks. Laughing, in that almost-hysterical way of women.

"Lia, can you hear me?" Luca asked, his hands covering my shoulders. His voice sounded far away, and I stared at him, wondering if I was really wounded, dying, and this was all some sort of vision.

"Luca?" I needed to hear his voice. Needed him to convince me he was well.

"I'm here, love." His face and tunic were splattered with blood, as I assumed mine were. He had fought so hard to get to us.

"I am so fiercely proud of you, Evangelia Forelli. So proud of you." He pulled me close, and I breathed him in, sweaty and soiled and all. My husband, here. Holding me. Me holding him.

We had fought so hard to survive.

And now, at last, it was over.

CHAPTER 45

GABRIELLA

I awakened from the middle of one of my old nightmares...the one in which I was pierced by an arrow and my sister stitched me up and I was disintegrating, from the inside out...

But this time, it was Mom doing the stitching.

I bit down on the piece of wood and wailed. She'd used some sort of herbal anesthetic, but it wasn't morphine by any measure. Better than when Lia did it...but I began to wonder if it had been better to have more pain and pass out than to stay partially conscious.

"Hold her, Ben," Mom said, when I tried to thrash loose. I wanted her to stop, stop what she was doing. But Dad wasn't the only one holding me down. Marcello held my other arm and someone was across my legs.

"Hang in there, kiddo," Mom said, eying me briefly as she worked. "I'm almost done." Her fingers looked like they were in red gloves, so covered in blood were they.

The wound was low and to the right. What damage had it done? How deep was it? I tried to gather the strength to ask, but all I could do was bite down harder on the wood as Mom moved. I looked to Marcello and for the first time, realized I was in our room, the fresco of stars above me. "For-Fortino?" I grunted, thinking for a moment beyond my own pain, but the name was intelligible around the wood in my mouth.

"Our sons are well," Marcello said, giving me a grateful smile. "Rest, beloved. We shall tell you more..."

But I was already fading. The room becoming black, my view of the stars narrowing and narrowing until I succumbed to blessed unconsciousness.

EVANGELIA

"It's good she wore that leather armor plate," Mom said, as she stitched up the last of Gabi's wound. I got off her legs, now that she was unconscious and slack.

Mom leaned back and wiped her forehead with the back of her wrist. Her face was covered with a linen kerchief, as were ours. "I think the dagger went straight in and when her attacker tried to lift up on it, the armor plate kept it from moving far."

I'd seen the wound. It was a few inches wide and according to Mom, deep.

"Her intestines?" Dad whispered.

Mom blinked at him, her forehead wrinkling in concern. "I just couldn't see well enough, or get in far enough. There was too much blood." Her blue eyes shifted to Marcello. "We can only hope that it missed anything vital. We'll know in a few days."

Cuts to intestines were most certainly lethal. We'd seen more than a few men die horrible deaths when intestines were free to leak into the abdominal cavity. The wounded slowly sickened and died. But based on where it was, so low and so centered, I was more worried he'd pierced her uterus. Would she be sad if she never had more children?

Giacinta moved forward to clean Gabi's skin and help Mom bandage the wound, quickly covering her with a blanket against the chill. The fire was still working hard to drive away the winter's cold that seemed to permeate the castello. Or was that the specter of death I felt, in every hall and every room?

Even now, Sienese knights were dragging out the Fiorentini dead, hauling them to wagons and driving out the castello gates. I didn't know if they planned to burn or bury them, but there were hundreds, and many of them exhibited the last throes of bubonic plague. Mom rose, washed her hands in the basin, and then turned to the doorway. Gabi had been her priority, but I knew she had a long day ahead. Wearily, I rose to assist. There were still many inside our walls that were wounded, our own brothers and sisters who might have a chance to recover and...what? Then battle the plague?

We'd been infiltrated by hundreds of men carrying the virus.

We'd survived one battle only to face a far bigger one.

"So..." I said, walking beside Mom through the courtyard. "So we all may be infected now."

"Indeed," she said. "It's out of our hands now. Let's say that you and I just do what we can for the people we love, and see what the morrow brings? Are you with me, Lia? Can you see this through? Or do you need a few hours' rest?"

I shook my head. While I'd collapsed in the tunnel when I was at last with Luca again, I felt a surge of energy after seeing Gabi stitched up. I was just glad it hadn't been me, this time, to do it. Once was enough...Still, I braced myself. It was likely that I'd have to lend my hand to other stitching this day.

Two Sienese knights lifted a dead Fiorentini from atop another of our knights and I did a double-take. "*Celso*? Celso!" I hurried over to him. He was so covered in blood that the golden Forelli tunic was more of a burgundy. His or his enemy's? I leaned down and felt for a pulse. It was there, steady and strong.

His beefy hand whipped up and gripped my wrist with frightening strength. I was both scared by his sudden action and elated.

His eyes bore into mine, the pupils wide and blank, unseeing.

"Celso, 'tis me, Evangelia."

"M-m'lady," he muttered, his head sinking back to the ground. "Saints be praised. You live."

"As do you!" I said with a smile, searching his body for the wounds that had downed him, as Mom began to do the same. "Where are you hurt?"

"Yes, where are you hurt?" Luca asked, behind me. "Because if my wife is going to have her hands all over a man, I would prefer it was me."

I laughed under my breath, and Celso grinned wearily, and then winced as Mom found his wound, at the back of his head. "Easy, easy," he cried.

"Forgive me," Mom muttered. She looked up at Luca. "Head wound. We'll bandage him, but he needs to stay as still as possible. Don't let the men lift him. We need blankets and cloth. Water."

"Yes, m'lady," Luca said, raising an arm to gesture to a girl carrying a bucket of water and strips of cloth for bandages. He grabbed a squire, Iacopo, and pointed to Celso. "Once the lady has him bandaged, tell anyone who approaches to leave him where he lies until we return, yes?"

"Yes, sir," said the boy, his eyes ringed with exhaustion. The squires had been amazing last night, supplying us as they had.

I called to a maid carrying a pile of woolen blankets, and we took one and tucked it around Celso's body to try and keep him warm.

"Stay still, friend," Mom said. "Don't move. Only rest. We'll return to check on you."

Celso did not respond. Again, I felt for his pulse.

"I think you'd best check for further wounds, m'lady," he said with a sly smile, peeking open one eye not to peer at me, but my husband.

I sucked in my breath, not sure whether to laugh at him or slap him.

"Keep toying with my *wife*, Celso," Luca said, leaning in, "and once you're up on your feet again, I'll gladly take your legs from under you."

Celso only grinned and laughed under his breath.

CHAPTER 46

GABRIELLA

I awakened later that day, my belly throbbing, but it seemed that there wasn't any internal bleeding. Mom was all about that, and I tried to act like I was happy too, but it still felt like...well, like I'd been stabbed with a dagger. Nothing like a knife to the belly to ruin a girl's day.

Mercedes came to visit me, with Benedetto in her arms and the kids clinging to her skirts. Rodolfo had set off with six knights to search for Alessandra. It turned out that the family had escaped the castello when it was attacked, and they'd hidden in the woods for a time. When the Fiorentini had discovered they weren't within the walls of Castello Greco, they set out to hunt them down. As they closed in, fearing capture more than death, they sent Chiara running to the village and turned to fight alongside the few knights that accompanied them. In the midst of that, Alessandra had gone missing, and Rodolfo had joined Marcello and Luca and their Sienese reinforcements in turning the tide against the Fiorentini.

I prayed that Alessandra still lived. That she hadn't been captured and taken to Firenze. That Chiara would have her mama back, and Rodolfo, his wife. I didn't think either of them could handle the grief of losing her...

Men continued to carry wounded on stretchers past my door, out to the western segment of the castello, where Mom and Dad were now treating anyone with the plague. They'd fallen back to a "mini" quarantine strategy, knowing it was fairly futile now, but determined to try anyway.

A terrible smell of roasting flesh filled the air. "What is that horrible smell?" I asked Mercede.

"The ground is too hard to bury so many," she said. "Instead, they burn them. It shall go on for days."

I winced over her words. Just the thought of so many dead, whether Fiorentini or Sienese, pained me. "Where?"

"That small eastern ravine. Lord Forelli has instructed that they build a tremendous fire and keep feeding it, in between the bodies, until there is nothing left but ash for the spring rains to wash away."

I shook my head. It was all so...cavalier, in a culture that traditionally made a big deal of honoring life and death with ritual and rites. "They couldn't use more of the Etruscan tombs?"

Mercede shook her head too. "There were too many for that, m'lady. Far too many."

Far too many. Sienese. Fiorentini. In the end, all the same, just men and women leaving the world with as much as they had when they entered it—nothing. Death, the Great Equalizer, Dad called it. Poor or rich. Beautiful or plain. In the end, we were all the same.

I sighed heavily, and then gasped, my exaggerated breath making my wound feel like it was breaking open. "What else goes on outside my door?" I asked Chiara, desperate to think of anything else.

"Cook is making soup!" she said, eyes wide with excitement.

I tried to concentrate on that a moment and wished I could walk to the kitchens to smell onions and garlic sautéing in oil rather than the putrid odors of the funeral pits.

Mercede looked at me with eyes that saw me, truly saw me, and said simply, "We'll find a nosegay for you."

"Thank you." They left me, then, intent on setting up a new sleeping space in the old den, with my blessing. The nursery was too close to the new plague infirmary.

Lia came in just as I started to nod off and knelt by my bed.

"Heya," I said.

"Hi. How do you feel?"

"Like I got stabbed in the gut. You?" She had a shiner under one eye and a cut on her jaw. Likely she had as many bruises and pulled muscles as I did.

"Like we battled for our lives all night." She took my hand. "But we stood our ground, Gabi. We stood with our people."

"That felt good, didn't it?"

"It did."

"Any news about Alessandra?"

She shook her head, eyes bleak. "No word from Rodolfo either."

"Think they got her?"

"I hope not."

I turned to look at the stars on the ceiling. Because this time, there would be no stealing into our enemy's city to set free one of our own. There were too many ways we could die, and too many counting on us to live.

EVANGELIA

I could see Gabi was fighting to not cry from the pain and fear. Sweat beaded on her forehead, even though the castello was pretty cold. "Lia..." she began, as I moved toward the door.

"I'll check on them," I said, knowing she was worried about the kids.

"Thanks," she said, closing her eyes.

I shut the door and almost wished I was the one who was injured and safely away, because what I faced in the courtyard was utter chaos. The stench of blood filled the air. A group of knights, their own various wounds bandaged, passed me, carrying another between them on a blanket, heading toward the Great Hall. The wounded man was moaning, his face a mask of pain and tears.

After a quick check on the kids, I went up to the wall to find my husband. Luca was directing men, making certain there was a mix of experienced knights and younger men keeping watch, ready for any further attacks. Patrols were out, our own knights augmented by reinforcements from Siena.

I waited until he finished talking to a guy around my age, thinking how, back home in Boulder, we'd be planning a biking trip on Saturday, not strategies on how to fortify the castle and drive any remaining Fiorentini out beyond the border. My life was so different here, but this was totally where I was supposed to be.

Luca turned to me and wrapped his arm around my shoulders, leading me a bit away. "Are you well, love?"

I nodded. "What can I do? How might I best help?"

"Be ready to return to the wall if we're attacked again. Other than that, see what you can do to assist your parents with the sick and wounded." His brows lowered. "The Sienese...they saved us, the castello, but there are sick among them too."

I nodded. "I know."

His eyes covered my face, as if wanting to touch me, but reluctant, here in this public space, with men passing back and forth. "Evangelia," he whispered, "if you become sick...the baby..."

I shook my head. "We cannot think of such things now," I said. "The only way through is through, true?"

"True."

"Any word from Rodolfo or Alessandra?"

He lifted his head, his lips falling slightly open. "You haven't heard?"

My breath caught. "No. What is it?"

"Rodolfo believes that Alessandra went across the border. To her father. It was the only thing he could think of."

I stopped breathing. Alessandra's father had disowned her. Believed she had betrayed the Fiorentini and ruined her good name during her stay with us, even though it was the farthest thing from the truth. I knew she had been so hurt from all of that...only Rodolfo's constant love and attention had brought her to healing. And Chiara's too. But her dad...would he turn her over to the Fiorentini?

"Luca, where are the Fiorentini troops? Those whom you drove back?"

He held back, but why? To protect me? Because I was pregnant? "Luca," I whispered. "I'm pregnant. Not incapacitated."

"Clearly," he said. "You showed me that last night. But still...you must take care. Your mother told me that further battle, trauma, may risk you and our babe. There are many, still, who pose a danger to us. But you shall be safe, here. Now that we have reinforcements."

So they lingered on the border, just a few miles distant. "And Rodolfo? He went after her?"

Luca swallowed. "With twelve of his best men. If anyone can get in and out, it's Greco."

I sighed heavily and looked north, toward the woods. I knew those woods. I'd hunted alongside Alessandra. She'd shown me the path she'd taken, chasing the boar on that fateful day. I could find it...

Luca took my hand and stood beside me. "Do not even think of it, Evangelia. I know how you and your sister feel about Alessandra. But leave it to Rodolfo. We need you here. *I* need you here. Understood?"

His pleading, frightened tone wilted any Gabi-like thought I had entertained for a moment of charging out there, saving Alessandra. One look over my shoulder to the courtyard, teeming with people, affirmed what he said. And with Gabi down, the children needed me too. "I'm not going anywhere," I said.

Looking relieved, he pulled my hand up for a quick kiss. "Take care, beloved."

I took hold of his tunic and pulled him closer for a kiss. "You too."

I turned to leave the wall and was heading down the circular stair to the bottom, passing several Sienese knights when I first heard it. *Strega.* Italian for *witch*.

I searched for who had said it, but all I saw were boots trudging upward. Had I misheard it?

But out in the courtyard, passing through two patrols of Sienese, I heard it again. Saw several men cross themselves and stare at me, half in open curiosity, half in distaste. I felt the blush and rushed forward, not liking the first feeling I'd ever had that some of my Sienese brethren were anything but supportive.

"Almeno lei é la nostra strega," said one. *At least she's our witch.*

That brought me full round, fist clenched. I looked from face to face, trying to figure out who had said it. I strode up to them and looked each one in the eye. They all deferred to me, bowing their heads as I passed, saying, "M'lady."

"Who said that? Who made such a foul claim?"

One man feigned confusion. "What is this you speak of, m'lady? What foul claim?"

"I shall know which of you did so. *Now.*" I still strode before the six of them, arcing around me.

"'Twas I," said a burly man just an inch taller than I, but twice as big across the shoulders. His eyes narrowed in challenge. A Sienese knight.

"You are dismissed," I said. "Go back to the city with your lies. You shall not remain here."

"You have not the authority to send me to the wall, let alone Siena," he said with a scoff. "I do not answer to you."

I acted without thinking. I grabbed his wrist, turned and flipped him to his back, knocking the wind from him. Kneeling on his shoulder and bringing a dagger to his throat to keep him still, I leaned close. "You *shall* answer to me. We have much to contend with in this castello. Death, disease! Lies, we have no time for. Now get out, or I shall tell my husband, who most assuredly has *authority* over you. But believe me, if he learns of this, he shall not be as merciful as I."

A crowd was gathering around us, some loyal Forelli knights among them, all poised to aid me.

I rose, shoulders back, head high, and sheathed my dagger, waiting for him to get to his feet. He lumbered upward, still struggling to get his breath, face red with rage. Forelli knights took hold of his arms. He tried to shake them off, but they held firm.

"M'lady?" Captain Pezzati asked, at my elbow. "What is this?"

"This is a traitor among us," I said, making certain my words sunk in for his compatriots too. "Spreading lies about me. I have told him to return to Siena. He is not welcome here."

"Indeed, he is not," the captain said, edging in to face the man, chest to chest, and stare him down. "Escort him to the gates. Give him a horse. We shall leave it to God to see if he makes it or not."

CHAPTER 47

EVANGELIA

T he men turned to drag the Sienese knight toward the gates. "Nay, please! Please!" he cried, clearly terrified. There must be more Fiorentini between us and Siena, I decided.

"M'lady!" he cried. "Forgive me!"

"Halt!" I called. I walked over to the three of them and again faced my adversary. "What is your name?"

"Zanobi Viridis, m'lady," he said, sweat streaming down his face, despite the cold.

"Do you understand now that I have all the authority I need?" I asked.

"Yes, m'lady," he said, all quick contrition.

"Is it the way of a witch," I whispered, leaning closer, "to be merciful, Zanobi?"

His eyes widened, as if he was caught. "Nay, m'lady," he said.

"Do you give me your word that you shall do nothing but defend my name and my reputation if I show you mercy?"

"Yes, m'lady. Yes."

I stared at him for a long moment. "Release him."

Captain Pezzati was again by my side, listening to it all. "Are you certain?"

"Yes."

The men looked to him, and seeing he had no argument, did as I asked.

"Thank you, m'lady. Thank you," he said, bowing repeatedly as he left us and returned to the others.

My eyes moved to Captain Pezzati. "How many Fiorentini are between us and Siena?"

His lips moved into a grim line. "More than five hundred."

"All of them ill?"

"Nay. But a higher portion than in our cities. Half, mayhap."

"How did these Sienese troops get through?"

"They divided when they arrived. Half retreated north, to the border. Half southward. There are five hundred Fiorentini prepared to attack that southern company today."

This made Luca's comments all the more clear to me. His desperation to keep me inside the castello. His need for me to be at the ready, to come to the wall, should we be attacked again. And his overarching desire to keep me and our baby safe. But now, even within these walls, I knew that we weren't entirely safe. "Thank you, Captain," I murmured, leaving them.

I turned the corner and leaned against the wall, thinking. So Barbato's mad claims had taken hold, even among our own. Everyone was going a little crazy... I rubbed my temples. What would happen if Siena turned against us? It had never occurred to me before now. Not when so many had shown us such devotion for so long. But the plague, the plague threatened to change everything.

Gradually, I became aware of the groans and cries from a window high above me. The Great Hall. It was time to go and assist my parents. Steeling myself, I turned and went in, stopping at a basin near the front door to wash my hands.

The entire hall was filled, the scent of decaying flesh making me gag. Those exhibiting signs of the plague were carried out, to the lean-to infirmary that had been erected outside our walls. There, they were given water, blankets, and could linger by fires, to see if they'd die or survive the dread disease. If we were attacked, they'd be killed. But there was no way around it; we couldn't keep them within. It was only due to our provisioning that we had the resources to take care of them at all.

And within, we still had more than enough to handle. From the weeping and amount of blood, I could see that several men had endured amputations of arms and legs. The scent of burned flesh rose above the others too—the cauterization that might save them. Maids moved back and forth with more linens, carrying away others so soaked in blood that they left a trail of drips down their skirts and on the stones behind them as they moved. Every table in the hall held men, most of them two abreast. Others lined the edges and the dais, leaving only space for maids and knights and my parents to move. The doctor, Sandro Menaggio, had returned to us, thankfully, and the thin man moved wearily down the line, seeking out his next patient. I knew he didn't seek out those hurt the worst—they were least likely to survive. He sought those that might survive if they only obtained a little help. Menaggio paused when he saw me, and his eyes darted to the corner.

For the first time, I noted that Mom and Dad weren't moving among the wounded. Mom was with Dad.

And Dad looked sick.

Mom was grasping at his tunic, and Dad was pulling away, shaking his head, as if arguing.

My heart pounded in my chest, stealing my breath.

On leaden feet, I moved toward them, wanting to know, but not.

Dad glimpsed me first and stilled.

I saw it then, as he turned to look at Mom.

The swellings under his neck, right under the jaw. Those that in a few days would become dark, black buboes.

No. No, no, no, no...

"I have to go outside, Lia," he said to me, in English. "Tell your mom. I cannot live by separate rules and—"

"All I want for him is to go to our quarters," Mom interrupted. "Where we can keep him properly comfortable and warm. Where he has his best chance."

"Where I have the greatest chance of infecting others," he said, swallowing audibly. "Please, Adri. I must. Even now I might have infected you and Lia."

Mom set her mouth in a grim line. "This is not going to kill you, Ben. We have immunities. Somehow, some way—"

Dad took her arms and shook her a little. "*No*. No," he said, his tone softening the second time. "Think, Adri. Even at home, people come down with it."

"I'll go then. To the tomb. And get what we need."

"No, Mom," I said in confusion. "You can't go out there. There are still Fiorentini about. And if anyone sees you going to the tomb right now..."

"I must," she said, gathering her skirts and already turning away.

It was my turn to grab her arm. "No, Mom. No! What could you need from there?"

She stared back at me. "There are medicines, I hope. Antibiotics," she whispered.

"What? How?"

She looked around us and then pulled me toward a corner where two men had just been removed. "Orazio and Galileo...they promised to bring back antibiotics and leave them for us."

"They did what?" I turned partway from her and took a deep breath. If anyone were to find those in the tomb...

"They promised. I'm not certain, obviously, that they were successful. But if they were..." She grabbed my hand. "If they were, they're in the back right urn. I must see. If we get some meds in him right away, he'll have a better chance."

"No, Adri," Dad said. "You and the girls are staying here. I have to go out anyway. If any of us are to try for the tombs, it's me."

I watched my mother as she considered him. I remembered her anguish, her grief at losing my dad the first time, and how it made my own grief nearly unbearable. Any time Gabi or I started to feel halfway decent, halfway normal, her grief unraveled us again, taking us back to the beginning, in a way. And now we were facing it again. What a terrible, wretched mess...

Dad moved toward the door, taking a blanket from the pile there. We intercepted him. "Wait here," Mom said. Her voice was tight, high. She was fighting to not lose it. "Just for a moment, Ben. I'll get your longer boots, an extra pair of socks and a woolen tunic and cloak. It will help, out there."

He nodded, wearily, but still insisted on waiting outside the Great Hall. I led him around the corner, away from most of the other traffic. He coughed, and I could hear the terrifying, heavy muck within his chest.

"Man, how long have you been feeling so bad?"

"It comes, fast. Just like we've seen in others. Yesterday, I felt weak. Last night, worse, but I just thought I was tired from the battle. The cough began this morning, but I hoped..."

His voice cracked, and that threatened to send me into sobs myself.

"I hoped it was just a cold," he said. "But this afternoon, I noticed the swelling in my lymph nodes. It took me a couple hours to come to terms with it. And to tell your mother."

I nodded, a ball of pain forming in my own throat.

"We're not going to lose you, Dad. Not again," I said, my voice strangled. I sniffed and blinked rapidly. He didn't need to see me cry. He needed only my strength right now. My confidence. "Luca survived it," I said. "You can, too. Maybe Mom's right. Maybe some of our vaccinations will aid us in fighting it."

"Yes, yes," he said, but I knew it was as much an effort to reassure me than any clear belief.

Mom returned and together, we escorted him to the castello gates. People grew silent as we passed, Dad clearly dressed to go outside, but just as clearly weak and ailing. Men and women crossed themselves and prayed under their breath, as if watching a man heading to the gallows. I wanted to shout at them to stop it, to not do that, but knew I couldn't. They meant well. It was commiseration, in a way. Shared grief. Only I wasn't ready to grieve my dad again.

Not again.

CHAPTER 48

EVANGELIA

A Forelli guard stood in my way. "Forgive me, m'lady, but it's the captain's orders that you are not to leave without his knowledge."

"My father is sick. I'll be just outside the gate."

He hesitated, and Mom and Dad and I pressed past him. I knew it wouldn't be long until Luca was out and with us. We found a place near the fire for Dad, and I tried to ignore the fact that the wide space available was likely due to others dying, their bodies removed. I flung out a blanket and Mom helped Dad to the ground. We quickly stretched his cloak around him and then covered him with another blanket.

I looked around for a squire or maid with a water bucket, then thought better of it. I'd bring Dad his own supply, with a clean cup to dip in. Who knew what else the common pail was now carrying.

The bigger issue was getting to the tombs. If Mom was right—if the Betarrini brothers had been successful in bringing us a supply of antibiotics—it just might prove to be the edge Dad needed to beat the monster back. But with people whispering of me and Gabi being witches, and their suspicion about us and the tombs, and my promise to Luca to stay in the castello—had I really promised?—oh, and the fact that there might be Fiorentini still about...I had some serious obstacles.

Two patrols came in then, and Marcello was at the lead. He caught sight of us as he passed, circled around and pulled up right beside us, his face a mask of concern. "Ben," he said, dismounting and taking Dad's hand. He forgot he should steer clear in his desire to get to Dad, in his need. And neither Mom or I seemed to have the energy to intervene.

"I'm glad to see you, son."

I had to turn away. Something about seeing Dad with Gabi's husband, their shared devotion—the same love he shared with Luca—threatened to break me.

Marcello turned to me. "Does Gabriella know?"

"No. We just discovered it ourselves."

"We should not tell her. She'll want to come to him."

"Oh, Marcello, I can't do that. You've seen it yourself. Dad has a battle ahead, and if he loses, he only has two or three days."

"Leave it until the morrow. She needs another day of rest."

I took a deep breath and shook my head. "I do not know if I can. She'll be furious."

"She shall insist we bring her to him. And in her weakened state," he whispered, "I fear she might be more susceptible to the plague. Do you not fear the same?"

I bit my lip, thinking. "On the morrow, then, and if he gets much worse, I shall tell her immediately."

He nodded, knowing it was my best offer. Luca arrived then, and as Marcello had, knelt by Dad's side and took his hand. "Ben, nay, nay," he murmured. Tears welled in his eyes and fell down his face, which did me in. He caught sight of me and rose, coming to take me in his arms. "It will be all right," he whispered. "Your father is strong. You shall see."

I tucked my head against the side of his neck. "Luca, I need something."

"What is it, love?"

"I need you to get us to the tombs."

He took hold of my shoulders and leaned away. "What? Do you intend—"

"Nay. We might lose Dad if we take him to the wrong time. And with me being pregnant..." For once, traveling through time was not going to be our answer. "The Betarrini brothers might have left some medicine in the tomb for us. At least, they were supposed to. If they were successful then—"

"Evangelia, you are not going out there. The woods are thick with Fiorentini. There is a reason I didn't want you outside the walls. There is a bounty upon our heads, but for you and Gabriella, especially."

"There has always been a bounty," I said.

"Except that Barbato quadrupled the offer for any Betarrini or Forelli." Even saying it made him move slightly in front of me and look about. "'Tis enough to make even a loyal Sienese think twice about moving north of the border," he said out of the corner of his mouth.

I frowned at that. "I cannot live in fear. And if I don't go, Mom will."

"I understand," he said, glancing her way. "But I shall go. Alone."

"That makes no better sense," I protested. "Then it shall be you in danger."

"I will be with him," Marcello said, drawing near. "We can trust no others in knowing where we travel, given the rumors that abound." So he'd heard it too, the rumors of witchcraft. "Let me look in on Gabriella, then let us be about this errand before nightfall descends."

My heart was in my throat. I knew no one was better qualified, but the idea of our husbands heading into further danger made me sick to my stomach. For the first time, I wished I was more like Gabi and had just slipped away to take care of it myself. Worrying about my own safety was less stressful than worrying about my husband and brother-in-law.

I set out to find a fresh bucket and cup to give Dad water, as well as some bread. When I returned, I saw that Luca had assigned a patrol of six knights to stand guard around my Dad and Mom. I wanted, with everything in me, to take care of him inside the walls of the castello, and when Gabi found out that he was sick and outside the walls...I sighed. The whole thing was such a wretched, terrifying mess.

Dad was shivering, his fever soaring. His eyes looked sunken in the sockets, his skin pale. Mom covered him with another blanket. Instinctively, I reached out to touch his arm, but Mom gave me a sorrowful shake of her head. "The baby," she whispered. "You must protect your baby. If you get sick...I will care for your dad. I've been more than exposed already."

I swallowed hard and settled to my knees, feeling the chill of the winter-cold ground. A smoky haze settled all around us, fed by the gruesome funeral fire that the men were still stoking. It lent a spooky feel to our beloved woods—making me all the more certain that enemy soldiers might attack us at any moment, or that Luca and Marcello might get captured.

Anxiously, I listened for their return, disappointed several times when it was merely new patrols, riding in to report, rather than the Forellis with medicine from the future. Medicine that might save my dad again. An hour passed. Then two. "C'mon," I whispered. *C'mon, c'mon, c'mon...*

Dad fell asleep, still shivering so hard that his teeth chattered. I wanted to weep when Mom curled up beside him, wrapping her arm across his torso. She cast aside the handkerchief that covered her nose and mouth, ripping it away as if it stifled her. She settled her face on his chest and tugged him closer. Tears drifted down the bridge of her nose and dropped onto Dad's tunic. I found another blanket and covered them both, letting my hand rest on her shoulder a moment, then turned to watch the path on which Luca and Marcello should have already appeared.

The gates came open and four patrols rode out, twenty-four men in pairs, heading directly north. I stood up and walked over to Captain Pezzati. "What is it? What's happening?"

"Lady Evangelia," he said, turning me aside as he eyed the horizon in protective fashion, "Might I ask—where were Lord Forelli and the captain heading?"

I paused, judging his expression, trying to figure out what was going on. "I think they hoped to find aid for my father. The same doctor that healed Orazio Betarrini," I said. It was close enough to the truth.

His gray brows furrowed. "Why did they insist on going alone?"

"*Captain*," I said sharply. "What is it? What has happened?"

"They've been cut off, surrounded. Our men are trying to get to them. I must insist you come inside."

"Nay," I said, my heart pounding. "I am through with hiding inside the walls. Even within, we are not safe, with the plague among us! Look there, to my parents. My sister is on her own recovery bed, and now my husband is in danger. I shall lend my hand to the effort in the only way I can."

"You don't mean to—"

"I do. Prepare two more patrols to accompany me to the front lines."

"Nay, m'lady. I cannot allow it."

"I am not asking you, Captain. I am telling you."

"But Sir Forelli specifically ordered me not to—"

I drew close enough to be nose to nose with him. "If Sir Forelli dies while I was here, arguing with you, I shall never forgive you, Captain. Now assign all the knights you need to give me adequate company. Or I shall be away on my own."

Turning on my heel, I strode into the castello, my heart pounding. I knew it was extremely dangerous, to head out. And there was no way I'd do it alone. But I couldn't just sit here. Not when I could do something to help Luca! It was something, *something* I could do to fight back the dragon that suddenly threatened to steal my joy from every angle possible—my sister, my father, my husband...

I got to the quarters I shared with Luca and hurriedly tucked my braided hair beneath a scarf and donned leggings and tunic—intent on masquerading as a man, hoping to be less of a target—then strapped on my quiver and arm guard, grabbing hold of my bow. I immediately felt stronger, more assured, armed. More She-Wolfy.

I turned and latched the door when I saw him. The dog, Gordo, on his side in the corridor, panting. Swallowing hard, I went to him, knelt and touched him. His nose was dry and hot. He was listless, not even raising his head when he saw me, only whimpering. I rose, closed my eyes, and went to the guard at the turret door. "The dog back there," I said with a strangled voice, gesturing over my shoulder, "is sick. See to it that he is put down and his body burned in the pits. Burn the gloves you use to carry him."

"Yes, m'lady," the knight said, face impassive, more interested in my curious manner of dress. To most in this time, animals were a nuisance, seldom beloved pets. Sick animals were put down without a thought. And in these years, that accounted for many. What was one more?

I trudged on, focusing on Luca and Marcello, refusing to give in to the tears that threatened to take me down. We'd already lost the cats and two other dogs to plague. Now, Gordo, my favorite. He was still the pudgy puppy in my mind that he was when we first saw him in Venice. The animals had likely spared us from infection for some time, keeping the castello free of rodents. But now the last had fallen victim.

It was all so wretchedly unfair. I wanted to shake my fist at God and shout, "Enough! Enough, already!" Inwardly, I did so, then freaked out, worried that God would then take my dad for sure to show me who was Boss.

But Father Tomas's words came back to me. *God is all about life, not death. Death is his enemy's domain.*

The enemy had taken Tomas and Adela. Our friends and neighbors. Luca and Marcello's blood brothers. Now, even, our last pet. I knew that Mom hadn't bought them as pets...they'd been meant as defense. But a girl couldn't just say no to puppy-dog eyes. And Gordo's eyes, and his dark black spots and curly fur...My breath caught.

I wouldn't cry. I refused to cry.

It wasn't the dog. It was everything.

Luca. I needed to focus on Luca.

But when I got to the courtyard, Gabi stood in my path. She was looking pale and scared, her hand against her abdomen. "Lia," she said, her mouth a grimace, "where is everyone?"

"Here, sit down," I said, grabbing hold of her elbow and ushering her to a stone bench. "You should not have left your bed."

She searched me. "You are prepared for battle," she whispered. "What is it? What has happened?"

"Gabi...Dad's sick." I paused a moment, letting her digest that. "And Marcello and Luca—they went to the tomb to get what Mom hopes was medicine, left by Orazio and Galileo."

"Orazio! Galileo?" Understanding dawned. The promise they'd made to Mom...the one we'd caught wind of, but didn't know the details about. "And now?"

"They are surrounded. I am going to aid in breaking through the line of Fiorentini who keep them from us."

"No, Lia, you can't."

I rose, unwilling to spend a moment longer in argument. "Don't you see? It's the only way. To save our husbands. Our dad."

"I'll go with you," she said, struggling to rise, her lips parting in a pained gasp.

"No. You won't. This time it has to be me, Gabs. Go help Mom and Dad, if you're up to it. If we don't get back..." My voice cracked, and I hurriedly wiped away the tears. "I don't think Dad has long." I bent and kissed her cheek. "I love you."

And with that, I ran for my gelding and rode away from Castello Forelli to bring back my husband, and hopefully, medicine that would save my dad.

CHAPTER 49

EVANGELIA

C aptain Pezzati sent Otello, Matteo and Falito with me, along with ten other knights. With the twenty-four that had gone ahead of us, I felt reasonably confident that we could approach the line of fighting and find out what was happening.

I was wrong.

Twilight—which came and went quickly in the winter months—was upon us. The smoke made it even harder to see. But when we heard the commotion ahead, we dismounted and crept closer. Marcello and Luca had run into the Grecos and some others, but they were surrounded. The Forelli knights that left ahead of us had engaged the enemy too but were outnumbered two to one.

Even with us, we'd still be outnumbered.

"We need to get them out of there," I whispered to Matteo, watching as Marcello moved woodenly, striking out and dodging swords, but plainly exhausted. Where was Luca?

"Follow me," said the man, the most senior knight in my patrol. He turned to the others. "We are going to make a way for Lord Forelli and the captain to make their way out, understood? We shall create a tunnel, and then a barrier, through which they shall escape. Follow our lead."

He trotted forward, half hunched over. "Otello, stay with the lady at all times. Work together with her. Falito, never leave their side. I'll do my best to be on the other one."

I thought we'd likely stop somewhere and find our best entry point, but either Matteo had already found it, or just decided that any place was as good as another. We paused only for him to gesture toward the backs of a group of twelve Fiorentini, and Matteo and I let our arrows fly, killing four before our men were cutting down others and then holding back more that moved toward us, alerted by the new line of conflict.

Otello and I stood back-to-back, our attention on taking down those who still were bent on killing our people within the surrounded circle. Our men attacked from two other angles of the circle as well, distracting the enemy, and now I could see why Matteo had chosen this third spot. It was the thinnest. But more were arriving, redoubling their efforts to kill our men, Rodolfo and Alessandra. With some relief, I finally spotted my husband.

I dispatched arrow after arrow, most finding their marks, when I wasn't jostled or pushed or pulled or stumbling over rocks in the swiftly falling darkness. But we were making progress.

The way opened, and our group pushed to either side, leaving a path of escape for Luca and the rest. But they were still pinned down inside. I took out or wounded three men as I ran toward him. He caught sight of me, did a double-take and faltered. Only Alessandra's scream, and Rodolfo's sword, kept him from being impaled by his opponent.

I killed a man who was then, in turn, about to kill Rodolfo, and wounded another moving to grab Alessandra. Otello, at my side, shot an archer out of a tree. "Well done," I muttered, having wondered where the arrows were coming from.

"Fine work yourself, m'lady," he said with a grin.

Two men came at us, screaming with a guttural cry, swords raised. We didn't have time to get arrows off, but Matteo and Falito were there. "Down," Matteo grunted, and together Otello and I ducked, letting the knights jump across our backs to meet our attackers.

I felt an arm go around my neck and I was dragged back. Otello advanced immediately, an arrow drawn tight across his bow. I drew my dagger and then wrenched my head to the right, giving Otello his target, and heard the disgusting sound of an arrow entering my attacker's eye socket. I rammed my dagger into his belly, below his breastplate, even as I turned. I could feel the warmth of his blood on my neck and swallowed back the vomit that rose in my throat.

"Are you all right, m'lady?" Otello asked, taking my arm as I gasped for breath.

"Yes, thank you, friend."

But he was already turning away, firing an arrow. Then another. I swallowed hard, forced myself to draw an arrow, and then was tackled by a large man.

"Lia!" I heard Luca call, but it was from far-off. I gasped for air and thought briefly about the baby. The man had knocked the wind out of me. He rose, and I tried to roll, aware that I had to keep moving—even if I couldn't breathe—that he was raising his sword, bringing it around to cut off my head.

But I was only as far as my hands and knees when Rodolfo was there, blocking the blow, then pushing the attacker back, with a series of parries and strikes.

Luca reached me, then, helping me to my feet before turning to fight another Fiorentini, this one plainly sick with the plague. "What in the saints' name are you doing here?" he grunted over his shoulder.

Wearily, I drew an arrow, moved to the side and shot his assailant. "Saving you, again, it appears," I said with a small grin.

He laughed under his breath and shook his head, half in fury, I knew, half in total dismay.

"Forellis, now!" bellowed Matteo, and I turned to see the opening was holding and for the moment, we had room to run. Rodolfo picked up an ailing, older man in his arms, Alessandra at his side. Otello turned to pull a wounded man's arm across his shoulders. The knight was bloody from head to toe, but alive. Marcello was ten paces off, near the edge of the woods, fighting a large knight.

"Did you get it?" I asked Luca, now working with me, Matteo and Falito in taking down any Fiorentini that drew near, even as we worked our way toward the exit point.

"We have it," he grunted. "*Down.*"

I crouched without question and felt the cold whoosh of metal near the back of my neck—setting every hair on end—and then heard the clang of sword against sword. I was rolling, rising, aware that my kerchief had fallen, when I felt a hand on my braid. The man pulled, and I was on my feet, wondering for a moment if he had pulled most of it out.

He wrenched me around to face him. He was huge. Twice my width and six inches taller. His mouth, filled with decaying teeth, opened in a wide grin of victory. I expected him to pull me back into a strangle hold, was preparing for it, but instead he shoved me with such strength that I lost my footing and yet covered a good twelve feet of ground. Two other Fiorentini grabbed my arms and rushed me toward the woods.

"Nay!" Marcello said, running to intercept them. "Release her!" he yelled, striking at the one on my left, forcing him to fight. An arrow came through the back of the neck of the one on my right, its bloody head sticking out as the man choked, dropping my arm. I turned to look over my shoulder. *Otello, God bless him.*

Instinctively, I ducked and turned, spotting one after another Fiorentini advancing.

"I know it's been enjoyable," Luca said, grabbing my arm, "but I believe it's time to leave this relaxing little picnic spot." We ran down the jagged corridor, past some men who were wounded but holding the line for us. Otello and I kept firing arrows all the way, easing some of the pressure, but I was thankful for Matteo's plan. Without it, we'd have simply become mired in the same tar pit as the others.

We were almost out, Rodolfo twenty paces in the lead, when another group of Fiorentini managed to get around the Sienese and came streaming down the hill on horseback.

"Get behind me, Evangelia," Luca grunted, lifting his sword.

I did as he asked, feeling the ground tremble as the Fiorentini came toward us, like shadowy soldiers from hell, their faces indescript in the darkness.

Rodolfo had set down the old man belatedly. He was just lifting his sword when a man rammed him off his feet as he galloped past, striking his shoulder with a spiked metal ball on a chain, then coming straight toward us. In quick succession I saw Greco fall, the rider perilously close, then felt Luca whirl and strike above me as I ducked.

The man cried out, his leg gashed to the bone. His horse pulled up and turned in a circle when he felt the release of his rider's leg. He turned and glared at me, at Luca's back, and then pressed in to come at us again.

Alessandra was screaming, but I pushed thoughts of her away, made myself breathe and draw an arrow and take aim rather than cry out to Luca, who was still concentrating on another group of knights, coming at us.

I shot him when he was just fifteen feet away, so close that the horse brushed past me, turning me, until I was again facing the monstrous knight who had grabbed me before. Two other Fiorentini rode between us, but the man remained focused on me, striding forward, as if there was no one else in the woods.

"Luca," I said.

"Hold, Lia," he grunted, pushing me a little to the left, unknowingly *toward* the knight, as another rider rode past us on the right, slashing with his blade.

"Luca..." I said. The big knight now ran headlong toward us. "*Luca!*"

My husband turned just in time to push me out of harm's way, kneel with the shaft of his sword against his thigh and impale the knight on the end of his sword, just before his own sword pierced Luca's breastplate. Luca let out a cry to match our attacker's and the two rolled, over and over, until they came to rest, Luca atop him, his sword half buried in the Fiorentini's chest.

I let out a mirthless laugh of wonder at my husband's skill, at the miracle that he hadn't been harmed too, when I saw Luca's face. He was looking in horror, past me.

Belatedly, I turned. Marcello was running toward Rodolfo, who was surrounded by three knights, trying desperately to defend Alessandra and the old man, while clearly wounded. One knight grabbed hold of Alessandra and dragged her backward, and when Rodolfo's attention turned toward her, another stabbed him in the lower back.

"Nay!" I screamed, taking aim with my arrow and managing to take down the third man. Marcello attacked the second, who had stabbed Rodolfo, even as his friend fell to his knees.

I turned my attention to Alessandra, fighting her captor as he tried to drag her off, away from the Sienese who now closed in to free us. But I was out of arrows.

Stealthily, I ran toward them, grabbing hold of another dagger. Four Sienese knights trailed the duo, keeping Alessandra's captor's attention. And in the same way that the Fiorentini's companion stabbed Rodolfo, I took down the man who held Alessandra.

He gasped, arched his back, and crumpled, Alessandra limping away from him. I left the knights to see to his end or his capture, going to Alessandra and giving her a brief hug before turning back toward Rodolfo. We moved toward him, together, with trepidation. More Sienese were between us and the Fiorentini now. We were reasonably safe. We were. But not Rodolfo.

I could see he was bleeding out, even in the feeble light. Alessandra went to one side, and I to the other, each taking a hand. The pointed steel ball had hit above his clavicle and nicked an artery. I was surprised he had been able to keep his feet as long as he had. And the wound at his back...gently, I turned him partway over to see and then looked with sorrow at his wife. I shook my head. I was sure he'd been stabbed in the kidney. Not even Mom could save a man with a wound like that.

Rodolfo lifted Alessandra's hand to his lips and kissed it. "I have loved you, Alessandra. Do not forget that. Thank you...thank you for loving me."

She wept, curling her head in toward his good shoulder. "Do not leave me, Rodolfo. Do not leave us. Chiara...and the baby..."

The baby? She was pregnant? I cried too. *Chiara*. Alessandra...what would they do without him? I could feel Luca and Marcello near, heard them panting for breath, spitting out blood and dirt, but my eyes stayed on Rodolfo.

He looked to me. "Take care of them, Evangelia."

I nodded, tears flowing down my face. "I shall."

He looked up to the men, behind us. "Take care of them all, brothers."

Marcello and Luca knelt by his shoulders. Marcello gripped his hand. "As if they were our own kin," he said. "You have my word, brother."

"And mine," Luca said.

Rodolfo took half a breath and then stopped, still staring at Marcello. I felt the life seep from him, the cold, still finality of death.

Alessandra wailed, and Luca forcibly lifted her up and away from her husband, a sight so terribly wrenching I thought I'd vomit. Marcello helped me to my feet, an arm around my shoulders. "We shall return for his body," he said, his dirty face now tear-streaked. "But now we must get you to safety. There are still Fiorentini about."

We paused by the old man. I saw, then, that it was Alessandra's father, in the last stages of plague, gasping for breath.

"Leave him," Marcello said, after kneeling beside him a moment.

"Nay!" Alessandra cried. "I must bring him with me! He may yet survive."

Marcello's brown eyes shifted from her to the old man. I felt the waves of futility and fury and mercy and sorrow wash through him. Here was a man who had disowned her, a Fiorentini, dying of the plague and yet...he sighed and turned toward two men. "Tie cloths about your faces and carry the old man to the castello."

"Yes, m'lord," they said.

The fight continued behind us as we trudged toward home—our horses scared off and lost to us for the time being—but it was waning. The Fiorentini had lost their most precious prey; night was closing in in earnest; and we were all battle-weary. After our own losses, I think we were all more than ready to rest behind Forelli walls.

But when we arrived at the castello, so thankful to see the row of torches illuminating the blessed, high walls of our sweet home, I saw something that made my heart freeze.

Mom and Dad—and the knights assigned to protect them—were no longer there.

CHAPTER 50

GABRIELLA

L ia, Luca, and Marcello burst into our room, looking half-crazed
  and totally battle-worn. Their faces were red-raw from the cold,
and blood and mud spattered their clothes.

"Dad!" Lia cried in relief, running to his side. Slowly, her eyes moved
to Mom, lying beside him, and she turned to me, silently begging me to
tell her what she plainly knew already.

Mom was sick too.

"I couldn't leave them outside," I said. "I just couldn't."

Dad reached out to touch Lia's cheek, weeping, then thought better
of it. "Thank God," he whispered, closing fevered eyes. "I was so worried,
Lia. So worried about you."

I hurried over to Marcello, hugging him in relief then pulling back.
"Did you get it? Was it there?"

Marcello released me, closed the door behind him, then reached
under the wide armhole of his tunic and fished it out.

"Oh!" I cried in relief, staring at the wooden box. The antibiotics.
Orazio and Galileo...they had done it. Saved us.

I opened it slowly, like it was a golden treasure out of an Indiana
Jones movie rather than a set of ten-buck antibiotics. To me, it was
priceless.

The wooden box was cheap veneer, but I thought it clever of the
boys to put the syringes in it. Far less conspicuous than the white plastic

First Aid box Mom had been forced to hide. And easier to burn when we were done. Inside were eighteen syringes, taped to the lid, and a note.

I read it aloud in a hushed, reverent whisper. "Forelli-Betarrini family, may this serve you in your greatest need, as you served us. Go with God, Orazio and Galileo."

There was another note, hurriedly scrawled across the top. "Dose for six adults," I read, "one per day; three days each."

My stomach somersaulted. This wasn't a miracle-medicine for eighteen, but only six. Still...it would help six. That was six more than we could save a minute ago.

I turned toward Dad.

But he was shaking his head.

"No, Gabi."

I frowned. "What?"

"No. You've already broken quarantine, bringing us in here. Exposing you all, repeatedly."

"There was no way I was leaving you out there—"

"You broke quarantine," he said sharply. "Our...first line of defense."

"Yeah, well, you went and got the *plague* of all things. Now we're going to fix that." I ripped off the first taped syringe and looked around for a basin of water and clean cloth. We'd need to clean his skin before inserting it...

"I thank you, son, for retrieving that medicine," Dad said in Italian. He was speaking to Marcello, man to man, who stood slightly behind me, to my right. "But 'tis not for me. There is medicine for six. You must save it for you and the children, should any of you need it."

I sucked in my breath, feeling slightly sick. I wasn't hearing him right...

"No, Dad." I fell to my knees beside Lia.

Mom pushed herself up to a sitting position and brushed back the hair from her perspiring face. "We've discussed it, girls," she said quietly, sounding confident, but I didn't miss the anxious glance she cast Dad.

"We shall put our lives in the hands of God. He brought us here. Gave us a second chance for your dad...for all of us, really."

I blinked. Mom...She didn't go in for this sort of God-talk. Not normally. But then...never before had we been confronted with death as we had in these last days. Never. I wished Tomas was still with us. There was so much I wanted to ask him.

"That is crazy," Lia muttered, rising and pacing, wringing her hands. Luca reached for her, but she brushed him off. "We almost died out there," she said, gesturing toward the door, "to bring you this medicine. Now you refuse it? In case we *might* need it?"

"I couldn't live with myself..." Dad said, working hard to form each word, "if I lived, only to watch one of you die, because I took one of the doses."

"And what of us?" I asked. "What if none of us ever contract it, and we sit here, with the medicine that might have brought you healing?"

Dad stared at me, silently begging me to stop arguing. But I couldn't. Not now, not on this point.

"What if..." he said slowly, swallowing hard, "we all take a dose, and Lia's babe is born, only to contract this dread disease? Or Fortino gets sick? Just the thought of burying one of you makes me want to die right now. And a grandchild? It's not the way it should be, girls. Not the way."

I stared at him, not allowing myself to look in Lia's direction. I couldn't say it. She had to.

But we were all silent a moment, the only sound our quiet sniffling. Mine. Lia's. Mom's.

Lia took Dad's hand, stubbornly holding on to it when he tried to withdraw. "Dad, we risked our lives to save yours. So did Orazio and Galileo, in a way. They didn't know if they could get back, but they risked it. We've lived our lives here for the present, not for the future or the past. Just the day. We've been thankful for each day we've been given. And to hoard this medicine, for my child, or Gabi's,"—she paused to look my way and I nodded my encouragement—"would be to live in fear of the future. We have to make our best decision today, for this day." She reached over to take Mom's hand too. "And trust God with our tomorrows," she said in English.

Mom and Dad both wept then, and we cried with them. It was wrenching, this decision, but it was right. Surely one of us here would survive the plague, saving a dose for Lia and Luca's unborn child...

Surely.

Surely.

Please, God, let it be so...

CHAPTER 51

GABRIELLA

We exited our rooms, after administering antibiotics to both Mom and Dad and posting guards, not allowing anyone else to enter or exit. It was lame to create a mini-quarantine room in the heart of the castello. But it was all I could do. One look at Mom and Dad outside, battling an illness and facing the threat of physical assault from the Fiorentini, and I knew I had to bring them inside, despite their protests. I was only glad they were too weak to fight me much.

And, truth was, the plague-zombies had fairly coated every wall and stone with the bug, during the attack. Add to that the fact that day after day, more inside the castello came down with the plague than those outside and...Any idea that we were safe from it was just plain ridiculous.

We all knew the antibiotics weren't a guarantee that they would survive, but we all might get a little sleep this night, feeling as if we had a good chance of waking to see them wake too.

So when I entered the courtyard and saw Chiara, hair in a mass of wild curls, crying, snot running down her nose, I rushed to her. "What is it, sweetheart? What has happened?" *Where was Alessandra? Rodolfo?*

But she cried too hard to tell me.

"Gabriella," Marcello said, soon at my side. Spying me with the grief-stricken child, Marcello had sent the boys with Mercede, the nurse-maid, who would see them to bed. I was glad Fortino wasn't here. Chiara's upset would set him to weeping too.

"What's wrong, Chiara?" I cooed. "Tell me."

The child shook in my arms. Empty. Wailing without sound.

"Gabriella," Marcello repeated.

I looked up at him then. The sorrow in his eyes. The open broken-ness for a...brother.

My mouth fell open.

I couldn't utter his name, but it echoed within me. *Rodolfo.*

Rodolfo.

Gone.

The pieces slipped into place. A child, missing a father; my husband, a brother...and my own jagged loss, of a friend.

"Nay," I said, tears welling and falling as I rocked the child, feeling her ache as my own. "Nay..."

I sobbed with Chiara a moment before pulling back and stroking her face. "Your mama? Where is she?"

"Outside," the little girl said, her breath coming in quick gasps, "with her papa." And then she fell into my arms again.

What? I mouthed to Marcello. Alessandra's father was here? Now?

He shook his head, brought a hand to his eyes and held it there a moment, wiping away tears of his own. He looked helplessly my way. "What could I do? They brought him across the border, Gabriella. They brought him with them. And he is sick."

I looked to the sky, dark and starless, trying for a breath. Was there no end to it? The illness? The death?

"We will go to them," I said, rising, then bending to take hold of Chiara's hand. "Your mama, and her papa—they need us."

"Gabriella," Marcello said in low warning. "'Tis night. There are yet enemies about."

"And we have family outside the gates," I said. "She needs us, Mar-cello," I said, softening my tone, reaching to touch his arm. "They need us," I added, gesturing toward Chiara.

He took a long, deep breath and then said one word. "Come."

We stood before the gates as they pushed back the massive steel crossbeam and opened the tall doors. Twenty knights watched in doleful silence as we exited. Eight stood in the gap, swords unsheathed. Four more stood between them, arrows across bows. Castello Forelli was taking no more chances.

At some point, I realized that Luca and Lia followed us. He, with sword drawn. She, with arrow upon bow.

But my eyes were on Alessandra, cape drawn around her shoulders—too loose for the winter chill—eyes wide and vacant. Chiara rushed to her, and she took her in her arms, and rocked her, but it was as a shell-shocked mama reacting on impulse, memory.

I knelt beside her, and it took a while for her to recognize my presence. But with one look, her eyes seemed to melt into cauldrons of tears and she uttered one word, "Oh."

I leaned forward, embracing them both—Alessandra and Chiara—now alone in the world, without their chief protector, the man who had loved them with his whole heart. Rodolfo.

Rodolfo...

Marcello put a warm hand on my shoulder, and I felt a shiver of betrayal for the momentary leanings I had had toward his friend years before. And yet what had drawn me were many of the same things that had drawn Marcello as his blood brother—intensity, intelligence, passion, drive. It had simply been...different between us. And yet in these last years, chaste, nothing but friendship. The mere acknowledgment that in another place, another time, under different circumstances...maybe.

But he had been wholly Alessandra's. And Chiara's. And now, now he was inexplicably, impossibly dead. After all we'd made it through. Survived. After all the battles and strife. It wasn't even the plague that killed him, but in the end, his fellow countryman's weapon.

I sighed as Alessandra keened in my arms, weakly beating my back with her fists, not wanting to hurt me, but in too much pain to embrace me. "I am sorry, Alessandra. So sorry."

She cried for a long time, and then she was silent. Wiping her face, her nose, with a dirty rag, she looked up at me, her face only half-visible in the torchlight. "He taught me what love was. How love could...heal."

I took her hand and held her gaze. "That he did. He loved you and Chiara very much."

She looked to Marcello again. "You will bring his body back? So that I can give him a proper burial?"

"He shall receive a knight's burial," Marcello said. "Honored in every way."

"What of your father?" I asked, turning to the old man. He looked far smaller and weaker than when we last met, years past. When he had turned away from Alessandra, disowned her.

She took his hand. "I know it shall make little sense. But when I was trapped, when I had no other place to go...I went home." Her dark eyes moved to meet mine, brows arcing together. "And he welcomed me," she added in a whisper, taking her father's hand. "When I discovered he was ill, I knew I couldn't leave him. Not after...Not now when..."

"I understand," I said, thinking of my own dad, battling for his life, above us, in my own room.

I reached out to take her hand. "Will you come inside for the night? I'll ask a knight to keep watch over him, and report to you any change."

But she was already shaking her head. "Nay. My place is here, with him. I shall stay."

I nodded, squeezed her hand, and rose. "Until the morrow."

"Until the morrow," she repeated, tugging her cloak closer, Chiara already asleep beside her.

Come morn, Alessandra's father was dead.

Mom was visibly improving.

But Dad was not.

Dad was not.

As soon as I entered the room that night, I closed my eyes against the putrid smell. I knew it well, by then. Buboes, bursting. Fetid poison of the plague, spilling outward.

No, I wailed inwardly. *No*.

Because from our experience, once the buboes burst, the patient was on the decline. The only relief, death.

Lia handed me a handkerchief, dipped in lemon oil water, and I wrapped it around my face, covering my nose and mouth. Mom was kneeling beside Dad, her shoulders shaking.

Dad's eyes were closed, and yet he still breathed. But each breath held the phlegm-rattle of death.

Candles lined the room, their flames dancing, impossibly lively and joyous in a room so full of fear and sorrow.

I wiped the tears from my eyes with the back of my hand and joined Lia on the bed, beside Dad, across from Mom.

"Girls," he said, big, brown eyes sad and lined with pain, "don't give me the third shot. Save it for…"

He dissolved into a coughing fit.

When he settled, I said, "Dad, one more. The full dose is three. It can work. You still have some time."

"Gabriella. Evangelia."

I dragged my eyes to meet his. I knew Lia did too.

"I am done. You saved me. Gave me…" He closed his eyes and shook his head, his mouth falling open, as if in awe, and then he smiled. "Gave me such a gift. These last years, here, with you…"

He reached out and touched my cheek and then Lia's. I closed my eyes, refusing to move. Even if he infected me, this was Dad. *Dad*. And I instinctively knew I might never feel that touch again.

"But what was it for?" Lia burst out. "To save you? Only to lose you again here? Now?"

His eyes were kind, caring, knowing. "Because this chapter of the Betarrinis' story..." He closed his eyes and shook his head. "I couldn't have possibly missed."

He fell into another coughing fit, and Mom raised him up. When she allowed him to sink back to the pillows, I saw there was blood on the handkerchief.

"To have missed this...to know you as women?" he said. "To know you at all, for that matter. What you are capable of...And to know your husbands? The joy of becoming a grandparent?" Tears slipped down his face, and I wept in earnest then, my vision blurring.

"Before..." He leaned back and closed his eyes. We waited for him to gain strength to finish his thought. "Before, we were so wrapped up in our work...Forgive us, girls. We missed you. Missed vital parts of your lives. But I'm so glad we had this. So glad. You saved me...and you gave me a part of life I am certain I never would have lived. Not just the medieval part."

We all laughed then, through our tears.

"And missing this would have made me less of a man. Less of a father. Less of a husband." He turned toward Mom, and she grimaced through her weeping.

"No, Ben. No..."

"You three are strong. My beautiful Betarrini girls. She-Wolves...all of you," he said, his words now coming in pants.

"I love you, Dad," I said, aware now that we were losing him.

"I love you," Lia repeated, crying as I was.

"Oh, Ben," Mom said, straightening on her knees, cupping his face with her palm. "How I have loved you."

"And I you, Adri. Live life in full, babe. Live it fully. For..."

His lips opened in a circle then.

His eyes widened.

His breath caught.
And there was a hint of a smile.
Before he left us.
Forever.
forever
forever

we'd lost him
and so many others
in the days that came after
to death
to death
to death
until the monster relented
leaving enough time for us to
bury our dead
at last

dad and rodolfo were buried as heroes
funeral pyres
tears
flames
ash
dust
dust

CHAPTER 52

EVANGELIA

On and on it went, one death after another. It came; it receded. Like an evil, monstrous tide. And in time, we received the daily report from the gate guards with wooden responses, incapable of grieving any longer. Were our hearts dying inside of us?

Three months later, word of Lord Barbato's death came as a hollow victory, thrumming against my chest. He died alongside his skinny wife, and after burying his three adult children, ensuring his particularly foul line was dead for good, but it gave me little sense of victory.

Instead, I felt robbed.

I wanted to sink my arrow into his throat. Hear it enter and exit with wet, bloody finality.

I know how wrong that might sound to others.

How sick and twisted.

They did not know what it meant to long for revenge.

But I did. To me, Barbato had been the first of many terrible dragons unleashed at our door. The one who had nipped and bitten and chased and haunted, and finally descended, wings sprawled so wide it cast a shadow over the castello for every day that followed.

I thirsted for revenge, my anger yawning within like a cavern cracking beneath the surface of the earth.

And it both hollowed me out and buried me at once, even as my body rounded with pregnancy.

CHAPTER 53

EVANGELIA

Tiliani Betarrini Forelli mewled with her borning cry six months later. Luca wanted to name her Adela or Benedetta, but it only reminded me of sorrow. Not joy. How long had it been since I'd felt joy?

Luca cried tears of joy as he held her.

Gabi cried and laughed.

But I did not.

I seemed to feel nothing but the ache of longing for my dad and the friends we'd lost. I felt nothing but the desire to see Dad hold Tiliani, as he had Fortino and Benedetto, and even Chiara Greco.. How unfair was it that I was here, holding his grandchild, and he was not?

As much as I was glad that the baby was here, safe, I felt like she was not mine, in a way. She was foreign, a squirming body, dangerous, now that she wasn't safe in my womb. Just another risk to my heart.

My milk went dry, scant as it was.

And Tiliani wept in hunger.

Luca wept in frustration.

Gabi wept in fear.

Mom wept for all kinds of reasons.

But I did not.

CHAPTER 54

EVANGELIA

M onth by month, the plague ebbed and flowed. People died. People lived. Dimly, I recognized that the tidal flow was increasing in span, the breaks longer. But still it returned.

Life, as they say, went on, but it wasn't the sort of life I bargained for. Fields were planted. Harvests were brought in. Winter came again, and so did our enemies, both Fiorentini and plague. Life became a cheap commodity, no one assured they would live long—all striving to get what they could, while they could. It was a particularly brutal year in Italia—that last year of the plague—and I retreated further. I knew I was retreating, but knew it from a distance, and found it impossible to change my direction.

Luca and Tiliani could still make me smile, but it was a small smile, like joy was but a memory. Daily he brought her to me, and I saw that at almost a year old, she was beautiful and thriving, and felt glad for it, but I dared not hope it would remain so. Everyone was a potential target. Would I bury her this year? Or next? Would she follow her cousin, Fortino, or lead him into death?

Just last month, Giacinta's sweet, red-headed daughter and Marcello's steward, Leo, had both died the same day. Twelve others within our walls went with them.

Luca placed our daughter in my arms, but she only remained there a minute before she reached for him again, whining. He took her, and his green eyes clouded with frustration. "Evangelia, this has gone on long enough. Where is the She-Wolf I took to wife? Is this what your father would want for you? For his grandchild?"

I turned my face away, to the window.

He came around, blocking my view, forcing me to look at them. "Evangelia, beloved, come back to us. We need you. I know it is a great deal to tolerate, but we are making it through. This plague shall finish its rampage soon, yes? We've made it this far. But we have today, *this* day. This fine spring morning. Come, come for a walk with me and our daughter in the woods. Or a ride?"

I shook my head slightly and looked to my hands. "Not now, Luca. I have a headache."

He stiffened, knowing I lied.

Turning him away, as I had so often in our bed.

He left me then, to my own morose thoughts and the minutes that passed, one after another, until night and blessed sleep again returned to me.

CHAPTER 55

GABRIELLA

My sister walked about like a ghost, spooking everyone but herself, as spring moved into summer. Lia looked serene, but mostly, she just freaked me out, she acted so weird. She ate, bathed, slept. But it was all robotic. She accepted news of the dead and news of the living with the same, monochromatic reaction. An *oh*-life, I took to calling it. Not "OH!" Or *Ohhh*...Just...*oh*. She lived in a sort of constant-sigh world and neither Mom, Luca or I could find a way to shake her out of it. To bring her back to us.

Tiliani was a gorgeous, impish child growing quite fat on a wet nurse's milk and flourishing in the arms of her auntie and papa and gramma and maid—but not the mama she needed most. Holding her in my arms, I knew I had to break Lia out of her trance.

Marcello helped me obtain a stack of large pieces of parchment, mounted to boards, along with some more easels from Siena. I placed them in the solarium, the dim windowpanes soot-covered in Dad's absence. I felt the cold, hollow ache of missing him every time I entered the place, despite the warmth of the summer sun. He'd been the only one who cared enough to wash the milky panes, commenting on the miracle of glass-making at all in this era, and wanting to reminisce about our time in Venezia.

And yet I knew the jolt of entering the room might be just what was needed to melt Lia's thickening layer of isolation, like coagulated, cool fat placed in a hot stove.

I took Lia's hand that afternoon and said simply, "Come."

She followed, as usual, complacent, willing, neither a sense of wonder or hesitation in her. Just...emptiness. The wide span of *oh*.

The only place I saw her falter was at the threshold. She placed a hand on the doorjamb and looked at me, a trace of fear in her eyes.

"C'mon," I said, gesturing toward a stool in front of the first, wide, blank canvas upon an easel.

She moved forward, walking in a stuttering, reluctant fashion but not voicing any complaint, as usual. She sank heavily to the seat.

I placed a chunk of charcoal in her hand.

"I want you to draw your pain. Your anguish. Your sorrow. Your fear. Your anger. Draw it out."

Her bright blue eyes looked to me, to the canvas, and back again.

"Draw it out, Lia," I insisted. "Show me what's buried in your heart. Show me what's blocking you from me. From Luca. From Tiliani. From Mom."

She remained still, staring at the canvas.

"Do it, Lia. Get it out. Get it all out. Because this? This way you're *living*? It's lame, Lia. Totally lame. It's not living. This is more like living-*death*."

She didn't move or say anything, and I began pacing.

"What you're doing is...horrible, Lia. It's a *sacrilege*, dishonoring all who have died to save us. Those who loved us. You are emotionally starving your baby, your husband, yourself." I sank to my knees beside her, tears dripping down my face.

"*Fight*, Lia. Find the fight again. Draw deep. Show me what pulls you from the light, from life. From love."

She remained where she was, slack, practically dropping the charcoal from her fingers.

"Lia!" I cried, pushing at her shoulder.

I was scared. Had I lost her too?

"You were meant for more than this, Lia," I ground out quietly. "You are a Betarrini. A *Forelli*. A She-Wolf. Delve deep, Lia. There is life yet, left to grab, and you have walked away from it! Let it go like it wasn't worth your effort anymore! *Think!* Think what Dad was willing to sacrifice so that we might live. And yet you turn away from it!" I let out a mirthless laugh, sitting back on my heels. "Come back to us, Lia. Show me what blocks you. What makes you angry. What makes you sad. What makes you feel anything at all! *Show me*."

I lifted her hand to the canvas and together we made a wide, black streak. A smudge that reminded me of the ash from the funeral pyres. The dirt of the burial grounds. "Show me," I repeated softly, slowly dropping my hand from hers, half expecting it to drop back to her lap.

But it didn't.

Her hand hovered there a moment. Then two.

And just as I was losing hope...she moved, drawing a jagged line all the way down the canvas. Paused. Lifted her hand halfway. And made another, deep, angry line. Paused.

After that came a flurry of lines, conscious smudges with the fat of her fist, more lines, moments when she leaned in, as if watching the image emerge herself, first tracing, then lining with authority. Shading. More smudging.

What evolved brought halted breath and tears that clouded my eyes.

She filled one canvas and then two, then the third. I tacked new parchment to the boards and she filled the next three as well.

It wasn't the dark, angry images I expected. Thunderstorms and waves. Tornadoes or birds with broken wings.

What Lia sketched were images of joy.

Mom and Dad. Laughing. Dad lifting a chubby Fortino, grinning in profile. Mom in Dad's arms. Tomas and Adela, holding hands. Rodolfo and Alessandra, cuddling Chiara. Giacinta, tickling Isabella. Knights we had known and lost—from the moment we got here to now—looking heroic, wrestling, laughing. On and on it went. For hours. Picture after picture.

I soaked through a handkerchief with my tears and running nose and was well through another when she finally stopped after her twentieth canvas.

This one was of Dad, holding little Tiliani.

Something he would never do.

She stared at it for a long, silent minute. "He died," she whispered. "He's gone."

"And yet not. Part of him lives on, in us, Lia. In Fortino. Tiliani."

Lia's shoulders curved in a wide slope, and she began to weep.

Deep, aching, sobs.

A keening so cutting, it sliced me in two.

But it was a breaking.

An opening.

A chance again, at last, at life.

CHAPTER 56

EVANGELIA

We had burned Dad's body along with Rodolfo's, upon funeral pyres, their hands placed around the hilt of each of their weapons.

But unlike the others in the mass graves, we had dared to gather the ashes and bits of bone after the fires cooled and placed them in ossuaries, small, marble boxes like the Etruscans had often used.

A year after the plague had waned, spit, and then left us for good, like the dying dragon it was, we stood at harvest-time at the edge of the Forelli cemetery.

Here, on the hillside within view of Castello Forelli, Marcello's ancestors were buried. Alessandra had asked that we bury Rodolfo's remains here, saying he had had no kin greater than Marcello and Luca. We'd honored him months ago.

Now we gathered, finally ready, really ready, to honor Dad's memory too, beside graves marked by Etruscan urns in which Gabi and I took to writing him notes he would never answer, but felt like he did, in our hearts.

The eight of us gathered at dusk—Marcello, Gabi, Fortino, Benedetto, Luca, me, Tiliani and Mom. No more. No less. Many more had loved Dad, but we were the ones who loved him most.

As the sun set, we shared stories of him. Of his bravery. Of his love.

As the stars came out, we shared his words of wisdom. Tales of how he wanted, more than anything, for us to flourish. Live life to the fullest. As we shared, we spoke of others, too, we had loved and lost. Of what they had added to our lives, the seeds they had planted. And as we did so, I set my illustrations atop the flames of a small fire, burning them—because the illustration technique might change history—commiting them solely to memory.

Gabi grabbed hold of a shovel, scooped up the ashes, and let them drop across Dad's grave. "Life is costly...but worth the cost."

"Indeed," I whispered, cuddling Tiliani close. She squirmed, rejecting my tenderness, wanting down, to play in the ashes, to reach for the fire. I laughed under my breath, liking the strength and stubbornness within my toddler, the littlest She-Wolf. Her cousins came to me, reaching for their cousin, and I set her down. Together, they ran off among the graves, holding hands, giggling. I thought that would have made my Dad smile. Life, among memories of death.

The fire died down to embers as we stood there in a circle, remembering, remembering all who had died so that we might live. And when it was at last out and we turned to go, we paused at the crest of the hill.

Because lining the walls of Castello Forelli, and in the distance, Castello Greco, were people, all holding candles and torches and lamps, warm, flickering light under a darkening sky.

"Oh!" I said, bringing a hand to my mouth, staring at the beautiful spectacle of it.

"Mama!" Tiliani cried, turning to look at it and point with her pudgy finger. Her cousins stood beside her, gazing out in awe.

"I know, baby," I said. "I see it. Isn't it wonderful?"

Luca wrapped his arm around my shoulders. "Our people love you, Lia. All the Betarrinis. They remember and honor you."

Mom came beside me, and Gabi by her, then Marcello. All of us staring at the spectacle that was our people. "Your dad would've loved this," Mom said, her tone melancholy, but with the edge of hope.

I smiled, through my tears. "Yes. He would've."

"Tuscan bliss," she said, gesturing toward the castello, the horizon's hills a silhouette against the last vestiges of twilight.

Bliss, I thought, so hard-won. A fable, most times, but scratching the surface in moments like this. Sheer, startling joy. Even though we'd been through agonizing grief. Faced death, over and over again. Here, *here* was life, before us.

I stared at the line of light, dancing before us, evidence of so many, within each castello, standing with us. Remembering. Commiserating. Honoring.

Here was community.

Here was love.

Here was life.

And in this place, the distant past—our future.

EPILOGUE

Summer, 1364

Tiliani Forelli laughed as she raced across the meadow and then up the steep ravine. She was bareback, her skirts up to her knees—which would make her Nona shake her head if she saw—but she was chasing Chiara, Giulio and Ilaria Greco, as well as trying to avoid her cousins, Fortino and Benedetto. Her little brothers, Rocco and Dante, were no serious threat. She considered letting them get closer before she claimed the prize, but the stakes were high. If she captured the flag, she'd get an extra portion of dessert tonight after supper. Papa had promised. And Cook had made her favorite sweetcakes...

There.

She spied the flag at last that Papa had planted earlier, the barest glimpse of red, waving from the limb of a tree. Sheer luck, she decided, even as she urged her mare in the right direction.

Together, they surged up the hill, all glorious muscle and strength and life. Never had Tiliani felt so alive. She wished this summer would never end, that the river of time would stop for once, so she could hold onto this moment. This perfect summer eve in her hand, eyes alight, smile on her lips, victory rumbling in her chest.

She leaned down as they crested the hill, tearing toward the tree, but then saw Fortino heading toward it, too, from the right. Benedetto was close too.

She paused, wheeled her mount around—ignoring her whinny of complaint—pulled her bow from her shoulder, nocked an arrow, and let it fly. It pierced the flag just ten paces before Fortino reached it.

Fortino wheeled his horse and glared at her as she rode up, smug. "Are you mad?"

"Not as mad as you, likely, given that you just gave me that extra dessert."

"Nay, I mean are you off in the head?" he said, gesturing toward his own, flicking fingers away from his temple. "You could have killed me!"

"Come now," she said, the tickle of a grin teasing up the corners of her mouth, "you know I haven't missed a target in over a year. Have you forgotten who my mother is?"

He shook his head, pulled out a handkerchief and wiped his sweating brow. "'Tisn't truly fair, Tiliani, using your bow," he complained.

"You could've used your dagger," she said, easing past him and pausing near the tree to rip down the flag. "A She-Wolf—or He-Wolf—uses every weapon at their disposal."

Giulio and Ilaria Greco rode up then too, Giulio groaning when he saw the flag in Tiliani's hand. "Again? I do not know why I try," he said. But there was a grin hidden behind his tone of mock-defeat.

Tiliani smiled. He was a handsome boy, just now showing the promise of manhood, with lengthening limbs and a face growing more angular by the day. His younger sister, Ilaria, rode beside him. His big sister, Chiara, would soon be too old to be out here with them. She should be back at the castello, entertaining suitors. As Tiliani herself should, in another year or two.

But when Tiliani gazed out over the hills—Forelli land as far as she could see—up until it gave way to Greco land—and to the horizon, where the sun set in an extravagant display of corals and golds and rosy reds...she knew there was time enough to enter adulthood.

She would live this day for all it was worth.

Just as her parents and aunt and uncle and grandmother had taught her.

I'll leave the morrow for the morrow. Today is enough and more.

Her little brothers arrived then, riding together on one horse. They scowled and groaned at the flag in her hand...as if they had ever had a chance.

"'Tisn't fair," complained Dante. "Making us ride together."

"Did she *shoot* the flag?" asked Rocco.

"She did indeed," Giulio confirmed, folding his arms.

"Never mind how I won or how *fair* it was," Tiliani said. "The victory is still mine. But I shall give you one last opportunity to redeem yourselves," she said, already turning her mare toward the castello. "The last one home has to help Cook and the kitchen maids with washing up."

It didn't take an additional word to send the rest of them tearing back toward the castello.

Tiliani paused, holding back her mare, wanting the thrill of coming from behind and passing them all, knowing that even if she didn't, it wouldn't be a victory if it hadn't been a challenge to begin with. And when the other three were halfway down the hill, she finally released her horse's mane, leaned down, and became one with her, each churning motion felt deep within, until they were going faster...

And faster...

Until time seemed to stop.

And joy fully enveloped her.

HISTORICAL
NOTES

As far as I can tell, most marriages happened in side-chapels and were fairly private events. But given their location and the doge's interest in making a spectacle of Lia and Luca's wedding, and their widespread fame, I made it a front-and-center event in the basilica—built as the doge's chapel.

Details on how they docked in Venice, and of the doge's palace, were out of my imagination and based on conjecture. I could find no definitive source on either of those subjects, in English.

The term *quarantine* did not come into usage until later in the 14th century, as the Italians began to figure out that they should keep sailors from other countries isolated for forty days before entering their city, to make certain no illness had come with them. The Italian word *quarante*, for 40, is where it comes from. The historical record in Dubrovnik notes keeping people isolated on an island for 30 days in this time too. So while they were slow to figure out that it would be a good means of keeping a lid on a disease's power to spread, and didn't officially use "quarantine," many nobles fled the city for their country houses, aware that to remain in the city seemed far more dangerous.

Oil of Thieves seemed to be mostly used by gypsies the second time the plague came hunting. But given Adri Betarrini's understanding of herbals and natural remedies, I thought it a logical addition to their cadre of tools to fight it.

❖ ACKNOWLEDGMENTS ❖

Many thanks to the team who made this book possible: my husband, Tim, for all his design work, Lindsay Olson for a solid edit; Kristin Hamm and Rachelle Rea for proofing; Julia Grosso for the help in Italian; and my "volunteer proofers" for this latest edition—Cheryl Crawford, Melanie Joy Stroud, Cori Crews, Sharon Miles, Alathea Melton, and Caroline Santilli. *Voi ragazzi sono fantastici! (You guys are awesome!)*

LOOKING FOR MORE OF THE BETARRINIS AND FORELLIS?

Check out the next-generation series, Oceans of Time, beginning with *Estuary*. All three books are available now!

www.ingramcontent.com/pod-product-compliance
Lightning Source LLC
Chambersburg PA
CBHW030543260626
47157CB00006B/2175